CARIBE DREAMER

THE SURFACE OF THE SEA

Donald Knoepfle

authorHOUSE®

AuthorHouse™
1663 Liberty Drive
Bloomington, IN 47403
www.authorhouse.com
Phone: 1 (800) 839-8640

Published by AuthorHouse 05/26/2016

ISBN: 978-1-5246-0506-3 (sc)
ISBN: 978-1-5246-0505-6 (e)

Library of Congress Control Number: 2016906697

Print information available on the last page.

Any people depicted in stock imagery provided by Thinkstock are models, and such images are being used for illustrative purposes only. Certain stock imagery © Thinkstock.

This book is printed on acid-free paper.

Because of the dynamic nature of the Internet, any web addresses or links contained in this book may have changed since publication and may no longer be valid. The views expressed in this work are solely those of the author and do not necessarily reflect the views of the publisher, and the publisher hereby disclaims any responsibility for them.

Dedication

To my loving wife, Jean and our daughter, Betsy for putting up with "the book" for all these years.

Acknowledgments

To my wife, Jean, for her love, patience and expertise in editing of the manuscript.

To Doug Olson, retired U. S. Navy Carrier Pilot, airline Captain and fellow Abaco cruiser and "boat buddy", for his editing the communication between both civilian and Navy pilots.

To Gene Jurrens, sailing friend, fellow cruiser and licensed Ham Radio Operator, for his editing the radio traffic and conversation between amateur radio contacts.

To the God loving, hard-working Loyalist descendants, who live on the edge of the Atlantic Ocean on tiny, out-island Cays of the Abacos. I thank you all for your love and friendship.

Foreword

Punta Gorda, Florida

My parents, Genevieve and Walter, along with two other sailing-friend couples from the Chicago Yacht Club, would spend a month each Winter chartering sailboats in the Caribbean. The boats were chartered from Nelson's Dockyard in Antigua, British West Indies. Some boats had a captain, while other charters were known as "bareboat", where the experience of the three Lake Michigan "captains" was adequate to bring the boat back in one piece!

In 1959, three couples were invited to join a yacht club member, Eddie and his wife Marge at their home in Nassau and cruise to the Abacos. The Abacos is a chain of Bahamian Islands one hundred twenty miles North of Nassau. Eddie and Marge had a small cottage on an out island and this would be home base for cruising to the nearby islands.

My parents fell in love with Man-O-War, a quaint boat building community populated by descendants of the Loyalists, supporters of King George III of England, who left New York in 1783. While the Loyalists were mostly farmers, they found the dense pine forests of the Abaco Mainland not suitable for farming. To survive, they had to become fishermen and move to the Cays (pronounced Keys) closer to the reef. The fishing business required wooden dinghies, as well as large sailboats. Man-0-War became well known in the Bahamas for the quality of their ships. They built hundreds of sailing ships, some as large as seventy feet. In 1960, my parents purchased a 1-1/2 acre plot with a yacht club friend, Clifford. They designed a one bedroom cottage to be built on the property.

The bi-level cottage, named "Long Look" was bolted together, as strong as a Man-0-War ship. Long Look has survived many hurricanes, including Hurricane Floyd that took direct aim on the Abacos with two hundred mile per hour winds! The cottage was completed in 1962 and it became the "go-to" vacation destination for our family.

Despite the lack of conveniences such as electricity or running water, the family, including my sister and brother and I would spend our Spring and Christmas breaks from college at Long Look. It was during one of these vacations that we met a young Canadian man, who was had vacationed there for many years. He was an extremely interesting and intelligent fellow and we would spend evenings with him and his Canadian friends, discussing the topics of the time. Through our relationship, we met the young people of the island and their families. In October, 1967, my bride, Jean, and I spent our honeymoon at Long Look. We pumped the water into a tank in the attic to get "running water". The stove and refrigerator ran on propane and the lighting was with gas lamps --- and we are still married!

In 1980, our high school friends and fellow sailors from Chicago, Dennis and Barbara and Jean and I chartered a CS 36 sailboat out of Marsh Harbour. One the suggested anchorages was the deep water just North of the shallow Tiloo Bank on the lee (West) side of Tiloo Cay. The water was warmed by the sandbank and the beaches were deserted. We anchored *Salty Five*, packed snacks and drinks in the dinghy and motored into the beach. Dennis and I tossed a Frisbee on the no-footprint beach. An errant throw caused me to walk into the underbrush to retrieve the Frisbee. It was here that I came face to face with a tripwire strung with empty tin cans, running from one tree to another. I had seen these devices during my infantry training in the U.S. Army. Someone wanted to be warned that danger was approaching from the beach. I looked inland, through the dense brush and saw "IT"! There, was an army green tent with a wash line hung with camouflage laundry! Who was hiding out on Tiloo Cay, and why? "IT" became the germ of the idea for this novel. I hope you enjoy reading this story wrapped in the terror threats of modern times and, someday, visit the beautiful people and the safe, azure blue waters of the Abacos.

Map of the Commonwealth of the Bahamas

The Commonwealth of the Bahamas is a former British Crown Colony that gained its independence in 1973. The Bahamas consist of 700 islands or "Cays" (pronounced Keys). There are only ten major islands including Great Abaco, which is the farthest Northeastern island, with many out-island Cays. The islands occupy more than 175,000 miles of the Atlantic Ocean and the population is estimated to be 350,000 people. The Bahamas are a cruise ship and tourist destination. The capital, Nassau, on New Providence Island is a financial center.

Manasota Key, Florida, Saturday, April 13

Still dripping from his shower, Scott gazes down at his blue, paint-stained hands and fingernails. *"Sure hope this new hand cleaner can whip these into shape," he thinks, as he works the brown paste into his hands.*

"Damn! -- that new anti-fouling bottom paint is insidious stuff. I wore a high efficiency respirator and my nostrils are still blue, wonder what my lungs look like," shouts Scott aloud to an empty shower.

Scott is not enthusiastic about getting all dressed up after a ten hour day at the shipyard, however 'Countess' Williams is trying to play matchmaker, again. She really isn't a countess at all, but to Scott and her friends, Lillian lives, loves, and entertains like one would imagine. Rodney, her late husband, earned his money as an executive for Sears Roebuck --- and there seems to be no end to the money. And, there seems to be no end to the supply of eligible, young ladies to introduce to Scott.

Scott's crisply ironed Tommy Hilfiger khaki pants are set off by a chocolate brown leather belt with a brass, shark shaped belt buckle. A white linen shirt is unbuttoned and shows his sun-bleached, blonde chest hair -- set off against his bronze tan. Around his neck is a wide, gold anchor-link chain. On his feet, he wears well broken-in, brown leather boat shoes, without socks. A yachting chronometer is strapped upside down on his right wrist. This is about as dressed up as Scott ever got.

"So what if my fingernails are still light blue — contemplates Scott as he gazes at his hands. Wonder where The Countess dredged up tonight's blind date? The last one was a fluff-head sales clerk Lillian met while shopping at the Burdines Store, in the mall. Who was more bored that evening? She or me," questions Scott to himself, as he drives East toward Punta Gorda and recalls the wasted evening.

Punta Gorda, Florida 6:30 P.M. Lillian William's home in Punta Gorda Isles

Scott's six year old, red Jeep Grand Cherokee winds its way past the well-manicured residences of Punta Gorda Isles, an upscale, deed restricted, waterfront community on the Southwest Gulf Coast of Florida. Translated from Spanish, the city name means 'fat point', however the Chamber of Commerce prefers their translation: 'broad point'. The lanais and pool areas of each home face canals similar to those found in the wealthy East Coast city of Fort Lauderdale. *Look at all those boats --- wonder how many of them ever move off the dock? Kind'a like swimming pools --- only one in three is ever used for swimming. The rest are just for --- oh, whatever rich people do with their time and money --- houses, boats, pools, cars, whatever.* Scott pulls onto an empty lot to avoid getting blocked in by other guest's cars. He notices a lone, white Mustang GT convertible parked in the driveway.

"Nice car --- not the muscle car of a fluff head. Wonder who's driving that? And, --- where are the rest of the cars," questions Scott.

'Countess Williams' landscaping is meticulous. Each flower bed is surrounded by tan concrete curbing and mulched with decorative stone. No 'Florida Crabgrass' lawn for her, she had special, drought resistant, hybrid of Kentucky Blue and Marion grass laid. To keep it green, she drilled her own agricultural well, so she could irrigate the lawn through the Winter dry season.

"Scottie, darling," shouts the Countess from the front door. "I'm so glad you are able to join us this evening. Step in, young man and give me a big hug. I'm really excited to see you and I want you to meet a wonderful young woman. Her name's Addie and she works in my dentist's office. Addie's waiting out on the lanai."

Breathless after her long introduction, Lillian grabs Scott's arm and holds onto him as he guides her to the lanai that overlooks the swimming pool. It isn't your usual Florida pool. The water cascades down from a large rock waterfall. Two cast bronze sculptures of dolphins are mounted at each end, spraying streams of water into the lighted pool. Addie is standing along the side wall of the Florida room, gazing at two large framed nautical charts of the Bahama Islands. She switches the champagne glass from her right hand into her left and turns to greet her host and date, as Scott and Lillian walk toward her. She holds out her hand to Scott.

"Hi, she smiles --- I'm Addie Weldorf, you must be Scott."

"Yes, Scott Lindsay, at your service ma'am," he replies as he extends his right hand and reaches out for Addie's outstretched fingers. Rather than shake her hand, he bends his head and softly kisses the back of her hand. Still holding her hand and looking into her beautiful eyes he says, "It's a pleasure to meet you, Addie --- in fact, it's a special pleasure to be in the company of two beautiful women."

"Oh, Scott, you're always so kind to this old woman — you make me feel like --- oh, you're such a charmer. I hope you won't be angry with me --- I arranged for the two of you arrive a half hour before the others. This way, you can have a chance to talk and get acquainted. You two get to know each other while I go to the kitchen and check on Joe."

Scott quickly takes measure of Addie. No fluff head this woman. Waldorf? Jewish perhaps? Ramrod straight posture and a great figure. Conservative dress — off white, a kind of wheat-colored woven texture, belted at the waist with a wide brown leather belt --- the straight skirt flowing just to the top of her knee. Nice knees. Very lovely legs. A small pearl and gold broche on her collar. Pearl earrings --- quite appropriate. And those piercing coal black eyes --- Addie is a very intriguing young woman, thinks Scott.

"Lillian certainly has some unusual artwork," says Addie breaking a short silence.

"Ah --- yes. As I entered, I noticed you were looking at those antique nautical charts. They are two of my favorites. The one on the left is from the late 1780's by the British Admiralty. Check out the one on the right--- it's almost a perfect copy of the English chart --- except, notice that all the names are in French --- and its dated 1786. Looks to me like the English cartographers were working, on the side, for the French Navy."

"Or, perhaps the French captured an English ship and copied all their charts --- how interesting," responds Addie, while sipping her champagne.

"A most interesting detail about the English charts is that the soundings --- that is the water depths --- are identical to those noted on the current British Admiralty charts of this area."

"Oh, that's interesting — and why would you be in possession of such a fact?"

"I'm surprised --- I thought that by now, Lillian would have briefed you on my personal dossier"

"No, Lillian has not --- however, I certainly would be interested in knowing a man who has a dossier --- sounds mysterious, or naughty --- perhaps bordering on the illegal --- kind'a like Rick Blaine in Casablanca," says Addie with a wondering glance.

"Perhaps dossier was a poor choice of words on my part. But, to answer your question, I expect to be sailing in these same waters in six months or so, ma'am."

"Oh, Scott, no need to be formal, it's Addie --- not ma'am. Your, ah --- trip sounds adventurous --- fitting of a man with a dossier," replies Addie.

"Addie, would you like to accompany me while I tend to some business on '*Good Hands*' --- the Countess' boat, says Scott quickly changing the subject. The Countess asked me to check the oil pressure on the port engine."

"Hey, I'm game to try if you think I can get aboard dressed like this," questions Addie.

"Don't see any problem except for your shoes. They'll have to stay on the dock. One word of caution, it will be quite stuffy on the boat 'til we get on the fly bridge."

'Good Hands', an Ocean 48 foot motor yacht, is tied at the dock behind the Countess' home. During the Winter season, Scott is the paid captain and in charge of maintenance.

"Addie, the tide is up, so it will be a high step into the cockpit." Scott steps over to help Addie, but she has already climbed aboard. "Wow lady, you did that very well. You must work out?"

"Why yes, I do work out. I take an aerobics class and StairMaster --- I try to get to the gym at least three nights a week," replies Addie.

"Which club do you belong to?"

"I'm a member at the Punta Gorda Club."

"Well, that's why I haven't seen you, I work out at Gold's Gym across the river in Port Charlotte," says Scott.

He works his way to the fly bridge with Addie following behind. The air is oppressive --- a warm mix of the smells of fiberglass resin, diesel fuel and tropical mildew. Scott flips the switch on the bilge blower, activates the bilge sniffer alarm, and unzips the port and starboard plastic curtains --- hoping to catch a breeze.

"There, it should cool down in a few minutes or so --- are you okay?"

"I'm fine, Scott. I've been in Florida long enough to get used to these temperatures. Do you mind me talking while you're troubleshooting --- do you?"

"No, lets continue the conversation."

"I understand from Lillian that you are visiting from Canada."

"Yes, I'm what you call a snow bird. I work in a shipyard in Toronto six months of the year and I'm down here in Florida for six months. I was born the U.S. and I've lived in the States so long, I don't even say ooout for out --- eh."

"That's what has me confused, you don't sound like a Canadian. Where did you live in the States?

"I was born in Milwaukee --- moved to Canada when I was seven."

"How interesting, --- I'm from Mequon."

"Gosh, what a coincidence. Mequon certainly is a beautiful suburb."

"So, if I've got this right, you're a sailor boy from Canada with a boat and you're itching to sail away to Margaritaville --- is that right?"

"Well, I do own a few Jimmy Buffet tapes, but I'm going to the Bahamas to feast my eyes on the most beautiful tropical waters, fabulous sunsets and endless beaches. And, I'm planning to make some money, at the same time. I'm going to charter my sailboat --- take passengers for hire," responds Scott.

"You're going to take a sailboat to the Bahamas --- all by yourself?"

"I am hoping that I can convince someone to join me --- do you have a valid passport," questions Scott.

"Yes, my passport is up to date," responds Addie with a quizzical look on her face.

There is an extended silence that is broken only when Scott turns the ignition key of the port engine and the engine roars to life. Addie climbs onto the white leather captain's chair and curls her legs under her. Scott is standing directly in front of her at the instrument consol. He can feel her knees against his buttocks. *H'm. --- works for me, he thinks.* Then, he starts the starboard engine and watches as the temperature and oil pressure gauges come to life. Glancing to the gauges, Scott notices that before the port engine is up to temperature, the needle on the oil pressure gauge begins to fluctuate from forty down to ten pounds.

"Looks like this problem is going to take some major troubleshooting. We should get back to the party --- don't want us to miss cocktails. I'll have to come back and spend some time to track this down. The oil pressure seems fine --- looks to me like it's a problem with the gauge."

Scott throttles the engines back to stop and turns off the ignition keys.

"We'd better get back to the party before the Countess sends out a search party."

"Oh, darn. I was just getting used to the lovely ninety degree cool breeze," laughs Addie.

Scott reverses the process of climbing down from the fly bridge and leads Addie back to the dock.

"Scott, please steady me while I get back into these stupid shoes."

"My pleasure, ma'am," he says as he put his left arm across her broad, strong back. She smells like a jasmine flower and he feels Addie melt into his hold. *Good, real good, thinks Scott.*

As the couple hurries toward the lanai, they are greeted by the buzz of spirited conversation from the well lubricated senior guests. The partiers are mostly retired neighbors; men with their golf tans setting off white, silver, or no hair. The women look a little tired, overweight and wrinkled. As they enter the lanai, The Countess hushes the crowd and introduces Addie and Scott.

"Ladies and gentlemen, I would like to introduce you to my dental hygienist, Addie Weldorf and --- most of you already know Scott Lindsay. Don't they make a fine couple. You all know how much I like to be in the company of young people -- it brings back the memories --- and it keeps me young, too. Please check the table for your place cards, as Joe is ready to serve dinner --- and thank you for joining me on this wonderful evening. You are all beautiful people. God bless you -- I love you all --- let's eat."

The dinner is carefully orchestrated by Lillian and exquisitely served by the house man, Joe. Starting with cold asparagus salad, the dinner continues with medallions of beef tenderloin topped with a béarnaise sauce, a crunchy green bean casserole plus assorted breads. It is finished off with a dessert of refreshing raspberry ice drizzled with creme de menthe. Scott and Addie sit at the far end of the table and make small talk with the guests sitting next to them. The subject of Scott's Bahamas adventure never enters the conversation.

"Scott, tell me about the house man, Joe," says Addie starting another conversation.

"Ah, an interesting story. He's an old friend of Lillian's late husband, Rodney. Joe is the youngest son of the Haritori family. They are Japanese-American and cooked and cleaned for the Williams family when they lived in Chicago. After Pearl Harbor, Rodney was commissioned in the Navy as a supply officer --- because of his position at Sears. When we began interning the Japanese, Rodney used his influence and had Joe's Dad assigned to his command. Somehow, he got them papers that said they were Filipinos. Rodney took good care of the Haritori family during the war and Joe took over for his Dad when he retired. Joe is a real handy guy --- he's as comfortable in his gardener's overalls as he is in his tuxedo. You should see him trim a boxwood hedge --- and he mixes some really exotic tropical drinks. But, Addie, fair warning --- you'll be well advised to stay away from a drink he calls a Spinnaker"

"Thanks for the advice, Scott, but remember, I am over twenty-one and, I can handle my liquor," responds Addie.

The Countess adjourns the dinner guest to the Florida room where she recites the names of a half-dozen after dinner liquors that are assembled on a large silver tray.

"Or, if you prefer, Joe is going to whip up a batch of his famous Spinnakers. Would anyone like a Spinnaker?" Addie waves her arm in agreement. She decides to try a Spinnaker. Joe rushes to her side with a frosted glass of pink liquid. Addie squeezes Scott's arm and gives him a wink.

"As you reminded me, young lady, you are of legal age," responds Scott.

"Scottie, darling," calls the Countess.

"Some of our guests are going to try Joe's famous 'Spinnaker' cocktail. Can you recite that little ditty of yours?"

Scott loves an audience and it didn't take much convincing to get him to perform.

"Oh, most assuredly, I'd be happy to, Lillian. Folks --- quiet please. I have an important announcement. I have some instructions for you on how to hoist a spinnaker. First, you need an ice cold, pink liquid in a frosted glass. Joe, a frosted Spinnaker, please --- mister!"

Joe rushes a Spinnaker to Scott and the guests raise their glasses as Scott slowly recites …. "Drink one at the most if you're able. Drink two and you're under the table --- drink three and you're under the host!"

Scott's recitation is followed by loud guffaws, a twittering of laughter and some back slapping among the male guests. Scott returns to Addie's side and is welcomed with an inviting arm which she wraps around his waist.

"Mister Scott Lindsay, you are one great actor. Now, I understand your earlier comment. You're really worried that I might consume three Spinnakers!"

"Me worried, Addie? No, I'm not worried. In fact, if you do consume too many Spinnakers, it will be my duty as a former officer and gentleman in Her Majesty's Canadian Forces --- to drive you home."

Soon, after the recitation, the guests begin to take their leave of the party --- after all, it is past nine o'clock --- sometimes referred to as 'Punta Gorda Midnight'. Addie didn't seem to be in a hurry to leave and she seems to be quite enjoying her frosty drinks. After the last guests leave, Addie and Scott help Joe and Lillian clear the glassware from the lanai.

"Hey, you two. Joe and I can clean up. You young people should be out dancing at some club --- not hanging with us old fuddy-duddies, protests Lillian. Scottie, darling, let me know the progress on the port engine. The boat club is planning a cruise to South Sea Islands Plantation the week after next and I'd like you to captain the boat for me and my guests."

The Countess reaches out for Scott and gives him a huge kiss on the cheek. Scott can feel Lillian's hand tuck something into the pocket of his shirt. He's pretty certain that it will be a fifty dollar bill.

"Yes, ma'am, I figure an hour of troubleshooting will handle it. I'll drop by during the middle of the week and get it fixed. Don't worry, you'll be on schedule for your cruise, darling."

"Mrs. Williams, interjects Addie. "I've had a perfectly wonderful evening. Thank you so much for inviting me. I'll see you next week for the final cleaning before doctor puts in your permanent crown. And, don't forget, avoid chewing on the temporary." Arm in arm, Scott escorts Addie to her car.

"Hey Addie, I'm thinking it might be a good idea to exchange cell phone numbers. That way, if you run into a problem, I can come help you."

"Good idea, Scott. Are you ready to copy? I'll dial up your phone. What's your number?"

"Mine is 625-2939 --- hang on a second and I'll key your number in ---."

"Addie, do you feel all right to drive? This county is full of DUI checkpoints."

"I'm okay --- I guess. I'm just a little tired. I worked 'til one o'clock today --- my problem is that I just can't remember my way out of here, Scott. The streets in Punta Gorda Isles, with all those cull-de-sacs and canals --- it's all very confusing."

"Addie, just follow me and when we cross the second U.S. Route 41 which is one way North bound, you will see the U-Save Supermarket on the right. Follow me into the parking lot and we'll say good night. If you're feeling woozy, just flash your brights and we'll switch to plan B --- Okay?"

"Okay, Scott. I'm glad you have a plan B. It's my plan A that is worrying me."

Left, right, right, left they wind their way to Olympia Avenue and across Route 41. A right turn into the parking lot and the two cars are parked driver window to driver window in front of the U-Save Supermarket.

"Scott, I'm so ashamed. You warned me and I went and did it --- the Spinnakers. My eyelids are so heavy. I don't think I can drive another block --- can you take me home? Oh, gosh --- I know, this sounds so bad, first date and all."

"Hey, hey, lady --- don't fuss. I'm a gentleman and you're the damsel in distress. I'd be flattered to drive you home. Turn off your lights, then turn off the ignition. I'll move your car under that light where it will be safe and you can pick it up tomorrow."

Scott shifts his car into park, gets out and goes around to assist Addie into the passenger seat. He reclines the seat and watches as Addie belts herself in. Scott moves her car under a light pole that is close to the street where it will be safe. When he returns to his car, Addie's head is slumped forward and she is out cold. Scott turns on the ignition and puts the air conditioning on high, while directing the vents toward the passenger seat in hope this will revive his passed-out passenger.

"Hey, Addie, if we're going to drive to your house, I'll need some directions."

Again, Addie's head bobs forward and to the left. Scott fumbles for her purse. *She must have brought her driver's license and that will have her address," he thinks.* Scott reaches into her purse, locates her wallet, and removes her license.

"Wisconsin, exclaims Scott. Oh, damn where's her Florida license? --- no Florida license in here."

MasterCard, American Express card, health insurance card, library card from Mequon, Wisconsin. There is nothing with Addie's Florida address. So, now to invoke Plan C., thinks Scott. He decides the only option is to drive Addie back to his beach house apartment on Manasota Key. Addie wakes, as Scott puts the car in gear and drives out of the pot holed parking lot.

"Scottie, I've been a bad girl and now I'm inconveniencing you --- I'm so sorry."

"No apology needed, lady. Scott Lindsay at your service."

"Drink two at the most if you're able --- drink three and you end up in your date's bedroom," babbles Addie.

10:45 P.M. Scott Lindsay's Beach Road apartment on Manasota Cay

Scott arrives at his coach house just off Beach Road on Manasota Cay. He helps Addie up the stairs and into his bed. Soon, he will find out just how uncomfortable his hide-a-bed is. Scott tosses and turns all night long and, finally, at first light, he hears the thawap of the newspaper hitting the driveway and he gets up. Scott walks down the hall toward the bathroom and peaks into the bedroom. Addie is still sleeping, fully clothed. She must not have even rolled over --- her hair is still perfectly in place. Scott grabs a pair of old gym shorts from the laundry basket and goes outside into the humid Florida morning to retrieve the paper. He glances at the headline --- nothing new here --- grabs the sports page and heads up the stairs for a shower and shave. After finishing in the bathroom, Scott puts the 'Tums' bottle in plain sight. He retrieves fresh towels from the linen closet and wipes down the sink and mirror. Fully revived after his shower, he opens the refrigerator and searches for breakfast for two.

"Let's see --- English muffins, jam, eggs, orange juice and most important, strong, black, decaf coffee --- that should do it, thinks Scott."

Addie stays for more than breakfast. Three weeks later, she moves in to share the expenses on Scott's quaint, one bedroom, beach house. On the weekends, she helps Scott get *Caribe Dreamer* ready to sail off to their new life in the Bahamas.

Two years later, Thursday, March 19, 6:30 AM, The Russian UN Mission, New York City

Josef Stanislaus, Second Agricultural Secretary for the Russian Republic flashes his I. D. card as he passes through the well- guarded gate of the Russian United Nations Mission on 7th Street. It is 6:30 AM and he has a long walk to the bus. Josef dislikes going to the eastern end of Long Island on Thursdays. Thursday's bus is the shopper's special -- a round trip for the price of a one way.

"Certainly, the bus will be crowded with shoppers going to the outlet mall in Riverhead," he surmises. Josef shudders at the thought of having to share a seat with some stranger. A plan forms in his mind -- he will push to the front of the ticket line to make certain he gets a window seat. Then, he can stare out the window to avoid having to speak to anyone and divulge his thick Russian accent. Josef presses his arm against his breast pocket and feels the reassuring bulge of the latest camera phone --- a phone with a high pixel camera lens. He buttons the neck of his trench coat against the early fall chill, puts his head down and trudges off toward the Mid-City Bus Terminal -- twelve long blocks away.

U. S. S. Topeka (SSN 754) a U. S. Navy Los Angeles Class nuclear powered Hunter-Killer Submarine

Topeka was launched October 21, 1989 at General Dynamics Electric Boat Division in Groton, Connecticut. Her complement is 12 officers and 115 enlisted personnel. Topeka is 360 feet long and has a beam of 33 feet and a draft of 32 feet. She is armed with Tomahawk Cruise Missiles, Harpoon Anti-ship Missiles and Mark 48 Torpedoes. Her wartime mission is to hunt and kill enemy submarines and surface ships. Topeka's home port is San Diego, California.

Nuclear Submarine running on surface

Thursday, 0730 Hours, aboard the *U S S Topeka*, Los Angeles Class Attack Submarine, sail number, SSN754, at the General Dynamics shipyard, in Groton, Connecticut.

Communication Chief Banacek walks hurriedly down the narrow corridor. He stops in front of the hollow aluminum honeycomb compartment door where a sign says, *'Private - Captain Craig P. Walters'*. There is a 'no knock' policy on all U.S. submarines, to avoid any unnecessary noise, so the Chief simply tries the door knob --- if it is locked, you use the telephone system. The door opens easily.

"Pardon the interruption sir, I've got an 'eyes only' message for you."

"Step right in, Chief."

Captain Walters is sitting in a leather office chair at a small pull down desk next to his bunk and is typing into his laptop computer. Chief Banacek closes the door and in a deep, but quiet voice, he speaks to the Captain.

"Sir, I have an 'eyes only' message from NORAD in Colorado Springs," he announces, as he hands the aluminum topped message clipboard to the Captain.

"Please sign on line seven, sir," announces the Chief, as he presents his special red pen. Captain Walters scrawls his initials on the message receipt, takes the message and returns the clipboard and pen to the Chief. Chief Banacek stands at ease while the Captain removes the message from the manila folder and begins to read.

"Chief, the Russian *Iris 58* satellite has just passed beyond our area. Next bird's not due over Groton until 1450 hours. Ah --- pass a message to the Exec to dial up the Dry Dock Supervisor and tell him to flood the dry dock and begin retracting the canopy. Our orders are to be ready for sea by 1300 hours --- and Chief, alert the maneuvering watch to stand by to assist the tug."

"Aye, aye Sir," replies the Chief as he performs an about face and disappears down the hallway.

Chief Banacek retraces his steps down the narrow corridor and returns to the communications room. He picks up the phone and to his surprise, gets a dial tone. *Good, the shoreline telephone is still operational.* Quickly, he dials into the General Dynamics switchboard. It is time for the Electric Boat people to remove the 'moon roof' that has hidden three months of modifications that have been made to *Topeka*. The crew will be very happy to be leaving 'The Evil Planet Nortog', as Groton is referred to. Living on board a dormitory ship is like being recycled through Great Lakes Naval Training Center for basic training. Lots of work parties and many hours of classes leads to a boring life. The crew is anxious to get back into the routine of being submerged under the sea.

The *U S S Topeka* is the first Los Angeles Class submarine to have a forty-four inch diameter vertical tube added to her amidships torpedo room. For all these months, the superstructure of *Topeka* has been hidden from peering eyes and satellites by massive semi-circular metal, culvert sections, while the modifications were being completed. The crew has nicknamed the sixty foot semi-circular structure 'the moon roof'. In less than three hours the dry dock will be flooded, the culvert sections will be retracted and *Topeka* will be towed out of dry-dock Number Four and prepare for sea trials. Captain Walters walks over to the squawk box. He turns the selector switch to position 1MC --- 'All Compartments' --- and depresses the handle. A recording of a Boatswain's piping resounds throughout the submarine follows by 'now hear this, now here this'. "Gentlemen, this is your Captain speaking ...."

Thursday, March 19th, 9:32 AM, Orient Point, Long Island, New York

Finally, the bus brakes to a stop at the end of the line. Josef eyes the bus riders and wonders if anyone has followed him. He is more than thirty miles beyond his allowed diplomatic status, travel distance from the Russian UN Mission.

"So, if I'm caught, I'll just say I fell asleep. But, most certainly the authorities would wait until after I get on the ferry. The minute I step on the ferry, the game will probably be up," thinks Josef. A few minutes later, he boards the 9:45 car ferry as a walk-on passenger. The next stop, in an hour and a half, will be New London, Connecticut -- home of the Navy's Submarine School, the U. S. Coast Guard Academy, as well as the Groton submarine shipyard of Electric Boat Division, General Dynamics Corporation. Josef moves quickly up the narrow staircase from the lower deck to the upper deck and locates a seat on a bench behind the wheelhouse. The door, behind the wheelhouse, is marked 'Crew Only' and Josef knows it is always propped open. Heat from the engine room pours out the door, warming the side of the bench where he will sit. Josef nods off into a sound sleep only to be awakened by the throaty sound of the ferry's engine, as it begins to maneuver inside the harbor. Josef walks back to the starboard rail and removes the cell phone from his breast pocket. He yawns out of boredom, as this is his fourth trip and, to date, none of his photographs has produced anything of value. Josef stares at the submarine dry dock. There, right before his unbelieving eyes, is a tug nosing a submarine out of dry dock. He notes the sail number painted on the coning tower ---754. It's the submarine he's been told to photograph. It's the *Topeka*! --- He begins taking pictures with his cell phone camera. Any modification to an American submarine is very important intelligence for the Russian Navy. Josef hopes he will be rewarded by The Rodina for his efforts. Quickly he dials the 201 area code number that is pre-programmed in his phone. Four long rings later, the phone answers and he transmits all ten photographs of the submarine. It is a long walk across town to the Amtrak station and, with any luck, the train will be on-time and he will have only a half hour to wait. Josef walks up the double flight of stairs to the windswept platform. He spots a newspaper vending machine at the middle of the platform. Josef walks quickly and inserts six American quarters into the machine to purchase a *Wall Street Journal*. No self-respecting socialist would read *The Journal*. Josef figures it is the perfect cover for a Russian intelligence agent. He spots an unoccupied bench in the warming sunlight and begins reading. A tall, Latino man in a beige trench coat approaches the bench. He addresses Josef while reaching inside his coat to remove his wallet and produce a badge.

"Josef Stanislov? I'm agent Carlos Fernandez of the Federal Bureau of Investigation. You have traveled beyond your permitted travel radius. You were observed photographing a United States Military Base. Photographing this installation is prohibited under the terms of your Diplomatic Visa. I must place you in protective custody and return you to your Mission. Your camera, please, sir." Josef breaks into a broad smile as he thinks of his timely sending of the photographs --- the possibility of a promotion and return to his family in Mother Russia.

Caribe Dreamer is a Lagoon 400, sloop rigged catamaran. She was built in France in 2002. The boat is 39' 3" overall length, 23' 9" in beam, and carries a draft of 4' 2". The boat has two private cabins aft with queen size berths. Both private cabins have separate, attached, head compartments. Forward on the port side is the crew cabin with single bunk beds. To starboard is the crew head compartment. The dinette in the salon converts into a queen bed when there are six cruisers aboard.

Twenty-one months after the Weldorf – Lindsay wedding. Friday, March 20, 8:30 A. M., aboard the forty foot, sloop rigged catamaran, *Caribe Dreamer* in the large, well-protected harbor at Marsh Harbour, Abaco, Bahamas.

"Hey, Scottie, we're on vacation," says Addie as she steers *Caribe Dreamer*. The occasional whoosh of the water cooled exhaust can hardly be heard over the noise of the twin diesels as the Lagoon 40 catamaran sloop moves through the harbor, past the boats at anchor. Some sailboats fly American, Canadian, German, French, or British flags. Each sailor --- a dreamer, comes from various parts of the world to anchor in this laid-back piece of Bahamian paradise on Greater Abaco Island they call Marsh Harbour --- a simplification of its original name, Marshes Harbour. Addie is at the helm and Scott is up forward making up the dock lines. Mittens, a White Coated Wheaton Terrier, scrambles about the teak decks trying to regain her sea legs after two weeks on shore. She sniffs at the sea breeze and occasionally barks at the bow wave.

"With the tide on rise, we should be able to steer North of Parrot Cay," suggests Scott as he moves forward to hoist the mainsail.

Scott is the consummate sailor --- always looking to add an extra tenth of a knot, and, with diesel fuel costing $4.80 a gallon, that is all the incentive Scott needs.

"I'm right on Parrot Cay on this course -- is this okay, questions Addie as Scott climbs over the combing and into the cockpit.

"Looks good to me -- how's our speed," asks Scott, while reaching for the main sheet and slightly trimming the mainsail.

"We're up to six and two tenths, since you put up the main."

Addie adoringly eyes Scott's well-tanned, muscular body. *I can hardly wait until tonight when we're together in the double berth in the aft cabin, thinks Addie. Eight straight, two week, charters -- sixteen weeks cooped up forward in the 'crew quarters'. Slaves' quarters is a better name. How romantic this life was supposed to be.*

"Not," Addie blurts aloud --- *but, now, I'll have you to myself for two whole weeks!*

"What did you say, hon?"

"Oh, nothing -- I was just talking to Mittens," replies Addie.

Armed with their U. S. Coast Guard 'Six Pack' --- a six passenger captain's license, hundreds of sailors bring their boats each year to various Caribbean ports hoping to make it in the sailboat charter trade. Only a few last more than one season --this is Scott and Addie's second season and they expect to end the year with a profit. They ran charters for seven repeat customers from last year. Is it just time that is finally working in their favor, or is it Addie's wonderful sense of humor, her genuine hospitality, or her excellent menu planning that is bringing in the referrals and repeat business? Scott searched far and wide for the ultimate charter cruising sailboat. While he had always been devoted to monohull designs, he realized that most cruisers could care less about sailing performance, they prefer a 'party platform'. In addition, they expect absolute privacy in their cabin, plus they want their own bathroom, or 'head'. Charterers want to experience new ports of call, and picturesque anchorages. They want to swim, sun and snorkel, eat island foods and party the nights away. Scott's research told him that the ultimate cruising platform is a sloop rigged, catamaran. Using his connections from his job at the shipyard, Scott spent years searching for a Lagoon 40 catamaran. The Lagoon 400 is molded in France, of glass reinforced resin. The builder used no balsa wood coring or wood stringers for reinforcement and, the Lagoon brand has a reputation as a true 'blue water' capable sailboat. In fact, Fountain-Pajot, the builder, delivers all of their vessels to destinations around the world 'on their own bottoms' rather than aboard a freighter or container ship. While working at the shipyard, Scott had the opportunity to interface with a number of adjusters from insurance companies. He is the 'go to' person when it comes down to repairing damage done by careless boaters or tropical cyclones. Hurricane Wilma crossed the Gulf of Mexico just in front of a cold front that was moving down from the North. The speed of the southward plunging cold front made the Hurricane Center's predictions somewhat uncertain and, in fact, Wilma developed into a Category 3 storm, not the Cat 1 storm Hurricane Center had forecast. As Wilma approached Florida's Southwest coast, she continued to confound the forecasters who were predicting landfall at Fort Myers. The cold front turned out to be much faster than the hurricane and the actual landfall was South of Naples. Naples, Marco Island and Fort Myers Beach were on the left or more powerful quadrant, of the storm. This last minute change in direction of the hurricane left many boat owners unprepared for Wilma's 100 mile per hour winds. *Cat's Meow*, a 2002 Lagoon 400 catamaran sloop became a victim of the hurricane when, tied to a dock behind the owners home on Marco Island, it smashed the port hull onto a piling sinking the entire port side of the vessel in salt water. Scott became the benefactor of this mishap, when Lloyds Marine Insurance Service towed *Cat's Meow* into the shipyard that October. The insurance adjuster declared her to be a 60% loss and offered her for sale 'as is, where is', at a sixty percent discount off of the BUC Book average sale price. Scott was the first person aboard the boat and he spent the entire evening looking at every inch of the port hull. Her mainsail was furled inside the mast, so it hadn't been damaged and the owner had removed the genoa jib. Luckily it was stowed in the starboard hull and remained clean and dry. The galley is to starboard and was in perfect condition. The Lagoon 400's port Yanmar

29 diesel engine showed no sign of salt water intrusion and her Panda generator set, while encrusted in salt, showed no signs of salt water in the crankcase. All of the port bulkheads were water stained and delaminating and the interior smelled like a rotten egg. These were small cosmetic items that Scott could take care of during his weekends and evenings. He set about raising the money to make a cash offer for the boat. He sold his collector car, a 1964-1/2 metallic blue, Mustang Convertible with a white top. He took out a second mortgaged on his small, two bedroom coach home on Englewood Beach. Three days after the boat arrived, Scott offered Lloyds Marine Insurance $111,000.00, a $6,000.00 overbid for the vessel. One week later, Scott got the call --- he was the high bidder. *Cat's Meow* was his! Scott's first repair to *Cat's Meow* was to apply new name decals to the aft portion of the hulls. Her new name is *Caribe Dreamer*. As the boat's repairs were coming to a conclusion, Scott and Addie met on that fateful Saturday night in November at The Countess' home in Punta Gorda Isles. Scott Lindsay and Addie Weldorf, after a ten month courtship, were married on the 23rd of June, at Temple Shalom in Milwaukee. Addie, a typical home-town girl, is the only daughter of Samuel and Sherill Weldorf. A straight-A student, cheerleader, captain of the volleyball team in high school, she wanted to be an author of children's books, but her father insisted that she continue in the Weldorf family tradition of serving humanity through medicine. Her brother, David, is a research physician at The Cleveland Clinic. Addie was born and raised in Milwaukee and graduated from Marquette University with a Bachelor Degree in Dental Hygiene. Her father, Samuel, a gynecologist and her mother, Sherill, a stay at home Mom, are part of the Mequon, Wisconsin country club set. Scott and Addie wanted a small sunset wedding with their bare feet in the surf, on the beach, in Hope Town or Marsh Harbour in the Bahamas. They would have preferred cash gifts, or West Marine Gift Certificates to help outfit *Caribe Dreamer*, but her parents insisted on a country club bridal shower with gifts of china and patterned silver --- all of which went into storage until the wanderlust finally wears off and they return to the States. A large, and very expensive, wedding at Temple Shalom was followed by an extravagant reception at the Mequon Country Club. A gift of cash from 'Mom and Dad' for $10,000.00, purchased a wind generator, a GPS chart plotter, an Emergency Position Indicating Beacon and other necessities to equip *Dreamer* to take one or two couples on charter, cruising in the Abaco Islands of the Bahamas. It is a two year tradition with Scott and Addie to anchor *Caribe Dreamer* off of Loyalist Cay on Saturday afternoons when they are between charters. It is an absolutely perfect anchorage with the island of Loyalist Cay sheltering them from the Southeast trades. Lubbers Cay to the North protects them in case of a sudden storm, from the Northwest. Loyalist has a beautiful deserted beach on the West Side --- seldom will you see another set of footprints in the sand.

"Hey Scott, be a darling and take the helm so I can go below and fix us a cocktail."

"Okay hon, I've got it," says Scott as he walks carefully through the cockpit so as not to disturb Mitten's nap.

He takes control of the wheel. Abeam of Parrot Cay, the water gets shallower, but on a rising tide, *Caribe Dreamer,* only draws four feet two inches. Straight ahead is the settlement of Hope Town, one of the first Loyalist settlements, with its picturesque red and white striped lighthouse. The alternating striped bands on the tower were actually the idea of a Madison Avenue advertising man, who was working for the Bahamas Tourism Bureau. His idea worked --- the Elbow Reef Lighthouse has become one of the most photographed objects in the Bahama Islands. Tonight, as it has since 1863, the Elbow Reef lighthouse will begin its nightly flash, flash, flash, flash, flash of white light --- five flashes every fifteen seconds, warning ships of the dangerous reefs on the eastern most islands of the Bahamas. Every two hours, the lighthouse keeper cranks the brass weight up to the top of the tower. The falling weight turns the clock-like mechanism, which insures five one second flashes and ten seconds of darkness, with every revolution of the Fresnel lens.

With the lighthouse to port and Lubbers Cay to starboard, Scott changes to a southerly course toward shallow, warm water of the Loyalist Cay bank and the evening anchorage. Addie is busy in the galley fixing slices of carrots, cucumbers and zucchini to be served with Ranch salad dressing dip. Rum and water with a squeeze of lime is the adult beverage of choice --- rum is cheap, everywhere in the Caribbean

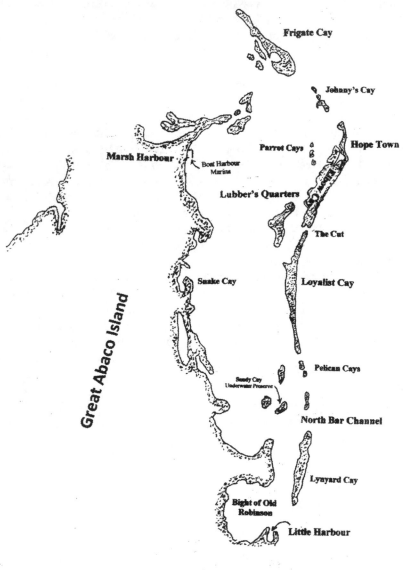

The Southern Portion of "The Abacos"

"I've whipped up some snacks --- I'm sure you're starving," says Addie as she places the snack tray onto the cockpit table.

"Hon, you're amazing --- you can make the best hors d'oeuvres out of almost nothing -- this definitely hits the spot.

"Yeah, if Mom and Dad could see me now --- galley slave, first mate, lover --- and sleeping with a Christian boy to boot -- wow! Some dental hygienist I am," interjects Addie as she returns to the galley for the cocktail napkins.

"Here's a toast-- to the Fergusons -- we hope they will book again next year and to my faithful crewman and love of my life --- Addie."

"To us -- I love you Scott Lindsay -- and to Miss Mittens, too," toasts Addie, as their plastic glasses touch together.

Caribe Dreamer passes close to the sand bar at Bikini Beach and soon is abreast of Loyalist Pond. Finishing the last of the snacks, Scott turns the helm over to Addie and goes forward to lower the mainsail. The wind is on their nose, out of the Southeast trades, and the main is simply flogging back and forth, providing no propulsion. Unexpectedly, the familiar shape of an Army surplus LCM landing craft, belonging to Island Freight, appears from behind the small cay flanking the entrance to the pond. Surplus landing craft are popular freight haulers in the shallow waters of the Bahamas with their three foot draft and thirty-two ton capacity. During dry weather, the landing craft can supply 20,000 gallons of valuable drinking water to out island residents. *"Hum, Scott wonders to himself -- did the Ives family finally find a buyer for their property? It has been on the market for at least five years. Wonder what Island Freight is delivering? -- probably pressure treated lumber for a dock or cement for a rainwater tank."*

"Hey, Addie. When you spot the shallows, bring her around into the wind and take her in --- until you're about twenty yards from the beach. I'll give you the usual hand signals when the anchor is in the water --- okay?"

"Honey, I know the routine -- hand signals are just fine with me. Please just don't shout me instructions with your back to me. With the engines running, I won't hear you."

Scott lowers the sixty-five pound Bruce anchor from the bow anchor roller. The chain races through the haws pipe with a clatter that sends Mittens racing back toward the cockpit. Scott watches the chain fall to the bottom in the crystal clear water, and gives the thumbs down signal to Addie, telling her to put the engines in reverse.

"Back her down hard," yells Scott hoping to set the anchor deep into the soft sand on the first time.

Friday, March 20th, 3:00 P.M., *Caribe Dreamer* anchored 100 yards off the beach that fronts the West side of Loyalist Cay.

"The holding on this sand bottom should be good. One anchor down with forty feet of chain will be enough to keep us comfortable for the whole night," Scott says to himself.

Slowly, *Caribe Dreamer* swings her bow into the light Southeast breeze and faces the beach. Already, Mittens is on the bow barking at the shoreline in anticipation of another opportunity to explore. Between charters, it has been tradition to go ashore to frolic and swim in the warm, shallow water off of the Loyalist Bank. Addie is below finishing packing lunch and the beach towels. She loads the foam insulated cooler with sandwiches, a couple of cans of Kalik beer, and some slices of cheese and apple.

"Scott, we'd better get Mittens into the dinghy before she decides to swim ashore -- I'm sure that after the long ride she needs to be watered."

"You're right, she could also use some exercise after being penned up at Mrs. Pinder's for two weeks," suggests Scott as he brings the Zodiac inflatable aft to the port side swim platform.

"Addie, while you're below, get Mitten's Frisbee, so we can play catch on the beach -- I could use some exercise, too."

Addie hands the cooler, canvas bag and finally Mittens to Scott in the Zodiac. Mittens takes her place up forward continuing her occasional barking at invisible things on the shore. Less than thirty seconds later, they beach the inflatable on the sandy shore.

"Still no footprints on this beach. I can remember the first time we anchored here and it looks exactly the same," declares Addie.

"Yeah, me too. Hundreds of charter skippers drop anchor here, but fortunately for us, few ever come ashore. I'm going for a swim, care to join me?"

"Sure Scottie, I'll join you but remember, rules are rules, --- no suits!"

"Okay, I'm game," responds Scott looking somewhat incredulously at Addie.

"Addie, what the devil is Mittens barking at now?" Please call her, so I don't have to chase her --- in the buff --- all the way down the beach."

"Mittens! Mittens," Addie calls as she claps her hands. The most always obedient Mittens comes racing back down the beach. "Good girl, Mittens. Good girl," says Addie petting the dog's head.

"Hey Addie c'mon in, I'm getting prunie --- the water is really warm."

Addie races off the beach and into the water, while removing her bikini top and throws it into the Zodiac. Scott is already in the waist deep water and Addie wades toward him.

"Hey, no fair, you've got your bottom on --- remember, rules are rules"

Addie reaches the waist deep water and removes her bikini bottom. Paddling back toward the Zodiac she throws her bikini bottom into the dinghy. Scott surges through the water toward her. Addie dives into the clear water and surfaces a few feet away from Scott --- her white breasts glistening in the setting sun.

"Gosh, you are gorgeous," Scott exclaims, as they embrace and their mouths find each other.

The two golden bodies melt together as they roll in the warm, gentle surf. Suddenly, Addie breaks away from Scott and paddles back to the privacy of the inflatable's hull, and retrieves her suit.

"Hey, big boy, let's play for real tonight -- after dinner. I like you hungry, Scottie. I'm going to use some of our precious water and take a shower, so I'll be ready for you."

Dejectedly, Scott retrieves his suit from the Zodiac and pulls it over his bulging erection.

"Hey, lady --- you know I prefer you naked."

"Scottie, it's not you, I'm really worried about Mittens. What is that dog into?"

"Okay, I'll take the Frisbee and go down the beach and find her. Why don't you pop the tops on a couple of Kaliks?"

"Okay fine, Scott --- but, do hurry, as the sun is going down fast and I want to get back to the boat and close the screens before we're inundated with no-see-ums."

What is that damn animal doing, questions Scott, as he bangs on the Frisbee and calls for Mittens. After a quarter mile jog down the beach, Scott hears Mittens barking. *She is way back into the brush -- probably chasing a land crab, thinks Scott as he carefully works his way through the foliage.* Suddenly, the glint of something shiny catches his eye. There, only a few feet in front of him, he sees it -- about shin high -- a trip wire tied between two small saplings. A wire strung with empty beer and soda cans.

Trip over this and you would really wake the dead, thinks Scott. He kneels down and inspects the wire. *Commo wire!* Two pair, twisted commo wire, like the kind the military uses to connect field telephones. *A trip wire, here on a deserted Bahamas island -- now isn't this a strange one -- why would anyone string a trip wire on a deserted island?* Eight years as an airborne infantry officer in the Canadian Land Forces reminded him --- *someone wants to know if their position is being approached from the beach -- not during the day, but more than likely, at night. He and Addie are probably being watched right now. Who, and why? Loyalist Cay has been for sale since the Ives family died when their plane crashed while 'going around' after aborting a landing at Marsh Harbour, during a Summer thunderstorm.*

"This place is giving me the creeps," comments Scott to no one.

"Where is that dammed dog," whispers Scott to himself, while trying to pretend that he has seen nothing unusual. He, again calls for the dog. Come on Mittens, we'd better get back to the boat."

"Mittens, Mittens," calls Scott, as he throws the Frisbee back toward the beach. Suddenly, Mittens races out of the brush diving at the Frisbee and throwing up a plume of sand. "Mittens, lets get the hell out of here, somebody doesn't want us nosing around this place."

Finally, Scott entices Mittens to go down the beach toward Addie and the Zodiac inflatable by playing fetch the Frisbee.

Saturday, March 21ˢᵗ, 0600 hours aboard the U S S Topeka, a Los Angeles Class Fleet Attack Submarine cruising at a depth of more than 200 feet in the 'Tongue of the Ocean', off of the U.S. Navy's Atlantic Undersea Test and Evaluation Center (AUTEC) Near Andros Island, Bahamas.

"Come left to a course of 270 degrees and bring the boat to periscope depth," commands Officer of the Boat, Kevin Anderson. "When you're level at six-zero, raise the Very Low Frequency antenna."

"Aye, sir --left to two seven zero degrees -- bring the boat level at six zero feet. Raise the scope and the VLF," responds the helmsman.

The submarine *Topeka* left Newport News just 70 hours ago after three months in dry dock for modifications to her amidships torpedo launching tube. Arriving off of AUTEC, the boat receives routine radio traffic over the Very Low Frequency radio. Five minutes later, an enlisted signalman approaches Captain Craig Walters with the familiar covered aluminum clipboard.

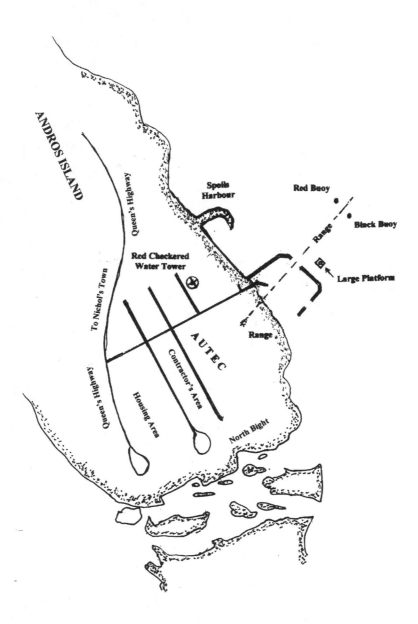

"Message, sir --- secret encoded traffic from COMSUBLNT sir," says the enlisted man. Captain Walters signs for the message and moves next to the conning tower ladder to read the communication.

RTTUZYUW RULSWCA0002 0020029 UUUU--RHMCSUU / /

ANR UUUUU / /

REF / OPORD / / SEA TRIAL TEST/ /

S E C R E T / / 030001Z MAR 20 / /

FR COMSUBLNT CMDR NORFOLK / / VA /

TO CMDR SUB OPS LNT / 051 / /

ASSGND PROJ BALLYHOO AUTEC ANDROS ISL BAHAMAS FM21 MAR TO 03 MAY / / CONTACT EVEREN ELEC PROJ OFCR S J BARTON 1300 HRS LCL 21 MAR/ CONTRACTOR HQ AUTEC / /

Captain Walters hands the clipboard to the Executive Officer, Lt. Commander Kevin Anderson. "Commander Anderson, here are our orders. Please post them in the officer mess for the crew to read."

"Yes, sir," replies Lieutenant Commander Kevin Anderson, as he reads the communication while walking toward the mess area.

Captain Walters moves to the 1-MC communications pod and lifts the telephone handset. The piping of the boatswains pipe sounds followed by 'Now hear this, now hear this, this is the Captain speaking'.

"Gentlemen, we have reached our destination and are about to surface off of the Eastern shore of Andros Island in the Bahama Islands. Some of you have been to AUTEC before. For those of you who have not, let me remind you that this is a sovereign, foreign country. We are here as guests of the Bahamas Government. This is a very small base with few recreational facilities. There is an Enlisted Club, an Officer' Club, a PX, as well as a movie theatre. Off duty hours ashore will be restricted to the base. No personnel will leave the base without the permission of the on duty Officer of the Boat. Weekend passes will be available to half of the crew each weekend for leave in Orlando." Captain Walters pauses to let the cheering and the refrains of M-I-C-K-E-Y M-O-U-S-E subside. Information that relates to our refit in Groton, our deployment to AUTEC and our training mission are Classified Secret and are on a need-to-know basis. Even the code name of this project is secret. Do not reveal anything, to anyone, regarding the movements of the *Topeka* or the nature of our modifications, or our mission. If you are approached by anyone, no matter their rank, regarding our mission, please advise your Section Chief or any of the boat's officers or chiefs. Despite our three months ashore in Groton and many new faces in our crew, you have handled the boat remarkably well. We need to continue to be alert and vigilant.

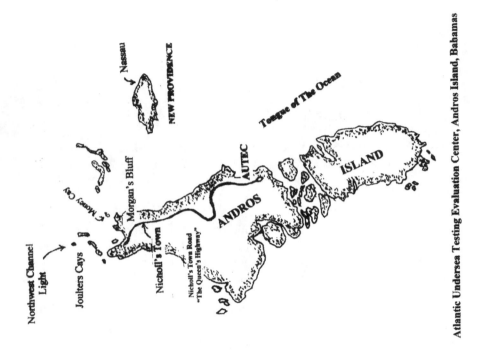

The entrance to AUTEC is narrow and the trade winds blow from port across the channel. Look smart as we tie to the tug and enter the harbor. Surface Watch and Deck Party report to the conning tower. Officer of the boat, prepare to surface. Communications officer, signal the tug to stand clear --- we are surfacing. Officer of the Boat, sweep the surface with the periscope. Sonar, identify any close in contacts."

"Sonar, no close-in contacts other than the tug at five hundred yards off the port bow, sir."

"Captain, the 360 degree sweep shows no vessels in close proximity to us," is the report from the Officer of the Boat.

"Surface. Chief, sound the surface alarm."

O-oooo-gah, Oooo-oooo-gah. Prepare to surface. Prepare to surface, sounds the speakers throughout the submarine.

Russian Intelligence Gathering Ship Khersones

The Khersones is a Mayak Class Ship of the Russian Navy that was named after the largest shipbuilding port in the Ukraine. The ship was built in 1968 in Lubeck, East Germany. Khersones is 178 feet long and is powered by one 880 horse power diesel engine. The ship travels at a cruising speed of 7.5 knots and has a range of 9,000 miles.

Intelligence Center or "Ice House" on Russian Intelligence Ship

Friday, 2000 Hours. On station aboard the Russian Intelligence Gathering Ship *Khersones* steaming due East at twelve knots. *Khersones'* position is forty-five nautical miles Northeast of Havana, off the Northern coast of Cuba, astride the Tropic of Cancer.

Grigory Kasimir completes the second jog around the ship -- his token 'physical exercise' after an artery clogging dinner. Now, he slows to a walk, as he completes his cool down lap --- while sadly surveying the rusting hulk, that was once a proud ship in the Soviet Navy. Grigory climbs the ladder leading to the *Khersones'* aft deck and enters the 'ice house', a cube shaped, windowless structure perched on the aft deck of the Mayak Class intelligence ship. Named after the largest naval shipyard in the Ukraine and launched in Lubeck, East Germany in 1968, *Khersones* is a modification of the basic Eastern European fishing trawler. Her fishing gear has been replaced, long ago, by an array of radio antennas of every description. The one hundred seventy-eight foot ship is grossly underpowered, with only a single 880 HP diesel engine, which produces a top speed of just sixteen knots. On station, the *Khersones* travels at a sailboat slow speed of 7.5 knots, which gives her a range of more than nine thousand nautical miles. The *Khersones* rolls gently in the ocean swells. Quickly, Grigory unlocks the only door and enters the air conditioned 'ice house'. His nostrils fill with the smell of hot radio vacuum tubes and stale cigarette smoke. For Grigory, the thrill is long gone, his life is full of routine and boredom. He secretly yearns for the good old Cold War days. During the Cold War, he would have relieved another Electronics Technician to go to dinner, but tonight, he is the only radio intelligence officer assigned to the *Khersones*. It is Friday night. Grigory loves the weekend because, even at the height of the Cold War, the U.S. Military always took the weekend off. He knows that AUTEC will close down for business promptly at 4:00 pm, and he is well prepared --- a fresh bottle of Polish vodka, and for a change of pace, some English brandy. He spins the dial on his intelligence safe and removes a few, worn issues of *Playboy* magazine. The only thing missing to build the weekend mood is his favorite American rock and roll music from a station in Miami. Grigory slides the well-worn reclining chair up to the radio counsel and bangs his knee on the edge of the cabinet --- for the hundredth time.

"Damn! Those effinging Germans didn't put a round corner anywhere on this ship," he swears into the empty cubicle.

Grigory spins the dial on the tuner of his sixties vintage AM radio trying to find his favorite rock and roll station, WOLD, Miami. It is 1745 local time and the big, thirsty, Tupolov TU-144 reconnaissance plane isn't scheduled to call until sometime after 1930 hours. Grigory will be able to listen to two hours of oldies but goodies before he has to go to work. The huge Tupolov turboprop, flying four hundred fifty knots at fifty-eight thousand feet, is completing its twice weekly photo and electronic reconnaissance of the Eastern coast of the North America-- a recon flight that is permitted by the Strategic Arms Limitation Agreement and continues to be in force, despite the demise of the Soviet Union. The *Khersones* will provide a radio beacon for the aircraft's approach to Havana and will download the photographic intelligence data for transmission to Moscow. Grigory will log the fuel requirements for the Tupolov's return trip over the United Kingdom, Norway and finally to its base in Murmansk Then, he'll radio the Russian intelligence base in the Havana suburb of Luyano, so they can 'make arrangements' -- a polite diplomatic term for bribe -- with the Cubans for thousands of kilos of scarce JP-4 jet fuel. Grigory sets his alarm clock --- just in case.

Friday, 7:15 PM Aboard the *Caribe Dreamer* anchored East of Loyalist Cay

"I'd better start the engines if we're going to have any hot water for your shower."

"You mean, I'll have hot water and be able to use real soap and shampoo," questions Addie, as she dries the dishes.

"Just give our trusty Yanmar diesels about twenty minutes and you'll be able to steam the varnish off the head door. I'm going up check things topsides and I'll see if the suits are dry."

Quietly, Scott retrieves his night vision scope from the canvas pouch under the port cockpit seat and peers anxiously to the East toward the island. Faint spots of green luminescence appear in the scope. Somebody --- or lots of somebody's --- are working in the dark on what was formerly a deserted island. Scott lets the scope dangle by its strap around his neck while he ties the Zodiac amidships on the port side. He locks the stainless motorcycle cable around the lifeline stanchion and sets the alarm. Sailing in the Bahamas is quite safe, but an expensive inflatable like his Zodiac, with a Mercury 50, has a penchant for disappearing without a trace. Scott checks the engine temperature gauge -- *nearing 180 degrees -- that'll make for a nice shower he thinks,* as he walks forward to check the anchors. Scott peers toward the top of the mainmast to check to see if the photo cell has worked --- it has, and the 360 degree, white anchor light at the top of the mast is lit. Scott shuts down the diesels and heads below into the cabin.

Friday, 2300 Hours, Central Intelligence Agency Headquarters, Langley, Virginia

Gerald Easterbrook is working late again. But it is only 11 P.M. Eastern Daylight Time -- he has worked a lot later into the night. Many agents work unusual hours while handling operatives who are positioned around the world in each of the eighteen time zones. Lots of divorced CIA types -- lots of marriages in trouble, too. Like many others in his trade, Gerry got his 'dear john' divorce letter five years ago when he was stationed in Panama. He dials the phone attached to his secure facsimile machine.

"Jack -- its Gerry Easterbrook here. I've got the latest satellite photos and intelligence report for your op. Ready to copy?"

A simple, gruff 'yes' is the only response and then the voice is gone --- replaced by the high pitched beeeep of the carrier tone on the facsimile machine. Line by line the satellite photo begins to appear on the paper. As they suspect, Loyalist Cay is loaded with dozens of wooden crates that could possibly contain military equipment. A radio intercept by the NSA indicates that military supplies are being 'shopped for delivery to an unknown Caribbean island location'. The supply list includes lightweight jungle fatigues, mosquito netting, jungle hammocks, combat boots, AK-47 rifles, 51mm Czech mortars, Belgian machine guns and surplus rations. Everything you would need for a small war. There is only one problem in connecting these dots --- there are few people visible in any of the satellite recon photos. All this equipment and no people? Maybe this stuff is going somewhere else, thinks Gerry.

"I wonder who dug up these 'C' and 'K' rations and when were these packaged? They're probably from the late 60's," thinks Gerry as he peers through the magnifier. *Wonder what this is down in the lower right corner --- looks to be an individual on his knees and, if the photo top is North, this guy is kneeling to the East --- A Muslim --- a rag headed Muslim?* Now, perhaps, we can connect the dots!" The fax transmission ends with a beep -- beep, indicating Gerry and Jack need to talk.

"Yeh Gerry, what's up?"

"Jack, check your copy of yesterday's high altitude photo --- look in the lower right corner --- under magnification, it looks to me like a person kneeling --- could that possibly be a prayer rug? What do you think?"

"Hold a minute --- let me get my mag stand."

"Well, I'll be damned, Gerry. You might be on to something. We need to tell Bing at Southern Air that he needs to get some better low level photo recon by tomorrow evening. I want that old DC-6 cargo plane of his snapping pictures of that island pronto! Or, we'll be contracting the next operation through his competition."

"Jack, that's a roger on the call to Bing. Remember --- look at the intel and try to connect the dots. Talk to you tomorrow."

"Damn, I hate these effing low priority operations. Why can't we get decent photography from our contractors," Gerry exclaims to no one in particular, as he slams down the receiver. Gerry presses the intercom button on his phone.

"Linda, I'm out of here for tonight! Make sure you call Bing at Southern and tell him that Jack is pissed. We need some really good low levels of Loyalist Cay by tomorrow, and tell him Jack is threatening to use Arrow Air for the next op, if he doesn't come up with some good photos. Okay, sweetie?"

"Yes, Gerry. I'll make the call --- then I'm out of here, too. See you early Monday."

Saturday, 0700 Hours aboard the *U S S Topeka* tied off of the Submarine Tender *U S S Camden Bay*, AUTEC Base, Andros Island, Bahamas.

Saturday is no exception, the harbor at AUTEC is crowded with ships. *Topeka* is the third submarine tied off of the Submarine Tender, *U S S Camden Bay*, on the South side of the main pier. The white-hulled Coastal Survey Ship, *U S S John McDonald*, is tied to the North side of the pier. Three smaller target towing frigates with their bright orange superstructures fill the only available space along the West side of the harbor wall. Two small tugs are tied up behind the *McDonald* waiting for a mission to guide a ship into, or out of the harbor.

Andros is a sleepy, off-the-beaten-path, Bahamian Out Island. It has few pretty beaches and only attracts a small number of eco-tourists. Its lone industry is the manufacture of 'Androsia' cotton fabric. The Negro Bahamian population is impoverished and has a forty percent unemployment rate. Andros has two very strategic and important attractions -- its location close to the Tongue of the Ocean, and lots of fresh well water, that is shipped by tanker to the thirsty inhabitants of Nassau. Missile and torpedo firing submarines love to practice in deep water and Andros just happens to be two miles from a deep ocean trench called the Tongue of the Ocean. Andros is home to AUTEC the Atlantic Undersea Test and Evaluation Center of the U.S. Navy.

"Sir, you sent for me," asks Lieutenant Commander Kevin T. Anderson, as he parts the curtain in the Wardroom and addresses Captain Walters.

"Yes, Kevin. Since this is a Top Secret communication, please join me in my quarters."

The two men squeeze into the Captain's spartan cabin. Captain Walters closes the thin aluminum honeycomb door and motions for Kevin to sit on the edge of his bunk. The Captain swings out the stool from under his desk.

"Kevin, as you know, the Navy has been developing an improved Mine Search System vehicle --- under the code name Project Ballyhoo. Clever name since a ballyhoo is a bait fish used to catch bigger bill fish, such as Marlin --- these guys in the Pentagon are clever with their project names. And, as you also know from prior briefings on this operation, *Topeka* is the first boat to be modified to launch the new MSS. Now, here is what you don't know --- but may have surmised --- we're at AUTEC to do a series of test firings and evaluations before the final contract is let. This is a very important test, as the Navy Department has authorized funding for the purchase of two hundred eighty-two of these weapons for deployment with both SSN and SSBN submarines. In addition, the contract authorizes one hundred additional vehicles to be deployed on surface ships as mine hunters. Kevin, because of your past experience with the Autonomous Underwater Vehicle program, I've assigned you as our liaison with Everen Electric, the MSS contractor. Your orders are for you to meet the contractor's representative, S. J. Barton, at Building J-21 here on the base. The contractor will be installing some special electronic control instrumentation in the amidships weapons control room over the weekend and the first test launch is scheduled for Monday, weather permitting. Any questions?"

"Sir, no questions right now, but I'm sure I'll have plenty after the briefing. What time do I meet the contractor?"

"At 1300 Hours. Here's the rest of the packet from the safe. I would suggest that you take it to your quarters and review it before the briefing. This is Top Secret material and it needs to be handled accordingly. When you're finished reviewing it, lock it in the Communications safe and sign it over to the Chief."

"Yes sir. I'm anxious to sink my teeth into this project. Thank you for having confidence in me and giving me this assignment."

"Kevin, you are an excellent Executive Officer and well on your way to your own command. I have every confidence that you can handle this assignment as well."

"Thanks Skipper," responds Kevin as he simultaneously opens the door and salutes the Captain.

Kevin takes the double sealed, Top Secret, manila envelope back to his bunk area and locks the door. The neatly typed tab on the file folder says: PROJECT BALLYHOO.

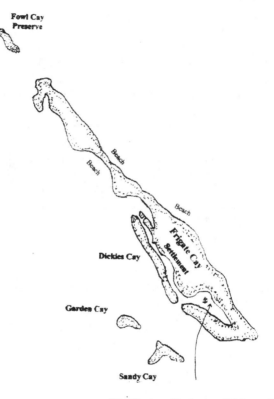

The Eastern Harbour at Frigate Cay

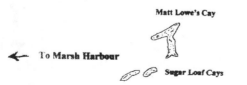

Saturday, 10:00 AM, aboard the *Caribe Dreamer*, at anchor in the Eastern Harbour at Frigate Cay.

"Addie, I'm going to take the Zodiac into the Settlement. I need to talk to Albert about hauling the boat to paint the bottom. You want to come with?"

"No thanks, Hon, I'll stay aboard with Mittens. Besides, I want to curl my hair and I need to get more visors painted to fill my orders. Scott, please stop by the Post Office and see if we have any mail."

"Okay, babe. I'll probably be gone for about an hour. I'll take the hand held VHF in case I get delayed. Just go below and put the ship's VHF on channel 9. That way we're in touch."

Scott seats himself on the gunwale of the Zodiac and speeds at full throttle, throwing almost no wake, through the crowded harbor toward the Frigate Cay Settlement. He waves greetings to his friends on sailboats at anchor in the two well-protected harbors. In the Settlement, he ties the Zodiac to the decrepit dock, next to the shipyard, and walks down the wide, crumbling concrete sidewalk toward the marina. At 10:00 AM, Albert would be 'holding court' with his island cronies at the Frigate Cay Marina offices. Scott walks past the Royal Canadian Bank and turns down the palm lined walkway toward the marina. The lineup of electric golf carts indicates that Albert is, in fact, 'holding court'.

"Good day, Albert and good day to all the gentlemen of the court," announces Scott.

"Well, by the Grace of God, it's good to see you, Mister Lindsay. I heard rumors that you and that lovely woman of yours were makin' love down in the American Harbour. Where's my favorite woman, Miss Addie?"

"That's a fine how-do-you-do, I'm here less than a minute and all you're interested in is my woman! Albert, --- Addie's just fine. She's getting beautiful, so she can come into town to see you later."

"Scott, you know that I'm just snooping on behalf of Mrs. Acton. Caroline will be asking me about Addie when I'm home for lunch."

"Okay, Albert, you're forgiven. How've you been? You're looking fine for someone who's seventy-two.

"I'm feelin' pretty good, Scott. I think they finally have my Insulin dosage right. How's Addie holding up to all that chartering?"

"Thanks for asking. She's doing fine. At least she hasn't asked me for the American Eagle Airlines flight schedule out of Marsh Harbour --- at least not today! How's Caroline --- and the boys?"

"Oh, she's fine. She's in West Palm with her mother. Another trip to the hospital for her Mom. I'm not sure how much longer her heart can hold out. The good news is that the boys and their wives and the grand kids are all fine."

"Addie and I will be up to call on Caroline next week. Say, as we sailed past Loyalist Cay, I saw a lot of activity. Did someone finally buy the island?"

"Yes, a rich newspaper man named Loomis --- he's from Oregon. He bought the whole damned island. He's got grand plans to bring plane loads of honeymooners here. Paid the Estate's asking price -- reported to be 26 million bucks, U. S. They're going to put in a hotel and two golf courses. Lots of business for the boys at Island Marine. Loomis has chartered two LCM's full-time for six months to take thousands of tons of crates from Marsh Harbour to the Cay. Water desalinizing equipment, air conditioners, bulldozers -- you name it, they're hauling it. And, its rumored that he's paying up front."

"Well, Albert, it's certainly good to see the young Frigate Cay people so prosperous --- that way their wives can afford to pay your high fuel prices and take their boats back and forth to Marsh Harbour to spend all that money."

"Scott Lindsay, you're like all the rest of the tourists. You think I'm raking it in by the bushel basket. Not true. We've both seen lots of development in the Abacos --- but, let's face it, most of the developers stay for a couple of years and go belly up --- then disappear without so much as a good-by --- let alone a check, or a thank you."

"Albert, you're probably right -- but, actually, I hope you're wrong this time. Hey, I almost forgot why I came into town. I need to make arrangements for *Caribe* to be hauled and have the bottom painted.-- have you seen Eddie?"

"Yes, I saw him this morning at Laura's Meetin' Place having a piece of coconut pie. I'll bet you can still find him there, Scott."

"Thanks for the tip. I'll head over there right now and then to the Post Office before lunch. Do you have any mail I can take up the hill?"

"No mail, but thanks for the offer. I've got to get my exercise, too -- doctor's orders. No more golf cart riding for Albert."

Saturday, 12:50 Hours Dock area, the harbor, AUTEC Base, Andros Island, Bahamas

Lt. Commander Kevin Anderson salutes the American flag flying from the coning tower of the *Topeka* and walks the gangplank across the hulls of two SSBN submarines tied to the sub tender. After showing his pass to the enlisted rank at the gangplank, leading to the *Camden Bay*, Kevin requests permission to board, again saluting the ensign flying on the stern of the ship. One more gangplank, one more I. D. check, one more salute and Kevin is finally ashore. He walks toward the navy blue, U.S. Navy Chevrolet, on the far side of the dock. The engine is running and the enlisted man has the driver's window down. He is dozing in the front seat. Kevin taps the side with his Annapolis ring and the driver awakes with a fright.

"Commander Anderson," the enlisted rank inquires with a salute.

"Yes seaman, please drive me to the Everen Electric contractors building, J-21."

"Yes sir. And --- sorry sir, about the dirty vehicle. I washed it this morning and then it rained and that turned every road on the base into a sea of mud."

Kevin doesn't bother to reply. He gazes out the window at the stark beige coral outcrops and the contrasting black asphalt pavement. There are a few scrawny palm trees and some flowering hibiscus bushes, but not a blade of grass in sight. Row upon row of pre-fab aluminum panel buildings line both sides of the street. Each building has a hand painted sign with black letters on a background of battleship gray. Finally, the vehicle comes to a stop in front of building J-21. The sign says simply: Everen Elect.

"Thanks for the ride, Seaman. How do I get a lift back to the dock area when I'm finished?"

"Sir, simply use any base phone and dial 1100. You'll reach the base motor pool --- just give your building location. Someone will be along immediately to pick you up. Have a fine day Commander."

Kevin returns the enlisted's salute and enters the front door. Immediately inside, he is greeted by a Boatswain's Mate seated behind a metal desk. On his left shoulder is a pinned-on badge with a Shore Patrol 'S P'. In the leather holster on his right hip, he carries the new Navy, standard issue, .38 caliber pistol.

"Lieutenant Commander Anderson of the *U S S Topeka* reporting. I have a meeting at 1300 with S. J. Barton of Everen Electric."

"Boatswain's Mate Miller, at your service, he replies. Your identification, please --- ah, sir --- and your briefcase, too --- ah, sir. Thank you, sir."

The Boatswain thoroughly searches the briefcase and returns it to Kevin along with his I.D. card. He hands him an adhesive badge that is imprinted 'VISITOR' on the top in red ink.

"Sir, please fill this out with your first name. Then, you can go through the door marked 'lab' sir."

Kevin scrawls his first name and removes the paper on the adhesive backed name tag. He plasters the name tag just above his Navy issued name badge, removes his cap, places it under his left arm and walks through the door. A young woman sits at a desk at the far end of the room and Kevin addresses her. "Lieutenant Commander Anderson here, I have an appointment with S. J. Barton."

"Hello Commander, I'm Jean Barton of Everen Electric --- nice to have you aboard."

Kevin steps forward as Jean rises from her desk and he reaches out his hand to shake hers. He touches her warm, soft fingertips --- something he hasn't experienced in more than eighteen months. He feels a rush go through his body. Jean is a beautiful woman and he feels an instant attraction to her.

"A pleasure to meet you Miss. Barton. I'm sorry I'm a little late. The *Topeka* is tied third boat out off of the *Camden Bay* and it took longer than I expected to get to the dock"

"That's quite all right, Commander. This is the islands and everything here operates on island time -- on island time, you're actually a little early," she says laughingly. Apology accepted, Commander. Let's get on with the briefing. By the way, please call me Jean --- and, have a seat right here."

"That's fine with me. We can skip the formalities if you will simply call me Kevin. Then we can get on with the show."

"Just a couple of formalities, Kevin. May I see your Navy Identification card? And second, I'll need to see your copy of the briefing packet to make certain it is a properly numbered copy --- security, you know."

"Not a problem with me, quite frankly I think there's too little security sometimes," states Kevin, as he stands and reaches into his back pocket for his wallet.

Jean *glances at his left hand as he retrieves the documents -- no wedding band and no tan line, either. Good, perhaps he's not married, she thinks.*

"Thank you, Commander -- 'er Kevin," says Jean as she hands back Kevin's I. D.

Jean walks over to the window side of the room and pulls the room darkening shades. Then she moves toward the movie screen with the computer projector's remote control in her right hand and a laser pointer in the left. The PowerPoint briefing is about to begin. Kevin quickly glances at Jean's left hand -- a ring on her fourth finger, but that's no wedding band. It is Miss Barton, not Ms or Mrs. Barton --- as he originally thought. Her auburn hair is pulled tight to her head and into a French twist. She is dressed in a plain khaki skirt with a simple blue denim, cotton blouse. Her bare feet are slipped inside well scuffed Reebok jogging shoes. A typical, Government Issue, black name badge stating, 'Susan. J. Barton GS-11', is pinned to the top of the blouse pocket --- she obviously prefers Jean over

Susan. A simple gold chain circles her neck and a small gold, bracelet watch fits loosely around her left wrist.

"Kevin, you're an expert submariner and I'm the resident expert on 'Project Ballyhoo'. So, our job for the next few weeks is to meld our expertise to make certain that the Navy ends up with a successful weapon system --- and I want to emphasize the word system. I'll move quickly through the first of these slides, as this presentation was developed for some non-submariner types at the Pentagon. I know that you have been briefed on the work that has been done on previous prototypes of Unmanned Underwater Vehicles. Ballyhoo is the project name for a very sophisticated UUV, or as it is now known a MSS or Mine Search System. By the way, ballyhoo are found in the waters around here. They are used as a bait fish to catch large deep sea trophy fish like sailfish and marlin. We hope that our enemy will take the bait -- pardon the pun. Are you a fisherman, Commander?"

"I'm not much of a fisherman, Jean, although I have baited a few hooks with ballyhoo. In my spare time above the water, I prefer to go sailing -- and please call me Kevin."

"Yes, Commander, er -- Kevin. As I was saying, MSS is the outgrowth of much smaller, and less sophisticated, decoy subs like the Autonomous Undersea Vehicles which are launched through thirty-six inch torpedo tubes. MSS is forty-four inches in diameter and therefore requires a special launch tube. *Topeka* is the first submarine to be equipped with such a tube. And … as you know, early AUV's such as the Mark 2 are simply Mark Forty-Eight torpedoes with the warhead removed and replaced with some special electronics. These early vehicles were launched like a regular torpedo. However, again, as you know, launching a torpedo means you have to make lots of noise --- first to open the outer doors and then there's the noise of the compressed air shot --- both noises are easily detectible by the enemy. MSS is a true miniature submarine that is almost as sophisticated as the mother boat that launches it. The Everen Mark 71 has a three hundred fifty hour duration battery and, with her titanium hull, can dive as deep as 10,000 feet. MSS is propelled by hydrogen liquid-fuel cells and, since it is launched vertically, it silently swims out of the launch tube of the mother sub with absolutely no noise profile"

"This next slide shows a cross section of the Mine Search System prototype. Here, you can see the section of the titanium hull that makes MSS able to withstand the enormous pressures at extreme depths. Note in this slide that the amidship launch tube is open and MSS, while in decoy mode, is starting to release the streaming noise generating array. A computer in the vehicle, can simulate the acoustic signature of any submarine -- and, I want to emphasize, underline any submarine, U. S., Russian, Iranian, Chinese, North Korean, British, French, Ukrainian, Cuban -- any submarine for which we have a recorded noise signature. MSS can trail one submarine target, while the mother boat trails another target. In Anti-Submarine Warfare mode, MSS can also deploy various types of ASW mines. This next slide shows the trailing external harness which contains four A/N dash Six mines. In Mine Search Mode, MSS, can search for bottom anchored or suspended acoustical mines. Once a mine is located, MSS deploys its acoustical array to generate the noise signature of a U.S. Navy or NATO surface ship or submarine to explode the mine. In our simulations in the lab, MSS has been able to explode mines at ranges of up to one quarter of a mile and still survive the explosion --- and, we can retrieve the vehicle either on the surface or below the surface. Hey, how about we take a break? I've been doing all of the talking and I've developed a real thirst."

"Good idea. I'll buy, what's your pleasure," responds Kevin jokingly.

"No need to buy, Everen Electric already did. There's some Goombay punch in the fridge, and there should be some Diet Pepsi's. I'm going to have a diet."

"I think I'll try a Goombay Punch, and, I'll put two quarters here in this Styrofoam cup --- we don't want any investigation of payoffs from the Navy to a contractor --- you know, no conflicts of interest here on this tropical paradise called Andros."

Jean wanders over to the test bench and hops up sitting cross legged. Kevin leans against the bench only a few feet from her.

"So, tell me what's ----

Jean interrupts and finishes the sentence. "---- a nice girl like me doing in a place like this?"

"Well Jean, I would probably have chosen my words a little more diplomatically."

"No problem, Kevin. I can sum it up in two words -- Neil Traxall. He's the reason I'm on Andros."

"So, who's Neil what's-his-name --- or am I being too personal?"

"No, Neil Traxall is the Senior Project Manager for Ballyhoo. He's my boss back at China Lake, California. His face appeared on the first slide in the presentation."

"Well, I guess I'd better change the subject, this sounds like something to steer clear of. Tell me, are there any facilities on base where you can quench your thirst with an adult beverage?"

"Nice job of changing the subject, Kevin. Remind me and we'll talk about Mister Traxall later. The 'O' Club has a pretty good bar -- but, I tend to avoid it, as I'm one of only nine females on base. There are some good local joint's as long as you have transport that can take the washboard roads.

Later? thinks Kevin. What's in store for later?

"I'm afraid that the only transport I have needs about thirty feet of water just to float in. After hours, it sounds like the 'O' Club for me."

"Kevin, --- I hope this doesn't sound too forward of me --- I've got a company car. Ah, actually, it's a pickup truck. I am planning on going up to Nicholls Town to a local place --- I know the owner and the reggae band is the best on Andros. What do you think? How about joining me?"

"Gosh, that sounds great --- as long as you let me buy the drinks and dinner. I don't want some two-bit Pentagon auditor questioning your expense account!"

"We'll go Dutch, and don't worry about my expense account. I get a per-diem and, with so little to spend it on in Andros, I'm way ahead of the game."

"Kevin, lets finish up the PowerPoint show, so we can get out of this metal box and get started on the weekend. This next slide shows a test we did at China Lake with MSS towing an acoustical array. Everen's engineers think that the future of anti-submarine warfare underwater will look a lot like todays above water deployments. Above the surface the fleet has helicopters dipping sonar and deploying sonobuoys, the undersea effort will use MSS just like a helicopter. Placing undersea sonobuoys will make it easier for our subs to find and kill the enemy."

"Any questions, so far?"

"No, Jean, not up to this point. Your presentation is very clear. I'll chime in if I have any questions."

"Good, this next slide gives a good overview of the electronic control console that will be installed onboard *Topeka*. And, over there on the workbench --- there's a full mock-up of the panel. Go take a look while I raise the curtains. That's the end of the PowerPoint presentation. The balance of our day will be spent familiarizing you with the mockup of the console."

1:00 P.M. aboard *Caribe Dreamer* at anchor in the Eastern Harbour, Frigate Cay, Abaco, Bahamas.

After arranging to have *Dreamer's* bottom painted and picking up the mail, Scott pilots the Zodiac inflatable through the harbor at full speed to return to *Dreamer*. A large tan canvas awning, with side curtains, shades the cockpit. Addie is busy working hand detailing tropical designs on the bills of sun visors, which she sells in various out-island gift shops. Mittens is curled up, asleep, near the helmsman's seat. The sound of the approaching Zodiac causes Addie to look up. A beaming smile appears on her face --- her man is back. Scott's been gone for two hours and she's been thinking of him --- and of last night.

"Hi, sweetheart, the postman is arriving. Four letters -- two from your Mother and, get this --- good news, no bills!"

"Hey, that's certainly good news. I've missed you. Here, let me help you tie up the dinghy," says Addie, as she takes the mail from Scott, leans over the lifeline and gives him a peck on the cheek.

"I've got lunch ready --- so wash up and then tell me the scoops you heard in the Settlement."

"Okay --- lunch can wait --- there's plenty of news to report" interjects Scott as he reappears in the companionway. "I spent about a half hour talking to Albert. Do you want to talk now or read the letters from your Mom?"

"No, Mom's letters can wait --- I can always tell when you've got something on your mind, Scott Lindsay."

"You sure can read me like a book, Addie. There's lots on my mind --- lots of trouble brewing, I think. Yesterday, when Mittens disappeared down the beach, I followed her. I only went into the underbrush about twenty feet when I came upon a trip wire -- you know what a trip wire is --- don't you?"

"It's obviously a wire someone can trip over, Scott."

"You're right, Addie. The military uses them when they want a warning that someone is approaching their position -- generally from the rear. A trip wire can detonate explosives, or you can simply tie old ration cans on a string and run the string about shin high across a path that would approach your position. An unsuspecting soldier trips across the string and the cans clatter together --- a very simple, but effective warning. Mittens and I came across a trip wire on Loyalist Cay!"

"Oh, come on, Scottie. You're imagining something. It probably was washed up into the brush by some storm."

"No, Addie, I'm not imagining -- the trip wire is real. Not only that, but last night, when I went on deck, I used the night vision scope to give a look see."

"And, what did you see?"

"In my scope, I saw the green phosphor shapes of what looks like men wearing military gear. They were working inside large wooden crates. I could see the moonlight glinting in their binoculars, as they gave us a look-see."

"Scottie, that's got me scared --- we were messing around in the surf ---ah stark naked and people were watching us with binoculars? Are you sure you're not hallucinating -- you're not re-living your army combat or something, are you?"

"No, Addie. I'm telling you the truth. I'm telling you what I saw with my own eyes. Somebody is using Loyalist Cay, as a military staging base. And, what they're doing is going to change these islands forever."

"Scott, settle down. Maybe there's an explanation. Maybe this is on the up and up. Why don't you run this by Albert?"

"Hon, whoever is doing whatever on Loyalist Cay is trying to hide this from the public and maybe even the Government of the Bahamas."

"So what? Why do you think you should get involved? If someone is doing something unlawful, then alert the Police Commissioner in Marsh Harbour."

"Addie, the Bahamas have been my second home since I was a teenager. I love these waters and islands and I make my living off of tourists that come to these peaceful waters because they are just that -- peaceful. There are no guns -- no violence and very little crime. We can anchor off of any beach or cay without worry. If my suspicions are correct, what's happening on Loyalist won't be good for business."

"So, you didn't mention your suspicions to Albert?"

"No, Albert is old. He's slowing down and, he's out of touch. Albert is just happy knowing that the local boys have six month charters for two of their landing craft running from Marsh to Loyalist. You know Albert, as long as there's prosperity, -- hear no evil -- see no evil."

"Come on, Scott, that's not fair to Albert. We both love these islands and their people. This is Albert's home and he loves them much more than we do. If he had any inkling of something sinister going on he'd be the first one on the phone to the Commissioner."

"Addie, you're thinking of the Albert of old. Albert has retired, ---- he's cutting out while the getting is good. He really doesn't care anymore --- you know, the Swiss bank accounts, the home in Florida. His heart isn't in it anymore. Heck for all we know he might even be on their payroll!"

"Scottie, I can't believe what I'm hearing from you. I can't believe that you would say that about a man who loves you and looks out for you. He's been like a father to you since your Dad died. You're just one person --- and you're a foreigner to boot. What authority do you have to nose into the internal affairs of the Bahamas?"

"I'm sorry for what I said about Albert, but I'll say it again, Addie. We make our living here in paradise and there are lots of people who are willing to take that for granted. I'm not! All I'm asking you to do is to help me satisfy my military curiosity. If, there's nothing going on -- I'll drop the subject. If there is something going on, I'll go straight to the Commissioner --- Okay?"

"Well, it's not okay. What's your expectation of me in this scheme? And, remember, I have a veto if I think it's too hair-brained."

"First, Hon, understand that I wouldn't involve you, if I thought it was a hair-brained scheme. And, if my plan is to work, we'll have to get moving -- there is a very small window of opportunity. I checked the computer and the tide is slack around nine o'clock --- and, the moon doesn't rise until after eleven o'clock. My plan is to move *Dreamer* to Hope Town and anchor her in Back Creek. Then, after dark, we'll take the Zodiac to the old Snake Cay day marker that's about half a mile off of Loyalist. You'll do the driving and wait while I SCUBA into the beach with the night vision scope. We will tie the inflatable to the marker and float on the current. I'll SCUBA in and do a quick recon from the beach --- then swim back to the dinghy. All of this shouldn't take me more than a half hour."

"Oh, Scott, that's it. I'm scared, and --- more than that --- it sounds terribly dangerous. What if someone sees us?"

"Addie, you may think it's an insane plan, but it's going be a lot more dangerous if I have to do it by myself."

"Okay, --- darn, you --- you stubborn Canuck. You're adamant about this -- I hope you haven't talked yourself into this --- like you could get shot --- killed. I hope you've thought this thing through, really well, Scottie. Since we're a team, we're in this together and I have no choice but to help. If we're going to sail to Hope Town, we'd better get going before the tide goes out."

Friday afternoon, 1545 hours, Building J-21
AUTEC Base, Andros Island, Bahamas

Jean completes the important background on the electronic interface between the sub and the MSS vehicle.

"There's certainly a lot of work for the electronic techs to complete on the weekend, Jean. I sure hope we'll be ready for sea trials on Monday."

"Kevin, I think my team can handle it. We've brought in two extra technicians --- one from Orlando and Matt Bowers is in from China Lake --- he's my best tech. Don't worry, we'll have you ready for sea on Monday."

"That's good news because my Captain is anxious to get back into rotation with the fleet. He's itching to get back on regular patrol status."

"I think we're finished here. If you don't mind, I could use some help with these manuals. They all have to be locked in the high security safe. I'll call the Shore Patrol guy in so he can verify that everything is shipshape and secure. If we've got a date for dinner at Big Big's, we'd better get you back to *Topeka*. It's about an hour drive to Nichols Town --- that is if it doesn't rain and turn the road into a quagmire. I'll ring up the motor pool to get you a car."

"That sounds like a fine plan, Jean. I'll need about a half hour to gather my gear and get over to the BOQ and get a room. What's the order of dress in Nichols Town?"

"I'll guarantee it will be hot on the dance floor, so shorts and a tee shirt are in order. Think you can be ready by nineteen thirty?"

"I'll be ready -- and hungry, too. See you in front of the BOQ at nineteen thirty."

"Kevin, I'm looking forward to this --- see you then."

The Enlisted driver deposits him at the pier and Kevin immediately notices that *Topeka* has been moved directly off the *Camden Bay's* port side. Already the air hoses and electrical cords are draped over the conning tower a sure sign that the Everen technicians are hard at work. Kevin goes directly to the Officer of the Day and has his briefcase locked in the security safe in the commo compartment. Kevin, anticipating his dinner date with Jean, begins humming one of his favorite rock n' roll songs -- 'something tells me I'm into something' that's good' as he heads to his cabin to pack his overnight bag. He meets Captain Craig Walters in the passageway.

"So Kevin, how did the briefing go?"

"Great, sir. Everen has really done a fine job on 'Project Ballyhoo'. I think you'll be impressed with the capabilities of this new weapons system."

"You movin' into the BOQ?"

"Yes, sir. I figure that the noise the technicians will make will turn *Topeka* into a base drum and sleep aboard will be at a premium."

49

"You're probably right, but having stayed at the AUTEC BOQ before, I'll take my chances on board. Besides, I need some time to review the ops orders for Monday's test. Have a good weekend -- I'll see you at oh-seven hundred in the ward room, on Monday."

"Yes sir, see you Monday at oh-seven hundred. Enjoy your weekend, too."

Kevin feels like a schoolboy who has just been dismissed for the Summer. He is really looking forward to this evening with Jean. *Jean Barton -- attractive, vibrant, sexy, intelligent and she just asked me out to dinner at a native joint called Big Big's.* "*Heck, I must be dreaming.*"

Kevin goes directly to his quarters and quickly packs his limited wardrobe of civilian clothes and his shaving kit. It takes ten minutes to walk the gang plank and pass through *Camden Bay* to the pier. The Enlisted rank is waiting with the same dirty blue Chevy.

"To the BOQ, young man," orders Keith.

The car follows the same stark route along the blacktop as it had earlier in the day. Brownish gray mud coats every vehicle that has ventured off base and this same mud is beginning to coat the blacktop. *Battleship gray mud -- great place for a Navy Base, he thinks.* Kevin closes his eyes and began to hum, La la la. la -- la - la -ah -ah --something tells me I'm into something that's good."

The Home Anchorage of Caribe Dreamer in Back Creek

7:30 P.M., aboard *Caribe Dreamer* on their mooring in Back Creek, Hopetown Harbour, Abaco, Bahamas

"Addie, its 7:30, we should get started," Scott announces. Addie doesn't reply, she simply gets up and finishes zipping up her wet suit. Earlier, she mentioned to Scott that she should bring her SCUBA gear and wear her wet suit --- just in case. Scott puts on in his Spring wet suit with bare arms and legs. The fully charged SCUBA tanks are already in the Zodiac. He attaches his night vision scope to his weight belt and straps his K-Bar knife to his ankle. Addie brings the waterproof light with the red lens from the locker below and places it in the under-the-seat bag in the inflatable. Mittens is safely locked in the forward head where the overhead hatch brings in a cool breeze. She curls up at the foot of the commode awaiting her master's return. Scott starts the big Mercury engine and the black Zodiac runs at idle through the harbor. The entire harbor is a no wake zone and it takes five long minutes before they pass the candy striped Elbow Reef Light. The lighthouse keeper is probably finishing dinner and soon will climb the stairs and crank the brass weight to the top of the tower. The falling weight will rotate the clock mechanism, which floats on a mercury base, and carries the heavy glass Fresnel lens. The light will begin its nightly five white flashes in fifteen seconds as it has every night since 1863. Outside the harbor, Scott throttles up to full speed and gets the inflatable up on plane. The Zodiac passes close to the north shore of Elbow Cay and into the Lubbers Cay passage. The sun is setting behind the Parrot Cays and the pink afterglow is fading fast. Kevin steers to the west side of Lubbers Cay, so as not to alert anyone to their strange course of travel, as darkness approaches. Scott and Addie strain to see the unlit wooden marker against the shadows of Loyalist Cay. The dilapidated day range marker is left over from the 1960's when tugs, towing barges loaded with Abaco pine logs, went from Snake Cay on the Abaco mainland to Jacksonville, to be made into cardboard for Owens Illinois Corporation. The marker, which formerly led the towboats in and out of the North Bar Channel, suddenly appears one hundred yards, directly ahead. When Scott is abeam of the marker, he swings the inflatable in a graceful left turn and heads due East. Throttling down to an idle, he glances at Addie. He can see the deep concern in her eyes and reaches out to touch her arm and give her a reassuring smile. Addie tries, but can't smile back. Now, the marker is only ten yards in front of them and closing slowly. Scott motions to Addie to take over the steering, as he moves toward the bow to prepare the mooring painter. Addie slips the outboard into neutral, pulls the kill switch cord and the Zodiac coasts up to the marker. Kevin ties the mooring line around the slimy, mollusk encrusted, splintered telephone pole. Pushed by the Southeast trade winds, the dinghy streams out toward the Northwest, its profile only slightly hidden behind the marker. The complete silence is interrupted by the lap of the slight chop against the marker and bow of the Zodiac. Addie and Scott gather amidships and she helps check out the SCUBA gear. Scott inserts the ITT Night Vision Scope into the waterproof pouch. He ties the pouch to the back of his weight belt. Finally, he breaks the silence with a whisper.

"Addie, check your watch so we can synchronize the time. I'm showing eight forty three."

"Scott, I'm two minutes fast, I've got eight forty-five --- I'll sync with you."

"Good. Figure that it will take me a half-hour to swim from here to the beach. Allowing ten minutes for me to recon the area, and about twenty minutes swimming back with the tide --- I should be back sometime round ten o'clock. Remember to give me one long red flash with the lantern every minute starting at nine forty-five."

"Scottie, this will be the longest hour of my life. And, tell me, how long is a 'long' flash?"

"Just count one, one-thousand. I'll need to get going before the tide changes. Love you, Mrs. Lindsay --- say a prayer."

Addie squeezes Scott's hand. He rolls over the gunwale and floats alongside the Zodiac to get his bearings. "Nothing heroic -- Okay, Scott? Be safe my love and do hurry back -- please don't take any chances on the beach --- please. I'll be praying the whole time you are gone."

"I'll be careful, Addie. See you in a little more than an hour."

With half the weights removed from his belt, Scott swims just below the surface toward the darkness of Loyalist Cay beach, one quarter mile to the Northeast.

Nineteen Thirty Hours in front of the BOQ, AUTEC, Andros, Bahamas

Kevin paces forth and back in the waning tropical sunshine outside the BOQ waiting for Jean to arrive. He has taken her at her word and is dressed in a pair of khaki shorts, a navy blue, Ocean Pacific tropical print, cotton shirt and Teva sandals. A gray Ford pickup truck approaches the semi-circular drive in front of the Bachelor Officer Quarters. A woman with neck length auburn hair is driving -- he isn't quite certain it is Jean until the truck comes to a stop.

"Hey sailor! Need a lift?"

"Yes, ma'am, but only if you're going to Nichols Town."

"Hop in, Kevin. Say, that's a very nice looking shirt. Actually, --- I think the blue matches my top."

"Well, you said it would be hot and with my limited wardrobe it is this or something that says N-A-V-Y all over it.

"Oh --- sorry about the condition of my truck. There are no car washes on Andros."

Kevin could hardly reply as he gawks at Jean's turquoise halter top --- no bra for sure. White short shorts, small white shoulder bag and white tie on sandals. She has let her hair down to her shoulders and pinned a pink Hibiscus in her hair above her right temple. Jean is a beautiful woman and she smells beautiful, too, he thinks.

"Say Jean, how about me driving?"

"Sorry, Commander, but this is a contractor vehicle and remember --- we don't want some Pentagon whistle blower type investigating our weekend."

"Okay, you're probably right. Then, I'll just navigate."

"No need to do that, there is only one road and if we turn right and go North, we will end up at Big Big's Restaurant. You can be in charge of the music."

The Zodiac tied to the Snake Cay marker, two hundred yards West of Loyalist Cay.

Scott holds the rope on the gunwale of the Zodiac. He glances up at Addie and gives her a thumbs up with his right hand. He adjusts his mouthpiece and moves the bezel on his watch to keep track of his submerged time. He disappears under the warm, dark water. Swimming into a slight tidal rip, Scott makes the quarter mile underwater swim to the island in less than twenty-five minutes. *Now, I need to find a way to the beach. A place where there is no coral to tear at my wetsuit or to clang my tanks against, he thinks.*

Scott works his way toward the north where there seems to be more sand. Then, he begins swimming East into the shallow water. Surfacing, he removes his mask and hangs it around his neck with the lens facing backward -- no need for the lens to reflect stray light back to the shore. He is in chest deep water and he struggles with his balance in the tidal current to take his position. He can see nothing but the black shoreline in front of him. The lapping of the waves makes it difficult to hear but --- there, he hears it! The distinct noise of a diesel generator pierces the eerie silence -- and then he hears a voice! *What language are they speaking?* The background noise makes it difficult to make out. *It certainly isn't Spanish --- perhaps Patois?* Scott works his way to the shore and kneels in the warm water. He reaches for the yellow waterproof bag hanging around his waist and carefully removes the night vision scope. He scans the tree line with the scope. *There! Off to the south are the outlines of what seems to be camouflaged netting. To his right he can see the faint shadows of men walking and shouldering something --- rifles? --- Kalishovnikovs? --or, is my mind playing tricks on me? Or, am I seeing what I expect to see? I need a positive sighting. I need to get closer,* he thinks to himself. Scott begins moving further South along the outcropping of coral holding the night vision scope above his head to keep it dry. He again kneels in the surf and sights through the scope. There, he sees it -- this time for sure. There are men using crowbars to remove the sides of the large wooden crates he had seen aboard the LCM's earlier in the week. He hears the faint screech of the nails, as the crates are being opened. *Did the crates really contain air conditioning parts?* The shadows of the men disappear into the open side of the wooden crate. Long, green aluminum boxes are being removed from the crate. Lots of military stuff is packed in those boxes. Scott has seen that particular type of box once before -- in the Canadian Land Forces -- while training on the new American, shoulder fired 'Stinger' anti-aircraft missile. *Anti-aircraft missiles! --- here on Loyalist Cay in the Bahamas. That's it - I've seen enough and I've overstayed my time -- Addie will be worried sick. I'm out of here!* Scott stows the scope in the waterproof bag and attaches it to his weight belt. He creeps backward through the surf until he is in chest deep water.

Checking his regulator, he glances at his luminous watch and compass for the course back to the marker. *There, he sees it --- a brief red flash from Addie's lantern. The course should be Southwest or about 240 degrees, he calculates.* The deeper water is cooler and feels good and the swimming is easier going with the tidal flow pushing from behind him. After breast stroking for a hundred yards or so, he surfaces and looks in the direction of the marker. He spots it --- one, one thousand. Another red flash coming from Addie on the Zodiac. A flush of adrenalin surges through his body and makes him swim faster. Scott approaches the Zodiac and can now see Addie hanging over the port side with the lantern. He stops and calls to her. "Addie, it's me. You can turn off the lantern."

"Scott, be quiet and get aboard -- I've been hearing voices for the last fifteen minutes, but I don't recognize the language... definitely not French or Spanish."

"Hon, they are probably Haitians speaking Creole. Let's get out of here."

Scott hangs on the rope at the gunwale of the dinghy catching his breath. He passes his mask, waterproof bag, weight belt and fins up to Addie and then rolls over the gunwale into the floor of the inflatable. Addie begins to smother him with salty kisses.

"Hon, stop it -- we've got to get out of here -- there will be plenty of time for kisses later."

Scott gets up and removes his SCUBA tanks. He, too, can hear faint voices. Are these men down by the beach looking for him or are they transporting men or material from the mainland of Abaco? Scott isn't going to spend time finding out. He quietly slips the dinghy painter from the marker and the inflatable begins drifting to the Northwest. The muffled voices fade off into the night and, after drifting for ten minutes, Scott starts the engine. Addie positions herself up in the bow to balance the load and Scott opens the throttle to full speed, setting a course for the Parrot Cays.

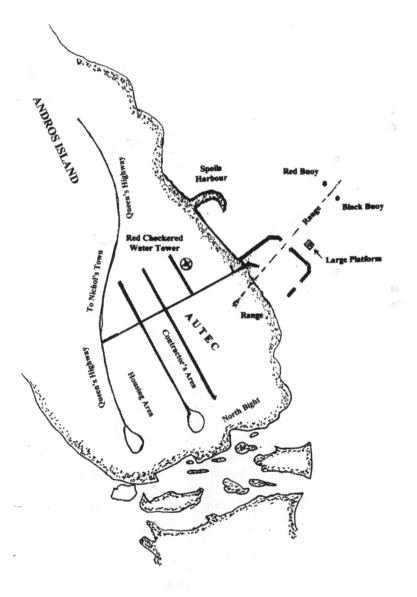

The Nichols Town Road, Andros Island, Bahamas

Jean maneuvers the pickup truck, as if she were on a downhill ski course. The road resembles a river bed and only the blaring sounds from Jimmie Buffet's Margaritaville tape drown out the groans from the pickup's suspension.

"Jean, you did say belt in for the ride of my life --- I'm just hoping that the shocks last long enough to get us to Nichols Town."

"Don't worry about the noises coming from the suspension, this is only a three year old truck and they tell me these are the original shocks. Just around the bend on the right will be Big Big's Restaurant. Kevin you've seen the TV commercials. This truck is --- or was --- Ford tough."

Jean is certainly right about the road, thinks Scott. The only things moving are pick up trucks or four wheel drive vehicles. They pass Chevys, Fords, Toyotas, Nissans and GMC pickups --- but, not one passenger car. Native, black Bahamians are flowing into the large, corrugated steel-sided shack which is Big Big's. Kevin is amazed to see so many scantily clad, native women.

"Hey, Jean, by the looks of the short shorts, even shorter skirts and tied-on halter tops, Andros is known for something other than loud music and native food," adds Kevin.

"Ah, sailor boy, you're with me -- you're not supposed to be looking at other women. Besides, this is the tropics --- on a night like this, you don't need to be wearing a lot of clothing."

The pickup dodges the water-filled holes, as Jean drives across the crowded parking lot, looking for a good parking space. The lot is occupied mostly by mud covered pickup trucks with missing tail gates. Big Big's Restaurant is constructed of corrugated metal and plywood. The top half of the walls are open, and screened and the solid shutters have been lowered by ropes to let in the night breeze. The crowd noise and clanking of dishes pours out of these openings and the open doors. Wonderful smells of fried foods, conch, grouper and french fries escape through a smoking vent atop the kitchen roof. Kevin rushes around to the driver's door of the pickup. He offers his hand to help Jean down from the running board -- placing his hand around her waist and swinging her to avoid a landing in a large mud puddle. They are the only non-native people in sight.

"Here Kevin, you take the keys. I'm taking my Amex card but leaving my purse under the seat. You hungry, Kevin?"

"Sure am -- m'am. The smells coming out of this place have me salivating."

The group of Native men at the front door welcome Jean with shouts of "H'uh'loh Miss Jean." The linebacker sized bouncer at the door even gives her a big hug.

"Kevin, meet my good friend Big, Big Martin. Big, Big -- meet Kevin."

Big, Big reaches out his huge right hand and high fives Kevin. He is big, big ---- NFL lineman big, and his white toothed smile mimics his name.

"Big, Big Martin does a great job keeping his business a fun, safe place by making certain no trouble makers get inside. And, when the Four Lix plays --- oh, never mind, I don't want to spoil your fun."

"Nice meeting you Martin. Now, I know where the name of your establishment comes from."

Jean reaches out for Kevin's hand and drags him across the empty dance floor toward a table for four in the far corner.

"This is the best table in the place --- away from the band, but close to the dance floor and, close to an open window facing the trade winds."

Kevin pulls a chair from the table and seats Jean. He seats himself in the chair directly across from her. "You seem to be a regular in this place?"

"I am a regular. Big Big is a friend of mine. He spent twelve years in the Navy, as a cook. Got his U. S. Citizenship and cooked in a New York City restaurant. Then, he got homesick, so he came back here and opened this place. He runs a tight ship. No drunks, no fights, no drugs, no prostitutes, no one under eighteen after seven o'clock. Later tonight, he'll probably stop by our table and buy us a drink or maybe dessert."

"So, what do you recommend for this hungry sailor?"

"The blackened grouper platter is the house specialty --- or you can have the grouper coconut fried. That's what I'm going to have. I'm told there's none better in all the Bahama Islands."

Kevin hates the next ten seconds of silence. He is anxious to find out more about Jean. He wants to talk --- before the band starts and they won't be able to hear each other. Fortunately, Jean brakes the ice.

"Kevin, tell me about how you ended up in the Navy."

"Well, it's a pretty boring story -- are you sure you want to hear it?

"Yes, I really do."

"I was fortunate to be born into a family that loves sailing. Almost every Fall, my parents would drag my brother and sister and me to Annapolis for the In-the-Water Sailboat Show. It was held on Annapolis Harbor right next to the Naval Academy. For a little diversion for us kids, Mom would take us on tours of Historic Annapolis or to the Academy grounds. By the time I was twelve, I had already decided to try to get an appointment to the Naval Academy. So, during high school, I took lots of math and science courses and I worked as an aid to our local congressman. That way, when it was time to select a college, I would be certain to get my appointment. And, everything worked out just like I planned it. Or, at least, most everything."

"So Kevin, tell me what didn't work out?"

"Oh --- no, it's a long story and I don't think we're ready for long stories yet --- besides, the band is going to start and I don't really want to go there --- at this time. This is about as happy as I've been in a long time --- and, I don't want to change the mood."

"Kevin, I'm sorry -- I didn't mean to get personal. You're right, the band should start playing any minute and you're hungry. I can tell. I'll place our order at the kitchen. Two coconut fried grouper platters, okay? How about you go to the bar and get our drinks, I'll meet you back here."

"Sure, what would you like to drink?"

"I'll have a Fuzzy Navel -- over crushed ice --- please."

Wow, thinks Kevin. Jean drinks Diet Pepsi on duty and Fuzzy Navels after work! -- that is my kind of woman!

Aboard the Russian Intelligence Gathering Ship *Khersones*

The rolling of the ship in the open ocean causes an almost empty vodka bottle to crash on the floor awakening Grigory. The radio is playing American rock and roll. He gets a towel and begins cleaning up the broken glass. Glancing at the alarm clock, he discovers that he has been dosing for more than an hour and a half.

"Stupid damn fool, I am. Wonder if the Tupolov has been calling," Grigory says to the glowing dials of the electronics panels in front of him. *They're probably just late -- headwinds or something, he thinks.* Seconds later, the speaker crackles.

"Mackerel Base this is Mackerel One -- do you copy?

Damn! They're still using fish call signs -- the Americans know this isn't a fishing trawler, but we insist on using fish call signs. And, you can bet the Americans and Canadians have scrambled the necessary fighters to keep the Tupolov from feeling lonely, as they work their way down the East Coast of North America. They know damn well we are not out here fishing, he thinks to himself. Grigory fumbles for the mike and responds.

"Mackerel One this is Mackerel Base -- I read you loud and clear, over."

"Base, my present position is Latitude 26 degrees 35 minutes North -- Longitude 79 degrees zero 5 minutes West. Please illuminate the navigation lights, over."

Damn! Damn them!-- they're continuing the charade. The Americans know that 'illuminate the navigation lights' is the command to begin operating the Visual Omni Range signal from the Khersones for the TU-144 to descend into Havana. Grigory flips the switch to power up the VOR transmitter. He grabs the mike to give the standard reply to the TU-144.

"Mackerel One, your navigation lights are visible. How much fuel will you require for tomorrow's trolling? Over."

"Mackerel Base, we will need 140 Kilos, over."

"Mackerel One this is Base, I copy 140 kilos. We will have it ready for you, over."

"Base this is One, roger that transmission -- have a good evening. This is Mackerel One out."

Grigory's face flushes red. He is tired of playing games. He quite doubts that the American intelligence services even bothers to listen to their transmissions any more. He would now have to get on the AM radio and encode a request to the Russian Embassy in Havana for 140,000 kilos of scarce, Cuban JP-4 jet fuel for the thirsty Tupolov. Later that evening when the communications satellite is overhead, he will transmit the latest recon photos to SVR Headquarters in Moscow.

10:30 PM, Twenty yards West of
Parrot Cay, Abaco, Bahamas

Scott presses the kill switch on the Mercury outboard and coasts due East hoping to get lost in the shadows of the coral outcroppings just West of the Parrot Cays. There is a slight glow over the darkness of the ocean foretelling of the rise of the moon. With the engine silenced, he retrieves the fiberglass paddle and, kneeling at the bow, begins to paddle toward the cover of the coral outcrop. Scott and Addie both listen intently for another sound.

"Good! Nothing seems to be moving out here," Scott whispers to Addie.

To the North, they can see the green and white running lights of one of the ferry boats on a late night run from Marsh Harbour to Frigate Cay --- but, other than that, they hear nothing but the gentle sound of waves slapping against the coral.

"Addie, I don't think anyone followed us --- other than that late charter ferry boat going to Frigate, I don't see or hear anything --- do you?"

"No, hon --- it's so quiet out here, I can even hear the ocean waves breaking on the reef --- other than that, I don't hear a thing."

"I think we should stay here for about ten minutes and then I'll paddle around to the other side of the cay before we start the engine. Why don't you join me here on the seat and we can cuddle and keep warm?"

Big Big's Bar, Nichols Town, Andros, Bahamas

Kevin returns with the drinks. A smiling Jean greets him from the table. Kevin raises his beer bottle to Jean's frosty glass.

"Clicks," toasts Kevin as their glasses meet.

"To us -- and to Project Ballyhoo, Jean. To us -- and to the twist of fate that brought us together. Kevin, do you believe in fate?"

"No, I don't believe in fate --- perhaps it is destiny, or God's plan."

"Kevin, think about it, if I hadn't been banished to Andros Island, Traxell would be giving you the PowerPoint presentation. And, think about it, your Captain could have assigned any senior officer on your sub, but it is fate --- or destiny, if you prefer. It turns out to be you, Lieutenant Commander Kevin Anderson."

Jean looks up at Kevin with misty eyes and then comes a long silence. Another lengthy pause that Kevin wants to end immediately, as his mind wanders and he thinks of Kathleen and their failed romance.

"So Jean, perhaps this a good time to finish the Neil Traxall story?"

"Yes, but -- I'll make it short because the band is going to start up soon. Neil and I were an item back at China Lake. Our relationship began to affect our work at the lab, so I broke it off. Needless to say, Neil didn't like that, so to get back at me, he decided to ship me off to Andros -- to have, as he said to me, some time to think. The interface between the boat and the vehicle is really the Project Managers job. He sent me here hoping I would fail, but, I've worked my tail off and I'm making darn well certain that this project isn't going to fail --- not on my watch."

The Four Lix begin to play 'Yellow Bird'. Kevin stands up from his seat and reaches out for Jean's hand to lead her to the dance floor. Right in front of them, on the stage, is Big, Big Martin with a steel pan hanging perpendicular at his large waist. Jean melts into Kevin's hold. *Gosh, she smells so good, he thinks.* Immediately he remembers the good times and of Kathleen --- but Kathleen was stiff and cold on the dance floor --- this woman is soft and warm. Quickly, the dance floor becomes stiflingly crowded. The natives are dancing very, very close -- the men suggestively have their hands on their partners buttocks, pulling them in close.

"This is one of my favorite calypso songs -- hope you don't' mind if we finish out this dance, Kevin." Suddenly, a short native man appears among the dancers on the crowded dance floor.

"Pardon me, Miss Jean, you's foods at the table, ma'am."

"Oh, Hi, Maurice -- Meet my friend, Kevin. Kevin, Maurice is the head chef --- and, he probably caught the grouper this afternoon --- right Maurice?"

"Dat's right Miss Jean. Dah grouper be fresh. You all eat, now."

"Pleasure to meet you, Maurice," says Kevin as they shake hands.

"Young man, les get you to your table -- my groupah plattah is bess eatin while tis hot," says Maurice, as he leads the pair through the crowd on the dance floor to their table.

"Mistah, this be one fine lady. Take good care o her -- and Big Big tell me the next round is on dah house. You ladys drinking a Fuzzy Naval and what for you, Mistah Kevin?"

"I'll have a Kalik Gold. By the way, the grouper is fabulous --- the best I've ever tasted."

"Thanks boss mahn. Mos days we catch it fresh --- 'cept when the winds up and It's too rough on the reef. I get you drinks -- enjoy dah meal."

"Thanks Maurice -- you're a doll," replies Jean, as Maurice gives her a peck on the cheek and then disappears among the dancers.

"Kevin, you're in charge of making sure that I don't drink that second Fuzzy Navel or you will be driving me home."

"Aye, aye ma'am -- after this meal, I'm not sure either of us want to get back on that washboard road, again."

Afloat in the Zodiac, East of Parrot Cay, Abaco, Bahamas

Scott presses the start button and the outboard motor roars to life. He switches on the running lights and pushes the throttle to full speed. The Zodiac inflatable leaps to life and heads toward the white flashes of the Elbow Reef light. At the harbor entrance, Scott throttles down to idle and weaves his way through the anchored boats in the harbor. He steers to the East toward the Hopetown Harbour Lodge and quietly approaches the Back Creek anchorage where *Caribe Dreamer* is anchored, from the East. On the trip from Parrot, Scott has changed out of his wet suit and stowed his SCUBA gear under the canvas in the bow of the Zodiac. Scott and Addie approach *Dreamer* on the starboard side where the boarding ladder hangs. Addie climbs the ladder and walks to the bow with the painter. Scott, proud of his perfect landing, raises the engine to get the lower unit out of the corrosive salt water. The moon has risen just above the roof of the Harbour Lodge. Not a word is spoken between them as they get ready for bed. Addie speaks first ---

"Scottic, hold me tight, I'm scared --- scared that you're about to do something that will change our future --- scared that you will do something stupid."

"Hon, wait a second -- I'm a little bit afraid, too -- but, as I promised you, I won't do anything foolish."

"Hold me Scott -- just hold me --I'm really afraid that this is going to go badly."

Coastal Operations Center, Central Intelligence Agency Headquarters, Langley, Virginia

Gerry Easterbrook swipes his I.D. card through the reader and waits for the sound of the printer behind the door. As soon as the printer records his entry, the door buzzes open. It isn't unusual for Gerry to be at his office on a Saturday night when an operation is getting hot. He moves quickly to his desk, lifts the phone and punches in a five digit number.

"Communications, this is Easterbrook -- do you have any traffic for me? Okay, I'm in my office, please   deliver it ASAP --and, thanks in advance for the good service -- bye."

He removes a key from his wallet and opens the panel on his security safe to expose the black dial of a combination lock. Twisting the dial left, right and then left again, the door opens and the ops file marked SEA FAN appears on top. He removes it and closes the safe. The manila envelope is stamped TOP SECRET in red ink on both sides. Gerry unwinds the figure eights of string that hold the flap closed. Inside is a manila file folder that is also stamped TOP SECRET. There is a knock on the office door. Gerry quickly places the secret documents inside his center desk drawer.

"Enter at your own risk," he replies half joking.

A young African-American male with a very short crew cut and a well-trimmed beard enters. He is carrying a clipboard that holds curled sheets of yellow paper.

"Here is the latest traffic for you, sir. You'll be signing for four pages of ciphers. Please sign on line   seven for receipt of four items."

Without a word, Gerry signs and the courier spins on his heel and leaves the office, closing the door behind him. He retrieves the file folder from his center desk drawer.

"What 'bon motes' do we have here," Gerry says aloud to the empty office.

He scans the header pages looking for any traffic marked 'Urgent'. His eyes spot the heading on the third page of ciphers --   URGENT   - SEA FAN

From: Beached Whale

To: Sea Fan Operations

Local sailboat charter captain, Scott Lindsay, CANADIAN, making inquiries of activities -- ref: Sea Fan. Owns 40 foot catamaran sailing vessel. His American wife and a pet dog are aboard. Extensive experience chartering in these waters. May inadvertently have compromised this operation. Other intel from LCM driver: Carried 4 boxes of West Marine. Part Number 100745, 53 gallon flexible diesel holding tanks. 2-55 gal. drums of methyl phosphonyl diflouride and 2-55 gal. drums of isopropyl alcohol.

Easterbrook reaches for the phone and enters a speed dial number.

"Jack, Gerry here. Got some intel from our man on the ground, a.k.a. Beached Whale. Seems we've got a problem on Sea Fan. A Canuck yachtsman, Scott Lindsay, and his wife have been snooping around there and are asking lots of questions."

"Hey, Gerry --- did you say last name is Lindsay? --- I think I know this guy, Lindsay.

"You know this guy, huh? Oh yah, now I remember --- Scott Lindsay. He's worked for the Company before. A guy named Scott helped us round up the bad guys on the Scotia Bank money laundering deal out of Nassau. Is that the same guy?"

"Yea, that's the guy. He's the accountant who figured out the bad guys, with connections to some   Islamic group in Syria, were slave trafficking in young girls. You think he can keep quiet?"

"Hell yes, as long as we get to him before he panics --- or does something stupid. Okay, Gerry. We probably need to meet face to face on this and decide on our next step. How about we meet in Miami?"

"Yea, I could use some sunshine. I'll take the early morning American flight to Miami --- gets in about   8:30 Eastern.

"Ah, Gerry, I'm online with Travelocity and they're showing a non-stop Delta flight from Washington   National that arrives at 7:40. Will that work for you? Let's meet in the Admiral's Club lounge."

"Okay, I'll see you in M-I-A, in the A.M. Bye."

"Son of a bitch, exclaims Gerry, as he spins the dial on the safe. Some damned Canadian is snooping about our operation and he turns out to be an ex-employee of The Company! How do you figure it?"

Let's see, thinks Gerry --- wonder what's the next hot intel in this damned stack of paper? Oh, here's something --- an intercept from NSA. Ruskie traffic from SVR Headquarters, Moscow to unknown surface ships of the Russian Navy operating in the Caribbean. Synopsis of message follows: American SSN Topeka identified by sail number 741 photographed by an on the ground agent. Aerial photograph recon shows SSN docked alongside of sub tender Camden Bay at U. S Naval facility AUTEC, Andros Island, Bahamas. Photo follows. Note modification to deck aft of sail completed during extended dry dock layup in Groton, Connecticut. Sources report a test firing of a new missile is imminent.

Big Big's Restaurant and Bar, Nichols Town Andros Island, Bahamas

"Kevin, let's dance over toward the front door. I need to get some fresh air. Okay?"

"Sounds good to me. I'm ringing wet. You lead the way," whispers Kevin in Jean's ear.

Big, Big is at the front door handling crowd control.

"Hi, Marvin. We're going to catch the cool sea breeze. We'll be right back."

"Okay, you two --- I bein watchin' you dance. The mister, he need to place his hans on you rear w'en you dancin' slow. I give you half an hour and then I come look'n fo yah."

"Oh, Marvin, don't give Kevin any ideas. You're going to scare him off -- this is only our first date!"

"Hey, Mistah Kevin -- you be doin' good for dee firs' date! Keep in mind, The Lix's goin' to play 'Hot, Hot, Hot' foh de next set - -you hurry back to dance so mor'."

"Big Big, we're already hot, hot, hot! That's why we're going up the bluff to catch the sea breeze." responds Jean, as she takes the lead and they walk hand in hand toward the bluff behind the restaurant.

"I think you'll like this view. The bluff is about seventy feet above the water -- and best of all there should be a good breeze from the Southeast. We'll look out to the East and see the glow of the lights from Nassau."

"A breeze of any kind sounds good to me. You lead -- I'll follow."

A quarter mile away, at the top of Morgan's Bluff, they can still hear the music and crowd noise from the bar. The surf, below, is barely audible. Flashes of lightning show in the North and Northeast. A small quarter moon is rising behind them into a star filled sky. Jean leads Kevin to a crude driftwood bench.

"Have a seat, Commander."

"Are you pulling rank on me --- Jean?"

"Yes, I am."

Kevin obeys and seats himself on the stone step. Jean sits on the grass in front of him and leans her head back between his legs. Kevin places his hands on her shoulders. Jean throws her head back and looks up at Kevin.

"Kevin, I love to look at the stars, but other than the Big Dipper and Orion's Belt, I don't know the names of the stars, or constellations."

"Well, I'm happy to teach you --- celestial navigation was one of my favorite subjects at the Academy. Unfortunately, we don't use it much in the undersea Navy. Look straight up, and you will see the three most important navigation stars in the sky --- Orion, Betelgeuse-- or 'beetle juice' as we like to call it --- and Rigel. They are the brightest stars in the constellation Orion. Betelgeuse is his head, Orion is his elbow and out just beyond the three shield stars of his belt is his foot, which is Rigel."

Kevin pauses. He notices that Jean is staring up at his face and not the stars. He tilts her neck back, leans forward and kisses her on the forehead.

"And directly behind us is....."

Jean swings her shoulders to the left and presents her lips. Kevin takes the lead and places his lips over Jean's --- simultaneously their tongues intertwine. Kevin's hands move down from her shoulders toward her breasts. Jean spins to the right and stands up abruptly.

"Kevin, no please! Not here! Let's get out of here and go back to my place. Besides, at this hour, there is no way you can get back into the BOQ."

"Okay, the navigation lesson is over --- to be continued. I'll lead the way back. And, by the way, --- it's dark and slippery, so I'm driving back and you're in charge of the music," announces Kevin.

"We'd better pray that there's no Everen whistle blower in the crowd at Big Big's, or we'll both end up in the brig."

"Sorry Jean, you lose --- I've got the keys and I'm pulling rank on this one. I'm not going to have this wonderful night ruined by us wrecking on this awful road."

"Hey, wait a minute, I'm a G-11 civil service grade and that outranks a Lieutenant Commander."

"Not in Kevin Anderson's navy, ma'am. Hop in."

Jean enters the driver's door, and slides over to the center of the seat and buckles herself into the middle seat belt. Kevin maneuvers the Ford pickup truck around the pot holes and turns south on the muddy road. Jean reaches under the front seat and retrieves her purse and begins to reapply her makeup. Then she selects a UB-40 tape, cranks up the volume and the sounds of 'Red - Red Wine' blend with the soft, tropical night air.

Aboard *Caribe Dreamer* at anchor in Back Creek, Hope Town Harbour

Addie is asleep in Scott's arms, but he lays awake thinking about what he has seen or what he thought he is seeing on Loyalist Cay. *Who should I tell? The Commissioner in Marsh Harbour? Albert? Danny Westerbrook, Member of Parliament? His contacts in the CIA? Most certainly this is some kind of U.S. operation -- or is it? The presidential election is only twelve months away. Is President Collins so desperate to win the State of Florida that he would invade Cuba? Not even plausible since we just spent ten years extracting our troops from that hopeless situation in Iraq. What a folly that would be --- but, desperate men do desperate deeds. Behind in the polls -- just start a war! And who is to say it is Cuba? It could be a jumping off point for Venezuela or Nicaragua for that matter. The befuddling thing is the men on Loyalist are not speaking Spanish -- and, it didn't sound like Creole either. What matters more is -- -have he and Addie been seen? What is going to be their cover story? Where were they going just before sundown?* Fortunately for Scott and Addie, not too many folks in the Bahamas pay attention to other people's business. The sun is starting to show behind the low clouds over the ocean. Soon it would be full daylight and they would take *Caribe Dreamer* back to Frigate Cay. Who could he trust? Certainly they could trust Albert, or could they?

The Queen's Highway Somewhere South of Nichols Town, Andros Island, Bahamas

Despite a road slickened by a light rain shower, the F-150 pickup truck in four wheel drive is able to handle every turn on the muddy Nichol's Town Road. *Thank God, thinks Kevin, that there wasn't a downpour. They would have been relegated to going ten miles per hour in four wheel!* Jean has fallen asleep and her head bobs back and forth with the ruts on the road. Kevin grabs her head and pulls her toward him.

"Here, this way at least you won't snap your neck and become paralyzed for life."

"Oh, Kevin, I'm sorry --- have I been sleeping?"

"Yes, but there is no reason for you to be awake -- it's not like I can't find the way -- this being the only sorry ass road back to the base."

"I'm really sorry -- it must have been the Fuzzy Navels. I'll stay awake and keep you company, I promise." Again, Jean's head began bobbing and weaving with every rut in the road. Kevin pulls her toward him again to keep her neck steady. Another ten minutes and they would pass the front gate of the base and be in the contractor's housing area. A particularly deep and jarring rut, requiring a sharp left turn, causes Jean to wake.

"Kevin, I can see the base water tower. Another five minutes and we'll be home -- nice driving."

"Jean, are you sure you want me to stay the night at your place? You could drop me off at the gate and I'll walk to the BOQ."

"No way, sailor. You're in no condition to be walking two miles back to the base. Besides, I have a sleeper sofa that has never been slept on. Slow down, and turn right at the next street --- all these places look the same. Mine is the one with the potted bougainvillea on the front stoop --- Everen number 3."

Kevin pulls the pickup into the carport -- Everen #3. He gets out and goes to the passenger side of the vehicle to help Jean.

"Oh, thanks, Kevin. It's good to be home. Thanks for driving."

"My pleasure to be in your service," replies Kevin as he hands Jean her keys.

The beige stucco exterior, with the light brown trim, has the look of base housing on any military installation, anywhere the U.S. Military resides. Aluminum jalousie windows line the side of the house facing the carport. A few scrawny cactus are planted around the foundation of the house. The front yard is white gravel interspersed with clumps of green weeds. Jean unlocks the handle and the dead bolt lock and turns on the light. The interior is as predictable as the exterior. The door enters directly into the living room. Kitchen is to the right. Eating area is behind the kitchen. Bedroom and bath are behind the living room.

"Kevin, be a love and select some music for the CD player. I'll be right back."

"Yes, Kevin Anderson at your service, ma'am."

Kevin moves over to the stereo and shuffles through the stack of CD's. Many of the CD's are duplicates of the tapes from the pickup. Kevin searches from something other than reggae or island music and finds some change of pace music --- *Eric Clapton -- that's not pure mood music but it's a step down from reggae.* He selects 'Unplugged' by Clapton, 'Love Language' by Teddy Prendergras and the movie music from 'Pretty Women'. He hits the shuffle button and the first song begins to play 'Hey Babe you got me on my knees ...." Kevin moves around the room looking at the photos that line the living room shelves. A photo of Jean dressed in her college cap and gown flanked by what Kevin assumes are her parents. Jean seated on a well-manicured lawn with a dog at her feet. Jean standing in front of a large navy anchor. The photograph was taken in an obviously tropical setting and the inscription on the pedestal where the anchor is resting reads 'Golden Anchor Award 1997 Barking Sands PMTF'. A good sign is there didn't seem to be any pictures of Jean and that fellow named Traxel. Suddenly, Kevin hears the sound of the shower running. *Wow! This could turn out to be a really great evening, he thinks.* Kevin sits impatiently on the couch listening to the music and staring at the ceiling. Soon, the sound of the shower ends and, after one more song is over, Jean appears in the hallway dressed in an oversized Mickey Mouse tee shirt that comes down to her knees. She is carrying bed linens and a pillow in her arms.

"Hope you didn't mind me admiring the family photographs. Noticed that photo of you at Barking Sands. I know a little bit about the facility on Kauai, but may I ask what PMTF stand for?"

"Oh, Barking Sands is another troubled little piece of paradise that the U.S. Navy has borrowed -- it's on the West shore of the Island of Kauai --in the Hawaiian Islands. PMTF stands for Prototype Missile Testing Facility. Remind me and later I'll tell you the whole story."

"Here, catch," says Jean, as she tosses Kevin a folded sheet. "You wouldn't mind helping me make up the hide-a-bed, would you?"

"Oh, not at all-- I'm really good at hospital corners."

"And, I'll bet you have a quarter to bounce on the bed when were finished," replies Jean.

"No --- no quarter. In fact, we don't do that aboard a submarine. No lose change is allowed -- it might drop at a very inappropriate time. Oh, by the way, I lowered the air to 76 --- is that temperature okay?"

"The temperature seems fine to me. Kevin, I put a fresh towel in the bathroom -- it's all yours. You will be amazed at how much better you will feel after a shower."

"Sounds good to me. I won't be more than five minutes -- I know water is scarce in the islands. Remember, save water -- shower with a friend." There is no response, only the soft sounds of Clapton's guitar.

Kevin exits from the shower, dries and wraps the towel around his waist. Walking down the hall from the bathroom, he notices that the living room is dark, except for a night light near the kitchen door. Jean lays curled up on the right side of the hide-a-bed. Kevin crawls in on the left side, rolls toward Jean and they embrace. Unexpectedly, Jean rolls to her right, sits up and swings her legs over the edge of the bed.

"Kevin --- I loved this evening. I love being held by you while we danced -- I love everything about the evening. Please, I hope you will forgive me, it's just that things are happening so fast, maybe too fast --- I need some time."

"Hey Jean, I understand. I was hoping tonight would never end, but it looks like it has."

"Sorry, sailor --- it's just a slow beginning. Sleep tight."

She kisses Kevin on the cheek and walks down the hall to her bedroom, closing the door behind her.

Aboard American Airlines Boeing 757 at 2,500 feet, ten nautical miles West of Miami International

The puffy early morning tropical clouds pass by the window of the American Airlines Boeing 757 on its approach to runway Nine - Right, at Miami International. Minutes after landing, Agent Gerry Easterbrook, walks through the doors of the Admiral's Club. He flashes his American Airlines Platinum Card to the receptionist and spots Jack Butterfield sitting on a couch in the back of the room.

"Hi, Gerry. Good flight?"

"Ah, the usual uneventful flight, but I swear they've removed another inch of legroom on the 757."

"Yep, as the price of fuel goes up, the legroom goes down. I've reserved a conference room at the far end of the hall. Definitely not a secure site, but at least its private."

"Good -- lead the way --- this is your home territory. I sure hope they've got some decent coffee."

The room has the expected conference table and ten chairs. A credenza is at the far end of the room. The end wall holds a white erase board and above it is the usual pull down projection screen.

"Jack, let's get started and since this is not a secure room we'll use our usual code."

"Okay, let's talk a little code. Do you have the background on our friend from the North country? --- anything in here confidential or secret?"

"No, we can talk about this guy in the open."

"Here's a synopsis of his bio. Quite an interesting fellow. Seems he's done lots in his thirty-two years. Born in Milwaukee. Parents emigrated to Canada when he was seven. Father was a professor at Marquette University and was listed as a Communist sympathizer during the McCarthy Hearings. Hmm, that's interesting. Graduated Cum Laude from York University with Bachelors in Accountancy. Scholarship from Canadian Land Forces for Reserve Officer Corps. Second Lieutenant upon graduation --- he volunteered for Jump School. S-2 Intelligence Officer for the Third Battalion Parachute Company --- promotion to Lieutenant. Third Battalion attached to NATO and sent to Bosnia in 1991. Scott wounded in firefight with Serbian Army --- returned to duty. Lots of promotions and commendations --- first to Captain and Para Company Commander then to Battalion HQ as their S-2 --- then to Major. Unit assigned as UN peacekeeping troops in East Timor to remove Indonesian Army. Honorable discharge after eight years. Licensed airplane pilot, Coast Guard licensed pilot to one hundred tons, PADI certificated SCUBA diver, HAM radio operator --there's more --- Chartered Public Accountant in Canada, CPA in the States. Member of MENSA. Lots of female interests during his travels in the Caribbean, Canada and the States. Currently married to a young American lass who is aboard his forty foot catamaran sailboat with a dog. No children. That's kind of a capsule version. You have the full bio in your packet."

"And Jack, keep in mind, he's been snooping around right in the effing middle of our operation. We need these people to think that they're transparent -- that no one is onto their Islamic jihad crap," says Gerry in a whisper.

"Yes, but Gerry, he's helped us in the past. Here's my thought process. Let's assume he's onto something at Loyalist Cay. If he is, just like us, he's not sure what to make of it. And, on top of everything, he's got an extensive military background. So, he's very curious and then, who does he go to? He's in a foreign country -- he knows that the bad guys know, or at least he thinks they know. So who does he talk to?"

"Hell, he's got his wife, on board -- so he tells her," states Jack in a matter of fact voice.

"Why, of course he confides in the wife --- but, who else does he tell? Who does he tell that can help allay his concerns? I say he calls us."

Gerry leans in toward Jack's ear and whispers. "Jack, you're probably right, but we've got to make sure he does call us and not the International Crime guys. They don't know poop about this operation. And, if this gets out --- poof, we'll have to move in early and blow them away --- before we know their weapon or their target. And, that doesn't even take into account the political fallout and embarrassment to the President for failing to nab the head guy from al-Qaida when that Somali war-lord offered him to us eight years ago."

"Jack, I think you should get into Bermuda shorts and a tee shirt, and get on the early American Eagle flight to the Bahamas. We've got to find this Scott Lindsay guy --- and pronto."

"You're probably right. I hope you've got a recent picture of this guy. And, by any chance do we know the name of his boat?"

"Jack, you're in luck -- there's half a dozen pictures of this guy -- each one with a different babe hanging on him. What's this guy got, anyway? Doesn't look like there's anything in the file on the boat. Maybe the Coast Guard can help us?"

"One of these photos will have to do. This guy won't be hard to find -- just go to the closest bar and look for a guy with a beautiful broad on his arm. As far as the boat is concerned, maybe Langley can help us 'caus I don't have time to waste going through channels to get info on his boat."

"While you're working that angle, I'll work with the commo guys on the amateur radio thing. And, here's another tidbit from Beached Whale. The young lads from Frigate Cay that work on the LCM's have been delivering some interesting chemicals as well as flexible rubber tanks to the island. I've got the science guys working on the two compounds."

"Sounds good --- I'm on the next flight to Washington National. Keep in touch and keep a low profile."

"Thanks for the advice-- I'll call you tonight."

Aboard *Caribe Dreamer* en route from Hope Town Harbour to Frigate Cay.

The humid ocean breeze has begun building land mass clouds that reflect the yellow of the rising sun. It is going to be another beautiful day in the Bahamas. *Dreamer* rolls gently under main and genoa as they pass the deep water leading to the ocean on their way to Frigate Cay. Scott is able to slip the anchor in Back Creek without waking Addie, who is now busy in the galley readying breakfast.

"Good morning, Scott, darling -- and thanks for letting me sleep in - -I feel great."

"You're welcome, hon. I'm glad you slept well -- I've been up all night --tossing and turning."

"I'll pass up the breakfast."

"Good idea --- it smells wonderful and, boy am I ever hungry. While I was awake, I was thinking about telling Albert what I saw last night. What's your opinion?"

"Scottie, I've also been thinking about our little adventure. I know you have known Albert and Caroline since you were fifteen -- and, I know you would never do anything to hurt them. Scott, I don't think you should mention any of this to Albert. What if he's in the know? You would be putting him in a terrible position of having to lie to you."

"Yea, that's exactly what I am thinking." Scott reaches over and pulls Addie close to him. He looks her in the eye. Addie, there's something I've got to tell you about my past. No, it's not about another woman. This is really serious stuff. In late 90's when I was working in the banking industry in the Caribbean, I was approached by the U. S. Central Intelligence Agency --- yes, the CIA, to help them put some sleazy guys away --- guys that were involved in the slave trade of young girls. They were laundering their money --- right here at the Scotia Bank in Marsh Harbour. I got the evidence that sent all of them to jail for twenty years. I know I can trust them. So, …. I've pretty much decided that I'm going to try to reach my old friends at the CIA. Are you comfortable with this?"

"Scott, just as I told you last night -- I'm scared to death and this morning I'm still scared to death. But, I don't know what other choice we have."

"Thanks -- hon. This whole thing frightens me, too. But, I think this is the right decision. We should tie up at the gas dock and top off the diesel. That way, I can use the phone booth at the post office, rather than making a spectacle by using the phone at the marina."

"I like the idea of tying up at the marina --- that will give me a chance to use the laundromat --- it's only twenty-five minutes to wash."

"You take the helm and I'll get the dock lines ready."

When *Dreamer* sails behind the southern tip of Frigate Cay, the wind dies. So, Scott rolls in the genoa and turns on the engines. Then he lowers the mainsail and powers into the narrow entrance channel. After managing the tricky entrance, a turn to port heads them to the settlement harbor and the marina. The mangrove lined channel opens up to a wide harbor ringed with the neatly painted cottages and businesses of the Frigate Cay Settlement. Five minutes later, *Caribe Dreamer* is tied to the west side of the fuel dock at the marina. Cliff, the white, Bahamian native gas dock attendant, a descendant of the Loyalists that settled on these islands after the Revolutionary War, helps take their dock lines.

"Morning, Cliff."

"Morning, Captain Lindsay. Good to see Yea. You're the first customer hov the day. Hit's good to see you and Haddie. Morning ma-am."

"Thank you, Cliff and how's the family?"

"Miss Phyllis his a little hunder the veather. But, she'll be hokay hin a few days. Fill er hup with diesel Captain Lindsay?"

"Yes, Cliff, top off the tank. Is Albert in the office?"

"No, Albert his hin Vest Palm for a few days."

"Cliff, okay if I leave *Dreamer* here for about a half hour? I need to tend to some business on the upper road."

"Hits hokay Captain Lindsay. Hi'll watch *Dreamer* for you -- take your time."

"Thanks, Cliff and don't worry, the dog is locked in the head -- she won't bother you. I'll settle up with you when I get back."

Scott walks down the dock, past the marina office and up the steep sidewalk that leads to the post office and Batelco Telecommunications where there is a pay phone. He pulls a well-worn calling card from his wallet and dials the long distance access codes. An operator comes on the line and Scott charges the call on his Global Net phone card. The phone rings, at least five rings, and to his surprise, a female voice answers the phone 'Central Intelligence Agency'. Scott asks for the extension number on the card and the phone rings and rings and finally, the voice mail system answers. Scott waits through the menu of selections and presses 'O' for operator.

"This is the operator, how may I direct your call?"

"M 'am, my name is Scott Lindsay and I'm calling on an unsecure line from a foreign country. I'm trying to reach Agent Easterbrook. It is very urgent that I speak to him."

"Sir, please hold the line while I page him."

This call is going to cost me a fortune. I hope Easterbrook is quick on his feet, thinks Scott.

"Sir, I have Mister Easterbrook for you. Go ahead."

"Easterbrook, this is Scott Lindsay calling from the Bahamas -- and I'm on an unsecure phone-- and we need to talk --- pronto! Do you understand?"

"We are aware of your situation. Where can we find you?"

"I'm aboard my sailboat *Caribe Dreamer* in the Northern Abacos in the Bahamas. Anyone at the Marina on Frigate Cay will know how to reach me. I've decided to take a powder until this situation blows over. I'm not sure who's in the know"

"Mister Lindsay, I agree that you should become scarce. We'll get someone to you -- I understand 'pronto'."

Easterbrook hangs up and the phone goes dead. Scott pretends to continue talking while he looks through the glass door of the phone booth to see if anyone is watching. There doesn't seem to be anyone around ---just a few school kids walking home. Scott hikes back down the hill to the dock to pay Cliff for his fuel and prepare to cast off.

"Hi Cliff -- how much did she take?"

"Honly took height and ha 'aff gallons, Captain Lindsay. That'll be $20.40."

"These trusty Perkins diesels have been really getting good mileage. Here's twenty three -- keep the change --- and thanks for the service. With the laundry done and the tide on the rise, I think we'll be shoving off, Cliff."

"Thanks fo the business, Captain." Ope ta see you hand the misses soon, Mr. Lindsay. The misses must be hay good cook -- she's been workin' hin the galley hay long time."

"That should be lunch, Cliff. Hope to see you soon. You know this is the only place where I buy fuel. You can cast off all lines. Thank you and take care, Cliff."

Addie surfaces from the galley holding a growling Mittens in her hand. Mittens has a thing about Cliff and she has to be banished below deck when fueling. Addie helps make up the dock lines and fend off as *Dreamer* moves slowly off the dock and into the busy activity of Frigate Cay Harbour. Scott makes a sharp u-turn to port in the narrow fairway between the fuel dock and a row of buoys with their captive boats. *Dreamer* steams out through the well-marked channel and into the Sea of Abaco. They steer West for a quarter of a mile and then turn to the North toward Great Guana Cay.

"Wow, you were certainly in a hurry to get out of there. What did your friends at the CIA have to say," Addie remarks.

"Addie, I'm afraid that what's happening on Loyalist may not be understood even by the CIA. They suggested that we get scarce. Those were their exact words -- get scarce. I think we should continue North toward Allens-Pensacola. It's going to be difficult to hide a forty foot catamaran, around here.

0715 Hours, Everen #3, Contractor's Housing Area, AUTEC, Andros Island, Bahamas

A beam of sunlight strikes Kevin's eyes and he awakes with a start. His legs ache from all the dancing and hill climbing. Except for the distant hum of the refrigerator, the house is deadly quiet. Kevin has a restless sleep --- - he misses the constant background noise of a submarine. Jean's bedroom door is still closed. No, he doesn't feel hungry --- but it is time to be hungry. Perhaps Jean is hungry? Kevin gets up and goes to the bathroom. He finds a tube of toothpaste, runs a blob on his finger and brushes his teeth. He quietly runs water in the bowl and washes his face, wets down his slept-in hair and goes into the small kitchen.

"The best place to start is always the refrigerator. In the tropics, almost everything is kept in the refrigerator -- bread, flour, sugar, coffee -- yes, coffee! Kind'a reminds me of the Folgers's commercial -- the best part of wakin' up --- Let's see, number of cups of coffee is four -- divided by two -- equals two plus one spoon for good measure. So, three spoons into the Mister Coffee. Add water, not from the tap, but from the bottled water dispenser in the corner," thinks Kevin. In ten minutes there will be coffee aroma wafting toward the bedroom. And, now for the toast. What cupboard holds the toaster? Kevin opens a cupboard door and the first try yields a toaster. Butter and the jam will be in the refrigerator --- and, since this is the tropics, the bread is there, too. Rye toast, lightly buttered --- orange marmalade on the side. Kevin pours a cup of coffee and a small glass of orange juice. Breakfast in bed is ready. Now to find a tray --- yes, next to the stove is a narrow cupboard. Kevin opens it. It holds trays and carving boards --- now he is prepared to wake up Jean.

Kevin walks the short hallway past the bathroom and knocks on Jean's door.

"Yes, --- Good morning, Kevin --- come in."

"No need for me to come in, your breakfast is ready. I'll place it by your door."

"Oh, don't do that, silly -- come on in, I'm starving."

Kevin opens the door and enters the bedroom with the breakfast tray in his hands. Jean lays in her disheveled bed, propped up by two enormous pillows.

"Morning, Kevin. How did you sleep?"

"Oh, I slept very well until the sun shone in my eyes. How 'bout you?"

"Not very well. I was extremely restless -- I kept dreaming that you were coming through that door to sleep next to me."

"Well, after our little talk on the hide-a-bed, I thought the better of it, not to mention that submariners are big believers in privacy. A closed door is just that --- closed. Here, have some coffee?"

"Thanks, Kevin," responds Jean cupping her hands around the warm mug.

"That really tastes great. Did you have your breakfast?"

"No, not yet. Mine's in the kitchen. Care to join me?"

"Sure, just give me a few minutes in the bathroom and I'll join you."

American Eagle Flight 1428 on Final Approach to Treasure Cay International Airport

American Eagle Flight 1428, an ATR-42, twin turboprop, banks left and turns on final for runway one-nine at Treasure Cay International Airport. Off the right side of the plane, the passengers can clearly see the skeleton of a Cessna 402 --- a reminder of a drug delivery gone wrong back in the early 90's. The pilot makes a 'no flare, fly right to the runway' landing and taxis the plane toward the tiny, yellow, stucco terminal building. The sign says: Welcome to Treasure Cay International Airport. A young native youth in tattered cutoffs and a tee shirt, is sporting a pair of one hundred-fifty dollar David Clarke hearing protectors on his ears, directs the plane to a stop. The aircraft is filled with natives returning from shopping trips to the States, as well as older American and Canadian tourists returning to their Bahamian cottages. There are a few starry eyed honeymooners wondering why their travel agent would ever book them to Treasure Cay. Jack notices one 20's something, bearded man who, while dressed in a business suit, looked like he could be a Middle Easterner. He immediately thinks about oil --- could the Arabs be financing oil exploration operations in the Bahamas? Jack can't remember if the oil experts even think there is oil under the shallow Bahama Bank.

Jack Butterfield plays the part of the tourist, well. He is dressed in beige Bermuda shorts and a light green tropical pattern shirt. Jack is wearing a Miami Dolphins cap to keep the sun off of the ever enlarging bald spot on the back of his head. In his hand he holds a small, red canvas briefcase and under his arm is the <u>Miami Herald</u>. Unlike most foreign assignments, there will be no one to meet him at this obscure international airport. Jack has removed the maroon "Official U. S. Government Business" jacket from his passport and now is simply: Jack Butterfield, U. S. Citizen, tourist.

White Sound and the Southern End of Green Turtle Cay

After clearing Immigration and Customs, Jack retrieves his canvas, Land's End, briefcase and gets in line for the next available taxi. Taxi cabs in the Caribbean islands are usually 1980's vintage Chevy or Oldsmobile station wagons. Other drivers make do with big, rear wheel drive, four door sedans. The sedans have deep, large trunks to carry lots of tourist luggage. The more fortunate drivers have fuel efficient Volkswagen or Toyota mini-vans. A young black boy, probably an illegal Haitian, holds open the rear door of a Chevrolet sedan and motions to Jack to get in. Jack thanks the boy and hands him a crisp one dollar bill. The boy beams a white toothed smile and says "Thank you 'suh. Have a great day."

"Cabbie, I need to get to the ferry dock for Green Turtle Cay, please."

"Mistah, you come to da right place.--- my name's Frankie. And you needin' to go to da ferry, so we will get ya to da ferry dock. Where you be stayin?"

"I'm not certain yet, where I'm staying. I am hoping that you could raise some hotel on your VHF radio and see if they have any accommodations for the next few nights."

"Be happy tah try for you, mistah -- 'tis all pard of de service fo' Taxi Nine," says Frankie as he picks up the mike and begins calling.

"Green Turtle Inn --- Taxi Nine on channel one-six." He waits for a reply, but hears nothing. Green Turtle Inn --- Taxi Nine, come in Miss Lydia."

"Frankie, you bad boy, 'dis Miss Lydia. Switch to one-zero," comes the static filled reply.

"This is Nine on channel one, zero. Miss Lydia, I've gots a tourist lookin' for a room for ta' night. You have a room?"

"Yes, Taxi Nine -- we've got plenty of room. Frankie, what's your tourist's name?" "Mistah' what's your name? Just shout it into dah' mike," says Frankie as he waves the mike across the top of the front seat.

"Butterfield -- B U T T E R F I E L D."

"Taxi Nine -- tell Mr. Butterfield to take 'da ferry to White Sound. We'll have our van at the dock. Thanks for 'da business, Frankie -- and you bad boy, don't be such a stranger --- you come see me nest time you're on 'da island. This is Green Turtle Inn, standin by on channel one-six."

"So, Mistah Butterfield-- yous gots a room for da night You sees Miss Lydia -- she be one of the finest looking women on Green Turtle --- you tell her Frankie sends his love."

"Sure will, Frankie -- you earned yourself a big tip, mon," says Jack in his best Bahamian accent.

Aboard *Caribe Dreamer* on starboard tack, broad reaching to the North, abeam of Guana Cay.

"Gosh, it's good to be sailing fast again. In fact, Addie, be a dear and take the helm. I'm going to set the gennaker."

"Wow, you are in a sailing mood aren't you? You haven't used the gennaker since we crossed the Gulf Stream two years ago, at Christmas time."

Scott goes below and raises the top on the chart table to expose the large sail bin. The air is filled with the faint smell of mildew mixed with the smell of fiberglass resin and diesel fuel. He returns to the cockpit with the blue sail bag with the 'N' logo of North Sails sewn onto the bag.

"Watch our speed and let me know if we pick up any after I have this trimmed in."

"Will do, honey. Right now, we're doing between five point six and five point eight knots."

Scott attaches the tack of the staysail to the fitting on the bow of the port hull. He goes aft to the mast to get the halyard and clips it to the head fitting. The sheet is fed through a block on the starboard rail. Scott hauls on the halyard and the white sail luffs off on the starboard side of the cockpit. Scott rushes back to the cockpit and trims in the flailing sail.

"Nice work, Scott, that seems to have helped our speed! -- we're at six point zero and climbing."

0815 hours, Jean Barton's residence, Contractors Housing Area AUTEC, Andros Island, Bahamas

They sit eating their breakfast at a round, glass top table in the kitchen. The day has started with a blue, cloudless sky, but now the tropical puffs of fair weather clouds are beginning to show. The sliding glass door is open and the smell of the sea breeze mixes with the coffee aroma.

"I've really have overstayed my welcome and should be getting back to the BOQ, real soon."

"Oh, no Kevin. I was so hoping that you would come with me to church -- it's a native church and you can go dressed casually."

"Are you sure you want me hanging around? And, just look at my clothes -- I can't go to church looking as if I danced the night away in them."

"We've got more than an hour till church. I'll wash and dry your shirt. The best we can do with your shorts is to put a fresh press in them. Okay?"

"Ah, the miracle of wash and wear. Jean, you certainly are persuasive. So, yes, I'll go to church with you, but only if you agree to join me for an afternoon of sailing. It's a beautiful day for a sail -- and I'm beginning to prefer moving about the surface of the sea rather than below. There's so much more for the senses to take in. Will you join me?"

"Kevin, I'd love to, but I have a million things to do -- laundry and shopping and just look at this place, it hasn't been really cleaned in over a week."

"You know, you really won't need to shop until next week, because lunch and dinner are on me. And, as far as the laundry is concerned, you will only need a swim suit, a cover-up, some reef runners, and a towel. And, while you're washing and ironing, I'll do a quick clean-up on the apartment -- you know -- the typical Navy 'clean sweep down fore and aft! So now what do you say to that?"

"Kevin, you're a real con artist. An hour at church in exchange for a sailboat ride --- that's quite a deal you've landed. Perhaps we can find some time for our long talk. By the way, where did you find the sailboat?"

"Oh, I haven't found the boat just yet. I saw a notice in the men's head at Big Big's that the Nichols Inn has daily sailboat rentals. Is it all right if I use your phone to see what's available?"

"Why of course, Kevin. I'd prefer something about 40 feet long with a captain and cook. While you're on the phone, I'll get to work on your shirt and pants."

Jean rises from her chair and reaches for a plate to clear the table, but before she can, Kevin grabs her wrist and spins her toward him. He pulls her close and wraps his arms around her in a tight embrace. Jean melts into his grip. Kevin kisses her on the cheek and ear and whispers --- "Thanks for making me aware of the wonderful world on the surface of the ocean. These last eight hours have been some of the happiest of my life."

"And for me, too, Kevin."

Kevin flexes at the knee and reaches behind Jean's legs, quickly lifting her into his arms. He carries her to the hide-a-bed where he gently places her on the right side of the bed. Kevin climbs over to lay next to her. They embrace, while kissing each other wildly. Kevin's right hand moves up beneath the Mickey Mouse night shirt and he cups his hand around her soft, round breast. His thumb and forefinger finds her aroused nipple and he softly massages it. Swinging his right leg over hers, he presses his thigh in between her legs and against her striped bikini panties so she can feel the full hardness of his erection. Suddenly, Jean rolls sharply to the right separating herself from Kevin and breathlessly she says:

"Wow, sailor boy, you turn me on. You are a hungry man and, I love my man to be hungry. But, I want you to be after me all day. If we keep this up, we'll be late for church -- and, right now young man, we both could use some churching. Okay?"

"Okay. To be continued --- I think," responds a disappointed Kevin.

Jean straightens her Mickey Mouse tee and returns to clear the table. Her aroused nipples are plainly visible through the shirt.

"Jean, since we're running late, let me handle the dishes --- or if you prefer, I'll press my pants."

"Oh, that's a deal I can't refuse, I hate to do dishes."

Room 117, The Green Turtle Inn, Green Turtle Cay, Abaco, Bahamas

Jack Butterfield sets his alarm for 6:00 and is up and jogging on the deserted beach by 6:30. As he jogs, he dodges clumps of seaweed that were brought up on the beach by last night's high tide. Jack thinks, *this beach isn't the clean paradise he had seen in the travel posters. In fact, a close inspection of the seaweed would show tiny globules of tar -- the remnants of some oil spill or the pumping of a ship's ballast tanks somewhere distant from these beautiful islands. Further down the beach is a debris field of every sort of plastic known to man --- Styrofoam cups and plates, P V C spoons, forks and knives dumped overboard by a foreign flagged cruise ship. Polyethylene titers of blood --- medical waste dumped into the sea off of one of the U. S. mainland cities --- perhaps New York or Atlantic City? And then, there is the military flotsam from Navy exercises in the Atlantic --- spent sonobouys and fiberglass rocket casings. Lots of Navy garbage and general junk gets tossed over the side in the dark of night. In addition, there are the scorched fiberglass panels from the last abort of a rocket launched from the Kennedy Space Center. Some of the beach debris actually looks like it belongs there. The well-worn wooden boards that may have been part of the hull of an inter-island freighter. The blue and white three inch braided hawser--- remains from some tug that had struggled to keep its tow in place in heavy seas. Who knows what kind of person does these terrible deeds to the sea? Only the sea knows and occasionally some sharp eyed cruise ship passenger with a video camera catches them in the act. Between the man made debris, there is lots of sand and coral -- and some signs of life.*

Jack Butterfield walks through his cool-down and stops at the foot shower to clean the sand from his shoes. The sign says: *Please, check your feet and shoes for tar. Use the tar remover and rags provided. Thank you, The Management.* Jack scrubs at the soles of his jogging shoes and removes most of the tar. He carries his shoes in his hand and walks the cement path to his room. Removing his room key from his jogging shorts pocket, he opens the door to his villa and goes immediately to the phone to call HQ in Langley, Virginia.

"Connie, J. B. here. Is Gerry in?"

"Good to hear your voice Jack and yes, Gerry is here. I'll put you through."

"Hi. Jack. I know you're on an unsecure phone so, the answer is no. The boys have been listening on the radio all night and day and nothing from that sailor boy of yours, but we'll keep trying."

"Well, keep me informed and let me know if you get anything for me."

"We will, Jack. Here's a good one for you. The science guys say the two chemicals you asked about, when combined, form a gas --- think Tokyo subway --- if you know what I mean. Keep on the line while I check with Connie."

"Oh, my God, Sarin gas --- these guys are playing for keeps," Jack thinks to himself.

Gerry calls Connie on the intercom. "Connie, do you have a trace on Jack's number yet?"

"Gerry, just hold the line for another thirty seconds more and we should have it."

The phone trace is completed and Connie gives the word to Gerry.

"Everything is A-okay, Jack. Now we know how to keep in touch with you."

"Yeh, good talking to you. Enjoy your day off, ha, ha. I think I'll do some fishing."

Jack disconnects with Langley and calls to the front desk to check on a fishing charter.

"No, actually I don't want to go off into the ocean. I'm looking for a guide and a boat and want to still fish with a hand line for yellow tails or go into the tidal flats and catch some bonefish. Do you have any suggestions?"

"Yes, Mister Butterfield, I would recommend Malcome --- actually, he like to be called Reggie --- Malone. He's one of 'da bess. Dah you want me to call him for you?"

"Yes, Miss Lydia, please call him and then let me know where to meet him."

"Mister Malone always meet his charter passengers at our East fuel dock. Be 'der around noon. Dah dock master will introduce you."

"Thanks again, Miss Lydia."

Jack needs to get the lay of the land, so he decides to walk to the East fuel dock and see if he can get a chart or guide book and maybe some information on where a charter yacht might anchor, if they wanted to get away from it all. The small yellow hut on the fuel dock is just big enough for a chair, a cash drawer and some shelving which held plastic bottles of two-stroke engine oil and a shelf of charts and spiral bound guide books. Jack peaks inside and startles a snoozing young boy.

"Hi, son. My name's Jack. What's yours?"

"Name's Ben, suh. Can I hep you?"

"Why perhaps you can, Ben. I'm looking for some kind of chart or guide book that I can use on my fishing trip this afternoon. What would you suggest?"

"Well, suh, we have the Cruising Guide to the Bahamas which covers the entire Bahamas Islands. It's pretty spensive. Or, we have the Abacos Cruising Guide which cover da local islands."

"Ben, money aside, which has the best charts of this area?"

"Oh, suh, there's no doubt, it's da Cruising Guide. It's spensive --- twenty-eight dollars, ninety five cents, U. S."

"Here's thirty dollars, U.S. Keep the change. And Ben, thanks for the help."

"You're welcome, suh. And, enjoy you stay at the Green Turtle Inn, suh."

Jack hurries back to his room. He only has two hours to study the guide book.

Aboard *Caribe Dreamer* in the Whale Cay Passage, Abaco, Bahamas.

Addie has the helm and Mittens is curled up at her side. The sailing is easy, as they move through the channel markers in Whale Cay Passage. You cannot go straight North from Frigate Cay to Green Turtle because of a shallow bank that stretches East from the Treasure Cay peninsula. You must sail East, out into the ocean off of Whale Cay. The steel I-beam markers tower twenty feet above the surface and are topped with numbered red triangles or green squares. Keep the green markers on your right and you would be in deep water. The markers had been placed in the channel by a cruise line that dredged a channel from the ocean to the northern tip of Guana Cay. Unfortunately, the channel ran Northeast - Southwest and every Northeast storm roared into the channel making it impossible to anchor a five-hundred foot cruise ship. Dozens of storms and dozens of canceled stopovers convinced the cruise line to quit calling in the Abacos.

Scott is below studying the charts of the waters North of Green Turtle Cay. He comes up into the cockpit carrying a chart. He opens the chart and spreads it on the cockpit table.

"Addie, take a look at this. Remember the little horseshoe shaped cove where we anchored at the South end of Manjack Cay?"

"Oh yes, now that I'm looking at the chart, I remember -- the hook shaped island is called Crab Cay. But, isn't the water really shallow?"

"The water in the cove is plenty deep, but there's very little water out front. We will have to hit the tide just right in order to get inside."

"Scott, I think it's a great place to hide out. Question is --- are we going to approach it from the East or the West?"

"It's a lot trickier to come in from the ocean side, but, if we come in from the West, everyone on Green Turtle will see us going by. Hon, we'd better sail a little higher. Steer toward that little cay just to the East of New Plymouth harbor. There's an opening in the reef and we can skirt by along the East shore on the inside."

"Okay, Scott. I'm locked in on the little cay. If I'm going to hold this course, it looks like the jib could use a little trim."

Approaching The Holy Gospel Church, just South of Nichols Town, Andros Island, Bahamas

Again, Kevin has to ride shotgun, as it is company policy that only employees could drive company vehicles. He is in charge of the Tape player and just holding on as best he can while Jean maneuvers around the pot holes in the road. The neat, hand painted sign simply states: Nichol's Town Gospel Church. It is a new building that has been constructed of four by eight sheets of rough sawn cedar paneling that have been stained gray. Red flower boxes filled with blooming impatiens hang under the jalousie, crank-out windows favored by people living in warm climates. Surprisingly, all the windows are cranked closed. Kevin climbs down from the passenger seat and hurries around the front to help Jean exit the truck. He grabs her around her waist and lowers her to the ground. Jean grasps Kevin's hand and silently they walk to the church. She is wearing a simple white cotton dress which buttons up the front with large brown buttons. Her waist is cinched with a braided two inch wide, white leather belt attached at the front with a large gold buckle. A simple gold chain with a cross adorns her neck. Jean's head covering is a Bahamian straw hat with a white sash above the brim. Most of the parishioners arrive on foot or by gasoline powered golf carts. A few have automobiles, and others arrive by pick-up truck. Most of the parishioners are Black Bahamians, although there are some Whites.

"Kevin, you seem so quiet. Are you uncomfortable going to this church with me?"

"I guess, just a little. I was raised Lutheran and going into a strange church still makes me a bit uncomfortable. You just lead the way and I'll follow."

"This is a very simple service and it will go by quickly. They sing at least six songs -- and they have a great four piece combo."

"Oh, that's good news. I love to sing in church."

There isn't a child in sight -- all the parishioners are adults. Sunday school is held simultaneously to the church service. Kevin likes the 'adults only' approach. Nothing peeves him more about Church than children misbehaving and worse, the parents that obviously have no control over their children's behavior. Kevin and Jean are greeted at the door by two Native Bahamian ladies, dressed in brightly colored cotton print dresses. As obvious visitors, they are each handed a Bible. Inside the Bible is a mimeographed piece of paper which says: Dear Visitor, Welcome to Nichols Town Gospel Church. *If ye not be a Baptized follower of Jesus, please do not partake of the elements of Communion when they are passed.* Kevin and Jean slip into the second from last pew on the left. Upon being seated, Jean begins paging through a hymnal. Using strips of paper from the notice, she marks

91

the pages of the six songs that are announced on the hymn board located at the front right of the altar. She hands the hymnal to Kevin and reaches for her Bible.

"I think I'm going to like this place. Air conditioning and a comfortable pew. Just nudge me if I begin to snore," Kevin whispers in her right ear.

"Kevin, I can assure you that you will not fall asleep -- see that amplifier on the stage --- I'll bet it can wake the dead."

At precisely five minutes to nine, four Native Bahamian gentlemen dressed in khaki wash pants and maroon polo shirts, walk onto the stage. One carries a saxophone, the others move into position to play bass cello, drums and keyboard. They begin playing a spirited, jazz rendition of "Praise be to Jesus." Exactly five minutes later, a white robed Native Bahamian man approaches the lectern and leads the applause as the quartet finishes playing.

"You all please stand and join the band with hymn number two eight five -- Praise be to Jesus," announces the pastor.

The congregation enthusiastically joins the band in four verses. The song seems to be one of their favorites. In some pews, the churchgoers hold hands and sway with the music. Others raise their arms toward the ceiling in praise of Jesus. Kevin and Jean join in the singing and swaying. Pastor Roberts leads the congregation in prayer and then gives a fifteen minute message entitled 'The Relevance of Jesus in the Modern World'. When the service ends, Kevin and Jean quickly exit by a rear door and return to the pick-up. They drive out of the parking lot and turn North toward the Nichols Bay Inn. The drive up the hill takes longer and the hill looks steeper to Kevin, than it had last evening. The Nichols Bay Inn reminds him of the Tara mansion in 'Gone With the Wind'. A circular driveway leads to a large portico supported by eight white columns. Beautiful flowering hibiscus bushes flank the ends of the portico. Large coconut palms with their curved trunks leaning toward the trade winds are scattered throughout the hotel grounds. Kevin directs Jean to the hotel office which occupies the first villa just beyond the circular drive. Kevin hops out of the pick-up and goes into the office to sign the charter agreement. A few minutes later, he returns to the truck rolling a large beverage cooler. Kevin and Jean proceed to the hotel washroom to change into their sailing clothes.

"Hey, sailor, where did you steel that cooler," says Jean laughingly.

"Remember, I said that lunch and dinner are on me. Well, this is our lunch -- and some cold drinks. Jean, park the truck over there along the beach. I'll meet you there and row us out to the mooring."

"Kevin, did you pick up any sun screen?"

"Hey, thanks for reminding me -- sun screen isn't something we think of on a submarine. I'll check in the office and see if they have some. Wait here --- I'll be right back."

Kevin turns around and walks back to the office returning in a few minutes with a bottle of spray, SPF-20 sun screen.

"So, Kevin, which boat is ours?"

"It's the second one out from the dock. The white, Cape Dory, sloop. --- and it's named '*Salty Two*'."

"Oh, what a cute little boat and I love the name --- it has the sound of adventure. And, it also sounds like we might get a little bit wet."

"Jean, as light as the winds are, it won't be wet, but it certainly could be adventurous. I haven't sailed a small boat since my sub school days at Groton."

"So, now you tell me! You invite me to go sailing and you haven't sailed in years."

"Oh, don't worry. Sailing isn't something you ever forget. The skills are transferable from boat to boat just like driving a Ford Focus is transferable to a Mustang. Here, help me launch the dinghy."

Kevin carefully loads their gear and the cooler into the dinghy. Kevin helps Jean sit in the rear seat. He sits in the middle seat to row while facing backwards, occasionally glancing over his shoulder to keep on course. They approach the *Salty Two* along the port side and stop to unload Jean and the gear into the cockpit. Then Kevin moves the dinghy forward and ties its tether to the mooring buoy float. He carefully rolls himself out of the dinghy and onto the narrow foredeck of the twenty-three foot Cape Dory Typhoon sloop.

"This boat is absolutely adorable," says Jean as she pokes her head out from the cuddy cabin. "Everything is in miniature. There are two beds and in between, in the front, there's a small toilet. And, on the left is a kitchen with a swinging stove."

"Whoa Jean, if I have any hope of turning you into a sailor, we need to get some of the terminology down. First, those are bunks, not beds. And, the toilet on the boat is called the head -- and up front is forward and left is the port side and the kitchen is called a galley."

"Okay, let me try. Bunk -- head -- and forward -- and left is port. Kitchen is galley. How do I remember port from starboard?"

"Easy, just remember that both port and left have four letters. Here, help me untie the mainsail cover --- this blue cloth thing."

"So this is the main sail and the blue thing covering the main is the mainsail cover. It all seems so logical. Tell me some more. Kevin, tell me everything you're doing --- by the numbers, just like sailing school."

"Well, once the main is uncovered, you can hand me that blue sail bag and I'll hank on -- that means attach the jib up forward with these spring-loaded brass clips. I'll clip them on the wire that comes from the top of the mast to the front of the boat -- it's called the forestay."

Soon, *Salty Two* is ready to sail. But, Kevin has a dilemma. *How do I slip the mooring and make certain the mooring pennant gets into the dinghy and the boat doesn't just float backwards to the beach. Should I have Jean on the bow or, back at the tiller in the cockpit?*

"Okay, Jean, here's the important part. You're going to go up onto the foredeck --- that means up front to the bow --- and you're going to release the mooring line. Simply remove the loop of rope from the metal cleat and throw it into the dinghy. I'll be here at the tiller ready to steer us away from the mooring."

"Kevin, do you really think I can do this and not screw things up? I've never been on a sailboat before."

"You will do just fine. I'll walk you through it. First, crawl forward on your hands and knees. You can use the jib sail as a cushion for your knees. Jean clambers over the cabin house to the foredeck where she turns her head back toward Kevin in the cockpit.

"Now, do you see the mooring rope coming up from the float?"

"Yes, Kevin, I see it."

"Simply unwind the line from the cleat in a figure eight motion and throw the whole she-bang into the dinghy."

"How am I doing?"

"You're doing just fine. Okay, throw the lines in the dinghy and then just stay put till I get the boat moving and then you can join me in the cockpit. Jean reverses the process and returns to the cockpit and seats herself next to Kevin on the port side.

"Say, that was nice work, you're well on your way to being an excellent crew."

"So far, this is fun.--- I can't believe it. I love to try new things. I'm actually learning to sail."

"Right now we're just sailing with the mainsail. I need to hoist the jib, so you'll have to steer, while I hoist. Are you ready for this?"

"Me --- steer, oh, no way. I don't know anything about steering a sailboat."

"Well, Jean, the best way to learn is trial by fire. Just hold your hand on the tiller and we'll do some test maneuvers. I used to tell ladies that steering with a tiller is just like steering a coaster wagon backward -- that is, until a women told me that most girls never owned, steered, or road in, a coaster wagon."

"You can put me in the same class as those women -- I've never steered a coaster wagon, forward or backward for that matter, or a sailboat."

"Okay, first thing we're going to do is to release some of the pressure on the tiller -- note that the boat wants to turn up into the wind -- or turn to the left. So, to make the boat go straight ahead, you need to apply a little pressure on the tiller -- so pull it toward your stomach -- but, just an inch of pressure -- not all the way toward your stomach -- or we'll end up going in a circle. Then release the pressure and repeat the process of pulling on the tiller. Pick out a landmark on the shore and try to steer toward it."

"I think it's going to take a long time to get the hang of steering -- but, its fun. How fast do you think we're going?"

"You're doing fine. With only the main up, we're only going about two knots. You can jog faster than two knots."

"Kevin, it sure seems like we're going faster than a jog."

"This close to the water, it seems like we're going fast -- but, sailing is about silence and grace and not about speed. See the small island ahead of us?"

"Yes, I see it."

"Think you can keep us pointed toward it while I raise the jib?"

"I'll sure try to, Kevin."

"Okay, here goes -- soon, we'll be going five knots which is a good speed for this little boat."

Kevin hoists the jib and cleats the halyard at the mast. Jean has done a good job of keeping on course and their destination, Morgan's Bluff Bay is only a little more than an hour away.

"Jean, see that small cay just off our port bow?"

"Yes, I see it."

"That's Money Cay and according to the people at the inn, we should anchor just to the West of it. The beach is supposed to be the perfect place for a picnic."

"Wow, that island looks like something from a Hollywood set -- its beautiful -- just look at all the palm trees."

"Yes, it sure is beautiful."

Jean sits close to Kevin. He holds the tiller with his large, warm hand on top of hers and his other arm is around her shoulder. She is very comfortable sitting next to this strong, patient man for the next hour. She's learning to sail. *I think I love sailing, she says to herself.*

"Here, take the tiller and steer straight toward the right hand edge of Money Cay. I'll take down the main and lower the jib. Then we'll start the outboard and motor into the wind and around to the other side."

"Aye, aye, sir. You know, Kevin, you're a great teacher -- I'm actually sailing this thing. Just let me know if I get too far off course."

"Don't worry, I'll keep us on course."

Kevin lowers the jib and wraps the jib sheets around the sail to keep it in place on the foredeck. He asks Jean to steer up into the wind while he takes down the mainsail --- she does a perfect job. Kevin furls the main on the boom by looping the tail of the main sheet around it. He moves the anchor from the cabin and places the anchor and the line on the bottom of the cockpit. Without any sail, the Cape Dory Typhoon bobs like a cork in the slight chop. Two pulls on the starter rope and the long-shaft Johnson outboard purrs to life. Kevin motors toward the North end of the cay. There is not another boat in sight -- in fact, they have seen only an occasional native runabout heading for Nichol's Town. With the tide almost high, Kevin motors in close to the beach. The bow touches gently on the soft, sandy bottom. Kevin retrieves the anchor from the cockpit floor and throws it toward the beach. The wind blows the bow off the sandy bottom and out into deeper water. The anchor rode pulls up tight indicating it is set deep into the sand.

"Let me get into the water first and take all the gear to the beach. Then, I'll come back for you."

"That's a deal. I'm getting hungry. I'll get the cooler from the cabin."

It takes two trips back to the boat to off-load the cooler, towels and snorkeling gear. Kevin goes back a third time to get Jean ashore. Standing by the starboard side of the boat in waist deep water, Kevin has Jean sit on the starboard side and dangle her feet over the side. He places his hands around her waist and lifts her toward him. Jean's arms drape around his shoulders and they embrace and begin kissing, their tongues searching for each other's. His left hand struggles to unhook her bikini top. Jean quickly reaches to the front of the bikini and unhooks her top. Her hands plunge into the waistband of Kevin's swim trunks and she pulls the trunks down below his knees. Kevin hops out of his trunks and throw them on the foredeck of the boat. Jean reaches for Kevin's erection as he bends down and places his mouth around her breast. Kevin reaches down and grabs Jean's thighs just below her buttocks and pulls her toward his erected penis. She wraps her legs around him and submits herself to his powerful thrust. For a few moments, their bodies moved up and down in the warm surf together. Breathlessly, Jean pushes away from Kevin, retrieves her top, and dives beneath the surface. Kevin follows her as she swims toward the deeper water. Then, with her top back in place Jean begins to swim toward him. They kiss passionately while in a tight embrace. Then, there is nothing but stunned silence, broken only when Jean begins to speak.

"Okay, sailor boy, it's time for our talk. I know that sailing is all about silence, but the time is now. We both want the same thing, but Kevin, please listen to me. I'm a very fertile twenty-nine year old woman. I have wanted to make love with you since you held me on the dance floor last night. Please, darling, don't think that I am leading you on. I am falling in love with you, but we need to take our time and we need to talk."

"Well hon, let's swim to the beach, have some lunch and start talking. You want to start by talking about Traxal or do you want me to talk about Kathleen?"

"Since you know about Traxall and this is the first time you have mentioned this Kathleen woman's name --- you probably need to go first."

"Okay, so, here's the short version. I'm in my second year at the Academy and we are allowed to have family and visitors. It's a home football game against the Air Force Academy so, my parents come to Annapolis with the family friend, the Congressman I told you about --- who, by this time is a Senator. Kathleen is his daughter and when I was a page, we had a brief --- ah --- summer-time romance. So, you probably guessed it, Kathleen comes, too. Again, keeping to the short version, we rekindled our relationship just like we hadn't been away from each other for three years. She is a beautiful woman and knew exactly what aroused a twenty-two year old male and, yours truly, knew how to make her happy. Our relationship blossomed and we were together every chance we got --- although my Navy career continually got in the way. We were married at the Academy Chapel just two days after my commissioning. Big wedding --- the Vice President and his wife were guests. Kathleen knew full well that I majored in Nuclear Engineering and that meant there was a good chance I would end up in sub school. She had convinced herself that her father could pull enough strings to get me a desk job at the Pentagon. If you're going to make the Navy a career, you won't go anywhere unless you get your own command. For me this meant working up the ranks until I was selected to command a submarine. In the end, our romance died while I was away on my fourth patrol --- she couldn't take the loneliness and soon found herself a shore bound sailor boy. Divorced. End of story. So, let's put away the crying towel and have lunch."

"Yes, sir, responds Jean with a salute. Hey sailor, dig your heels into the sand and listen to it bark."

"Oh, so that's where the term barking sands comes from?"

"Yes, Barking Sands, is on the North Coast of the island of Kauai. Andros, this little piece of paradise, reminds me of a lot of Kauai. It has some of the beauty -- although Kauai is the most beautiful piece of God's world that I've ever seen --- unfortunately, it too, has the Navy. But, like paradise everywhere, there are people trying to screw it up."

"Yes, it seems that the Navy has tried to screw up some of the prettiest places in the world."

"But, it's really unfair to blame it all on the Navy. Look at Kauai -- who would have thought that the world would ever have too much sugar? – or, that chemists would produce artificial sweeteners --- or that you could get sugar from beets and corn?"

"So what's the price of sugar got to do with paradise?"

"Kevin, it's got everything to do with it, because behind every paradise, there's people. People working to feed families. People on small islands that will never have enough money to get on a jet plane to go on vacation. People falling in love. So, then comes the end of the Cold War and the dissolution of the Soviet Union --- how much longer will we be testing torpedoes or missiles at Barking Sands in Hawaii or at AUTEC in the Bahamas."

"So, what you're saying is that you're are worried about our collective futures. Heck Jean, don't kid yourself. The Cold War may be over, but there's another kind of war starting -- a religious war. It will take its place and we'll be testing weapons forever --- and the Navy will be here in paradise, no matter what the price of sugar --- or, unfortunately, the price of people. Just look at the mess the President has created over in the Middle East. This religious war between the Muslims and the West is just getting hot. How about we adjourn this conversation and have lunch?"

"Only if you promise that we can continue this conversation--- the great sugar debate --- later. Till, later, then?"

Kevin grabs a beach towel and hands it to Jean. He seats himself on the edge of his beach towel and spreads it on the sand and reaches out to help

Jean sit in front of him. He wraps his arms around her and pulls her tight to his body while nibbling at her neck and ears. Jean turns around and kisses Kevin full on the mouth.

"Kevin, I told you I want you hungry. I'm not trying to lead you on, but the one thing neither of us needs is for me to get pregnant. Spend the night with me in my apartment. We'll put some good music on the CD player and fluff the pillows on my bed, okay?"

"Hey, that's a date no red blooded submariner can refuse. I'm still hungry -- let's eat! -- okay?"

"Yes Kevin, let's have our picnic."

Soon it is time to up anchor as '*Salty Two*' must be back on its mooring, by sunset. The trip back is a close reach into the southeast chop and it will take an extra half hour to get back. Kevin raises the sails while Jean handles the tiller. As soon as they are East of Money Cay, they are able to broad reach to Morgan's Bluff. From Morgan's Bluff, the sailing becomes a little more difficult. Kevin must trim the sails close hauled and beat into the chop toward Nichol's Town.

"Kevin, I just love our time together. This is the best Sunday I've had since I was a kid. Thanks," says Jean as she kisses him on the cheek.

"Mega dittos to that. I'm looking forward to spending at least the next five hours together."

"Oh, I hope we have more than five hours together in the future. I'm really dreading the thought of driving you back to the BOQ."

"Speaking of the BOQ, they're going to get off cheap -- I never did sleep in my bed," exclaims Kevin and breaks into a laugh.

"Jean, come sit next to me on the high side. You can stretch your feet across the cockpit and it will help you hang on while we're heeling and bucking into these seas. Besides, I want you close to me."

"Sure, I'll join you on the high side. Hopefully, my one hundred pounds will help to level this tippy little boat."

Kevin holds the tiller with his left hand and puts his right hand around Jean's shoulders, pulling her gently toward him. Jean places her left hand on his right thigh, gently rubbing back and forth with the motion of the boat.

8:00 AM, The West Dock, Green Turtle Inn, Green Turtle Cay, Abaco, Bahamas

Jack Butterfield spots Mister Malone seated in the open Boston Whaler outboard boat. It is a center console model with a white canvas bimini top. Large red letters on the hull spell out WHALER. Aft along the gunwale are rod holders rigged with light tackle for bone fishing.

"Mister Malone?"

"Yes, sir, you must be Jack Butterfield --- and, please call me Reggie," came the reply in the most perfect Queen's English.

"Say, Reggie, I've been studying the charts and it looks like some good bone fishing territory up to the North end of the Cay. Do you think we can find some good fishing up there?"

"You read your charts real good, Mr. Butterfield. We're going to head North up between Green Turtle and Manjack."

"Sounds good to me, Reggie, let's go get us some bonefish!"

"Jack, you'll be more comfortable if you stand next to me and hold on to the console. This Whaler has twin one-fifties on the stern and there's a pretty good chop to the sea, so it may be a little rough."

"Say, Reggie, did you ever do any sailing," shouts Jack over the sound of the engines.

"Sure did, Mister Jack. You see, my family were sponge fishermen in these parts, long before there were steam engines. I come from a long line of sailors. Why you ask?"

"Oh, I am just wondering if you see many sailboats in these parts."

"We don't see too many sailboats up here. If they're coming from the States, they stay out in the ocean until Whale Cay channel. Here on the inside, we see mostly power boats. They come down from Walker's Cay and Allans-Pensacola Cay or Vest End. If we do see a sailboat around here, it is usually a well-seasoned sailor in an around-the-world type boat. Ya know, the one with the solar panels and wind generators to keep the batteries charged --- the type of person who doesn't need the marina services or shore power."

"What if some person wanted to get away from it all. Would a sailboat come up to these parts?"

"Hey, Jack, what's this -- twenty questions? It's none of my business, but I thought were up here to do some bone fishing -- and we ain't even wet a line, yet. What are you fishing for, anyway?"

"Sorry about all the questions, Reggie. You're right, I'm fishing for more than bone fish -- I'm looking for a friend of mine who needs my help."

"Hey, Jack, you've paid up front for a half day. We can talk --- or we can fish, it's your money."

99

"Well, Reggie, the man I'm looking for owns the sailing catamaran named *Caribe Dreamer*. And, all I can tell you is that locating him is vital to the security interests of the United States."

"Listen, Jack. There's lots of people who come here to escape whatever, the process server, the ex-wife, the IRS --- or the law. I make my living here in the Abacos hooking into bonefish. I have an impeccable reputation. People know they can trust me and, I ain't no snitch. Quite frankly, people in the Bahamas don't give a rat's behind about the security interests of the United States. The U. S. has mucked over the Bahamas for all two-hundred plus years of your existence. You put import quotas on our sisal, our pineapples and even our rum. So, mon, what makes you think I would help you? Actually, my gut feeling, mon is Yanqui Go Home."

"Sorry, Reggie, I'm not conversant in 200 years of relations between the U.S. and the Bahamas, but seems to me that your countrymen supported the King of England during our war for Independence. You gave supplies and protection to The Confederates during our Civil War and you protected the lawbreakers who wanted to overturn our Prohibition Law but, I understand your position perfectly well. Here's my calling card. And yes, I know, anyone could have this card printed up. If you care to, just call the toll free number and speak these four letters into the phone. You will hear a verification message that I think will put your mind at ease."

"Oh, mother of God, you're a spook from the CIA --- Reggie Malone is carrying a spook from the CIA. We be turning back, mister!"

Aboard Caribe Dreamer sailing on the East side of Green Turtle Cay.

Scott is at the helm. Addie is up on the bow trampoline, with Mittens, calling out the location of dangerous coral heads that stand in their path.

"Honey, bear a little to port -- about five degrees. There's a large dark brown patch of coral just off of starboard," shouts Addie toward the stern of the boat.

"Thanks, I see it now. In a few minutes, we can bear off about twenty degrees and reach right between Addle and Manjack. Tides on the rise and should be near full by the time we get there."

"That's good news. I'm a nervous wreck watching for these coral heads."

"The best news is that we haven't seen any boat traffic since we left Whale Cay passage."

"Hon, you spoke too soon. There's a pretty good size Whaler heading West, just off the North end of Green Turtle."

"Looks to me like he's in a hurry to get back to Green Turtle, Addie. I'm showing six feet and rising on the depth sounder. We're in deep water, so you two can come back and join me in the cockpit."

Addie and Mittens move aft to the cockpit. They are sailing about a mile from the South shore of Manjack Cay where a small peninsula of coral, called Addle Cay, forms a perfectly secluded harbor. Inside the pool, there is ten feet of water over a grass and marl bottom. At low tide, a drop of more than three and a half feet, *Caribe* will be aground for a few hours each day and night. Scott knows the dual keels of the catamaran will keep *Dreamer* fairly level. The stern of the boat will be tied to a large coral outcrop on the shore with the bow anchored pointing to the Southeast into the trades. A large stand of Australian Casuarina trees on the peninsula will block the view of *Dreamer's* mast. If Scott and Addie arrive unseen, they will have been successfully in making themselves scarce.

"Addie, please take the helm, while I furl the sails. As soon as the speed drops below five knots, you can fire up both engines."

"Okay, Scott, but don't be too far away in case I get us into trouble."

"Sure, just watch the depth. If we get below ten feet, give me a holler and I'll take over."

As their speed drops below five knots, Addie turns the key and the port diesel roars to life followed shortly by the starboard engine. Soon, Scott has the sails furled and covered. He returns to the cockpit to join Addie and Mittens.

"We'll take this really slow. As soon as I can, I'm going to swing to starboard into the wind. Then, we'll coast toward shore and that patch of mangrove. Think you can handle the anchor?"

"Yes, I think so, Scott. The only thing I'm not sure about is the color of the depth marker on the chain at fifty feet. Is it yellow?"

"Yes, it's yellow. In any case, it's the second marker on the chain. The first, which is red is at twenty-five feet."

The anchoring goes per the plan. Scott uses the Zodiac inflatable to get ashore to fasten the stern line to a large Casuarina tree. When he finisher, Scott joins Addie in the galley to help fix dinner of dolphin steaks, a mixed greens salad, and peas and rice. She has a chilled bottle of California Chardonnay in the fridge. After dinner, Addie and Mittens curl up with a good book and Scott goes up to the cockpit, under the canvas top to set up the ham transceiver. He attaches the twelve volt power connection, the ground wire and plugs in the antenna which runs up the boat's rigging. The transceiver comes to life and Scott tunes the receiver up to the twenty meter band and puts on his headset.

"C Q, C Q, C Q. This is C6AIAC --- Charlie, Six Alpha, India, Alpha, Charlie, calling C Q. C6AIAC --- Charlie Six Alpha, India, Alpha, Charlie from the Bahama Islands calling C Q on 14.285 megahertz, monitoring and standing by."

Scott begins hearing calls in reply to his C Q and he tunes his receiver to the loudest signal.

"C6AIAC this is WA1BON --- Whiskey, Alpha, One, Bravo Oscar, November calling from Weymouth, Massachusetts in the good old U S of A, over."

"This is C6AIAC thanks for the callback. The name here is Scott and your signal is five by five. I'm talking to you on a Deltastar DXC-25. My antenna is a nineteen strand long wire which is the insulated backstay of the rigging on my sailboat. WA1BON this is C6AIAC, how copy?, over."

"C6AIAC this is WA1BON, the name here is Warren and I'm reading you also loud and clear on a home built remake of an old Hallicrafters HT-425. That's an amazing signal strength considering you're using a long wire. My beam antenna is currently aimed South and mounted on a thirty foot crank-up tower. By the way, Weymouth is a suburb southeast of Boston. I know a little about the Bahamas. My wife and I own a sailboat which we sail here in the Summer. On various occasions, we have cruised in the Bahamas -- the Abaco out islands, out of Marsh Harbour. Is your QTH close to that area? C6AIAC this is WA6BON over."

"WA1BON -- C6AIAC great to meet you Warren and nice to know that you had fun times in the paradise we call the Abacos. My QTH is currently about twenty miles Northeast of Marsh Harbour near the island of Green Turtle Cay. My wife and I run a charter operation on my forty foot Lagoon Catamaran named *Caribe Dreamer,* out of Marsh Harbour. We take one or two couples for one, two or three week cruises throughout this area. We also do SCUBA diving trips. I'll mail you a QSL card --- it has a picture of our boat and all the information on scheduling a charter. Please QSL back to me, Scott Lindsay in care of Marsh Harbour Marina, Marsh Harbour,

Abaco, Bahamas. Back to you Warren for your QSL address and some final chatter. WA1BON --- C6AIAC, back to you."

"C6AIAC -- WA1BON good to hear that the Abacos are still the paradise my wife and I remember from our cruises. We, and another couple, did a Moorings charter through the Abacos, about four years ago. One of our favorite stops is at Frigate Cay. We especially enjoyed the dinghy rides in from the Eastern Harbour to get ice cream treats at the take-away joints in the settlement. By the way, my QSL address is 43 Bradrock Lane, -- that's four, three B - R - A - D - R - O - C - K Lane, Weymouth, Mass -- 02191. It's been great rag chewing with you and --- if my memory serves me right --- you're my first contact in the Bahamas." C6AIAC from WA1BON --- back to you for final -- and have a good evening."

"WA1BON -- C6AIAC I, too, enjoyed our chat. Warren, have a great rest of your evening and remember, it's Scott Lindsay and --- you have a friend in the Bahamas. This is C6AIAC clear."

"Break - Break this is C6AZAZ -- C6A, Zed, Alpha, Zed calling C6AIAC -- come in Scott."

"C6A Zed, Alpha, Zed, this is C6AIAC -- how are you, you old coot? Over."

"C6AIAC -- C6AZAZ I'm only twenty two days older than you, old man. How's that beautiful woman you're shacking up with?"

"Why Harold Pinder -- you nosey old codger. My business with my woman is exactly that -- my business. And, I've told you a dozen times that we were married two years ago in Milwaukee. By the by, the charter business is great -- best it's been in a couple of years. We're between charters for a couple of weeks for R & R. We do need to meet soon and talk about some important matters over a couple of Kaliks. How about tomorrow at eleven o' clock at the Leaky Tiki? Over."

"C6AIAC --- C6AZAZ. eleven o'clock at the Tiki is fine with me. Bring your better half --- okay? By the way, the gang has pretty much gone over to six meters for their net. They were being harassed by lots of interference from the Cubans on twenty. We talk at eighteen hundred on Tuesday, Thursday, and Saturday. Why don't you call in on Thursday."

"ZAZ this is IAC. Thursday night would work for me. I'll try to get cranked up after dinner."

"IAC this is ZAZ. Nice to visit with you. See you at the Tiki."

"C6AIAC, this is C6AZAZ clear"

"C6AZAZ -- C6AIAC Goodnight Harold, see you tomorrow. This is C6AIAC clear. Remember, you have a friend in the Bahamas. 99's and good night."

9:30 P.M. Room 107, The Green Turtle Inn, Green Turtle Cay, Abaco, Bahamas

"Langley Ops Center operator. How may I direct your call?

"I'm on a non-secure line and I need to speak to Guy Cable. Can you activate the encryption, please?"

"Certainly sir. Your conversation in now encrypted. Unfortunately, Mr. Cable has his phone set to 'do not disturb'. Do you want to leave a voice mail message?"

"Sure, put me through."

Jack waits through the usual voice mail prompts and finally hears the beep. "Guy, this is Butterfield. Just wanted you to know that the bone fishing wasn't very good and my guide wasn't very helpful, either. In fact, my guide was downright hostile and anti-American. If you need me, you know how to reach me."

"Wait, Jack, don't hang up! Guy, here -- sorry about the voice mail nonsense, but I needed to get some work done. Too bad about the fishing trip, but I've got some good news. Just got a call from the guys in commo. Your sailor boy is talking on the radio and we have a pretty good idea of his location. He's meeting another Ham for breakfast at a local place called the 'something Tiki' -- tomorrow, at eleven o'clock."

"Wow, that *is* good news. I was beginning to think I had lost my touch. I'll call you sometime after one o'clock and report my progress. Talk to you then. Bye."

Jack is encouraged by the turn of events -- tomorrow, he's finally meeting Scott Lindsay, face to face. But, first he needs to find out where the 'something Tiki' is located. Jack recalls seeing a very large telephone directory in one of the dresser drawers. He searches and quickly locates it. The phone book is at least three inches thick and is organized by island groups starting with Grand Bahama Island and working south, through the Out Islands. The white pages are followed by yellow page advertisements. Jack finds the listings for the island of Green Turtle. Behind the white pages he finds the yellow page advertisements and pages back to 'Restaurants'. The Leaky Tiki is located at Harbour Front and First Street. Nothing is far from this place, so it will only be a five minute walk imagines Jack as he calls it a day and heads to bed.

4:50 A.M., Room 107, The Green Turtle Inn, Green Turtle Cay, Abaco, Bahamas

It isn't a very loud explosion -- it is kind of a dull thud followed by a crash, as the front door to his room comes tumbling inward. Bright orange flames illuminate the room for only an instant. Instinctively, Jack rolls left -- out of the bed and falls on the floor. He is still clutching the pillow that was covering his head. Jack removes the pillow and stares at four small burn holes in the pillow case.

"Damn, that could have been my face. What the eff is going on here? I thought the Bahamas is considered to be a friendly, touristy place?"

Jack quickly pulls on his bermuda shorts, slips into his sandals and runs across what had been the front entrance to his room. The area in front of his door is littered with smoldering trash -- it looks to Jack to be burnt newspaper, as well as lots of splintered pieces of plywood and a strong smell of gasoline.

"Man, that fishing guide really wants to send me and the Company a message. I'd better call the front desk and get this place cleaned up."

AUTEC, approaching the Main Gate, Andros Island, Bahamas

"Jean, it sure has been nice to have such a beautiful chauffeur for the weekend, but I think that I should get back to the BOQ."

"I understand, Kevin. Tomorrow is the big day. But, I keep hoping this day will never end," says Jean her voice choking with emotion.

The dirty Ford pickup approaches the main gate at AUTEC and slows as the Navy S P appears from the guardhouse. Jean and Kevin flash their I. D. cards, at the guard and he waves them through the gate. Jean pulls around the circle drive in front of the BOQ and stops. Kevin squeezes Jean's hand and looks into her eyes.

"Well, goodby for now -- I'm pretty comfortable on my turf -- under hundreds of feet of water -- no sunlight -- no smell of the sea -- just the smell of well-oiled machinery. But, this weekend, you made me realize there is life on the surface of the sea, too -- and that, unlike my life on a submarine, we could share the beautiful sights and sounds, of the surface world -- with each other."

Kevin turns, reaches for his overnight bag and slides across the seat toward the door. Jean pulls on his left arm but his momentum carries him out of the truck. On the pavement, he turns and looking through the open window -- he stares into Jean's tearful eyes.

"Don't forget sailor, you still have to tell me the whole story about Kathleen, okay?"

Quickly, Kevin blows her a kiss, turns and walks briskly toward the main entrance of the BOQ. Bravely, Jean throws him a salute and drives off in a cloud of gray dust.

Monday, 0630 Hours, aboard the *U S S Topeka*

"Now hear this, now hear this. All Operation Ballyhoo personnel report to the enlisted mess-- all Operation Ballyhoo personnel report the enlisted mess." pipes the Boatswain's Mate over the squawk box.

The *Topeka* is starting to come to life after a weekend liberty. Half of the crew had R & R and were flown to Disney World in Orlando while the other watch is scheduled for Orlando the following weekend. Most of the officers spent the weekend aboard the boat. Kevin Anderson spent the last six hours of his weekend in his room at the BOQ going over the operation orders for today's mission.

"Chief, are the SP's posted at all the mess entrances," inquires Kevin.

"Yes sir," responds the Chief.

Kevin enters the mess area to the command --- "Attention on deck." The assembled group stands in silent attention.

"Carry on, gentlemen --- er' and lady."

"Let me first introduce some of the riders that are sailing with us this morning. I would like to introduce you to Miss Jean Barton. Miss Barton represents the Navy's contractor, Everen Electric, and is the Senior Technician in Charge of Project Ballyhoo. Also, I would like to introduce you to Matt Bowers, and Nick Belmonte, technicians from Everen Electric based here at AUTEC. On this side of the table from Naval Weapons Facility, China Lake, California we have Lieutenant David Warmann and Boatswain's Mate Charles Morse. I think that's everyone. Did I forget anyone? --- no, then Miss Barton, would you like to say a few words?"

"Oh, thank you, Commander Anderson. I would just like to say that I'm really excited to be able to go undersea for the first time. All of my experience with the vehicle prototype has been at the simulation trench at China Lake, so this will be a new experience for me. I would like to thank all the officers and enlisted men of the *Topeka* for the countless hours of time you spent this weekend --- Jean steals a smiling glance at Kevin --- and that each of you has worked very hard, to see that this operation will be a success. The men of this ship --- oh, excuse me --- the men of this boat and your fellow shipmates on other Navy ships, need every advantage over the enemy that our skill and technology can produce. MSS will give us a huge defensive and offensive capability that cannot be matched by any of our potential enemies. I would like to extend a special thanks to Boatswain's Mate Richardson and his crew for the excellent work they did in loading the vehicle into the tube. May God bless this boat, her crew and this mission. And, God bless America."

"Thank you, Miss Barton. Before we disperse to man our stations, we need to assign each visitor to an emergency re-breather or EBA as we call them. Boatswain's Mate Richardson will demonstrate how to don this device in case of an emergency. Take the re-breather with you to your assigned station. Also, when you arrive at your station, you will be given a talker set. All Ballyhoo personnel will be able to communicate with one another on channel 3 on the 3-MC circuit. The entire boat can be reached by switching to 1-MC. Any questions? Not noting any questions, you are dismissed." The personnel begin to disperse toward the amidships torpedo room and their duty stations.

"Oh, Miss Barton, could I speak with you -- privately -- for a moment?"

"Why, yes, Commander Anderson. Where would you like to talk?"

"Oh, right here will be fine, as soon as everyone files by. Can I buy you a cup of coffee?"

"No thanks, Commander. My nerves are already on edge and, I don't relish the thought of visiting your washroom --- 'er head."

"So, speaking frankly, what do you think of my office?"

"A submarine is a magnificent piece of machinery. I like everything about the *Topeka*, except the lack of a window in your office."

0430 Hours Aboard the *Caribe Dreamer* at anchor in the lee of Manjack Cay

It is low tide and *Dreamer* is listing to port. Scott rolls to the edge of the bunk. Startled, he is instantly awake. Quietly, without waking Addie, Scott pulls on his swim suit and a hooded cotton pullover. He goes on deck to check the spinnaker pole. It is dark -- first light is about an hour away. Everything on deck -- seems fine. Tide is on the rise and soon they will be floating upright. Now, he is wide awake. Returning to bed would certainly wake Addie, so Scott decides to go to the galley and brew a pot of coffee. Over a cup of coffee, he thinks about his plan for the breakfast meeting. *Will he take Addie or leave her here with the boat? It will be mid-tide and perhaps they should move 'Dreamer' to the West dock at the Green Turtle Inn?*

"Honey, what are you up for," asks Addie from the aft cabin.

"Good morning, darling. I couldn't sleep. I think it was the list to port that woke me. How'd you sleep?"

"I slept great. Had some wonderful dreams about you and when I rolled over, you were gone. Can you come back to bed?"

"Oh, Addie, don't I wish. My mind is a clutter with details, about today. Why don't you get up -- we need to talk."

"Okay, hon. I'll get up and join you. Is that coffee I smell?"

"Sure is. I'll pour you a cup."

Aboard the *U S S Topeka* off of AUTEC, Andros, Bahamas

"Diving Officer of the Watch, prepare to dive."

"Aye, sir. Preparing to dive -- sound the alarm."

The Dive Officer reaches for the klaxon switch on the consol and the gong starts ringing throughout the boat.

"Dive, dive," he shouts into the microphone of the 1-MC bitch box.

"Maneuvering --- make turns for fifteen knots."

"Planesman, ten degrees down bubble."

"Ten degrees down bubble. Aye, aye, sir" responds the senior bow plane operator.

"Report passing sixty feet. Helmsman, report your course."

"One-Eight-Zero degrees magnetic, sir."

"Passing sixty feet, sir"

"Roger, passing sixty feet and still diving"

"Level off at niner-five feet," orders the Diving Officer.

"Yes sir, coming level at niner-five feet"

"The boat is level at niner-five feet, sir."

"Captain Walters, the boat is level at one niner-five feet, speed is fifteen knots --- our course is one-eight-zero degrees magnetic. We have eight hundred seventy feet of water below the keel."

"The Captain has the con."

"Well done, Lieutenant," responds Captain Walters. "Exec, what's the plot for our turn to the North?"

"We've got three minutes, fifteen seconds until the course change, sir."

"Roger, three plus minutes. Commo, this is the Captain. Do we have communications with the rest of the group?"

"Commo here, sir. We have both the *Harkness* and the S-3 Orion aircraft on Com Channel One, sir."

"Roger, commo. Sonar, do you have a range and bearing on the *Harkness*?"

"Sonar, aye. *Harkness* bears forty five degrees on the starboard bow at two thousand yards. Her speed is sixteen knots."

"Roger, sonar. Maneuvering Officer, make turns for sixteen knots."

"Roger, sir. Increase speed, make turns for sixteen knots."

"Plot, call the turn"

"Aye, aye, sir," responds Kevin.

"Helmsman turn left to zero, zero, five degrees on my mark." "Five, four, three, two, one, mark!

"Coming left to zero, zero, five degrees, sir. Steady on zero, zero, five"

The crew all instinctively reach out to hold on to something solid as the *Topeka* banks to the left like an airplane.

"Well done, Chief. Commo, I want the Executive Officer, Commander Anderson and the Ballyhoo team on the talker."

"Commo, roger."

"Anderson, 'er Weapons, this is the Captain. You have the con."

"Roger, sir. Chief of the Boat, this is Weapons, decrease speed to dead slow."

"Roger, Weapons. Maneuvering, reduce speed to dead slow."

"All engines slow, making turns for dead slow. Speed is twelve knots and slowing."

Aboard the Russian Intelligence Ship, *Khersones* in International waters, twenty miles South, South-West of Andros Island, Bahamas.

Ah, Monday. How I love Monday, thinks Grigory. The American Navy at AUTEC is back to work. And, I've got a live one! It has been a long time since he needed all three receivers tuned up. There is ship to shore traffic from 'Duck Blind' --- probably a P-3 Orion submarine tracking aircraft. His old friends at AUTEC Telemetry Control, radio call sign 'Pheasant Hunter' are on receiver number three.

Grigory powers up the radio direction finder. He wants to get a RDF fix on 'Duck Blind' to determine her course and speed. Is AUTEC working the North or South end of the range? Ten minutes and a second fix would tell him. The adrenalin was flowing just like it had off of North Vietnam when he was a Cadet in training and kept track of the American aircraft carriers patrolling on 'Yankee Station'.

Ten minutes later, Grigory hand cranks the RDF antenna to the Northeast and waits for a transmission from 'Duck Blind'. He places the earphones on his head and waits, and listens. There it is, a routine position check from AUTEC. Grigory slowly moves the antenna, first to the South -- nothing, no null -- they're moving North. Yes, the azimuth ring confirms it. 'Duck Blind' is moving North -- at about fifteen knots -- the usual speed for a surface vessel when a torpedo test firing is taking place. Another fix in ten minutes would confirm both course and speed of the surface ship.

The Amidships Torpedo Room, *USS Topeka*, on the North Test Range at AUTEC submerged in the Tongue of the Ocean.

Kevin stares at Jean's back. She is sitting at the starboard console, intently staring at the telemetry data on the displays in front of her. Dressed in Navy issue, khaki trousers, blouse and baseball cap, her hair stuffed inside, it is difficult to recall images of her in her peach colored bikini but, for just a moment, he closes his eyes and tries.

"Weapons, the Captain, here, came the jolting voice over the headset. Kevin reaches for the microphone button and replies, "Weapons."

"Weapons, the *Harkness* is on station and air is overhead. We're dead slow ahead at one hundred feet. Tell the Contractor that it is her call when we release the vessel."

"Roger, sir. Miss Barton, you heard the Captain -- it's your show."

"Thank you, Commander Anderson. Men, let's get the video rolling -- lights, action, camera. Matt, are you ready to disconnect?"

"Yes, Miss Barton, everything is go from here."

"Nick, are you ready on telemetry?"

"Yes, Miss Barton, we're ready for launch."

"Miss Barton?" inquires Lieutenant Commander Anderson.

"Yes, Commander."

"Switch your talker set to 1-MC which is channel one and you will be piped directly into Captain Walters location in the coning tower. The boat is all yours."

"Thank you, Commander Anderson. Captain, this is Miss. Barton, we are ready to launch."

"Roger, Miss Barton, we're ready up here -- just give the word and we'll begin the sonar track."

"Yes, sir, you may start the sonar track. We should have swim-out in just a few seconds."

All eyes focus on the television monitor as the picture shows the hatch rotating to the side and exposes the nose cone of the first prototype of an unusual weapon --a thirty-five foot long titanium cylinder with the warhead nose-cone painted in day-glo orange stripes. Slowly, MSS lifts out of its vertical tube with only a few bubbles marking its assent. Five seconds later, Nick announces that the vehicle is clear of the coning tower and periscope. Immediately, Jean begins working the joystick to maneuver the vessel on its first voyage. The three Everen employees work in virtual silence. Nick is watching the telemetry data coming back from the MSS. Matt is in communication with AUTEC. Jean glances at the training scenario placard and begins the first test maneuver -- a simple rotation of the vehicle from a vertical attitude to the horizontal.

"Rotation successful," she announces.

One half hour after successful completion of ten simple maneuvers, the vehicle is ready for its most important test -- a pre-programed maneuver controlled by the onboard computer.

"Captain, the vehicle has been perfect in the checkout phase. The contractor personnel are ready to turn control over to the onboard program," announces Kevin.

"We copy that in the Maneuvering Room, Commander Anderson. We're ready up here, too."

"Nick, -- ready? Matt, -- you ready," queries Jean.

"Excuse me, Miss Barton, before you start the program, I would like to have sonar verify my distance and range calculations," interjects Nick.

"Okay, Nick. Give me your positions and we'll have Commander Anderson verify them with sonar."

"I'm showing the MSS vehicle at two thousand five hundred yards ahead and approximately ten degrees off the starboard bow."

"Sonar, can you give me range and distance to the target?"

"Sonar, here. Range is two thousand eight hundred, seventy yards. Bearing is starboard zero-one-one degrees. The target is stationary in the water at a depth of four hundred feet."

"Roger sonar. Nick, are you okay with this?"

"I'm go with those numbers, Miss Barton."

"Send the signal"

"Miss Barton, the acoustical downlink program is running."

Aboard the *Khersones* Twenty One Nautical miles Southwest of Andros Island, Bahamas

It is a short, but panicky transmission from 'Clay Pigeon' to 'Duck Blind', that catches Grigory's attention. "Duck Blind --- Clay Pigeon, I've got your vehicle on the surface. It looks like a sailfish -- it's crashing through the wave tops --- at --- I'd estimate about twenty to twenty-five knots -- over."

"Roger, Clay Pigeon -- stand by one."

Now, there is a flurry of radio activity as the Americans on the surface and in the air report on the status of their target.

"Pheasant Hunter --- Duck Blind, what's your telemetry telling you? --- over."

"Duck Blind --- yeh, we've got a problem --- the vessel is on the surface and is making a slight turn to starboard. We'll need Clay Pigeon to keep a close eye on her."

"Pheasant Hunter, roger -- we'll stand by."

Oh, Damn, this figures. We get Khersones in position to the West and the Americans move away from us at twenty knots. At our best speed of fifteen knots, it would take this rust bucket two days to get close to the American position, thinks Grigory.

Quickly, Grigory tunes up the UHF transmitter. It is time to talk to his SVR 'handler' in Havana. *Perhaps the Navy has some other assets in the Southern Atlantic that can assist the* Khersones? Grigory scrawls his message to Fleet Naval Intelligence on the encoding pad in groups of five letters. Then, he swivels his chair to the encoding machine --- an exact copy of the IBM KLA-7, used by the Americans in the 1960's in Vietnam. Grigory pages through the encoding manual for today's date code. Carefully, he rotates the plastic lettered wheels into the correct position shown in the code book. Once the wheels are in position, Grigory types his message and the encoding machine disgorges three feet of three-quarter inch paper tape with the encoded five letter groups. Swiveling his chair further to the right, he positions himself in front of the chrome plated Morse Code key. He flexes his thumb and forefinger and then sends twenty practice dots and dashes that resound as clicks and clacks throughout the ice house. His warm-up over, he sends the message out over his powerful AM radio. His message is received by the Fleet Naval Intelligence Office at the SVR Russian intelligence complex overlooking the Bahia de Havana in the suburb of Luyano, Cuba. Simultaneously, the message is received and stored on a low priority server at the National Security Agency in Langley, Virginia.

1622 ZULU 260996 MACKEREL ONE URGENT LAT 24 015' 15"N; LON 75 12' 45"W

COMMANDER FNI HABANA.

INTERCEPT RADIO TRAFFIC AUTEC TORPEDO TEST. MK-48 RUNAWAY TO THE NORTHEAST AT 20 - 25 KNOTS. WHAT ASSETS AVAILABLE IN SOUTH ATLANTIC TO ASSIST IN SEARCH. REQUEST PERMISSION TO MOVE AT FULL SPEED TO POSITION 20 KM EAST OF NEW PROVIDENCE.

MACKEREL ONE

The Settlement at New Plymouth, Green Turtle Cay, Abaco, Bahamas

Scott and Addie had enough of hiding out and they decide that it will be best to move *Caribe Dreamer* to the West Dock at the Green Turtle Club. Scott knows the dock master well, so the boat will be safe, at a well-protected dock. Addie can easily walk into town to do her shopping. *Dreamer* arrives on a rising tide and they tie her in a vacant slip just North of the gas dock. Scott leaves the boat at once, as it will be a fifteen minute walk to the Leaky Tiki Restaurant. Addie will stay aboard to tidy up the galley and wash the breakfast dishes. Scott kisses her goodbye and powers the inflatable across the strait to the North Shore of Green Turtle Cay. After stashing the dinghy in the mangroves, he starts walking to the restaurant. The narrow streets are almost void of people or golf carts. Part way there, he meets up and walks with a group of happy-go-lucky, young girls dressed in their uniforms, on their way to the island school.

The Leaky Tiki is a hexagonal shape barge that floats in the harbor, a few hundred yards to the North of the government dock. As Scott approaches, he can see some of the local boats tied to the deck that surrounds the floating restaurant. The clear plastic weather curtains that protected last night's patrons from a tropical thundershower, are still rolled down. An unattended yellow ringer bucket stands in the center of the pine board floor.

'Hi, Mister," Scott blurts out, as he spots Harold Pinder on the last bar stool guarding his first beer of the morning.

"Scottie, good to see you lad. Where's the misses?"

"Oh, Addie's doing some cleaning on *Dreamer*. How about you?"

"Other than a little bursitis, arthritis, and an occasional hangover, I've been fine. So what's all the hush - hush about, Scottie?"

Scott put his finger to his lips as the bartender moves in their direction, with a mop in his hand.

"Good morning gentlemen, what can I get you," asks the bartender of Scott.

"I'll have a Kalik Gold, and get my friend one, too."

"Need a glass with that?"

"No -- a bottle is fine."

"That will be ten dollars."

"Ya know, Harold, I've never been able to understand beer prices in the Bahamas. Heineken from Holland has to travel half way around the world to get here, and its forty-five dollars a case. Budweiser comes from Tampa and they have to pay import duty --- its thirty-eight dollars a case. Kalik, the beer of the Bahamas -- only has to travel one hundred and sixty miles, pays no duty and it costs forty-five dollars a case. So, Mr. Bartender -- how come Kalik is so expensive?"

"Mister, I don't know. I don't own the place, I'm just the bartender."

"So, Harold, what's the answer?"

"Hell if I know, Scottie. It must be the cost of the water in Nassau. You know they bring it by tanker from Andros."

Scott hands the bartender a U.S. twenty dollar bill. Since American currency is coveted, he returns the change in Bahamian dollar bills. Scott leaves two Bahamian on the bar, for a tip.

"We should be enjoying this beautiful morning -- how about we move to that table outside in the shade?"

"That's fine with me, Scott."

"Harold, have you been down past Loyalist Cay lately?"

"Nope, I haven't -- no reason I can think of for me to go that far South. But, I did hear some scuttlebutt that the property sold."

"Well, you're right that the property sold. Seems the new owners are into assembling their own army."

"What do you mean --- an army? We don't need an army --- we've got The Bahamas Defense Force, that's all we need."

"I mean army troops --- complete with jungle fatigues and weapons!"

"Aw, come on --- you and I both know you can't bring firearms into the Bahamas without declaring them."

"Harold, I'm not talking about a Saturday night special, I'm talking about Kalashnikov's and fifty-one millimeter mortars."

"Holy crap, Scottie, are you sure about this?"

"I'm a sure as I can be. I SCUBA'd into the beach and took a look for myself with my night vision scope."

"Scottie, this is not making sense -- why Loyalist Cay. Is this some kind of a U.S. led invasion of, say --- Venezuela? And, why, in heavens name, would the Government of the Bahamas help the United States after the crapy way the U.S. has treated us for the past two hundred years?"

"I'm thinking it's CIA --- Addie's pretty certain that she heard the bad guys speaking Arabic. Well, as far as I could tell, they're not Haitians? They certainly aren't speaking Creole or patois --- I'm thinking they're might be a Middle Eastern, Islamic terrorist group called al- Qaeda."

"Al --- who," blurts out Pinder.

"Keep it down, man. I said al-Qaeda. They're Muslim fundamentalists and they haven't forgiven our Western Culture for the Christian Crusades They refer to all non-Muslims as infidels and they go around shouting death to the infidels"

"Aw shoot, Scottie --- you, me, Addie --- are you telling me that everyone of us is an infidel?"

Aboard the *U S S Topeka*, submerged in the Tongue of the Ocean

"Maneuvering, this is the Captain, all ahead standard, make turns for twenty knots."

"Maneuvering, aye sir. Making turns for twenty knots."

"Amidships torpedo. Commander Anderson, can you give me an update?"

"Yes, Captain. The telemetry readings confirms the visuals from the P-3. We're showing the vehicle doing twenty knots and making a very slight turn to port. We need to keep the vehicle in sight, so, we'll need to know how much air time the Orion can give us."

"Roger, Anderson. I'll have Commo contact the Orion and find out how long he can stay with us. We'll call Patrick Air Force Base and see if they can get another Orion into the air as backup. Also, I'll check with the Coasties to see if they have a Falcon, in case we can't get a P-3. As soon as I have any information, I'll let you know."

"Roger, sir. The contractor personnel are huddling right now. They're trying to decide if they should send the abort signal to the vehicle. I'll keep you informed."

"Excuse me, Commander Anderson, we need your input, interjects Jean. You know the waters around here. If we don't abort, what's the chance that the vehicle could end up on a beach somewhere?"

"Well, that's a pretty unlikely scenario, Ms. Barton. Other than the Berry Islands that lie North and West of here, there's deep water all the way from here to the West end of New Providence Island. I guess what we need to know is how far can the vehicle travel on its cells?"

"Matt, how many more minutes can the MSS go at this speed"

"M'am, the last battery reading registered one thousand, two hundred amp hours. At this speed, she can run on the surface for at least six hours -- maybe more."

"It'll be dark by then, says Jean to no one in particular. If we send the abort signal, the MSS is programmed to surface and go into a twenty degree continuous left turn --- like a Jet Ski. We don't want a MSS to fall into the enemy's hands, so it's designed to be at neutral buoyancy at four hundred feet, when it finally runs out of juice, it should simply sink to the bottom. The vehicle will detonate if it remains motionless, at neutral buoyancy, for more than sixty minutes. Kevin, can you get us a chart of the area North of here?"

"Certainly, Jean --- er, Ms. Barton. I'll call Navigation for a chart."

There are lots of raised eyebrows in the amidships torpedo room. They just heard Miss Barton call Lieutenant Commander Anderson 'Kevin' -- he answers her back with a familiar sounding 'Jean'. No one ever calls Miss Barton, Jean.

Aboard the *Khersones* rolling in the Atlantic swells, en route to New Providence, Bahamas

Grigory is half way through his exercise regimen of five laps around the *Khersones* deck. Down the starboard ladder to the well deck --- under the cargo boom, up the six steps of the port ladder to the cargo deck -- along the passageway below the bridge -- up two steps to the aft deck-- along the port side the ice house -- left behind the ice house -- left again along the starboard side of the ice house and back to the starboard ladder. Each lap takes four minutes, fifteen seconds. The entire circuit takes about twenty-five minutes --- then another cool down lap of five minutes.

Captain Mikoyan will have finished his lunch, and now while his stomach is full, will be a good time to approach him, thinks Grigory, sweating profusely, as he walks up the ladder to the bridge wing and knocks on the door.

"Comrade Captain? This is Grigory Illich. May I speak to you?"

"Certainly, Grigory. Please enter."

Captain Sergei Mikoyan is a sixty year old Byelarus Russian, who was born in Mensk. During his Navy career, he worked his way from the lowest enlisted rank to Captain of the Soviet, top of the line frigate, *Razitelny* -- only to have the bad fortune to run aground at the entrance to Vladivostok harbor during an early Fall blizzard, five years ago. The sea has been cruel to Sergei -- cruel to his career and cruel to his health -- his face has been etched by the sea and sun into deep wrinkles. He looks like a man of seventy years. Nearing the end of his career he will soon make one final entrance to Vladivostok --- to take *Khersones* to the scrap yard.

"Sir, I trust that you had an enjoyable lunch."

"Yes, I did. Now, you didn't come all this way to discuss my lunch. What do you want?"

"Sir, I want you to move *Khersones* to New Providence Island -- at full speed."

"And, why, may I ask do we need to go to New Providence?"

"Comrade Captain, we are both nearing the end of our careers. This could be the break we need to end our careers on a high note -- and hopefully we will be rewarded a full retirement. I have listened to messages from the American torpedo range on Andros Island that indicate the Americans have a problem with their current test. One of their new Mark 48 torpedoes is a runaway. It is moving toward the West end of New Providence Island. I think we have a shot at finding, or at least marking the position of that torpedo."

"Grigory, is what you're asking me to do is to take my ship into the territorial waters of the Bahamas?"

"Yes, sir. That's what I'm asking you to do. If you don't change course, even the fastest ship in the Soviet, 'er, Russian Navy wouldn't be able to get into position to help search for this runaway torpedo."

"And, what makes you so sure that anyone -- even the United States Navy will find this torpedo. The waters North of Andros are more than six hundred fathoms deep."

"Comrade Captain, you may be right. But, the American's have only a few very slow ships in the area and their P-3 may have to return soon to base for fuel. Besides, how will we know where to search if we can't get close enough to get a good RDF fix on the American ships?"

"You make a good point, but, may I remind you that we are a military vessel and we must have permission of the Bahamian Government to transit their territorial waters."

"Sergei, we both know this. Take this chance and we may both be able to retire to a dacha on the Crimean coast. Stay put and you and me, and the *Khersones*, will all rust away -- together. Besides, what can they do to us? Once they scrap *Khersones*, you and I will be surplus personnel."

"So, okay, you've made your point. I'll change course for Nassau. We can always say we need emergency repairs -- and, if you insist on pushing this rust bucket at sixteen knots, we probably will. Good Day, Grigory."

Elated by the Captain's decision, Grigory charges down the ladder from the bridge, sprints aft along the deck and returns to the ice house. Before leaving to talk to Captain Mikoyan, Grigory has recorded all transmissions onto the reel-to-reel tape recorder. Now, he is really busy. Before he tends to his tape recorder, he needs to get a current fix on the next radio transmission. Then, he will analyze the recorded transmissions. *Oh, to have the help of an eager, young apprentice technician -- like in the good old Soviet Union days!, thinks Grigory* The first live transmission he hears is from the P-3, Orion, 'Clay Pigeon'. The pilot reports that he has visual contact with the vehicle, but he is low on fuel and will need to return to Patrick Air Force Base in twenty minutes. 'Duck Blind' asks for the speed and direction of the vehicle. *Why all this talk of 'vehicle'?, thinks Grigory.* Usually, the Americans call torpedoes 'fish' or just torps' -- not vehicles. Grigory gets a pretty good null with his Radio Direction Finder on the transmission from 'Clay Pigeon'. He thinks the action will move into the open ocean, Northeast of Andros Island and *Khersones* is heading that way.

1300 Hours. Aboard the *U S S Topeka*, thirty-five nautical miles Northeast of AUTEC Base, Andros Island.

An Enlisted Rank brings the rolled paper chart to the amidships torpedo room. Kevin unrolls the chart and carefully folds the Andros Island section to the top. The Everen Electric contractor personnel gather around, as Kevin begins pointing with his finger.

"This is our position right now. Here is the position of the MSS --- about six nautical miles to the Northeast. This is the position of the *Harkness*. She is heading on a more easterly course to intercept the vehicle since it seems to be turning slightly to the West. As you can see, there's nothing out here but deep water. The only land in the way is New Providence Island and a few small cays to the East. Any questions?"

"Well, from my perspective, we have no option but to send the abort signal states Jean in a matter of fact tone.

"It's the right choice, Miss Barton, says Nick. "If we don't abort the vehicle --- hell, it could turn right and end up on a beach in Cuba."

Matt simply nods his head in agreement. He flips back the red protective switch cover and takes another glance at Jean -- she nods her head and Matt pulls down on the red breaker marked ABORT.

"Abort signal sent to the acoustical downlink, Miss Barton."

"Do you have a confirmation?"

"No, Miss Barton. --- there is no response from the vehicle. It's continuing to run in a Northward direction at twenty knots."

The Leaky Tiki Restaurant and Bar, New Plymouth, Green Turtle Cay.

Jack Butterfield walks across the gangplank and enters the restaurant. Despite an assortment of craft tied to its outside deck, the place seems to be empty of any customers. He walks past a yellow mop wringer bucket and approaches the bar.

"Anybody home?"

"Good Morning -- we're open for business. What can I get you?"

"Actually, I'm looking for a friend -- Scott Lindsay."

"My only customers are outside on the South deck -- go through that door and turn left."

"Thanks," responds Jack as he walks toward the opening that will lead him to the deck. As he approaches the doorway, he stops to get a good look at the two men sitting at a table on the deck. One man seems to be much older, is bald, and has a full beard. The other man is well tanned and has thinning brown hair. The second individual meets the size and facial characteristics of Mister Scott Lindsay.

"Good morning, gentlemen. Would one of you be Scott Lindsay?"

"If one of us is, who might you be," questions Scott as he stands up and turns toward the stranger.

"I'm Jack Butterfield."

"Good to meet you Mister Butterfield -- and what business might you have with this Mister Lindsay?"

"Well, you might say that I'm a friend of a friend."

"Heck, any friend of Scott Lindsay is a friend of ours, care to join us, Mister Butterfield?"

"Thank you, gentlemen. You sir, certainly look a lot like the description I was given of Mr. Lindsay

"Well, that description was pretty good, because I'm Scott Lindsay and this is my friend Harold Pinder."

"I'm glad to meet both of you, but with my apologies to Mister Pinder, I'm wondering if I could speak to you, alone?"

"What ya say, Harold? How about buying Jack a Kalik," says Scott as he pulls a Bahamian five dollar bill from his pocket.

"Sure thing, Scott. Is a beer okay, Jack?"

"You bet. Kalik is the local beer, isn't it?"

"Yes, and Scottie, keep your money. I'll get us three Kalik's," says Pinder as he disappears inside the bar.

"Jack Butterfield, United States Government," says Jack as he places a business card in front of Scott. It has the Eagle Seal in gold with the words United States of America around the edge. In the lower left corner is a phone and fax number, an e-mail address and on the right is simply: Langley, VA 23665.

"It sure is good to know that you sensed the urgency of my phone message, Jack."

"Phone message, what message? I'm not here because of any message, unless you mean your ham radio transmissions. I'm here because an intelligence operative of the United States Government reported that you were making inquiries about some activities on Loyalist Cay. I'm here to ask you to stop your activities, as they involve a security matter of interest to both the United States and Bahamas Governments."

"Well, Mister Butterfield, this is all very interesting. You seem to know all about my comings and goings. You've eavesdropped on my radio conversations, and I know nothing about you -- except you claim to be from the U.S. Government. First, you --- oh, here comes Harold with the beers."

"Sorry to interrupt you guys -- here's your beer. I'm going back inside. The rest of the Hams are here and the QSL card meeting is about to start. Nice to have met you Mister Butterfield. I hope you have a pleasant stay in the Bahamas."

"Thank you, nice to have met you, Mister Pinder."

"Mister Lindsay, all my government is asking is that you keep the information you have acquired to yourself. The activities by the Government of the United States on Loyalist Cay has been cleared with, and has the approval of the Government of the Bahamas."

"Well, Mister Butterfield, that's very reassuring --- in fact, here comes a representative of the Bahamian government. The guy in the black pants with the red stripe is a Bahamian policeman and he seems to be coming this way."

"Good day, Gentlemen. Is one of you Mister Butterfield?"

"Yes, I'm Jack Butterfield."

"I'm Corporal Sanders of the Green Turtle Constabulary. I need you to accompany me to your hotel. There has been a fire in your room and we need you to come down to Headquarters to answer some questions."

"Yes, Corporal I'm aware of the fire. In fact the fire was at the outside door of my room and I put the fire out with an extinguisher. Could I speak with you in private for a moment?"

"Why, certainly sir. Let's step inside to the bar for a moment. Please excuse us, sir."

"Corporal, I'm a representative of the United States Government."

"Mister Butterfield, do you have any identification that would substantiate your claim to be on official U. S. Government business?"

"Nothing official sir. I'm traveling as a tourist," Jack responds, as he passes the officer his calling card. "I'm traveling as a tourist and am only carrying my business card. You can call the toll free number and enter the six digits on the front and you will get a verification directly from my headquarters."

"Since you have no other official identification, I think you have only two choices --- accompany me now to my station or I will have to arrest you and put you in hand irons. Which will it be?"

"You win, Corporal. I think you have, as they say in Britain, you have the leverage. However, I would ask just one small favor --- allow me to talk to Mr. Lindsay for sixty seconds."

1500 Hours aboard the Russian Intelligence Gathering ship *Khersones,* 100 nautical miles Northwest of Havana

The VHF radio comes to life with a burst of static. It is Havana calling with a reply to his message. Grigory reaches for the code book and checks the receiver to make certain the paper tape will feed properly. The first code groups start coming across --- K 5 L A K, V B 9 X 8, 7 N K K S. Only the decoding machine will know the content of this message. In a matter of just minutes, the paper tape stops feeding. Quickly, Grigory inserts the lead end of the tape into the decipher slot in his encoding machine. He has already rotated the plastic wheels to the cipher book's proper setting. The string of five code groups will now print as a readable message.

0600Z MV81 Khersones

SVR HQ, Habana

SUBMARINE SUPPORT SHIP FEDOR VIDYAYEV LOCATED BAHIA DE HABANA.

DESTROYER FRIGATE ADMIRAL TRIBUTS STEAMING SOUTH LAT. 24 13 05 N. LON 83 22 02W. COMMUNICATE AT 18 PLUS ZULU.

"Wow!" Grigory exclaims to the empty icehouse. "The *Admiral Tributz is* a thirty knot Udaloy Class Destroyer Frigate from the Black Sea fleet. She will be carrying two Ka27 anti-submarine search helicopters. They will certainly arrive before the *Khersones. Fedor Vidyayev* is definitely not going to be of much help at anchor in Bahia de Habana as it steams at only seventeen knots. It will be days before it can get close to New Providence Island. But, thinks Grigory, perhaps it will be carrying a submarine rescue vehicle which will come in handy in an undersea search. Grigory will begin a continuous plot of the activity of the Americans. There are plenty of transmissions from 'Clay Pigeon'.

"Ah, Ice House, this is the Captain," came the voice over the squawk box. "Aye Captain, Ice House here," replies Grigory.

"The engine room is reporting that we cannot continue at this speed -- Alex thinks we have picked up barnacles on the propeller and this is putting a strain on the shaft bearings -- despite constantly oiling them, they're starting to overheat."

"Yes sir, I understand -- whatever speed you coax out of this rust bucket is okay by me. The U.S. Navy radio announced that the target has taken a more northerly course -- perhaps we can still intercept it just South of New Providence" And, thinks Grigory add on three knots for the Gulf Stream current and perhaps we'll be in position by daybreak.

The Leaky Tiki Restaurant, Green Turtle Cay, Abaco Bahamas.

"Mister Lindsay, the constable consented to allow us to have sixty seconds to talk before I accompany him to the station. I know that you have assisted the Company on another occasion --- with the Scotia Bank operation. I also know that you are a Canadian Citizen. I'm only asking that you cool it for a while. We're trying not to spook the people on Loyalist Cay. We want them to lead us to their target and then take them out before they can do any harm."

"I completely understand you, Mister Butterfield. I'll take your suggestions under advisement. Thanks for the calling card --- who knows, I might be calling."

"Thank you, Mister Lindsay ---we'll be in touch," replies Butterfield as he walks to the door, in the company of the constable.

"Hey, Pinder. Okay if I join your meeting?"

"Sorry Scottie, the meetings is almost over. The guys are just adding up the points for the most QSL's from the former Soviet prefects. Care to add yours in?"

"No problem, mon --- I haven't been on the air in the last few weeks so I don't have any."

"Sure, Scottie. What have you and the misses been doing --- starting a family?"

"No, Pinder, this Loyalist Cay situation is getting all of my attention. It turns out that our Mister Butterfield is some kind of an intelligence operative for the U. S. Government."

"So he's a spook -- who's he with? --- CIA, NSA, Naval Intelligence?"

"Well, here --- he gave me this business card. --- it says CIA."

"Oh, what the hell Scott, anybody could print this up on the office copier."

"Well, whatever Mister Butterfield is, he knows about my snooping around Loyalist the other night. What really bothers me is that he said his information came from an informant."

"Oh, c'mon Scottie. You know how everybody in the harbor knows what everyone else is doing."

"Hey, Mister, this is deadly serious. I suggest that we make plans to keep in touch on the radio. I would also suggest that we use 2-Meters --- and, operate at low power. Then, the spooks won't be able to listen in. What do you say?"

"You're right Scottie -- let's keep in touch --- say at sixteen hundred hours?"

"Okay, see you on 2-Meters at sixteen hundred hours. I'm out of here. I need to find Addie and help her with the groceries."

Aboard the submerged Attack Submarine *USS Topeka*, 50 Nautical miles North of Andros Island

"Kevin, the Skipper wants to see you in the Wardroom -- pronto."

"Thanks, Jack."

Kevin makes his way from the Amidships Torpedo Room, forward one compartment, to the Wardroom. An enlisted man wearing a sidearm is standing by the doorway. He pulls aside the curtain for Kevin as he enters, nodding toward Captain Walters who motions for him to sit on the bench. Kevin slides onto the bench facing his Captain.

"Commander, I needed to talk to you in private because it's beginning to look to me as if this situation could be within minutes of getting away from us."

"How so, Skipper?"

"First, Kevin, it's starting to get dark on the surface --- then we lose our air cover and, now we have company," says the Captain as he passes the decoded message from COMSUBLANT across the table in front of Kevin.

"Oh Damn, ah, excuse me sir, those effing Russians are just as much a pain in the ass now, as they were during the Cold War."

"Yes, we both know the war out here with the Russian Navy hasn't ended. You probably notice, in the message, the *Admiral Tributs* is on the move from Cuba. She's a very fast and capable warship --- she's the flagship of the Russian Black Sea Fleet. In the meantime, I want you to know that I'm closing in on a decision to terminate this mission and ask the *Kennedy* to launch some airpower and blow this thing to kingdom come."

"Blow up the only prototype, sir?"

"Yes, Commander, blow it up. Unless we get a change in our orders from COMSUBLANT, our treaty with the Bahamas prevents us from steaming North of 25 degrees, 40 minutes. We'll be there in less than thirty more minutes at our current speed."

"Sir, may I suggest something?"

"Certainly Kevin --- what's your plan?"

"If we're not going to be able to track the MSS vehicle until it runs out of fuel, I suggest that we begin to change course to the North. Obviously, the Russians are using RDF bearings on our radio transmissions to try to locate the vehicle. If we keep following it, they'll be in a better position to find it. If we go North now, before the *Tributs* gets here with her sonar, the Russians will be searching two hundred miles East of the MSS's actual location."

"That sounds like a plan, Kevin, but what makes you think the Russian ships will enter Bahamian Territorial Waters?"

"Sir, there is nothing they won't do to catch up with our latest technology. What's the Bahamas Government going to do to the Russian Navy? Protest at the UN?"

"Kevin, I think you're right. What we can really use now is some radio traffic between us and that P-3. Or, --- how about this? We'll use the VHF radio on an open channel, call the *Harkness* and send her steaming to the East -- over toward New Providence. Certainly, the Russians are monitoring the AUTEC frequencies. Hopefully they have a good RDF man on watch."

Captain Walters reaches for the telephone. "Maneuvering? This is the Captain, come left to zero-one zero degrees. Communications? Get me the Chief."

"Chief Banacek, get us patched in to Patrick Air Force Base and find out when we can expect the next P-3. And Chief, call the *Harkness* on the regular AUTEC open channel and tell them to change course to zero, seven zero."

"Sir, you really want me to call *Harkness* in the open on the VHF?"

"Yes, Chief -- as I said, the open channel --- so the Russians can listen in."

"The Russians! Aye, aye --- sir."

1900 Hours Central Intelligence Agency, Langley, Virginia

Guy Cable reads the Flash traffic message for a second time. The Office of Naval Intelligence is asking for Agency help in the Bahama Islands. The test firing of a super-secret naval weapon has gone awry and the Navy needs help --- fast. Meanwhile the Ruskies have put two ships to sea from Cuban ports and they are heading toward the Bahamas. Does the Agency have any assets that can assist the Navy? Cable does a quick mental analysis. *"Assets? Let's see --- we've got Butterfield in the Northern Bahamas with the Canadian, Scott Lindsay --- Scott's not on the payroll, but I think he can be trusted. Other than satellite surveillance, we've got nothing else to offer. Need to get a heads up to Butterfield on some kind of secure telecommunications --- but, what? Ham radio to Scott Lindsay? Not secure, but about the only thing immediately available. First, I need to have the communications guys to get a reply to O N I. Then, the commo guys need to try to reach Jack through Scott Lindsay."*

"C6AIAC, calling C6AIAC on 147.420 megahertz. This is WA6GCI, calling. C6AIAC, C6AIAC, this is WA6GCI, come in Scott." There is no reply. Every half hour, the same transmission goes out over the 20 meter band from CIA headquarters.

1530 Hours, The North End of Green Turtle Cay

A five minute brisk walk has Scott back to the inflatable. He removes his Timberland boat shoes, rolls up his pants and wades to the Zodiac that he has hidden in the mangroves. A few strokes on the oars and he is in deep water. He starts the engine and heads for *Caribe Dreamer,* safely tied up at the West Dock. The boat is completely dark, just as he has instructed Addie.

"Scottie is that you," comes the whispered inquiry from the cabin. "Oh, thank God it's you -- I've been so worried."

"Addie, darling --- I'm really sorry. Wait 'til you hear about my day --- but first let me give you a kiss and then I'll go to the head to freshen up."

"Scott, please tell me everything --- don't leave anything out."

"Hon, this will have to wait. I have to get on the radio on two meters and talk to Pinder. I'm going to set up the radio and the antenna trimmer and talk at 1600 hours."

"That's only ten minutes from now --- how can I help you?"

"Addie, just grab my gear bag and lay out the patch cords. I'll work on the antenna tuner."

By 1555 hours, Scott has his system up and running and is tuning his radio to the two meter band. Promptly at 1600, Pinder is on the air.

"C6AIAC this is C6AZAZ calling on 147.420 megahertz. Come in Scottie."

"C6AZAZ this is C6AIAC back. I reading you five --- five."

"IAC this is ZAZ --- Scottie, you've got some Whiskey Alpha Six guy from the States trying to reach you every half hour on twenty meters --- what gives?"

"ZAZ --- IAC here. Pinder --- it beats the heck out of me why he's calling. I talked to a guy from 'One Land' a few days ago -- someone from Massachusetts. Right now, I can't get up to twenty meters without retuning my rig. How about you relaying for me and find out what's on his mind?"

"IAC --- ZAZ back. Sounds like a plan, man. Stand by on two and I'll venture up to twenty --- talk to this yahoo and call you back in half an hour."

"ZAZ --- IAC I'm standing by on 147.420 Simplex for your call back.

"C6AZAZ is clear with C6AIAC and switching to the twenty meter band.

1700 Hours, The Amidships Torpedo Room aboard the *U S S Topeka*, operating in the 'Tongue of the Ocean'

"Excuse me Miss Barton. May I have a word with you?"

"Certainly, Commander Anderson."

"The Skipper is of a mind to just hit the destroy button on this mission. And --- glancing around the room Kevin whispers and puts his finger to his lips --- this is really top secret stuff --- the Russian Navy is in the area and they are snooping around. A Russian Navy frigate is on the way to the Central Bahamas. So, I offered up a plan and I think this will buy us some time."

"Oh, my God, Commander. I never thought this test would end up this way."

"Right, no one did --- that's why we test. Here's what Captain Walters has agreed to do. *Topeka* will continue to follow the vehicle underwater. The Captain is sending the *Harkness* off on an easterly heading --- hoping to lead the Russians in the wrong direction. The P-3 Orion aircraft is going back to Patrick Air Force Base to refuel. At daylight, we'll have more aircraft available. The Coast Guard has offered us their Falcon Jet as well as a C-130 Hercules. Meanwhile, the Office of Naval Intelligence is contacting all the agencies who might have assets in the Bahamas to help us in the search. It's going to be a long night -- so get some rest. And, no mention to any of your personnel about the Ruskies nosing around. Okay?"

1730 Hours aboard the Russian intelligence gathering ship *Khersones*

Grigory is monitoring only two frequencies, now. 'Clay Pigeon' has gone home and nothing much has been heard from 'Pheasant Hunter'. 'Duck Blind', the surface ship, continues to movie to the Northeast -- toward New Providence and closer to the location of the *Admiral Tirpitz* steaming in from the deep Atlantic Ocean to the East.

"This is all good news, thinks Grigory. The pieces of the puzzle are falling in place. The Captain and I will be rewarded with full pensions --- perhaps a dacha on the Black Sea."

1800 Hours aboard the *Caribe Dreamer*

"C6AIAC this is C6AZAZ Calling. Come in Scottie."

"C6AZAZ this is C6AIAC --- come back Pinder."

"IAC this is ZAZ --- Scottie, you're going to have to read between the lines on this transmission --- if you know what I mean. That Whiskey Alpha Six caller is a commo guy working for your former employer, out of Virginia. A major sea power has an operation going in the Eastern Atlantic and they think they'll need your services. It's all hush - hush and they want you to get back into contact with their salesman, with --- of all people, that sales guy we met at the Tiki, over."

"ZAZ this is IAC --- so it looks as if our 'salesman' is who he said he is. I know where he is staying --- so, I'll sign off now and take a hike and see if I can find out what services he is interested in. Over."

"IAC this is ZAZ -- sounds like a plan, man. Just keep me posted in case they also need the services of an old coot, like me."

"C6AIAC is clear with C6AZAZ."

Addie and Mittens are snoozing in the cockpit and unaware of the exchange between Scott and Pinder. Scott kisses Addie on the cheek to wake her.

"Hon, sorry to wake you. I just talked to Pinder and it seems like the guy I met at the Leaky Tiki is, in fact, a CIA agent. Seems there's some Navy operation going on off of Andros that may need my attention. I'm going to the Green Turtle Club to look up Mr. Butterfield. The wind is calm and the tide is out, so you two should be fine. I'll be gone no longer than an hour. Okay?"

"Scott, be safe. I love you."

Scott hops into the inflatable and powers around the point into White Sound. He ducks into an opening in the mangroves and hides the rigid inflatable boat. A five minute brisk walk takes him to the Green Turtle Club. It is dinner time and the patio bar and restaurant are hopping with dinner guests. Scott surveys the area and spots a male dining alone --- it is Jack Butterfield. Scott approaches his table.

"Good evening, Mr. Butterfield."

"My gosh! --- Scott Lindsay. I thought it would be *me* searching for *you*. That sure was fast. How'd you find out we were looking for you?"

"Seems your friends at the Company found me talking on my Ham radio. They indicated that you may need my services. Although --- I must say, this sounds a little more serious than a simple money laundering scheme."

"Yes, Mr. Lindsay, this is some really serious stuff. It's so sensitive that we can't talk about it here --- and, I'm not certain where to talk, since it seems that my room has been compromised."

"Well, then, let's walk into New Plymouth and we can talk, while we walk. If we need to do more talking, we can always sit in the back of the

Anglican Church --- it's never locked --- and few people sit in the pews, at this hour at night.

"Okay, so we walk and talk. Follow me, I'll need to pay for my dinner at the bar and then I can brief you on the secret nature of this matter. Before our little talk is over, you will know about two top secret initiatives of the U.S. Government --- and, since you are a Canadian Citizen, that just complicates matters --- 'caus, if you were a U.S. Citizen, we could threaten to jail you and throw away the key. In this case --- ha, ha, we would just have to kill you! No, just kidding, but this is extremely sensitive, top secret poop." Jack calls the waitress and signs for his meal, putting it on his room tab and the two men leave the Club.

"Scott, since I have no idea where we're going, you lead, I'll follow --- and I'll do the talking. Okay?"

"I'm walking --- you're talking, Jack. Just a correction to your file on me. Yes, I am a Canadian citizen however, you may have noted that I was born in Milwaukee to a mother and father that, at the time were both U.S. Citizens. So, you won't have to kill me!"

"I'll see to it that our records are corrected. It's my turn to talk --- please listen carefully. Our military contractors have been working with the Navy on a revolutionary new weapon. Seems that when Western Navies play hide and seek with Russian or Chinese subs, the enemy simply waits submerged, off of our known submarine bases. The enemy subs just wait off of Puget Sound, Norfolk or King's Island following our every move --- and, we do the same thing to them. When a sub leaves port, they just tail it. Recently, the U.S. Navy developed a torpedo-type miniature submarine which, when released by the mother ship, produces an identical acoustical noise signature. The real sub plays possum and the mini-sub leads the enemy sub on a wild goose chase. Two problems --- first, the cost. The torpedo is only good for a single shot. Once fired, it cannot be retrieved. Second, the noise of the compressed air, as the torpedo is launched --- this noise can easily be detected by the enemy. So, our 'Military/Industrial Complex', ha, ha, came up with a better idea. Refit existing subs with a vertical tube, where the mini-sub would be launched silently, by swimming vertically out and away from the mother --- no compressed air needed. And, after its mission is over, it returns to the mother ship --- 'er boat, or it can be retrieved later by another submarine or surface ship. The first of the converted subs, the *U S S Topeka* has been deployed to the undersea testing base on Andros. The first test of a prototype was run this morning and, unfortunately, the multi-million dollar thing has run wild. And, just to complicate matters, the Russians are nosing around the area hoping to get to the 'vehicle', as we call it, before we do."

"So, Jack --- where do I fit into this scenario?"

"The vehicle has ignored all commands to abort and is making a turn to the East - Northeast. Based upon the battery life and the speed and direction of the vehicle -- the Navy's best estimate is that this thing could end up on the reef at a place called Lynyard Cay or, perhaps a bit further North at Loyalist Cay. And yes, you heard me right --- I did say Loyalist Cay --- which is another complication to this matter that we must discuss. The Agency, in preparing for this possibility, has asked me to have you organize a group of trusted Bahamians who can operate small boats, to search for and retrieve this vehicle, if it continues to come this way."

"Well, Mister CIA Man, that's quite a tall order. You stop talking and I'll start thinking. We're almost to the Anglican Church. We can continue our conversation there. I'm thinking out loud, now --- small boats --- trusted people --- people who know the area. I'm thinking --- Albert Alton."

"Okay, Mister Lindsay --- who is Albert?"

"He's Albert Alton the owner of Frigate Cay Marina. He provides free dockage to the Frigate Cay Ferry Service. You probably got off a ferry at his dock. The drivers are Bahamians and they know the waters ---- they've been sailing and running outboard boats here since they were six years old."

"Scott --- it's all right that I call you Scott? You don't need to tell me about Albert Alton's credentials. He's an informant in another top secret case that the Agency is following --- and, I will need to brief you on this at a later date. Your idea of using the Frigate Cay ferry fleet is a good one."

"Excuse me, Jack. And, yes, you can call me Scott. You're telling me that Albert Alton is a CIA informant?"

"Yes, Scott. He's code named Beached Whale."

"Jack, I need to get back to my boat and my wife. She'll be pretty worried about me. Knowing that Albert is your informant has taken a lot of worry off of both our minds. When do we put this plan into action?

"We'd better get some sleep, as my next contact with the Company is 0400 hours. I suspect we will be underway by daybreak, when the air assets arrive."

"Air assets?"

"Yes, the U.S. Government is throwing everything they have at this situation. We'll have a P-3 Orion, sub hunter, from Patrick Air Force Base, a Coast Guard Falcon Jet as well as a Coast Guard C-130 Hercules, search and rescue aircraft out of Melbourne. The Navy has redirected the aircraft carrier *Kennedy* from its planned stopover at Mayport, to assist us with air cover --- if necessary."

"Wow, you guys sure move fast."

"Yes, we certainly can coordinate better since the Nine-Eleven attack. Think of this --- now, different branches of the military can even talk to each other on our radios!"

"That's good news. Okay, Jack. I'm out of here. I'll meet you at 0600 in front of the Leaky Tiki."

2000 Hours aboard the *Caribe Dreamer* at West Dock, Green Turtle Club

"Hey Addie, I'm back --- and I have lots of good news to share."

"Oh hi, Scott. Sorry I'm a little groggy. Mittens and I were sound asleep. What's the good news?"

"Agent Butterfield briefed me on some really interesting top secret stuff. Here's the bombshell --- Albert is an informant for the CIA and, he's the one that reported our activities --- so, the heat is off from that aspect. And ---"

"Slow down, Scottie --- I'm just waking up and I'm having a hard time following all this. You mean to say that the CIA is behind what's been going on at Loyalist Cay?"

"Hon, I'm not sure, yet. Butterfield says he will brief me on that, later. Meanwhile, I'm supposed to help the Agency coordinate a search for some super-secret Navy thing-ama-jig that's broken loose from its mother ship --- a submarine --- off of Andros. It's coming this way --- and, here's the stuff I'm *not* supposed to tell you --- some foreign naval forces are trying to get this thing --- before we do."

"Scott, if this is good news, I guess I'm not following you. It sounds terribly dangerous."

"Well, the good news is that, we can go back to our mooring at Back Creek. As far as the danger is concerned, I'm not too worried --- Albert and his boatmen are going to be doing the shallow water stuff. All I have to do is coordinate. So, let's get some sleep since I'm meeting Jack at the Leaky Tiki at 0600."

2200 Hours aboard the *U S S Topeka*, submerged at 100 feet, 75 Nautical Miles North of Andros Island

"Commander Anderson, Captain Walters, here. Would you assemble Miss Barton, as well as the rest of the Everen contractor's group in the Wardroom --- and, make certain that they leave someone in charge who is capable of keeping tabs on the vehicle."

"Yes sir, we'll be there in just a few minutes."

The group of five enter the Wardroom and pull the curtain. The SP guards armed with side arms are at their posts in the passageways near both entrances. Captain Walters moves to the center of the room and begins to speak.

"Lady and gentlemen. The information you are about to hear is classified Top Secret. Obviously, you would not be assigned to this program if you didn't have a top secret clearance --- so let me begin. This room is certainly not soundproof, which is why I have posted guards and removed all personnel out of earshot of this area. The guards are from our Communications Section and have Top Secret, Cryptographic clearance. The Operation Ballyhoo test launch is certainly not going the way it was planned. A new weapon system always has some initial problems --- and, unfortunately this one has developed more than a minor glitch. To make matters worse, the problem has developed into a possible international crisis that has been brought to the attention of The President. He has directed the Chairman of the Joint Chiefs of Staff to place all the resources of the U.S. Government at our disposal. The Commander, Submarine Force Atlantic will coordinate all the agencies including the CIA, NSA, Office of Naval Intelligence, the submarine fleet, the surface Navy and the Coast Guard. The Department of State has briefed the Government of the Bahamas. Our orders are --- simply, to keep tabs on the vehicle as it approaches the end of its battery life. COMSUBLANT will decide if we are to attempt to recover the vehicle, or if it is to be destroyed. We all need to get some rest as *Topeka* will be at battle stations at daybreak. That is when we expect our air cover, to help in the search for the vehicle. We will have substantial assets, including an air wing from the aircraft carrier *Kennedy* at our disposal. The *Kennedy* is steaming at full speed to a point twenty miles due East of the Elbow Cay Light and will be ready to assist as needed. Lieutenant Commander Anderson will coordinate with Miss Barton to establish a watch schedule, so that our contractor personnel get some rest, while we continue to monitor the position of the vehicle. Miss Barton, do you have a current position report on the vehicle?"

"Yes, Captain. The vehicle continues to porpoise on the surface and its course is being affected by the waves and swells from the Southeasterly trade winds. It is turning ever so slightly, a few degrees East of North. I have provided the actual latitude and longitude coordinates to your Navigation Section."

"Thank you Miss Barton. This is good news, as this track will keep the vehicle away from New Providence Island. Any questions? Hearing none, you are dismissed --- good luck and God Bless the United States of America."

0400 Hours, the home of Albert Alton, on the Upper Road, Frigate Cay, Abaco Bahamas

Albert is used to his phone ringing at all hours of the night. His Marina is the lifeline of Frigate Cay with its docks and fuel for the ferry service. The ferry boats have carried pregnant women, the sick and injured, as well as the bodies of loved ones that didn't stand a chance to make it by airplane to hospitals in Nassau or West Palm Beach. Some lived --- some died en-route. Albert never asks what the emergency is. He does it because these are *his* people and he loves each and every one of them. This morning, his emergency phone rings.

"Albert here, how can I help?"

"Jack Butterfield, from the Agency calling"

"Oh, Hi Jack, I didn't expect to be hearing from you so soon."

"Mr. Alton, the flag is going up --- and we need your help. This is a separate issue from the activities on Loyalist Cay. Seems our Navy has lost one of its most secret weapons. I've been in contact with your friend, Scott Lindsay, and he suggests that you might be able to roust out some ferry boats --- with boatmen --- that we can use to do a possible shallow water recovery of this secret thing the Navy calls a vehicle."

"Mr. Lindsay is right. Currently tied in my marina are three ferries of different sizes. And --- as far as drivers are concerned, I'm pretty certain that I can round up three --- plus myself to assist you. Just give me fifteen minutes and I'll get back to you with the numbers and then we can coordinate our movement. Two of the boats will need fuel, so I will call my marina and arrange to get the diesel pumps turned on. What's your phone number?"

"Albert, I'm in Green Turtle and my phone, direct to my room is 367-2224. And, by the way, all of your expenses will be reimbursed by my Agency."

"Don't worry about me getting paid. I'm a proud Bahamian, but when I was a teenager, during World War II, I volunteered to work in the States. In fact, I did man's work on a chicken farm in Nebraska. After the war, I went into heavy construction and worked on building expressways in the Saint Louis area. I love the USA --- and, don't worry, Albert always gets paid."

"Thank you, Albert. We need to coordinate communications with your vessels. Can you give me their call signs?"

"Yes, just wait one. --- all of the ferries are named 'Davie', however each boat has an individual number. Here's the information from the white board in my office. Waiting for maintenance, is 'Davie Three' and 'Davie Seven'. On charter backup is 'Davie Ten' --- which is one of the larger vessels and 'Davie One', which is the smallest and oldest in the fleet. I would suggest that we communicate on VHF Channel 71 --- is that okay with you?"

"That's great, Albert. Channel 71 is fine, if you say so. Get back to me with the numbers and I'll pick up Scott. Riding in his inflatable, it will take us at least an hour to get to Frigate Cay and another half hour to North Bar Channel. We should rendezvous two nautical miles East of a place called North Bar Channel. Does that make sense to you?"

"North Bar is fine with me. It is the last place you can get into the Atlantic from the Sea of Abaco with a deep draft vessel. At the ferries speed, it will take an hour and a half to get there from Frigate Cay Harbour. That should put everyone off of North Bar at about 0630 hours."

"Thanks, Albert. The plan seems to be shaping up nicely. Now, all we need is some cooperation from our run-away and this will end up being a routine matter."

0600 Hours in front of The Leaky
Tiki Bar on Green Turtle Cay

Scott arrives dressed in his black spring wetsuit and carrying his diving bag. He's wearing his favorite Milwaukee Brewers baseball cap.

"Hi Scott. We need to reverse course and get back to your inflatable. I've been on the phone with Albert and he's been able to come up with three drivers plus himself for the ferries that are available. We're going to rendezvous at a place called North Bar Channel around 0630."

"Good going, Jack. Sounds as if the plan is coming together. Let's double time back to the mangroves, as it will be a long, rough ride to North Bar in my inflatable. What about communications?"

"Albert suggests VHF Channel 71. Our call sign will be 'Lighthouse.'"

"Channel 71 is a good choice --- the only guys that use that channel are the boats entered in the sportfish tournaments and they won't be coming here until next week."

0600 Hours aboard the *U S S Topeka*, nine Nautical Miles North of Andros Island

The squawk box sounds with one bong, followed by a single tone on the Boatswain's pipe. "Now hear this, now hear this. Battle Stations. This is not a drill. Battle Stations."

"Officer of the Boat, the Captain has the con."

"Aye sir, the Captain has the con. The course is zero-one-zero magnetic and the speed is 20 knots. We have two hundred twenty feet of water below the boat."

"Roger, course is 010 True. Speed is 20 knots. Water under the boat is two-two-zero feet. Bring the boat to periscope depth. Raise the VHF antenna."

"Aye, sir --- up on the bow planes and bring her level at periscope depth --- raise the VHF antenna," repeats the Diving Officer.

The crew braces as the bow of the submarine makes a swift assent to just sixty feet below the surface.

"Reporting the boat is at periscope depth, VHF antenna is above the water, Captain."

"Communications, this is the Captain. Contact 'Lighthouse' on VHF Channel 71 and advise them that we are submerged, ten miles East of Channel Cay, awaiting daylight and the arrival of aerial assets. Advise them that sunrise is 0744 local time and we should have first light at 0714 hours local."

"Roger Captain. Communicating with Lighthouse' on VHF Channel 71."

"Officer of the Boat, search on the infrared periscope for any vessels on the surface. Sonar, report any contacts."

"Negative contacts on the infrared periscope, Captain."

"Captain, this is Sonar. We have propeller noise from multiple small boats approximately fifteen thousand yards to the West of our position. These are recreational vessels and pose no threat to us. We will continue to monitor these contacts."

"Roger, Sonar."

0645 aboard the Zodiac Inflatable off of Loyalist Cay

"Hey, Jack," Scott shouts. "You're bouncing around like Shamu at Sea World. Why don't you climb into the bow, grab the bow line and ride this thing like a bucking bronco. That way, you can take some of the shock of these waves with your knees and arms."

"Hell, Scott, I've had two back operations and I doubt I could stand up there for more than ten seconds. I'm not sure you can hear me over the roar of the outboard, but this might be a good time to brief you on the Company's operation on Loyalist. This is Top Secret information and, as you surmised, those people are up to no good. The Agency has had them under surveillance for the last four months. Seems that the money to buy Loyalist Cay came from a Saudi prince who laundered it through some kook newspaper guy from Oregon. The Saudis are supporters of this world-wide rebellion against Western Civilization --- they call it a 'Jihad' --- and they have three major targets --- all Westerners, especially Jews and Christians, United States assets and the State of Israel. They consider any non-Muslim to be an 'infidel' and all infidels must be killed."

"Wow, Jack, that's a tall order to take on the whole of Western Civilization --- do they have nukes or some other means of destroying the West?"

"We know they're trying to get nukes, but worse than that, Scott, they have much of the Islamic World on their side. They have hijacked the Muslim bible, the Koran, and have turned it against the West. They have thousands of potential suicide bombers who have been told that when they die, they will be greeted in the hereafter by a bunch of virgins. The umbrella organization is called al-Qaeda, and they have splinter groups and terrorist cells all over the world."

"How come the average guy, like me, has no idea of how great a threat these bad guys are to our society?"

"Hell, they've been talking to us and threatening us for years now. But, we just laughed them off as a small number of radicals. Remember the bombing of the Marine quarters in Beirut and the attack on the U.S.S. Cole --- and the biggie on 9/11?"

"Yea, all that made the news --- some suicide bombers took out a small building with a truck load of TNT and they ran a small boat into the side of the Cole then they flew two hijacked jets into the World Trade Center towers and three thousand people died --- but why haven't we mobilized against this threat?"

"Basically, it's because our government is burying its head in the sand. They had plenty of intelligence, and they knew that al-Qaeda was behind

145

the bombing of the World Trade Center and the U.S.S. Cole --- that was them, too."

"Why isn't the White House on the lookout for these Islamic guys?

"Oh, seems that the Collins administration viewed the organization as a group of law breakers and sigged the Attorney General and the Justice Department on them.

"Hell, you have to be kidding me --- these guys have explosives and rifles --- and Rocket Propelled Grenades. They're beheading a bunch of Western looking guys and doing the same to the Christian minorities. What good are courts and lawyers against a bad guy with an RPG," questions Scott.

"You're right and that's why public pressure has caused the Administration to take a war-like posture with this group of bad guys --- simply put, they're terrorists. And, we need to kill them, before they kill us."

"So, what you're telling me is that there are terrorists are on Loyalist Cay?"

"Yep --- and our only problem is trying to figure out what they're targeting --- and to stop them, before they are able to pull this off."

"Hell, Jack this is easy to figure out --- they hate Israel and Jews, right? And they hate Americans, right? I'll tell you their target --- how many American Jews do you figure live on the East Coast of Florida --- or, just in Miami Beach? That's their target, plain and simple. Just explode a couple of canisters of mustard gas a few miles off shore and let the Southeast trade winds take it inshore and wipe out thousands of Americans --- half of them would be Jews."

"You're right, Scott. That's exactly what the Agency is thinking, too. We don't want to spook them into moving until we're ready to move in." So, we have them under heavy surveillance --- Satellite photography --- electronic monitoring, photos from a DC-6 cargo plane that flies out of Marsh Harbour three days a week --- and, our best man on the ground is Beached Whale, your friend Albert."

"Boy, that info is quite a shocker, although he's probably the only person on Frigate Cay that could have handled that job."

"You are right, Scott. Albert has been one of our best informants on the ground."

"We should be off of Channel Cay in a few minutes and then we can throttle back --- the ride will get better. Hey, check out all the white stern lights and all-around 360 white lights ahead of us. Looks like Albert got all four boats out and on their way. A few minutes ago, I heard a transmission between Lighthouse and a call sign of 'Pheasant Hunter' --- that's the sub and the message indicates they are submerged four miles East of here They're saying that we should have first light at 0714 or so --- then we should be hearing some aircraft overhead."

"That's good news, Scott --- keep it coming."

0700 hours aboard the *Khersones*, twenty Nautical Miles East of New Providence

Punched paper tape comes streaming out of the receiver --- it continues to roll in great white waves onto the floor of the 'Ice House'. Grigory is sound asleep at his console --- another wasted night with the vodka bottle. He awakens as the propeller noise indicates a sudden slowing of the ship. Where are we? Perhaps, Nassau? He opens the door of the 'Ice House' and sees nothing but a trailing foamy wake and the rolling sea behind the ship.

"Wonder what's going on?" But, the operations of the ship are completely out of his control. To know where we are, or where we are going is the exclusive province of the Captain --- Grigory has heard that a hundred times on this trip.

"Damn, look at the mess on the floor. Wonder when these messages came in," he shouts out to no one. "Better get them decoded."

"I really need a visit to the head for a shower and a shave, but under the circumstances it is probably prudent to skip that and set the decoder to the correct date and code parameters."

Grigory references his code book and adjusted the five wheels of the decoding machine. He feeds the punched tape into the opening and watches as the message prints out one character at a time.

"Oh, Mother Russia, this is a flash message to the Captain. It came in at 0430 hours --- I'll have to reformat this message to change the time. The Admiral Tirpitz and the Khersones have permission from the Bahamian Governments for a port call for the ships and crew. Both ships will put in at the Prince Edward Dock tomorrow at 0900 hours. I'd better run this up to the bridge and let the decoder print away," thinks Grigory, out loud.

Grigory quickly makes the long, staggering walk against the motion of the ship and finally reaches the bridge. He delivers the message directly to the Captain.

"Ah, Grigory --- finally some good news. A port call. I can't remember our last. Was it Havana?"

"Yes, sir it was Havana --- two months ago. Pardon me sir, but I've got to get back --- there are more messages."

"Certainly, Grigory --- be on your way."

Grigory retraces his path to the 'Ice House', unlocks the door and stares at the decoder.

"Oh, crap another 'flash' message for the Captain. Oops, this one's not good news --- seems that urgent fleet matters will prevent the Tirpitz from making the port visit. Both ships will rendezvous at a point twenty miles East of the Sal Salvador Lighthouse on the Atlantic side of the Bahama Islands. Looks like another walk up

to the bridge --- this time, I won't hurry," he thinks, as he opens the door to the humid tropic air and starts his walk to the bridge.

"Captain, another flash for you."

"Humph, --- the Captain is silent as he continues reading. I doubt that there ever was a port call in the works. Looks like a ruse, so our ships can operate in Bahamian Territorial Waters. So, Grigory --- back to your dungeon. Sorry to have crushed your dreams of a dacha and a pension. This cruising in circles in a derelict vessel is downright boring. Even a partial pension sounds good to me right now --- even orders to be stationed in Vladivostok in the Winter would be acceptable over this effing command."

0714 Hours First Light in the North Bar Channel. Aboard the *U S S Topeka*. The Captain has the con.

"Maneuvering, make the speed of the boat 12 knots. Perform a five minute, 360 degree turn to starboard. Communications, stream the Very Low Frequency antenna so we can communicate with COMSUBLANT as well as the *Kennedy* --- if need be."

"Aye sir, maneuvering speed to 12 knots with a standard 5 minute turn to starboard. The VLF antenna has been deployed."

"Communications, open up the Very Low Frequency link with COMSUBLANT as well as the *Kennedy*. Also, contact the Coast Guard Falcon --- or, by now it may be a C-130, on VHF Channel 16. We need to let them know that all VHF traffic will be on Channel 71."

"Roger skipper. We will make the links with COMSUBLANT as well as the *Kennedy* and the Coast Guard. We're monitoring both Channel 16 as well as 71 and are in contact with 'Lighthouse' as well as 'Spyglass' on 71."

"Thanks gentlemen and well done, commo section."

"Amidships Torpedo Room, this is the Captain. What's the range and speed to the target?"

"Captain -- we show it on the surface and it is slowing to seven knots. The vehicle is seven thousand yards to the West of our position --- and one nautical mile to the South.

"Roger Amidships. Ah, -- Communications -- patch me through to the closest air asset."

"Sir, Como here -- at the current time, that would be the Coast Guard Falcon Jet. They're overhead and patrolling from the Hole-In-The-Wall Light -- North as far as Loyalist Cay. Patching you through, sir. The Falcon's call sign is 'Spyglass'."

"Spyglass, this is Pheasant Hunter --- over."

"Pheasant --- this is Spyglass. Can we be of assistance? Over."

"Spyglass, our telemetry is showing the vehicle to be on the surface --- or close to the surface porpoising through the wave tops at a speed of only seven knots. She's Northbound and we show her to be about one nautical mile South of North Bar Channel. Can you do a low level fly by? Do you copy? Over."

"Roger that transmission, Pheasant Hunter. We'll make a run from the South to the North at 300 feet. Understand that we're looking for something about thirty feet long with orange day-glo stripes on the nose. Is that a roger? Over."

"Ah, Spyglass, this is Pheasant Hunter --- that's affirmative. Spyglass is standing by on VHF Channel seven-one."

"Lighthouse, this is Pheasant Hunter, over."

"Pheasant Hunter, Lighthouse on Channel 71. Over."

"Lighthouse, what is your current location --- and what is the plan for your small boat flotilla? Over."

"Pheasant Hunter, Lighthouse. We just passed over the North Bar Channel heading Northwest. We're out in the open ocean. I have split the fleet in half. Davie 3 and Davie 7 --- a large boat and a smaller boat are turning South toward Lynyard Cay. Davie 1 and Davie 10 are turning North toward Loyalist Cay. Over."

"Lighthouse, this is Pheasant Hunter. Roger your last and agree that this is a good plan, as we have telemetry showing the vehicle Northbound about a mile out in the ocean. The Coast Guard Falcon, call sign 'Spyglass' is making a pass from South to North in your vicinity. They will drop a smoke flare if they see the target. Over."

0730 Hours, the 'Ice House' communications shack aboard the *Khersones*

"Damnation, --- this situation is --- Grigory stops cursing and surveys his surroundings --- is why the West is going to win the new Cold War. They have all the money, all the assets. Here we sit with one person, me, attempting to gather all the intelligence --- one lone man against the assets of the United States military. I have no effing help and I'm supposed to keep track of Pheasant this and Lighthouse that --- it sounds as if the U.S. Navy has mobilized half the effing Atlantic fleet. And the mighty Russian Navy --- the mighty *Admiral Tributz* has decided to play it safe and hide out in international waters. Mother Rodina, you deserve better. But, not from me. I quit --- I'm through. Give me port leave in Nassau and I'll go on a drunk for 48 hours. Damn it --- there must be ten meters of incoming messages that need to be decoded. Where's my effing assistant? eff ----- the whole effiing Russian Navy and double eff ----- to the SVR and the intelligence establishment --- those worthless effing bureaucrats.

0745 aboard the *U S S Topeka*, submerged thirty nautical miles Northwest of Nassau

"Captain, this is commo --- we have communications from a 'Davie 10' --- ah, that's one of the small boat flotilla. They've spotted the vehicle and we've called for confirmation from the Coast Guard. The Coasties have their C-130 Herc above us --- call sign is 'Golden Coconut'--- the Falcon has gone back to Melbourne. I'll pipe you through on VHF Channel 71 --- okay Skipper?"

"Roger Commo. Ah, get a message to COMSUBLANT on the VLF and copy the *Kennedy*. Then, pipe me through to 'Golden Coconut' --- who, the hell, makes up these call signs?"

"Commo here --- heck if we know, Skipper, but we roger your order to contact COMSUBLANT and keep the *Kennedy* informed. Now, we have you piped directly to 'Davie 10' on VHF Channel 71."

"Davie 10, this is Pheasant Hunter, how copy?"

"Pheasant Hunter, this is Davie 10 --- read you loud and clear. Over."

"Roger, Davie 10 --- please give us your location and advise if the Coast Guard C-130 has over flown your position?"

"Pheasant Hunter, this is Davie 10 --- a big turboprop with an orange tail and U.S. Coast Guard markings on its wings is about half a mile East of our location. He's going North --- away from us. Over."

"Roger, Davie 10 --- we'll give him your location and send him your way --- just keep the vehicle in sight. Over."

"Roger, Pheasant Hunter. This is Davie 10 standing by on Channel 71."

"Golden Coconut, this is Pheasant Hunter, over."

"Hunter, this is Nut, we've monitored your last transmission and are turning back to the Southeast and will sweep the area looking for a small boat and the subject vehicle with the day-glo orange stripes. Over."

"Golden Coconut, this is Pheasant Hunter. Roger that, we're standing by on VHF 71. Lighthouse, this is Pheasant Hunter, over."

"Hunter, this is Lighthouse, over"

"Lighthouse, how large a vessel is Davie 10? Over."

"Hunter, the Davie 10 is a forty footer."

"Beached Whale, does Davie 10 have the capability of taking a line around the vehicle to keep it from crashing into the reef or ending up on the beach? Over."

"Hunter, this is 'Lighthouse' --- there's only one man aboard Davie 10 --- don't think this is possible until I get there with Albert. I'm just a half mile behind Davie 10 in my inflatable and I have extra lines and fenders. The three of us could probably do it --- and, I have the driver from Davie 1 available to help, too, over."

"Hunter, this is Nut. We have confirmed the sighting of the vehicle. A small, blue/over gray cabin cruiser is following. A smaller blue/gray cabin cruiser is about 100 yards behind --- followed closely by a black inflatable outboard with two souls aboard. Over."

"Golden Coconut, this is Pheasant Hunter. Thank you for the report. We're standing by on VHF 71."

"Captain, Commo here. We have an Urgent --- Eyes Only for you from COMSUBLANT --- we're sending it up to you right away."

"Interesting --- wonder why they didn't use voice on the VLF?"

"Yea, Skipper. We were wondering the same."

"Sir, I have an Eyes Only Message for you. Please sign on line 3. Thank you." The communications clerk retrieves the aluminum clipboard, salutes smartly and returns to his station.

1410 ZULU URGENT-EYES ONLY-COMMANDER, U S S TOPEKA.

From: COMSUBLANT

ADVISE ALL ASSETS IN RECOVERY PROCESS OPERATION BALLYHOO TO STAND DOWN. ALL UNITED STATES MILITARY ASSETS ARE TO RETURN TO A LOCATION 12 MILES EAST OF THE NORTH BAR CHANNEL. LOCAL RESCUE ASSETS ARE TO RETURN TO THEIR HOME PORTS. AIR ASSETS FROM THE *U S S KENNEDY* WILL DESTROY THE TARGET WHEN IT RUNS OUT OF FUEL.

"Commander Anderson and Miss Barton. Report to the Ward Room immediately."

0815 hours aboard the Zodiac Inflatable

"Shoot, Jack --- that thing they call the 'vehicle' sure looks a lot longer than 30 feet."

"I agree, Scott. Think we can get a rope around the front of this thing and bring it alongside of Davie 10?"

"Hell, it's worth a try, Jack. I'll maneuver alongside of it --- and, I'd better tell Davie 10 what we're up to. Perhaps, his bow wake will squeeze it towards us? Check with Albert and find out who's driving her?"

"Beached Whale, this is Lighthouse --- who's driving Davie 10?"

"Lighthouse, this is Whale --- Darvin is driving."

"Scott, its Darvin --- let's get to his port side --- he's got the driver's window open and he'll be able to hear us if we shout."

"Hey Darvin --- we're going to try to get a line around this thing--perhaps you can squeeze it toward us with your bow wave."

"I'll give it a try, Scott."

"If we get a lasso around it, the rope should slide down the tube until it gets to those stabilizer fins at the ass end."

"Give it a go, Scott. If this works, the vehicle will simply tow us to where it's going to stop."

The VHF radio sounds --- "To call signs Lighthouse, Beached Whale, and vessels with Davie in their call sign, this is Pheasant Hunter. All civilian vessels involved in the recovery of the Naval Asset of the United States, please stand down and return to the position you occupied at 0700 this morning. I say again, please stand down and return to your 0700 position. Pheasant Hunter out."

"Albert, I've got it --- the lasso is sliding down the tube and soon, we'll have it alongside."

"Scott, throw the end of the rope in the sea."

"What the eff, Albert --- are you crazy?"

"No, Scottie. The Navy has decided to quit and go home."

"Aw, hell, you gotta be kidding. Here, cleat this through the ring in the bow bridle while I get on Davie 10 and make the rope fast to her bow cleat."

"Scott, okay, go ahead --- but then we've got to confirm the transmission from 'Pheasant Hunter' and get out of here."

"Pheasant Hunter, this is Lighthouse, over."

"Lighthouse, over."

"We have attached a rope to the vehicle and have the rope attached to the bow cleat on Davie 10. Do you still want us to abort the mission?"

"Lighthouse, abort and return to your position as of 0700 this morning. Please confirm receipt of this transmission."

"Pheasant Hunter, this is 'Lighthouse'. We copy your last --- loud and clear. We're getting out of here --- and fast."

"Scottie, look to the Northwest --- see all that black smoke? What the hell is that?"

"Hell, Albert --- that's a Russian TU-144 Recon aircraft. It looks like its flying at one hundred feet above the ocean. Watch as it goes by --- check the red star on the tail --- it's the Ruskies alright. Heck, they're acting like the Cold War is still going on. We can't let them see the vehicle. What about shifting into reverse --- do you think we can cause it to stop and sink?"

"Scott, it's definitely worth a try. I'm in reverse, now. Hell, at one hundred feet and at that speed, all they will see is foam. Call to Darvin, have him come alongside. Get out two fenders and some lines. Perhaps his shadow will hide the vehicle from being seen from the air."

"Hey, Albert --- look to the South. Just as I suspected, the Ruskie aircraft is making a sweeping U-turn to the West --- he's coming back for another look-see. We've probably got only two minutes to make this work. Here, help me with this fender. Darvin --- get in close, and hurry it up," shouts Scott over the noise of the diesel.

"Scott, this seems to be working, the Easterly swells are pushing the bow around and we're facing Northwest. The vehicle seems to be on the last of its electric cells -- it's no longer towing us, we're actually making progress in reverse. As soon as the Tupolov flies by, we can drop the lines and get out of here."

"Good idea, Albert. Before we ski-daddle, hit the Man Overboard button on the GPS so we can keep the position of the vehicle in memory. You know, just in case the you-know-what hits the fan. What's the reading on the depth sounder?"

0820 Hours, the Ward Room of the *U S S Topeka* submerged 150 miles North of Nassau

"Lieutenant Commander Anderson and Miss Barton --- I've summoned you here to tell you of a decision by COMSUBLANT to use carrier jets from the *U S S John F. Kennedy* to destroy the MSS prototype. There is some top secret background information that I cannot divulge to you that has resulted in this decision by higher ups in the chain-of-command. This information is highly sensitive and is, of course, top secret. Again, I have posted guards from our Communication Section, so that this information is kept among the three of us. Is this understood?"

"Yes sir" is the coordinated response.

"Miss Barton, it is a more than a little bad luck that MSS ended up here --- on this particular piece of reef. Unfortunately, under the conditions encountered by the Bahamians, the vehicle would continue to tow the civilian ferry boat into the beach of a island called Loyalist Cay. The CIA has determined that the island has been occupied by a small number of armed terrorists from the Islamic Group called al-Qaeda. They are a Muslim para-military force and are training on this piece of land for a mission that is thought to involve an attack on the East Coast of the United States with weapons of mass destruction. This group has been under surveillance by the Central Intelligence Agency for more than four months, and our presence --- virtually on their door step --- could possibly upset the timing of the Agency in apprehending these bad guys. Therefore, COMSUBLANT has deferred to the orders from the Director of the CIA as well as the Presidential Assistant for National Security, in the White House. I am extremely sorry that I have to be the one to tell you this news. I'm certain that you have a jumble of thoughts going through your head as to why this mission failed. And, --- in the near future, I'm certain that the Navy will convene a Board of Inquiry, so that all the facts will come out."

"Captain Walters, you've got to be kidding me --- a Board of Inquiry into a test where the prototype vehicle failed because of some electronic malfunction. Not to mention that the corpse is going to be destroyed and the evidence, as to the cause of this malfunction, will never be known. And, to top it off, we had it tied alongside a rescue vessel. You have to be kidding me," stammers an enraged Jean Barton.

"I'm sorry, Miss Barton. This is just speculation on my part, but that is how the Navy works. They're following orders, they're not looking for blame, only for answers."

"Oh, Captain Walters, I only wish your last statement was true. There's millions of dollars at stake here. My employer, Everen Electric, is going to want to be reimbursed for the destroyed vehicle --- they are going to want to find a scapegoat, so they can write off any financial loss and keep performing on this contract."

"Well, Miss Barton ---- this discussion is exactly why a group of impartial Naval Officers will go over each and every detail. You will get your chance to testify."

"Testify! Excuse me, Captain! This sounds like the Navy is going to be both the judge and jury in this inquiry. It doesn't look like this proceeding is going to have a very positive affect on my career with Everen. With your permission and with apologies to Commander Anderson, I would like the opportunity to speak to my fellow employees."

"Certainly, Miss Barton --- with the one caveat that you not mention any of the top secret information that you heard here."

"Yes, sir. I will not divulge any top secret information. Thank you, sir."

1900 hours aboard the Zodiac inflatable, West of North Bar Channel

"Well, Jack. This is a fine how-do-you-do! We get this multi-million dollar machine lassoed and hog-tied and they tell us to let it go."

"Scott, I'm certain the Agency was concerned that as we went further and further North toward Loyalist Cay that some trigger happy Jihad person was going to open fire from the beach. Can you imagine the news report on that --- Albert's ferry boat is blown out of the water by some guy with an AK-47. Not to mention the jig would be up and we'd never know if the target really is Florida's East Coast --- let alone what type of weapon and what delivery system they plan to use."

"We'd better get some kind of communication going with Albert and his drivers --- probably should meet at 'Dine Inn -- Dine Out', the restaurant at the marina on Frigate Cay."

"Good idea, Scott. This way, I can get some names and an estimate of the expenses incurred by Alton's Ferry Service. I don't want Albert to be waiting a year to get his money. Let's go back to Green Turtle."

0830 Hours, Flight Operations, the aircraft carrier, *U S S John F. Kennedy*

"Gentlemen. Our mission is to destroy a secret Navy prototype torpedo that has finally come to rest on a sand bar --- just inside the reef of a Bahamian Out Island named Loyalist Cay -- which is located here on the chart."

"Lieutenant Olsen, you will fly lead and Buck-O will be your wingman. Buck-O will illuminate the target and you will launch one AGM-65 Maverick, to the target. It should only take one missile, however --- in case of an ordnance problem, you will each be carrying two AGM-65's. Any questions? Yes, Buck-O."

"Sounds simple enough, Commander. I know the Bahamas is a small country --- and probably doesn't have a Navy or an Air Force, but have we been cleared to bomb this ---ah sand bar, this piece of a sovereign nation?"

"Excellent question. Yes, we have. Our permission came all the way from the Secretary of State and the White House."

"Thanks for telling us --- we'd better not screw up, Buck-O or we'll be on the national news."

"Okay, you two, you are scheduled for engine start at 0845. Let's make this quick and painless."

"Roger that. We don't want to keep the White House waiting."

Wednesday, 0800 Hours AUTEC,
Andros Island, Bahamas

"Excuse me, Miss Barton."

"Yes, Commander Anderson."

"I'm sorry that these last forty-eight hours ended up this way."

"Yes, and me, too. Looks like the next time we'll see each other is up in Norfolk when the Board of Inquiry convenes."

"Unfortunately, you are probably right. I'm not having great vibes about this inquiry thing. My time in the Exec slot is just about up. I've completed all the schools and course work and am just waiting for my own command. These kinds of incidents can become a little messy --- if you know what I mean."

"Sure do. I sent an e-mail yesterday with my letter of resignation to Everen HQ in Saint Louis --- and their answer was; sure, you can resign, but don't venture outside the U.S. because you will be required to testify. So, I might as well stay on the payroll."

"Oh, boy -- that sounds like trouble to me. Let's keep in touch by e-mail. Oh, by the way, my parents have a beach house on the North Carolina shore near Kill Devil Hill and Kitty Hawk -- it's only a couple of hours from Norfolk. Winter may not be the best time of the year to be there, but perhaps we can spend some time getting sand between our toes, again."

"Commander Anderson, I really like that idea. I'll e-mail you my schedule. Meanwhile, it's back to Building J-21 and then to the test bench in China Lake, to see what may have caused this malfunction. We don't have the remains, but we do have the telemetry data. Till then --- Kevin," says Jean as her hand traces down his arm toward Kevin's hand and with a squeeze, she turns and walks down the dock and disappears in the bustle of activity.

0600, aboard the U S S Topeka at the dock in AUTEC harbor

The Boatswain's Mate's whistle sounds through the boat. "Now hear this, Now hear this, prepare the boat for sea. All men to your stations. Deck party to the conning tower."

"Gentlemen, this is the Captain. Our orders are to proceed directly to Norfolk where we will re-provision and perform some maintenance. At Norfolk, we will be placed in the rotation for a thirty day patrol. As more information becomes available, I will keep you informed. Our departure from AUTEC will be stern first with one tug aft pulling and one tug forward to steer us into the channel. Let's look smart on deck. Make your turns sharp and by the book and --- we don't want a reef off of Andros Island named for the *Topeka*. That is all."

Wednesday, 1100 Hours, a flight of two F-18's from the *U S S Kennedy,* circling over the North Bar Channel

"Bahama One, this is Bahama Two --- you see anything down there with day-glo orange stripes on it?"

"Negative, Bahama Two. How about I circle at Angels Two and you make a slow, on-the-deck pass from the South to the North. Then join me up here, over."

"Roger, Bahama One --- I'm going down on the deck for a look see."

"Yea, I saw it, Bahama One --- just for a second. Its way South of our coordinates --- right off the tip of that island --- the one with the sand bar going off in a Westerly direction, over."

"Roger Bahama Two --- glad you saw it, cause from up here I can't see anything. Illuminate the target and I'll send a Maverick on its way."

"Bahama One, I've illuminated a patch of ocean where I saw the vehicle. Arm and shoot when ready."

"Roger Bahama Two -- missile away -- report any secondary explosion."

"Tally ho -- I've got lots of sand, coral and water in the air --- no secondary explosion noted, but the day-glo nose cone is no longer in sight."

"Roger. Let's go home."

"Roger, Bahama One --- I'm behind you and climbing to join you at Angels Two."

December 13, 2003, Naval Station Norfolk, Norfolk, Virginia. Building K-5, Room 3. Court of Inquiry Proceedings. Vice Admiral Thomas Phillips presiding.

"Officers of the Inquiry Panel, we have before us, the written testimony of Mr. Matthew Malone, a civilian member of the Everen Electric Contractor Team. Mr. Malone, please raise your right hand and repeat after me. I do solemnly swear that the testimony I will give before this panel shall be the truth, the whole truth, so Help You God," reads Admiral Phillips.

"I do."

"Sir for the record, please tell the panel what your position was with Everen Electric when the test vehicle incident occurred," continued the Admiral.

"I was the Senior Electronics Tech --- which means that I was in charge of the linkage between a submarine and the MSS vehicle.

"And, what was your experience while working on the simulator in China Lake --- 'er did you have any linkage problems between the console and the vehicle."

"No sir, we didn't experience any problems but, keep in mind, that the vehicle was operating in a six thousand foot long trench that was only seventy feet wide, and forty feet deep. That's quite a bit different that operating in the open ocean."

"Yes Mr. Malone, that's exactly why we test --- sooner, rather than later, you have to go from the lab into the real environment," responds Admiral Phillips.

"That is correct sir."

"Can you tell me, as best you can recollect, that morning off of Andros Island, of any situation that felt out of the normal --- or, perhaps didn't follow the routines or procedures that you had in place at China Lake?"

"Well, sir --- there is only one thing that has remained in the back of my mind all these months."

"And, Mr. Malone, what's that?"

"Well, when the MSS vehicle refused to run the pre-programmed test --- and, literally, all hell was breaking loose on board the sub -- Miss Barton addressed Commander Anderson by his first name, 'Kevin' and he responded to her with her first name, 'Jean'. I glanced over at her station and her face had flushed, bright red. She was blushing --- I could see it in the color of her skin. It was like they had a personal relation --- not just a business relationship. As employees, we were never allowed to address her as anything but Miss Barton."

"Mister Malone. Is this information in your written testimony?"

"No sir. No one from the Navy ever asked me a question like that."

"Excuse me, Admiral," interjects Lieutenant Frazier. "This is new testimony and it may lead to questions regarding command and control issues between the Weapons Officer, Lieutenant Commander Anderson and the Contractor's representative, Jean Barton."

"Ah, Lieutenant --- are you asking for a recess?"

"Yes, Admiral. We will need to have Jean Barton and Lieutenant Commander Anderson present, so we can delve into this situation more completely."

"Lieutenant, in addition - -- to be completely fair to both Miss Barton and the Commander -- I would suggest that you interview other personnel who were in the amidships torpedo room, when this exchange that Mister Malone is testifying to --- occurred. This proceeding is dismissed until 0800 on Monday."

1630 Hours, BOQ Norfolk Naval Base

"Holiday Inn Express, how may I direct your call?"

"Room 117, please."

"Hello, Jean --- Kevin, here. How'd your day go?"

"It was pretty boring --- I sat in the hall for the entire day and was never called for any testimony. Two of my people paraded in and out --- but, I was never called --- and the coffee was really bad. How'd your day go?"

"Sorry to hear that your day was so bad, mine was pretty routine. We're planning our next patrol --- looks like another 30 day tour. How about I pick you up and we go to get a good cup of coffee, as well as some dinner. I know a great place --- not a Navy hang out --- The Island Grill --say, in about half an hour, in the lobby of your hotel? Oh, by the way --- pack your toothbrush and make certain you have a warm jacket with a hood. I've booked the family cottage on the ocean --- if that's all right with you."

"Wow, from a dinner date to an entire weekend at the beach --- any girl's dream. A half-hour will be just fine. See you then. Bye."

Kevin answers his ringing cell phone. "Lieutenant Commander Anderson, here."

"Hello, Commander, this is Lieutenant Elizabeth Frazier from the JAG office. I'm the Adjutant in Charge of the Inquiry and am calling on behalf of Admiral Phillips. I just want to inform you that you will need to be in attendance at the hearing on Monday morning at oh, eight hundred."

"Thank you, Lieutenant. I will be there, well before oh, eight hundred."

"Yes sir, and have a nice weekend."

"I'll try, Lieutenant. Bye."

Friday, 1700 Hours, Holiday Inn Hotel lobby

"Hi, Jean, I hope you were not waiting, long?"

"No, I've only been waiting a minute or two, Kevin," says Jean as they embrace and share a quick kiss. "Here, let me help you with your bag. Let's get out of here --- I'm starving. My car is right over there under the portico."

"Wow! Kevin, some car --- an Audi T Type convertible --- and it's Arrest Red which is my favorite color. This sure is a far cry from that F-150 pickup we drove on Andros."

"Yes, and the best part is --- heated seats", says Kevin as he places her overnight bag into the back seat.

"Hop in, belt up and we'll get ready to sit in traffic going across the bridge. Despite this cold spell, there will still be plenty of traffic. This time, you are in charge of the XM Satellite Radio. Play around with it and find some traffic jam music."

"You okay with smooth jazz?"

"Sure --- fine with me. If this traffic congestion continues, we may have to skip the Island Grill and stop at the breakfast-all-day place at Kill Devil Hills."

"Or, how about we just stop at a convenience store and I'll buy some groceries and cook you dinner."

"Hey --- a great idea. In a few miles we'll pass a Harris-Teeter grocery store. We can browse around the take-out counter and put together dinner --- and something for breakfast."

"You sure sound upbeat --- do you have some insight into how the inquiry is going?"

"Well, just a little. An old friend of mine, a Chief from sub school. He's now at JAG and I saw him in the hall a week ago. He says that he's sat in on lots of these proceedings. His take on this deal is that with millions of dollars down the drain, someone is going to be made a scapegoat. I guess I'm upbeat because I've had time to adjust the realization that any inquiry on my record will probably put an end to my goal of commanding my own submarine. And, maybe it's for the best. If our relationship is going anywhere, I don't need to be away on patrol for the next thirty days."

"Kevin, I'm really sorry if that is the way things are going to turn out. But, I'm sure happy to hear that you won't be going on patrol --- especially since we just spent the last sixty days of our relationship corresponding by e-mail."

"You know Jean, the last time we were together, you were scheduled to tell me about *him*."

"Oh, about ah --- Traxel --- Jack Traxel. I guess a traffic jam is as good a place as any to tell you the story. All was going well in our relationship until he wanted to get really serious. The kind of thing that would have jeopardized both of our jobs with Everen. As it was, we were violating the company dating guidelines for employees holding Top Secret clearances. I told him --- nothing doing. I suggested that we cool our relationship and that one of us should request a transfer to another program. And, did he ever transfer me --- as far away as one could get. All the way from California, to Andros Island in the Bahamas. But, in the end, I made the best of it. I'm all over Jack. Last month he sent me an e-mail and said he left Everen and went to work for Northrop-Grumman in San Diego. I deleted the message and never replied. Spammed him, so I haven't heard from him since."

"I'm certainly glad to hear that he's gone from China Lake. I had visions of him harassing you on a daily basis."

"I'm glad he's gone, too. Looks like I'll have to go back to China Lake, for a week or so, after this is over, to get de-briefed and do all that corporate exit interview baloney. They've got my resignation --- all I need is for this inquiry to be over."

"I've accumulated seventy-five days of leave. Maybe we can meet up in China Lake. I'll put a hitch on this thing and we can load your stuff into a U-Haul and head to Las Vegas."

"Vegas? Why, Vegas?"

"I am thinking we could get married in Vegas."

"Well sailor, you've got to propose to me first and that will require a ring and for me to say yes. I'll say it now --- I love you Kevin Anderson and I would love to be your wife --- forever and forever. That's my acceptance --- now we only need a proposal and a ring --- ha, ha."

"Hey, if we get back early enough on Sunday, we can go to the twenty-four hour pawn shop in Norfolk. There will be plenty of rings. Sailors are always getting jilted or divorced."

"The ring can wait. I'm still waiting for your proposal."

"In due time, in due time. Meanwhile, I want to say that I'm madly in love with you and want you to be my wife. Oops, almost missed the Harris-Teeter parking lot. Let's hit the take-out counter and sample some of their salads. I just love their German potato salad."

"I'm more partial to the three bean salad," says Jean laughing.

"Hey why don't we just do a bunch of salads. One thing is a must --- strawberry Jello with whipped cream."

"Okay, you can have your Jello as long as I can have my pickled beets," responds Jean.

"That's a fair trade --- I assure you, I'll never steal one of your beets."

"You know, instead of going to Vegas, we should visit my parents and give them the good news. Mom and Dad live in Petaluma, California. It's a long, two day drive from China Lake, but in the Audi --- I'll bet we can make it a fun trip."

"Good idea --- ah, parents. I'll bet they'll be asking all sorts of questions. Like, how are you going to support my daughter when you don't have a job."

"Or, Kevin --- the big question from my mother. Have you spoken to Kevin about having children. Come to think about it, we haven't talked about it --- and the Harris-Teeter take-out counter is probably not the right venue."

"You're right Jean. While you get your beets, I'm going to the liquor department and pick out a few bottles of wine. Then, I'll stop by the cocoa aisle and get us some milk and mix for hot chocolate. Come to think about it --- I may need to pick up a cord or two of firewood. I'm not certain if Dad put in any wood for the winter --- he's been complaining lately of a bad back."

December 14, 2007. *Caribe Dreamer* anchored in the Eastern Harbour at Frigate Cay, Abaco Bahamas.

"So, Scottie anything important in the mail.?"

"Yeah, look at this envelope. Sure looks important. Office of the Director, The Central Intelligence Agency, Langley, Virginia. Postage Paid for by The U. S. Government."

"Hon, open it --- quick --- quick. Read it to me."

"Mister and Misses Scott Lindsay, The Sailing Vessel *Caribe Dreamer* Frigate Cay, Abaco, Bahamas.

Dear Mr. and Mrs. Lindsay,

Each January, The Central Intelligence Agency holds a banquet which honors persons and institutions that have helped the Agency complete its mission and protect the lives of millions of freedom loving people all over the world. I hereby extend the invitation for you to join us on January 11 - 12, at Agency Headquarters in Langley, Virginia. You will be guests of the Central Intelligence Agency for those two days and all expenses will be paid by the Agency.

At the banquet, you will be honored as a "Friend of the CIA," for your help on two occasions when we needed feet on the ground so we could complete our mission. Your friend and fellow Bahamian resident, Albert Alton, will also be honored, at the dinner.

The Agency will provide a U.S. Air Force Gulfstream Jet for your round-trip flight from Marsh Harbour International Airport to Washington National Airport, where you will be met by a private car.

Dress for the banquet will be semi-formal with sport coat or suit and tie for gentlemen and formal party dress or tailored pants suit for the ladies.

Please reply at your earliest convenience to my secretary at (212) 355-5544. I am personally looking forward to your visit.

Sincerely,
George T. Morris
Director

"Wow, Scottie. We're going to Washington ---- and flying in our own private jet. This is really exciting."

"Actually, I'm flabbergasted. A Canuck flying on the CIA's private jet. That's really something. And, think of it, Albert is going with us. Should be a good time. We'll have to do some shopping for a sport coat for me and new dress for you."

Harris Teeter grocery store, Kill Devil Hills, North Carolina

"Excuse me, Miss Barton. I'd like to introduce you to --- ah, Mike. He's the Assistant Produce Manager and I spotted the Navy Anchor tattoo here on his forearm --- so, I figure he is the right person to witness my proposal. And, on the way back to the carry out area, I stopped in floral and got you this bouquet."

"Kevin, you're a riot --- isn't anyone taking pictures?"

"Darn, forgot to stop by photo, on the way here. Hey, Mike, can you run to photo and get one of those disposable cameras?"

"Certainly, sir. I'll be back in less than sixty seconds."

Breathless, Mike returns to produce with a camera. Kevin stoops down to one knee and Mike begins snapping photos.

"Jean Barton --- I love you. Will you marry me?"

"I love you, too Kevin Anderson and, yes, I will marry you. And, the flowers are fresh and beautiful."

"I love you Jean Barton and I'm flattered --- and thank you, Mike, for officiating at our engagement."

"My pleasure, Mister Anderson --- go Navy, Beat Army."

"Kevin, what's that in your cart?"

"Well, I stopped by the deli and got some sandwiches for tomorrow --- then to aisle ten and got some Quaker Instant Oatmeal. Next aisle over, I got a package of light brown sugar, for the oatmeal. Then to dairy, where I got a quart of 2% milk and then, to bakery for a loaf of Cuban Bread --- plus a loaf of butter crust for toast. Then on to frozen foods for a couple of pizzas. And, finally to the liquor department for a couple of bottles of wine. So far, how am I doing?"

"Kevin, you're doing great. I've got the salads -- I think we might need butter and jam for our toast and perhaps some coffee --- if you think there is an automatic coffee pot. --- and, it's always good to have a half-dozen eggs."

"Yea, I'm sure there is a coffee pot, my old man is a three cup a day person. Don't let me forget the firewood --- we'll need one birch and two oak. I think that will do it. So, we need to head back to dairy and then to aisle thirteen for jam. Then to checkout and, don't let me forget the firewood," says Kevin, as they cruise with their cart past the checkout area."

"Excuse me, Katie. Would you ring up the disposable camera first? Then, if you don't mind, please page Mike from produce to come up front. I'd like a picture of the three of us --- we just got engaged."

"Oh, you're engaged! That's really exciting --- actually, Harris Teeter has been the scene of a couple of weddings, but I think your engagement is the first I've ever heard of."

"Mike to register four for a price check. And sir, your fiancé said not to forget to pick out three cords of wood from the display outside."

'Long Look', a sea-front cottage tucked in behind the low sand dunes at Kill Devil Hills Beach, North Carolina.

"Kevin, what an absolutely adorable place --- and the hand painted sign 'Long Look'. Where did this name come from?"

"Oh, my Dad named it that because he and Mom had looked long and hard up and down the shore for just the right place on the beach. He's the only person in the family with any art talent --- he painted the sign. Wait here by the front door, while I go around back and retrieve the key."

"So, you just hide a key?

"Yes, pretty much that's what people around here do --- everyone looks out for the other person's property. They'll see the owner's association decal in my back window and should recognize my car."

"Here's the key --- now, let me go in first and turn off the alarm system. No need to get a visit from the sheriff."

"Okay, come on in --- I'll head to the fuse box and get the electricity going. Next step will be to light the pilot on the furnace --- and finally, when we get some heat in here, I'll turn on the water and light the pilot light on the water heater. Then, we'll empty the car and get a fire going."

"Kevin, I love the knotty pine paneling --- and the antlers --- and fish on the wall. This is exactly what I had seen in my mind's eye view of this place. Thank you for bringing me here."

"This is a great place to come and just think and talk. We've both got some thinking to do and talking it out among ourselves, will certainly help."

"Yea, all the way on the drive up here, I had this gnawing feeling in the back of my mind that this inquiry is not going to go our way."

"Me, too. The information from the Boatswain that I knew from Sub School in Groton, doesn't sound good. He said you can rest assured that the Captain is in the clear. All he had to do was get the boat into and out of port without running aground. He thinks I'm the guy on the hot seat --- and, since you're a civilian, I'm the only one the Navy can blame. However, keep in mind that this is only an inquiry not a Courts Martial."

"Hey sailor, that statement doesn't give me much faith in the Navy's inquiry system."

"Kevin, I'm not going to let their little game ruin my engagement weekend with you. How about making it official and --- here, use my cell phone and call your parents in California."

"Great idea --- with the three hour time difference, they're probably back from golf --- watching Fox News and thinking about cocktails. I'll use my cell --- I've given up memorizing phone numbers, since my cell phone does it for me."

"Okay, how about you hand me your phone and I ask for your Dad ---
and then I'll spring the news on him that I'm asking for your hand in
marriage? What's your Dad's name? And, you Mom?"

"Sure, why not. The phone's ringing --- just ask for Thomas. Mom's
Diane --- he'll probably insist that you call him Tom. Here, I put it on
speaker."

"Hello, Barton residence."

"Why, hello Mrs. Barton. Would Mr. Barton be at home?

"This is Lieutenant Commander Kevin Anderson of the U. S. Navy
calling."

"Oh, yes --- hang on. Thomas, darling, a Lieutenant Anderson from the
Navy on the phone."

"Someone from the Navy for me?

"Yes, Tom, its for you. Find out what he wants."

"Hello, Tom Barton here."

"Hello, Mr. Barton. This is Lieutenant Commander Kevin Anderson
of the United States Navy. I'm a Navy submariner and I work with your
daughter, Jean. I'm calling to ask for your permission to marry her."

There is a long silence at the other end of the phone.

"Well, Commander --- I'm quite pleased that you would even consider
making the call. Seems these days that you young kids just go about doing
whatever you like and --- hell to convention or custom. I appreciate the
call --- only one question --- when you popped the question --- did she
say, yes?"

"Well, Jean got me chocked up --- there was a moment of hesitation
before she answered --- you see, we were in the middle of a Harris-Teeter
grocery store, but she finally did say, yes."

"Congratulations, young man --- and, let me put her Mother on the
phone before she has an attack --- she'll want to speak to Jean about the
details."

"Jean, here --- it's your Mom. I'll get to work on the fire."

Jean switches the phone off of speaker. "Hi, Mom. Yes, off course. ---
we work together on a top secret Navy project. --- yes. Oh, I'll send you
an e-mail on that. --- We've known each other for seven months. --- He's a
submariner. --- Yes, I know they go on long patrols --- but, Kevin is thinking
of leaving the Navy. Why, of course, he'll have a job, he's a Naval Academy
graduate. Ah, we haven't talked about that, yet---.- Brown hair, brown eyes,
about 5 feet 10 inches --- great build. I'll e-mail you our engagement photo ---
no, but soon. I've got to go back to China Lake to be de-briefed. Yes, mom,
I'm quitting my job. --- No, I don't think I'll have any trouble getting another
job, Mom. --- We haven't talked about a big or a small wedding. His parents
live in Winchester, Virginia and are retired. I love you, too. Give my love to
Daddy. I'll e-mail you when I get back to Norfolk. Bye."

"Sorry Kevin, about the one sided conversation. You know, girl stuff.
Like the first question out of her mouth is --- you're practicing birth control,

aren't you? And then the fourth question --- have you talked to him about having children? So, how about we call your Mom and Dad?'"

"I'll leave a message --- they're on a cruise ship going through the Panama Canal --- won't be back home until next week."

December 16, 2003, 0800 Hours, U. S. Navy Base Norfolk, Norfolk, Virginia. Building K-5, Room 6, Court of Inquiry Proceedings, Vice Admiral Thomas Phillips presiding.

"Lieutenant Commander Anderson, Miss Barton. As you may know an inquiry is not a strict legal proceeding. It is more like an interview. And, after the interviews are over, the Board may decide if any other form of Proceeding is necessary. During most Inquiries, seldom are two persons interviewed at the same time. However, considering the information that has been presented to us, I felt it would be prudent to present it to you and Commander Anderson, at the same time. We have a written transcript of the testimony of one of Miss Barton's employees. My staff has additional corroborative testimony from other individuals that were in the amidships torpedo room at that same time. You may have as much time as you need to review the transcripts. And, if you have any questions, you may approach the table and we will attempt to answer them."

"Excuse me, Admiral."

"Yes, Commander?"

"May Miss Barton and I talk among ourselves?

"Yes, you may."

Kevin and Jean begin reading the two page typed transcript. Kevin finishes first and glances up at the Admiral.

"Admiral Phillips, sir. May I address the Board?"

"Yes, Commander, you may. Please step forward to address the Board.

"Gentlemen, every word written on these two pages is the complete truth. The one problem I have with this statement is that nowhere is there any linkage between my, or Miss Barton's, after-hours activity and the performance of our duties aboard the *U S S Topeka*. And, furthermore --- I didn't know that the after-hour activities of Navy personnel was within the jurisdiction of the military code of conduct --- unless, of course, the activities involve espionage, treason or some other illegal activity --- or that we used recreational drugs, or were under the influence. Neither Miss Barton, or me, consumed any alcohol or any illegal drug within twelve hours of our mission."

"Thank you, Commander. Miss Barton, do you have any comments regarding the information contained herein?"

"Admiral, I echo the words of Lieutenant Commander Anderson. Our after hour activities were not done in seclusion. We went to dinner and danced at Big Big's Restaurant, which is a public establishment on Andros Island. We did not over consume alcohol, nor did we make a spectacle of ourselves on the dance floor. Because of the road conditions on Andros --- there had been a number of thundershowers that evening and the mud and gravel road was very slick --- we arrived back at base too late for Commander Anderson to go to his room at the BOQ. So, I offered him the pull out couch in my living room. The next day was a Sunday and we went to a public church and then spent the afternoon sailing. We drove back to the BOQ, said good night and Commander Anderson returned to his room at 2100 hours, to begin preparation for Monday morning's test. I don't think that our activities had any bearing on what, in my opinion, was an obvious problem with the electronic interconnect of the prototype and --- if I might surmise who the person was who wrote this --- I'll just bet that his job was integrating the electronics for the vehicle to the submarine."

"Thank you Miss Barton. Ah, Board, if I may take the liberty to speak for the rest of you --- Commander Anderson and Miss Barton, you have stated your view of the facts very well We certainly will take your statements under advisement in finalizing this proceeding. Does any other Board Member want time to address either Commander Anderson, or Miss Barton."

"Yes, Admiral. Captain William Blake --- for the record. I want to address both of you. I whole heartedly agree that the Navy does not have the right to meddle into the after-hour affairs of its personnel. However, when you are in a command situation --- many times it is simply the *perception* on the part of individuals that can cause a mission to fail. My personal opinion is that your date, if I can call it that, had nothing to do with the failure of the test --- however, in my mind --- I can see that one individual's perception of events causing confusion with the chain of command and control. That is all I have to say."

"Thank you, Captain. Does anyone else on either side of the table have anything to say? --- not hearing anything, I declare this proceeding to be in recess."

Kevin rises from his chair and salutes the officers and exits the room into the hallway and out a side exit. Jean follows a few steps behind him.

"Hey, lady. Great performance. Academy Award performance. That may have been a career saver."

"Kevin, am I ever glad that inquisition is over. I'm sure it was Matt that wrote all that garbage. So now, all I have to do is wait for Everen to send me a plane ticket or a bus ticket, ha, ha, to China Lake. No matter how this turns out --- I'm quitting."

"Yea, me, too. I didn't like the 'however' that our friend the Captain inserted into his comments. I think I'll get my resignation paperwork in the works --- before the Inquiry Board meets again. I know personnel will try to put the brakes on my request, but at least I won't have to wait around here very long to get mustered out. Hell, I'm on TDY while this inquiry is going on --- and, the proceeding has been put in recess so, there's no need us being apart while these guys make up their mind how they're going to blame us for this malfunction. Why don't we hang out at Long Look for the weekend? And, once they complete their 'fact finding', we can get back here in less than two hours."

"Kevin, you come up with the best ideas. You're right, they have our cell numbers and the phones work just fine at Kill Devil Hills. Let's get your stuff from the BOQ and then drop me off at the Holiday Inn and I'll get my clothes and we'll head back to our little love nest in the sand dunes."

0830 CIA Headquarters, Langley, Virginia

"Easterbrook, did you get a look at those low level recons on our Bahamian friends?"

"Yeh, I'm thinking what you're thinking --- too many large crates stenciled as 'generator' for me. How many friggin' generators do you need on this effing little island, questions Jack.

"The crates are one thing, Jack --- how about the people on the grass mats facing East? And, the fishing must be good on the South end of that place --- have you noticed all the boat traffic in and out of here?"

"Yeh, replies Butterfield looking through his photo magnifier --- see what you mean. I think we should get in touch with the Islamic Jihad Group and see what they think --- this Muslim prayer thing is a little beyond my job description."

"That sounds like a plan. We need to get the ball moving down the field on this situation --- and quick. We probably should to go to the Old Man and see what the Bahamas Section has, too. He'll want to coordinate since we're moving onto other people's turf."

Gerry picks up the telephone, punches in five digits and waits.

"Hi Pam, Gerry Easterbrook here. Need to speak to the Old Man. This will only take thirty seconds. Yep, I'll wait."

"Hello Guy, Easterbrook here. Jack Butterfield and I have been discussing a situation we are following in the Bahamas --- Operation Sea Fan. It's getting hot and we need to run this by both the Jihad Group as well as the Caribbean/Bahamas Group. He thinks you should coordinate this thing so no one starts thinking we're stepping on their turf. Time is of the essence."

"Yeh, great, Guy. We'll prepare a PowerPoint and include all the recon stuff we have. See you at 1400 hours in Secure Conference E --- and thank you, sir."

"Jack, looks like we're off to the races. How good are your PowerPoint skills?"

"Sharp as ever, Gerry. I'll work on the on the ground assets and the timeline if you don't mind scanning in the recon photos --- okay?"

"Let's get a move on, Jack."

Secure Conference Room E, CIA
Headquarters, Langley, Virginia

"Good afternoon, ladies and gentlemen, please take your seats. I'd like to get started right on time. For those of you who don't know me, my name is Gerry Easterbrook. I'm representing the U.S. Coastline Group and this is my associate, Jack Butterfield. You each have a PowerPoint presentation on the desk in front of you, so if you would like to follow along, let's get started. Note the Top Secret designation and the serial number on this presentation. Please follow protocol and handle these documents properly. To get the lay of the land, the first photo is a NASA shot of the Northern Bahamas, an area named for the large island and generally referred to as The Abacos. The major islands are Grand Bahama, Little Abaco and Great Abaco. The only city is Marsh Harbour ---note the spelling of Harbour. This is not a typographical mistake, this is the Old English spelling. 'Marsh" is located on the main island of Great Abaco. The smaller towns are called settlements and are so noted --- notice Fox Town up in the North of Great Abaco and Hope Town to the South --- they are referred to as settlements. The small, out-islands of importance are: Loyalist Cay, Elbow Cay and Frigate Cay. The Abacos are a tourist area that caters to sailing, sport fishing, SCUBA diving and beach combing. The inhabitants are a mix of the descendants of the Loyalists who left the Colonies in 1783. They make up the White population. The descendants of their freed, former Negro slaves and a large influx of illegal Haitians make up the Black population. An additional population consists of well to do Americans, Canadians and a smattering of other foreign property owners from Europe who own vacation property. There is scheduled air service into Marsh Harbour from the large cities on Florida's East Coast, as well as flights from the national carrier, Bahamas Air, to and from Nassau. Travel to the out islands is by private boat or scheduled ferry service from Marsh Harbour. That concludes my background briefing. Additional details are in your packet. Any questions?"

"Hearing none, let me continue on to 'Situational Details'. You have your timeline on this. I'll summarize. Our first contact regarding Loyalist Cay was from the owner of Frigate Cay Marine, Albert Alton, Code Name 'Beached Whale'. He's a White Bahamian who was born on Frigate Cay. He worked in the States on a farm in Wisconsin during World War Two. After the war, he worked heavy construction in the Chicago area and then returned to build a marina on Frigate Cay and got married. Last year, Loyalist Cay was sold to a wealthy, eighty year old newspaper publisher from Oregon. His cover story is that he is developing the island into a family vacation compound. Island Marine is chartering two, converted Navy surplus, LCM's to run all the construction materials to the island. Two young men from Frigate Cay are captains on the LCM's and the one of the young men got 'vibes' that some of the items they were hauling weren't listed correctly on the Customs House manifests. So, he mentions his misgivings to his parents and they call Albert Alton who called the FBI. The Bureau checked the newspaper guy out and seems he's been cozy with the Saudis --- so they called our section. Stick with me, people --- it's complicated, but here comes the bottom line. Enter a sailboat charter captain, Scott Lindsay, Code Name, 'Ladies Man'. He and his wife anchor their catamaran off of Loyalist Cay. He's on the beach exercising their dog and comes across a trip wire in the underbrush. Since he's ex-Canadian Land Forces Paratrooper, he's curious about the goings on at Loyalist so he recons the place by SCUBA one night --- he hears strange voices, sees personnel shouldering weapons and said the place had a military smell --- only a military guy would know what that smells like. So, we get this intel through 'Beached Whale' who says 'Ladies Man' at first thinks he's hearing Haitians speaking patois, but now thinks he was hearing Arabic. So, Jack and I begin some low level photo recon using a DC-6 that flies groceries from West Palm Beach into Marsh Harbour Airport. Note on your map, the only runway at MHH is East-West. With the trade winds out of the Southeast, takeoff is to the East and climb-out is over Loyalist Cay. The latest photo intel appears after the narrative on page four. We sent Jack Butterfield to Green Turtle Cay, which is the northern most, notated island on the photo, to meet up with Scott Lindsay, the Canadian. Mister Lindsay thinks the group on Loyalist Cay are Muslim extremists and since they have sworn to kill Jews and Americans --- they're planning to attack Florida East Coast cities that have large Jewish populations with poison gas or a dirty bomb. So, that is the short version. Let's go around the table and hear what you think."

"Thank you, Gerry. Nice job on the intro. I'm Greg Short from Jihad Group. Quite frankly, I think the Canadian chap may have this right. It seems to fit into their most recent threat pattern. They've given up on flying in and now with more Border Patrol agents and troops on both of our borders, the coast is one flank they figure we're not paying much attention to --- that is until now. What do you think, Linda?"

"Greg, I've got some reservations, but the more I sit here and read through the narrative, the more I'm becoming convinced. What about you, Don?"

"I'm pretty much on board. I'd like to look into the background of this newspaper person from Oregon. Isn't this the guy that paid a large fine for trading with the enemy --- does anyone remember?"

"Greg, I think you're on the right track, it wasn't with the Saudi's though, I think he was providing money for weapons for the Irish Republican Army. Anyway you slice it, this newspaper guy seems to know his way around military gear," interjects Fred from the Caribbean/Bahamas Group.

"So, it looks as if there may be some dots that we can connect. Muslim extremists are looking for our weakest line of defense. With the recent arrests on the Mexican and Canadian borders, they're looking for another way in. There's a ton of yacht and sailboat traffic, as well as commercial traffic, approaching Florida's East Coast from the Bahamas. They could blend right in --- they could use a couple of Grady-White's or Contender fishing boats with twin 250 outboards. They run fast without lights at night and, when the wind is right, they do their mischief. If the Coast Guard shows up, they abort and blow themselves up. Simple isn't it? Damn simple," sums up Guy.

"Sir, what do you think our next move should be," asks Jack.

"I'm going to let you and Gerry run this op. Your group doesn't have as much on your plate as the other groups, so I think you can give it the attention it needs. In addition, I'm going to assign a twenty-four--seven recon analysts to your group, so we don't miss any moves the bad guys make. I note on the low level photo that there's a second dock under construction on Loyalist Cay. It's shaped like a T and it's close to the house that is under construction. If you look right here, it seems as if they are installing boat lifts on each end of the T. When we see two go-fast boats show up in those lifts, it won't be long before the flag goes up. Then, we get twenty-four hour infra-red satellite coverage. We link up with the Navy in Mayport and have them move a couple of frigates to say, ah --- West Palm Beach, which is notated on the chart as the Lake Worth Inlet. West Palm is a very busy commercial harbor and two Navy patrol craft won't arouse suspicion. That's my view of things. Excuse me, but I've got to get back upstairs. I'll take care of contacting Navy Intelligence and briefing them on what help we'll need. I will get a memo off to you when I have confirmation of the Navy's involvement --- we may have to let the Coast Guard in on this, too. The other groups are welcome to stay and give Gerry and Jack all the intel you think may help this operation. Good day and good hunting."

Guy picks up his presentation and places it in his brief case. He locks the case and walks out of the room. As soon as the door has closed and the green 'secure' light reappears, the room comes abuzz with the remaining five voices.

May 20th, 0730 Hours, CIA Headquarters, Langley, Virginia, U.S. Coastline Group

"Hello Jack, what brings you in this early this morning?"

"Couldn't sleep last night --- I was mulling over that Bahamas threat --- and a question came into my head. What events occur in the Abacos in the early Spring? So, I went out online to Bahamas.com and checked. Beginning tomorrow, there's a big bill fishing tournament out of a marina in Marsh Harbour --- by big, I mean that the entrance fee is ten thousand dollars for each boat! --- certainly not something for your average bloke. The tournament lasts for ten days and then on the 31st, it moves to Fort Lauderdale. The bad guys will need cover as they cross the Gulf Stream and approach the coast. Plenty of boats will be making their way from the Abacos to the U. S., right after the tournament ends."

"Hell Jack, you could be on to something. Couple your research with the recent photo intel of the two Contender fast fishing boats arriving at Frigate Cay and the balloon could be going up, soon. I think a meeting is in order --- and we'll need to give a heads-up to the Navy."

0900 Hours. Aboard the guided missile frigate, *U S S Rodger W. Simpson* (FFG-56), West Palm Beach Commercial Harbor, Lake Worth Inlet, Florida, Dock L-42

The Executive Officer, Lieutenant Commander Lance Arnold is meeting with the ship's commanding officer, Commander Thomas Blake, in his cabin aboard the U S S Simpson discussing the next day's schedule.

"Sir, we've got a new group of Reservists coming aboard at ten hundred hours for Annual Training. They're from Glenview, Illinois, a Chicago suburb. They were aboard last year at this time --- they're a very well trained unit --- the Commander is Lieutenant Commander James Stephens," states the Executive Officer.

The U. S. S. Simpson (FFG-56) a U. S. Navy Guided Missile Frigate

The Simpson is an Oliver Hazard Perry class guided missile frigate. She was commissioned on September 21. 1985 at Bath Iron Works in Bath, Maine. The ship is 453 feet long and has a beam of 45 feet and a draft of 22 feet. Her maximum speed is in excess of 29 knots and has a range of 5,000 miles. The ship's complement includes 15 officers and 190 enlisted personnel. The Simpson is armed with Harpoon anti-ship missiles, as well as torpedoes and Standard anti-missile/aircraft missiles. She carries two SH-60B anti-submarine helicopters armed with Penguin and Hellfire missiles. Her wartime mission is fleet and convoy protection. The Simpson is assigned to the Naval Reserve Fleet at Mayport, Florida.

184

"Yes, Lance. I do remember that group --- they helped us with the Haitian relief effort," replies Captain Thomas Blake. Their conversation is interrupted by a knock at the door.

"Come in."

"Excuse me, Captain Blake, Radioman 1st Class Thomas, reporting. I have an 'eyes only' message for you. Please sign here --- line 4, sir," says the radioman, while handing the aluminum clip board to the Captain.

"Thank you Radioman Thomas. Please post yourself outside my door. We don't need any visitors. The XO and I need to review this message. We may need to reply, so I will relieve you when we are finished --- shouldn't be more than five minutes."

"Yes, sir. That won't be a problem, sir."

Commander Arnold escorts the radioman to the cabin door. He locks the door and returns to his stool at the side of the captain's desk.

"Hey, what do you know, it's a 'top secret' from Commander Surface Naval Force, Atlantic. Intel has it that the bad guys --- whoever they are --- are getting ready to move from their base in The Abacos. We are to put to sea tomorrow in support of 'Operation Fast Boat'. Our patrol area will be North along the Western edge of the Little Bahama Bank, then Northeast to eighteen nautical miles North of Walker's Cay, then we turn Southeast and steam to a point fourteen nautical miles East of the Elbow Reef Light. Then we are to proceed Southeast toward the Northeast Providence Channel and a point fourteen miles East of Hole-In-The-Wall Light, where we will turn Northwest and proceed through the Northwest Providence Channel, to a point twenty miles West of West End, Grand Bahama Island. Our patrol speed will be 18 knots. We are to keep one SH-60B heli and an armed boarding party on standby, at all times. Our call sign is 'Nimbus 56'. Refueling will be by tanker off of Freeport, Grand Bahama, on an as-needed basis. We will continue to patrol this loop until relieved by *U S S Roberts*, FFG-58. Acknowledge and respond at once."

"Commander Arnold, give this reply to the radioman. Send the following: Making preparations for sea. 05/21, 1400 Hours. Signed Nimbus 56. Then inform the Chief Boatswain's Mate to prepare to get us underway tomorrow, after we board the reservists, but definitely before those damn cruise ships start coming into the channel at 1600 hours. Then, meet me in navigation. I'll need to pass these coordinates on to Lieutenant Hernandez."

"Aye, aye, skipper. Consider it done. See you in navigation."

1100 Hours, May, 20th, Secure Small Conference Room H, CIA Headquarters, Langley, Virginia

"Good morning -- I count five bodies, so everyone is present and accounted for. In front of you is a copy of the plan from Operations. It is titled 'Operation Fast Boat' and is classified Secret. Here's a synopsis of everything that I know to this point in time. A guided missile frigate, the *USS Simpson*, is being moved from Mayport to the Port of West Palm Beach on Friday. She will start patrolling the Northern Bahamas tomorrow. The ship is assigned to the Navy Reserve and they get a new group of reservists at ten hundred hours tomorrow. The port is just North of the Palm Beach Airport, so this gives the ship's deployment to West Palm a good cover story --- you know, it's all about saving travel time to and from the airport and saving money for the taxpayers. We've already had local television news do a story for the evening news. *Simpson* will have one of their two helis and an armed boarding party on continuous standby. We have twenty-four -- seven infra-red satellite coverage over the target area, so we will know the instant those fast boats move off their lifts. Meanwhile, Beached Whale is keeping us posted on everything they see and hear on and around Loyalist Cay. The last piece of intel we've had is that there have been six, well dressed, males with dark complexions --- in summer suits and ties --- 'investor types', I guess --- delivered to the Cay. Two of them have returned to Nassau --- so, obviously that leaves four on the Cay. Two Contender 32 fast boats with twin 250 horsepower Yamaha engines are still in place on the boat lifts. Jack thinks the bad guys will use the completion of a local fishing tournament to provide them with the cover they need to make their run to the East Coast --- lots of boat traffic coming from the Bahamas will certainly overwhelm the Coasties. All of our Naval ops will be in International waters, so we will not notify the Bahamian Government, until the fast boats have left Bahamian territorial waters. Then we will request that the Bahamas Defense Force take control of Loyalist Cay and prevent the movement of any locals, on or off the island."

"Any questions to this point?"

"Yes, Janet --- your question?"

"Gerry, why the need for helicopters on twenty-four hour standby?"

"Oh, good question, Janet. It's a matter of two things --- speed and the possibility that the two boats might take different routes. On speed --- the *Simpson* can do 30 knots but the Contenders can do 45 to 50 knots. The helis can do 180 knots. Then look at the chart of the Northern Bahamas --- on page three. The green post-it arrow is Loyalist Cay. The whole island of Great Abaco lays between the bad guys and Florida. If they decide to go North, they will run along the shore of Great Abaco, then they turn

Northwest and parallel Little Abaco and continue past Great Sale Cay. Here the water becomes shallow and they will follow some markers and leave the Little Bahama Bank to enter the Gulf Stream near West End, Grand Bahama. If they take the Southern route, they will run along these mostly uninhabited cays to a point on the chart where there is a blue post-it arrow. This marks the North Bar Channel and deep water. Then, they can proceed toward the Cherokee Sound Settlement. Their next landmark is the lighthouse on the South end of Abaco, at Hole-In-The-Wall. From there, it's a right turn and a straight shot West to the Florida coast."

"Any other questions?"

"Yes, Robert."

"Quick question, Gerry. If the bad guys are going to leave with vessels that participated in the fishing tournament, aren't we going to have too many infra-red targets --- couldn't our targets get lost in all the clutter?"

"Good question. Once the bad guys move and we know which way they are going, we want the take down to occur in international waters --- before they get a chance to get lost in the clutter, we can mark them on our plot screen --- as we get the real-time satellite feed."

"Other questions? Noting no other questions, the meeting is adjourned. Read your packets and wait for the flag to go up. You're going to be very busy when they make their first move -- so get some rest."

1030 Hours. The navigation area, just aft of the bridge, aboard the *U S S Simpson*

"Okay, Lieutenant Hernandez, please show me see the plot of our patrol."

"Yes sir Captain, come take a look. I have the chart on the plot board and have posted all courses and GPS waypoints, so we can safely circumnavigate the shallow water around this group of islands. I went on the Internet and found some great sketch charts of the Abacos. The charts are intended for cruising yachtsmen, but they're a lot better than the ones we get from NOAA. First, here's the harbor and channel chart for the Lake Worth Inlet. For departure, we will have a pilot aboard. Our speed will be limited to 10 knots and he will turn over the helm one mile West of the Outer Marker -- which is this white lighted, floating buoy, right here. I have reminded the Chief to have the Jacobs Ladder ready on the starboard side, so we can deposit the pilot on the pilot boat after we pass the Outer Marker. As we continue East for about two miles, we will enter the Gulf Stream --- the Northward current will carry us slightly Northeast. At six miles, while steering zero, one zero magnetic, we will turn to zero one eight degrees and make turns for eighteen knots. With the Stream, our speed over ground should be twenty-three knots. There are no problems out here, as this is all very deep water. Then, we turn Northeast and skirt the Little Bahamas Bank. This is where we need to be on our toes, as the Mantanilla Reef projects North away from West End, Grand Bahama. There are no navigation aids on the Northwest corner of the reef. Our D R plot will need to follow the position of the red light on the water tower at West End to keep us out of the shallow bank. Then we turn due East -- zero niner zero, to our waypoint twenty miles North of Walkers Cay. Walkers is well lighted with red anti-collision lights on a 150 foot radio mast located at the North End. The balance of our patrol is in the deep water of the North Atlantic Ocean."

"Great job, Hernandez. What kind of ship traffic can we expect?"

"Shouldn't be too much. After dark, when we're nearing Walkers Cay, we may encounter some cruise ships, but they're lit up like Christmas Trees --- shouldn't be a problem --- may see an inter-island freighter going back to West Palm or, perhaps, a tanker heading to the bunker oil terminal at Freeport, Grand Bahama."

"Did we get a weather briefing from the Met Office at Mayport?"

"Yes, sir. Weather looks good, we may experience a light shower late in the afternoon and right after sunrise. The wind will be East -- Southeast at eight to 15 knots. Seas should be no higher than two feet with additional ocean swells of one to two feet."

"So, anything that might have you lay awake at night thinking about, Hernandez?"

"No sir, this is all deep water. As long as the GPS system keeps working, it should be a piece of cake. Of course, we will follow standard navigating procedures and keep a dead reckoning plot on paper charts, in case we have a GPS failure."

"Hernandez, I have complete confidence in you --- just give me a big margin of error up North by the Mantanilla Reef and, most important --- keep the *Simpson* off the beach, Okay?"

"Yes, sir --- that won't be a problem, sir."

0410 Hours, U.S. Coastal Operations Office, CIA Headquarters, Langley, Virginia. A phone call from inside the building.

"Mister Easterbrook? Sorry to bother you. This is Satellite Analyst Jay Grissio. I am under instructions to call your phone number when I see a heat signature appear on either of the two vessels, at the target island. They're warming up all four outboards --- looks as if they are getting ready to move out. Yes, sir. Both those names are on my alert list. As soon as we hang up, I'll alert the other personnel."

0415 Hours, The Communications Section, the guided missile frigate, *U S S Simpson* at sea in the Atlantic Ocean, sixteen nautical miles East of Great Abaco Island.

"Officer of the Bridge? Signalman 1st Class, Broderick reporting. I have a message for the Captain."

"At ease, Signalman, wait one minute. I will wake the Captain. He is sleeping in his sea cabin."

"Yes sir."

When at sea, or during any high alert situation, most ship captains and executive officers sleep in their work uniform in a small sea cabin behind the Navigation Station. This is the case, when the Ensign, who is the duty officer on the bridge knocks on Captain Thomas Blake's compartment door. Only a dim red bulb over a small desk provides any light in the cabin.

"Sir, Ensign Malnar here. Sorry to wake you, sir. A signalman is on the bridge and he has a message for you."

"Thank you, Ensign. If it's from COMSUBLNT, that means the balloon is going up on our operation. Ensign, use the intercom and wake the Exec, as well as Lieutenant Hernandez --- and the Air Officer on duty. Tell the messenger to give me a minute or two to use the head --- I'll be on the bridge directly --- and have the duty officers assemble in Navigation."

"Aye, aye, sir. I will contact Lieutenant Commander Arnold, Lieutenant Hernandez and the Air Ops Officer --- and have them meet you on the bridge."

"And, Ensign ring up the Chief --- we may need to assemble the boarding party."

"Aye, aye, sir."

0423 Hours, The Bridge of the *U S S Simpson*

"Attention, the Captain is on the bridge," shouts the helmswoman, as Captain Blake appears in view, entering the red night lighted bridge, from behind the navigation area.

"Stand at ease, everyone. Signalman, tell me where to sign and I'll have you on your way." The signalman presents the clipboard to the Captain.

"Yes, sir. Please sign on line one, sir."

Captain Blake signs and removes the message. He reads as he walks back toward the Navigation Area where there is better light to read. The Executive Officer, Lance Arnold joins him.

"Morning, Captain. Would you like a cup of coffee?"

"Thanks, Commander--- yes, I would. Sure need something to knock the cob webs away."

"Balloon going up, sir?"

"Yep, looks like the intel boys have noticed some early morning fishing --- they have infra-red signatures on all four outboards."

Lieutenant Hernandez, the Navigation Officer, joins the group.

"Morning Captain, morning, Commander whispers Lieutenant Hernandez. I heard you say the balloon is going up. Let me check the plot and tell you where we are -- out in this dark ocean. A few seconds ago, I saw five flashes, from a lighthouse that is off our starboard beam. That should be the Elbow Reef Light which is on the Eastern side of a small cay which parallels Great Abaco Island. Yes sir, the plot puts us fifteen miles East of Elbow Reef."

"Hernandez, how much time until first light," asks the Captain.

"Sir, we're showing about forty minutes to first light and then another thirty-five minutes to sunrise."

"Okay Commander, I want you to relieve the Reservist Ensign, ah what's-his-name --- ah, Palmer --- as Officer of the Bridge. Tell Palmer to stick around, we may need him. Then, make turns for fifteen knots and start a slow turn to port, until we are heading zero-nine-zero degrees -- or whatever course puts our bow on the rising sun. We'll have the light of the sunrise in front of us and on an easterly heading, we will show as little of our silhouette as is possible. Hernandez, I want you on the plot. When the Chief and Air Ops arrive, send them to my cabin."

0448 Hours, Captain's Sea Cabin located behind the bridge, Aboard the *U S S Simpson*.

"Come in, door is open. Good morning, Chief."

"Morning, Captain. Morning Lieutenant McCormick. Looks like something big is happening."

"Yeah, things are heating up --- literally and figuratively. The four outboard motors -- two on each boat -- are showing infra-red signatures. Chief, we're going to go to 'General Quarters' at 0630, right after breakfast. This could be a long day, and I want the crew to be fed, prepped and fully awake. Advise the section chiefs to wake the "off watch," so they can get chow, too. Get your boarding party and the launch party ready."

"Yes, sir --- I'll be ready. May I be excused, sir?"

"Certainly, Chief --- you've got lots to cover. If you need help, use Ensign Palmer, the Reservist. He seems to be a pretty sharp lad."

"McCormick, I want a fresh crew on the chopper --- your best crew. Push the Number Twelve bird onto the launch pad. Move the Number 16 bird into position just inside the hangar door. Oh, and what kind of ordnance have you loaded?"

"Sir, we have two door mounted fifties and we'll have four Penguins, two each hanging off of either side of the ordnance pods --- I'm figuring that if they put up a fight, we'll use the 50's. If we decide it's prudent to stand off and fight, we'll take them out with the Penguins --- sound okay?"

"Good plan, McCormick. Make certain that both helis are armed in the same configuration. Okay?"

"Yes, sir. --- anything else, sir?"

"Yes, Lieutenant, go brief your men and make certain all watches get breakfast. Here is a copy of the call signs. The twelve heli is 'Acrobat 12', the sixteen heli is 'Cormorant 16,' Home Base is 'Nimbus 56' and the boarding party in the black rigid inflatable is 'Black Fin'. If we need to reach the guys running this show from Langley, their call sign is 'Sea Fan Base'."

"Aye, aye, sir," responds Lieutenant McCormick as he returns his notebook and pen to his breast pocket and bolts for the door.

The 0630 Hours call to general quarters will be of no surprise to the crew. The enlisted mess has been abuzz all morning with the news and most of the crew are already dressed in their flameproof coveralls, flak jackets and are cradling their Kevlar helmets in their laps.

0515 hours, Secure Communications Room 4, CIA Headquarters, Langley, Virginia

Row after row of gray, foam waffle cone shape, sound absorbers are mounted on the walls, insuring that what is said inside the room stays inside the room. The door opens and the 'unsecure' light starts flashing, as a male enters the room.

"Morning, Gerry --- how was the ride in?"

"Not much traffic on a Sunday Jack, what do you have so far?"

"Looks like we've hit it pretty lucky. The *Simpson is* only forty miles South of the North Bar Channel and they've turned East to avoid presenting a warship silhouette at sunrise. They go to General Quarters at 0630. I think we're in perfect position if the bad guys take the Southern route."

"And, if they split up or both go North, what then?"

"*Simpson* has both copters on standby --- one is ready to launch and the other is at the hangar door and ready to go. We'll have to just wait them out."

"Right, Jack. What's the commo guys name?"

"Justin."

"Hey, excuse me, Justin. My name is Gerry and I'm supposed to be running this circus. So, what do we have for commo links?"

"Ah, just wait a few seconds and they'll all show on the big screen --- up front. First thing you'll see are the call signs --- and we have these cool silhouettes next to them --- Yah know? A silhouette of a helicopter and a frigate. Then, in the top corners, we will have the real time satellite images. Right top is the infra-red. Left top is regular high definition photography. We have a camera feed from the *Simpson*, so you will be able to see the face of the personnel your talking with on the horn."

"Looks like we'll just have to hurry and wait, Jack. Sure hope we have plenty of coffee."

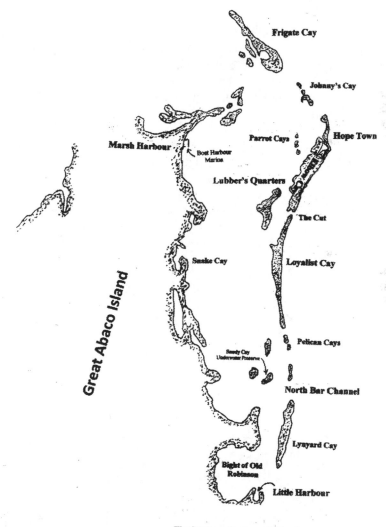

Frigate Cay

Johnny's Cay

Parrot Cays

Hope Town

Marsh Harbour

Boat Harbour
Marina

Lubber's Quarters

The Cut

Snake Cay

Loyalist Cay

Great Abaco Island

Pelican Cays

Sandy Cay
Underwater Preserve

North Bar Channel

Lynyard Cay

Bight of Old
Robinson

Little Harbour

The Southern Portion of "The Abacos"

0640 Officer's Wardroom, *U S S Simpson*, 18 nautical miles East of the Hole-In-The-Wall Lighthouse. All 16 officers are assembled.

"Morning, Gentlemen"

"Morning, Captain," comes the sleepy, muddled reply.

"Please congratulate your section chiefs, the General Quarters went quite well. Here is where we stand right now. Soon, we will have sunrise and we expect our targets to start moving. We don't know the direction, however intel thinks they will attempt to mingle in with other tournament fishing boats, as they return to Ft. Lauderdale. The odds are that they will split up and move toward two different targets on the Florida coastline. The Central Intelligence Agency is running this operation. We're in the chain of command through Naval Intelligence and then through Commander, Surface Fleet, Atlantic. The CIA is providing both an infra-red and a photographic real-time satellite link for this mission. As soon as our targets move, I will alert the entire crew on the squawk box. Meanwhile, have your men stand at ease until we get some orders. Any questions? That is all --- you are dismissed."

0718 hours, Secure Communications Room 4, CIA Headquarters, Langley, Virginia.

"Check this out Jack, looks like we've got some movement. Look at the infra-red. The boats are running single file and moving North in the Lubbers Channel. They're moving really fast -- like twenty knots."

"Yah look, the second boat is peeling off to the right --- on the chart that's marked as 'The Cut'. With the smooth sea state and the slack tide, it must be okay for them to run in the open ocean outside of Elbow Cay --- then North outside the reef. My guess is that the second boat is heading directly for the Walker's Cay area. What are you thinking, Jack?"

I'm thinking they're going to run in the ocean as long as they can --- there are dozens of places they can cut through the reef and run on the inside --- if the sea get too rough. They may still be heading for West End."

"Hey, has anyone been watching the other bad guy," questions Gerry to no one in particular.

"I've got my eye on him, responds the communications tech, Justin. He's heading due West toward a number of yachts that look as if they are at anchor." Pointing with his laser, Justin illuminates Boat Harbour Marina on the mainland, at Marsh Harbour.

"Figures, that's the headquarters for the fishing tournament, Gerry," reminds Jack.

"Just as you thought --- he's trying to mingle with the large yachts that are leaving for the next tournament stop at Ft. Lauderdale. These guys have definitely split up. We need to alert the *Simpson,* so they know we will need both of their 'copters in about three to four hours."

"Justin, get on a secure circuit to the *Simpson* and send a FLASH message --- we need them to stand down from General Quarters and rest the crew until early this afternoon."

"Affirmative Gerry. I'll send the message, FLASH, secure."

"Gerry, do you think the *Simpson* should move?"

"No, Jack. I don't think so. The *Simpson* isn't fast enough to keep up with these guys when they get going. I think they are in the perfect place. They're in International Waters and this is starting to look as if it's going to be a naval air operation. We have permission from the Bahamas Government to overfly their territory.

"Justin, send another message. The *Simpson* may as well disband the boarding party --- their part in this is over for now."

"I don't want us to lose track of either of the targets. I think we should split up into two teams and move to opposite sides of the room."

"Good idea, Gerry. Lady and gentlemen --- let's split up --- half those on the right side of the room keep track of the target that is going

North -- Contender North, or right on the big screen. Left wingers --- keep track of the target on the left of the screen -- Contender South. We've got about three or four hours of this, so assign everyone a one hour watch ---- this way no one will get bleary eyed. Okay?"

Combat Information Center, U S S Simpson in the Atlantic Ocean, fifteen miles East of Hole-In-The-Wall Light

"Captain, Lieutenant Hyland here in CIC with Lieutenant Olsen. We've been watching the two targets and, as everyone expected, they are splitting up. We'll need both SH-60 dippers up in the air --- and, Olsen suggests that we contact the *Kennedy* and have them on standby in case we need in-air refueling."

"That's an excellent contingency plan, Olsen. I'll get the folks in Langley that are running the show to run that by the top brass. I'll keep you posted."

"Commo, patch me through to Gerry Easterbrook at the Agency."

"Aye, aye, sir."

Secure Communication Room 4, CIA Headquarters, Langley, Virginia

"Easterbrook -- message for you from the *Simpson* requesting air to air refueling assets on standby from the *Kennedy* -- in case this turns ugly."

"Thanks, Justin. Hey, Jack --- come over here. Check out the message from the *Simpson*. I think it's time to have the *U S S Roberts* go to sea --- just in case something gets mucked up."

"Gerry, you're right. Remember that 'Bravo Sierra' from headquarters about all the assets of the U.S. Government being thrown at this terrorist thing. Well, it's put up or shut up time."

"Justin, do you have a circuit open to the *Roberts?*"

"Yes, Gerry. Her call sign is Neptune 58 since she's frigate FFG-58."

"Get their Captain on the horn. We need these guys to get ready for sea --- pronto."

"Gerry, I've got Captain Davis of the *Roberts* on the horn. As a contingency, COMSFCLANT has ordered them to keep both turbines on stand-by. They can be off the dock, as soon as they get clearance for a tug and a port pilot."

"Good job, Justin. Ask the Captain to estimate how many hours 'til they pass the Lake Worth outer marker."

"Gerry, Captain Davis says to stand-by one minute while he consults with his Exec and Navigation Officer."

After a short delay, the Captain of the *Roberts* returns to the phone. "Thank you, Captain Davis --- I'll pass on the word."

"Gerry, Jack --- the *Roberts* can be at sea in two and a half hours --- it's all depending on the cooperation from the tug operator at the West Palm Beach dock. He'll keep us updated."

"Thanks, Justin."

"Jack, come with me over to the Abaco chart for a minute. I'm thinking we should send the *Roberts* North to a position just to the West and South of West End, Grand Bahama. Then, I like your idea of having the *Simpson* shadow Contender South that's moving toward the Northwest Providence channel. With both ships moving toward our targets, this will continually decrease the distance the helis have to fly."

"Gerry, I'm one hundred percent on board with this plan. We need to get the officers on the *Roberts* updated on what we're facing. Both ships need their dippers on stand-by --- and, we'll probably have to reconstitute boarding parties on both ships."

"They're probably pretty busy on the *Roberts* getting ready for sea, so we'll have to do this on-the-fly."

"Yea, Gerry. While this is not the best of circumstances, right now, we have time on our side."

"Jack, get me a GPS. At least we can come up with the some lat and lon coordinates for their station off of West End."

"Five miles is a little close --- it could spook the bad guys --- how about moving them further North and West?"

"Good idea, Jack --- the bad guys will be moving due West if their target is West Palm Beach. We should be about ten miles North of their course. Moving *Roberts* North will give us a very small silhouette --- she'll look like any other commercial ship. That's definitely the right position for the *Roberts*."

"And, having *Simpson* shadow Contender South will keep closing the distance so the helis don't have to drive too far. So, now all we have to do is wait and watch the satellite images. How about a cup of coffee and a Danish, Gerry?"

"I'll pass on the Danish --- but I will take you up on the coffee. Who's buying?"

Pouring two Styrofoam cups of leaded coffee, Jack replies, "I think this one's on the Agency."

"Hey Easterbrook. Hey Jack. Come over here --- check this out," calls Justin. Follow my laser on the overlay chart. We've been marking the course of 'Contender South', as we're calling it. Note that they have been following the one hundred foot depth curve all the way into the Northwest Providence Channel. Their course has been a gentle turn from almost due South, to Southwest. In the last few minutes, they have turned back to South. What do you make of this?"

"Hell, Justin! I'm not sure what to make of this, exclaims Gerry. Looks as if this course will take them close to the Eastern most Berry Islands group."

"Perhaps they have to re-fuel and they're going to Spanish Wells or Harbour Island," wonders Jack aloud.

"If they are going to either of those places, they would be heading more Southeast. Besides, satellite intel shows each boat getting fuel from six, fifty-five gallon drums of gasoline back at Loyalist Cay. I doubt they need gas. The only piece of land that's dead ahead of them is New Providence Island -- you know, Nassau --- the Capital."

SH-60B Helicopter takes off from the deck of the *U.S.S. Simpson*.

"Yea, like Nassau is synonymous with cruise ships --- and Paradise Island --- this isn't looking good," remarks Gerry.

"Get Guy on the horn --- we need more help down here. Justin, get the *Simpson* on the radio. They better get one of their SB-60's in the air."

"Roger, that. Since we've been talking --- Contender South is really haulin' --- they're moving at forty knots and are less than twenty-four miles from the Nassau harbor entrance --- if, in fact, that's where they're heading. I'm calling the *Simpson*."

"Nimbus 58, this is Sea Fan Base, over. Launch your first dipper --- I say again, launch Acrobat 12. Target coordinates and engagement instructions to follow. Did you copy?"

"Sea Fan Base, this is Nimbus 58 --- roger your previous transmission. Nimbus 58 standing by."

Guy Cable enters the room and walks toward Gerry and Jack. "Hey you two. If their target really is Nassau --- we're in deep do-do. Get this. The Jewish-American Friendship League is holding their annual convention at the Casino on Paradise Island --- and to complicate matters, they have a cruise ship full of people aboard the *Excaliber*, which is tied up at the Prince George Wharf."

"Justin --- where the heck is our target", shouts Guy across the room.

"Guy, just follow my laser --- they're right here --- about fifteen miles from the harbor entrance --- notice that they have plenty of ship traffic to blend in with, as there are three --- what look to be cruise ships --- waiting outside the entrance for harbor pilots."

"Justin, bring the photo satellite image down as close as you can to 'Contender South'

"Sure, Guy --- here goes. Watch the left top of the screen --- you can see that they're bouncing pretty good and kicking up quite a bow wave. Check out the bad guys --- they look like they have wet suits on --- oh, hell no --- those aren't wet suits --- they're chemical decontamination suits."

"Justin --- get the State Department situation room on the horn."

"Affirmative, Guy --- I'll have them on speaker in fifteen seconds."

"State Sit Room --- Reed speaking."

"Reed, Guy Cable, CIA here. I'm coordinating Operation Sea Fan and, we've got a problem. I'll be brief, as time is critical. One of the vessels we have been monitoring has changed course and looks to be heading toward Nassau. The satellite real time picture shows the bad guys geared up in gas masks and decontamination suits. We're thinking a sarin gas attack. And, get this, Bahamas Tourism tells us that the Jewish-American Friendship Group is meeting on Paradise Island. We've got a Navy heli following them --- however we can't blow these guys out of the water in Bahamian Territorial Waters, without an okay up the chain of command. They're less than fifteen miles from the harbor entrance -- we need authorization to launch a Penguin missile in the next ten minutes."

"Sea Fan --- wait one."

"Sea Fan, Under Secretary Reed here --- I'm told this info has to go to the White House or the Secretary of State. We're trying to get into contact with Secretary Randall --- she's walking on the tarmac at Andrews toward Air Force Two --- she's flying to Nairobi for a meeting on AIDS --- wait one."

"Nimbus 56, this is Acrobat 12. We're within five miles of the target at three thousand feet --- we're keeping our distance --- this guy is weaving in and out of the heavy ship traffic outside the harbor."

"Hey Justin. Tell him to keep his distance and arm one Penguin missile and stand by."

"I've got it --- Guy. "Acrobat 12 this is Sea Fan Base. Keep your distance. Arm one Penguin missile and stand by for orders."

"Sea Fan --- Acrobat 12. Affirmative. Slowing this bird and maintaining level Angels Three --- have acquired the target and am locked on. Awaiting your order and standing by."

"Excuse me, Mr. Secretary. With all due respect, whiskey tango foxtrot is taking you guys so long --- another minute and all hell is going to break loose on New Providence --- the loss of life could be staggering."

"Hey CIA --- we share your pain. They're trying to connect to the Veep -- the President's golf cart communications is down and he's miles from the clubhouse."

"Bravo Sierra, what the eff is going to get these people off their asses and make a decision?"

"Sea Fan Base --- Acrobat 12 here. The target has turned away from the harbor entrance and is going directly South toward the opening into Paradise Beach. Advise status for Penguin missile."

"Justin --- tell him thanks for the update. Stand by one."

Acrobat 12 --- Sea Fan Base. Thanks for the update. Stand by one."

"CIA ---- we got a hold of the VPOUS --- the Vice President --- permission granted. You are authorized to shoot. I say again --- okay to shoot."

"Roger that Sit Room. Sea Fan, out."

"Justin --- tell the SB-60 to shoot.

"Acrobat 12 --- Sea Fan Base. Affirmative --- fire your missile. I say again --- launch your missile."

"Sea Fan --- Acrobat 12 --- bad news, guys --- we're too late. Oh, my God --- the bad guys beached the boat at high speed and blew it up. All we can see are flames and heavy black smoke. The beach is in chaos --- bodies everywhere and --- people are running into the water to get away from the gas and the flames. We're staying upwind at Angels Five, as we have air traffic going into Nassau International. Over."

"Roger Acrobat 12 --- return to base. Sorry our timing was off --- but we did our best."

"Sea Fan --- Acrobat 12. Roger, disarming the Penguin and returning to the *Simpson*."

"Damnation --- Gerry --- Jack. --- Justin. If they really are carrying sarin gas, there is nothing more we can do for Nassau except to advise the Situation Room at State --- they'll have to send in the Marines to help with the dead and wounded and to decontaminate the disaster site. Now, we have to concentrate on 'Contender North'. What have they been up to? --- Justin," yells Guy

"Infra-red shows 'Contender North' has just passed to the North of Mangrove Cay ---- they're slowing down. This is the beginning of the shallow water and a circuitous route through the markers is ahead of them."

"Gerry, Jack --- gather 'round. Despite our best efforts, the Islamic Jihad won the first battle. We assumed they were going to Florida's Gold Coast --- wrong! Now we have to make certain they don't win the next battle. I'm going to suggest to the State Department, and the effing White House, that we take these guys out, as soon as they cross into International Waters."

"I think that's the right decision, Guy. The sooner we intercept them --- the longer any sarin gas cloud would take to reach our coast. This sounds like the best scenario to me --- after what we watched in Nassau. They faked us into believing they were going to go West and then they turned South and hit the throttles --- we were caught off guard."

"Hell, Gerry --- we never saw any evidence they knew that *we* knew. They planned it this way --- just in case we made the effort to tail them. They split up --- smart, real smart --- that doubled the area we'd have to keep track of. And, their timing was perfect. They knew all the cruise ships would be waiting for pilots to take them into the harbor. They knew they would have cover and have an easy time making a run for Paradise Beach. Nassau was a sitting duck --- I doubt that the Bahamian Government ever thought they would be considered an al-Qaida target."

"Good after action analysis, Jack. I'm calling that Reed person at State. I want to give them our plan ---very early in this operation, so we don't have another snafu --- another group of innocents gassed by these effing Jihadis."

"Justin, get me over to State."

"Yes, Mister Cable."

"Gerry, get with the Skipper and Air Officer on the *Roberts*. We must nail these bastards the moment they cross into International Waters."

"Okay, Guy --- I'm on the line to the *Roberts*," replies Gerry.

Department of State, Washington, D.C.
Assistant Secretary Reed's Office

"Okay, listen up -- here's the way we are presenting this to the public. Secretary Randall was unavailable --- and because of a tight airport security schedule, the aircraft had to take off. So, the Secretary instructs the pilot to make a u-turn, and return to Andrews. She lands fifteen minutes later. The Secretary will be holding a press briefing at 1730 hours. The White House is staying out of this because of the snafu with POTUS's ground communication on the golf course. This is important, the entire Sea Fan operation is still Top Secret. The Secretary is simply going to express her condolences to the relatives of the casualties in Nassau and condemn the action of whatever splinter al-Qaida group pulled this off. So, Barb --- write some words for Secretary Randall. The usual stuff about providing humanitarian aid --- finding out who did it and punishing them. You know, the usual blah, blah, blah. We'll need it on the teleprompter by 1715 hours."

"Yo, Reed. Are you serious? You're telling me we're not going to push this up the hill to the White House where it belongs --- duh, replies Barb. We still have a boatload of bad guys floating out there off the Florida Coast hoping to do some harm to our people. So, are we just going to ignore the fact that we've had two Navy ships chasing the bad guys and that one of our helicopters was within minutes of blowing up the boat that hit Paradise Beach?"

"Barb, that's the spin the White House wants us to follow. President Collins is adamant that this whole thing take on a low priority. Their cover story is going to be that one of our Navy ships, on routine drug interdiction patrol in the Gulf Stream, just happened upon a boat load of terrorists carrying sarin gas --- and we blew them out of the water. Case closed. Excuse me, Barb. I've got the CIA on the line. They're looking for orders regarding how to handle the second boat."

"CIA? Guy Cable here."

"Under Secretary Reed speaking. The Secretary just called from her motorcade and she has given permission for the Navy to use deadly force to blow up the remaining boat."

"Thank you Reed. We'll pass on the happy news to the *U S S Roberts*.

"Roger that, Cable. Tell the *Roberts* --- happy hunting."

"Nimbus 56 --- Sea Fan Base calling for Captain Davis, over."

"This is Nimbus 56. Captain Davis speaking. Over."

"Guy Cable, CIA. I just spoke with the State Department and the Secretary has given you permission to take out 'Contender North', as soon as it leaves Bahamian Territorial Waters. They don't care how, they want you to make an observation of the craft, so you will have to scramble one of your copters. You may use a Standard missile from your ship or let the copter do it with a Penguin. You should be receiving a message from Commander, Surface Fleet Atlantic, in Norfolk confirming this order.

"Sea Fan Base --- Nimbus 56. Roger your instructions. We are awaiting the decoding of a message from COMSFCLNT. Nimbus 56 standing by."

WFLD-TV the Fox Television
Network Affiliate in Chicago

"Good afternoon, WFLD - TV Fox News, Chicago. How may I direct your call?"

"Brandt Marshall, please."

"Mr. Marshall's extension is five, six, two, three. I'll put your call through. Have a pleasant day and thank you for calling Fox News, WFLD - TV.

"Marshall, here."

"Mr. Marshall, you don't know me. My name is Sabrina and I live in Glenview. My husband, Darryl, is a Navy Reservist. He just returned from his two week summer cruise aboard the *U S S Simpson,* a Navy frigate, home ported in Mayport, Florida. Mr. Marshall, --- are you listening --- are you there?"

"Continue, Sabrina. You have my full attention."

"I'm sure your familiar with the gas attack -- a few days ago -- that killed all those Jewish people and lots of innocent Bahamians -- in Nassau. Well, my husband --- his job, in the Navy is to load ordnance on rotary wing aircraft --- helicopters. The *Simpson* has two --- two helicopters that is. He told me that one of our helicopters was sent on a mission to sink the terrorist's boat. When the helicopter returned to the *Simpson,* the crew told my husband that they had a missile locked on to the terrorist's boat, but they couldn't get permission to fire, because of some communications screw-up. They came back with all their ordnance and my husband --- he was really upset. He had to disarm and unload them."

"Sabrina, that's quite a story. I've taken some notes and I would like to call you back in the next day or two for some clarification. Would you allow me to contact you in the future?"

"Mister Marshall, I've probably said too much already --- and my husband could get in big trouble. I think its best that we hang up now. And, my name is not Sabrina."

The telephone goes dead. Brandt dials the extension for Connie Newsome, the News Director.

"Hello, Connie Newsome, speaking"

"Hi, Connie -- it's Brandt. I need to meet with you. I just got a lead on a story from an informant. Sounds like it could be something pretty big."

"Come on up. I'm all ears --- especially on a slow, Summer news day. See ya."

Brandt takes the stairs up to the third floor and knocks on Connie's door.

"Come in Brandt --- sit down, what do you have for me?

"Here's the story in a nutshell. Anonymous phone call from wife. Husband is a Navy Reservist on Summer cruise out of Mayport, Florida. Husband loads missiles on a helicopter. Helicopter returns to ship --- hadn't fired any missiles. Crew tells him they had locked onto the terrorist's boat off of Nassau --- couldn't fire because of some communications screw-up. I ask for her phone number and she hangs up on me. What do you think?

"Well, we do know that the Navy sunk an outboard boat in the Gulf Stream, the same evening that the attack took place on Nassau. Perhaps they were following two boats? Perhaps there was more than one Navy ship involved in this? Who knows? The best way to find out is to ask the Pentagon. This story needs to go to the Network 'Big Wigs' and have Kelly Lockwood ask the question at tomorrow's Pentagon briefing."

"Good idea, Connie. And, don't forget --- this is my story."

"Brandt --- I won't forget. I'll send Kelly an e-mail and copy you on it."

Press Room, daily briefing, The Pentagon, Washington, D.C., Alex Williams, spokesperson.

"Okay, people --- that's my prepared update for you for today. Now it's your turn for questions or just clarifications. I'm ready --- shoot. Yes, Kelly, Fox Television."

"Alex, I need an update and some clarification on the al-Qaeda gas attack in Nassau. I've received information from a source that a Navy frigate --- ah, the USS Simpson was tracking the terrorist's boat and that the Simpson launched one of its helicopters --- the crew reported to my source that they had locked a missile on the terrorists, but never got the order to fire --- because of some communications screw-up with the White House."

"Wow, Kelly, you've really caught me off guard on that one. I have no information on any other Navy operation in that area --- other than the briefing I gave you on Monday. I'm not prepared to provide you with any additional background on that --- I'll work this angle over the weekend get back to you on Monday --- okay?"

"Certainly, Alex. Same time, same place --- I'll see you, Monday."

"Anyone else --- with a question I can answer? If not, that's all from me. We'll see you a 0900 hours, Monday -- same place. Have a great weekend and thank you."

The room breaks into a buzz as correspondents from CNN, Associated Press, ABC News and others surround Kelly. Mitchell Andres from CNN is the first to get face to face with Kelly.

"Hey, babe --- so where did that little fire bomb come from?"

"Oh, Mitchell --- it is an anonymous tip through our affiliate in Chicago --- so, don't try probing me. --- I'm not telling anyone, anything."

"Well, speaking for all the other press members, Chicago is certainly a long way from Nassau --- seems a little strange, but I can assure you we'll all be working this story from our sources."

"Have at it --- the more we probe on this, the better chance we have to break this story loose and determine the truth. See you guys, Monday," says Kelly, as she gathers her attaché case and walks toward the door.

Friday 1:00 P.M., Kelly Lockwood's office, Fox News, Washington Bureau

Kelly Lockwood is meeting with her news director, Kent Richardson.

"So, Kelly, we're getting nothing further from the Pentagon on this until Monday. Looks like we're on our own. Hell, there are four hundred sailors on a frigate. If the Pentagon won't talk, I'll bet we can find someone from the crew --- it's Friday and perhaps the crew will have weekend liberty. These guys will be heading for the bars in Jacksonville or Mayport --- all we have to do is buy them a few beers. Who's our Florida guy," inquires Richardson.

"Kent, it's the young kid, you remember him, Neil Webster. Come to think about it, he came to work for us after a tour of duty with the Coast Guard. I'll bet he's shared a few beers with the Navy. Want me to get him on the phone? He's in my speed dial."

"Kelly, hand me your phone. Let me talk to him, so he knows this assignment is coming from the top."

"Neil? Oh hi, it's Kent Richardson from the Washington Bureau. Need your help. Where are you? Oh damn, you're in Miami --- well, we have to get you to JAX as soon as possible. I want you to catch the next American Eagle flight --- or, whatever can get you to JAX, fast and cheap. Now, here's your background brief. We want you to hang around in bars that are frequented by sailors on leave from Mayport. See if you can get close to some airdales or commo guys from the frigates *Simpson* or *Roberts*. Yea, write this down --- they're Navy frigates, the *Simpson* or *Roberts* --- both based in Mayport. A Navy Reservist said that a chopper from the *Simpson* had a missile lock on the al-Qaeda terrorist boat that struck Paradise Beach last week --- the shoot order didn't arrive because of some communications glitch with the White House. See what you can find out. Kelly Lockwood is working the story from the Pentagon side. If you find anything, call her on her cell phone --- night or day. Got that?"

"Yea, got it. I'm on my way to Miami International. I figure I'll be in Jacksonville by three-thirty -- or four, at the latest. I'll get a rental car and wait by the front gate at Mayport, to see where the first taxi load of swabbies go for R and R."

"Okay Neil, stay cool and don't get into a bar fight. You know what the Navy thinks of you Coasties."

"Don't worry, Kent --- I'm too much a pacifist to get into a fight with anyone. I'll keep you posted. Bye."

"So, Kelly, where do we go from here?"

"The only thing we have is a story from a Reservist's wife whose name is Sabrina --- although she said that wasn't her real name. And, we have her phone call into WFLD --- wonder what kind of phone system they have? Think we can get her number from their incoming phone calls? Worth a try --- I'll call Chicago and see what they can find out."

"I'll check with some of my old sources and if I come up with anything, I'll call you. Have a great weekend, Kelly and good hunting."

The Lockwood residence on a quiet street in Annandale, Virginia, a Washington, D.C. Suburb

"Hi Hon, hi kids --- Mom's home. It's the weekend, it's time to have some fun."

Kelly's husband, Bob, greets her with a hug and a kiss followed by the four year old twins, Ellie and Charles, who race out from the kitchen to hug Mom's legs."

"Mommy, mommy --- Ellie and I have been helping daddy bake our dinner."

"Oh, really --- what have you been baking?"

"It's a secret --- it's for dinner," whispers Ellie.

"Wow, I can't wait --- you two go back into the kitchen and Mommy is going upstairs to change into something comfortable."

As she reaches the top stair on the second landing, her cell phone rings. Kelly looks at the screen ---

"Oh, damn, it's Neil Webster from Jacksonville --- I suppose I'll have to answer." says Kelly to the empty bedroom, as she sits on the edge of the bed, kicks off her shoes and answers the phone.

"Kelly here. What's going on in JAX?"

"Some good, some bad. The bad is that both the *Simpson* and the *Roberts* are in the Reserve Fleet and they are manned by Reservists, on their two week cruise."

"And --- what's bad about that?"

"Both ships are tied to the pier and the Reservists have gone back to their home base --- they're not here in Mayport, drinking beer."

"So, Neil --- what's the good news?"

"Good news is that the air groups --- the helicopter pilots and ground crews, are full time Navy. I've got a lead on a drinking establishment they frequent. I'm on my way there. Just wanted to keep you up to date."

"Thanks Neil --- I'll talk to you later. Bye."

"Oh, hi Bob, honey --- that was Neil Webster, our Florida guy. He's working on a big story that could come out of the al-Qaeda gas attack on Nassau. I'm hoping this won't mess with our weekend."

"Me, too. It won't be the first time --- and we've always managed to work around work. Hey, want to see your segment on the Evening News?"

"Nah, no thanks. I'm all 'news-ed' out. Okay if we let dinner wait? Let's open a couple of cold beers and sit on the patio. The kids can update me on what went on at school --- and, perhaps we can have some alone time? Just you and me?"

"Sounds like a plan --- You get changed --- I'll get the beers and meet you downstairs, Kel."

8:25 P.M., Pilot Pete's Bar, American Beach, Florida

Neil Webster knew this would definitely be the sort of place pilots would hang out in. Lots of autographed photos of men standing in front of airplanes. Overhead hangs a real J-3 Piper Cub training plane painted traditional yellow and large scale models of various warbirds. Seating in the waiting area consists of old aircraft seats and the wait staff are dressed like flight attendants. Neil seats himself at the apex of the 'L' shaped bar --- there are three seats to his left and six seats to his right. He orders a Coors Light and runs a tab on his American Express Corporate card. The bartender brings him a bowl of pretzels. Neil starts to analyze the clientele --- about four to one males over females. Military haircuts outnumber civilian hair by five to one. A Jacksonville Jaguar pre-season NFL football game is on the TV and the music is country and western from Satellite Radio. Electronic darts and bowling are the activities preferred over pool. Two young, good looking guys with Navy haircuts sit down to his right. They order a Becks and a Corona Light. Neil stares straight ahead at the football game and sips his beer. Finally, Neil breaks the ice.

"Hi gentlemen. Care for any pretzels? --- there's enough here for the whole place."

"Thanks, mister," replies the taller man, as he reaches into the bowl. My name's Ben --- this here is Kyle."

"Oh, hi --- my name's Neil. Nice to meet you," says Neil, as they shake hands all around.

"So, Neil. You from around here?"

"Nope. I'm up from Miami."

"You look like a Navy Contractor type --- what's you line of work?"

"No, not a contractor --- my girl is a Reservist and her two week cruise just ended. I'm supposed to meet her about nine thirty."

"What ship's she on?"

"Ah, a frigate named the *Simpson*."

"Yes sir, know it well. Kyle and me, along with our Air Wing is assigned to the same detachment --- we are on the *U S S Roberts*. Spent the last week in West Palm Beach on some kind of public relations gig for the local TV stations."

"Well, you guys are pretty famous now, after dispatching that al-Qaeda boat to the bottom. Nice shooting."

"Thanks, Neil. We personally can't take any of the credit. Our job is to keep the helis flying. Seems that the *Roberts* is always where the action is. During the Gulf War, she shot down an incoming Exocet missile fired at them by the Iranians. The *Roberts* responded with a Standard missile and took out the Iranian ship --- they reported that the biggest piece of the

Iranian gunboat they could find was a two foot piece of plywood --- ha, ha," laughs Ben.

"Hell, we unleashed a single Penguin missile from a chopper five miles away and, according to our pilots, all they saw was a huge ball of flames," adds Kyle.

"Yah know, Neil --- I'm wondering if you are going to see your girl tonight. The SP's were guarding the pier when we left on liberty. No way you could get close to the *Simpson*. Scuttlebutt has it that they missed a chance to tallyho that terrorist outboard off of Nassau --- and, get this, the word is --- the big SNAFU was that the President was golfing and the hi-tech commo on his golf cart went haywire. Go figure --- good thing the Chinese or the North Koreans weren't launching. We'd have been caught with our pants down. And, finally the order came from the Vice President. Unfortunately, they were too late."

"Man, that's some serious stuff --- if it's really true."

"Yea, scuttlebutt is fifty percent fact and fifty percent Bravo Sierra --- but, in this case, we have it from a very reliable source in our commo group."

"Say, gents --- how about me buying you guys another round?"

"What you think, Kyle?"

"Thanks, mister --- but I think we're going up into Georgia. There's a joint there that is overrun with college girls on the make. We'll take a rain check, Neil. Thanks for the conversation. See you around the Base, maybe."

"Guys, thank you and, stay safe. Enjoy the weekend. Adios."

Neil grabs his cell phone and speed dials Kelly. Her phone goes direct to voice mail. "This is Kelly Lockwood, please leave me a message."

"Hey Kelly. Met up with Kyle and Ben two Navy guys from the air wing, on the *Roberts*. They say the scuttlebutt is that the *Simpson* couldn't shoot because --- get this --- the President's communications on his golf cart was down! And, that finally, the order came from the Veep --- but too late! Call me back when you pick this up. I'm still in this Navy hangout in a town called American Beach and I'll keep my ear to the ground. Only wish I had gotten a haircut --- I'm standing out like a sore thumb."

Saturday 6:30 A.M., The Lockwood Residence in Annandale, Virginia

"Darn, Bob --- turn off that alarm clock. Six thirty? --- on a Saturday. Why do we have to get up so early?"

"Oh, I was planning to go for a run with the dog and --- remember we have two soccer games --- one a ten and Ellie's game at one. Plus, I need to get to Home Depot and buy some more stone for the dog run."

"Well, maybe we can sleep in tomorrow?"

"Yea, hope so. I'll shower after my run --- so you go ahead and shower. You probably need to check your phone for messages --- the damned thing was beeping all night."

"I thought this was the weekend and that I only worked for Fox, Monday through Friday?"

"Not when you're in the news business --- Kelly."

"You're right, Bob. Hand me my phone," responds Kelly dejectedly.

"Wait, Bob --- got a voice mail from Neil Webster last night --- he's was in a bar North of the Mayport Navy Base and he got some really good stuff regarding the terrorist attack on Nassau. Seems the President was out of contact with the White House Situation Room, while he was out golfing. If this is true, I can hear the Republicans --- they've been really critical of all his golfing --- now, they can tie it to national security. This could be big, really big."

"Doesn't sound to me like we're going to sleep in late tomorrow --- Don't worry, I'll take the kids to soccer. Kelly, get on the phone to the bureau. They'll want to follow up on this bombshell."

"First, you go for your run with the dog --- he certainly needs to go out. Next, I need to get to Neil and thank him for his hard work --- then to Connie at the news bureau."

Kelly speed dials her cell phone. "Neil? --- did I wake you? Tough night, huh? Not a bad assignment working a beach bar in Florida."

"Yah, Kelly --- it's all in a day and night's work."

"Any more information other than what is in your voice mail?"

"No, I didn't have any more luck --- although I met a really nice young lady from Northern Florida University."

"Okay, enough about your love life. Tell me --- the Navy types --- did they seem credible? Were they in positions to actually know this, or is it just a lot of bilge water?

"No, Kelly I don't think this is bilge water. These guys are believable --- they are the mechanics that work on the helicopters on the *Roberts*. While the frigates are manned by Reservists, the Air Group on board is Regular Navy. They said the information came from a radioman who is attached to the Air Group. That seems reasonable since they were probably listening in on the same frequencies used by the *Simpson*."

"Okay, this all seems to be fitting together. Stay where you are. I'll call Connie and see where she wants you located --- either Connie or I will be calling you back. Thanks again, Neil. Bye."

"Oh, another voice mail with a Washington area code --- oh my God --- it's from Alex Williams at the Pentagon. I'd better listen to this, pronto."

"Kelly, Alex Williams here. I was asking around for some corroboration of your story regarding the Navy action last week. I wasn't able to get anything --- however, it was noted in the Secretary of State's security detail minutes, that she was about half way up the ramp on Air Force Two when one of her security detail called out to her and met her on the ramp. The minutes say they briefed her about a security issue. That is all I have to report. I do note, also, that Air Force Two returned to Andrews about fifteen minutes after takeoff to check out some small maintenance issue. See you at Monday's briefing. Have a great weekend. Bye."

"Humph, interesting --- but nothing definitive, thinks Kelly. Oh, rats --- another voice mail --- who's this one from? Looks like a Chicago Area Code."

"Hi Kelly, Connie here calling back about our phone system. I talked to our techy types in charge of the phones and they tell me that we can call A T & T and give them a date and time and they will provide a printout of our inbound calls. The only calls that won't print are for unlisted numbers. We're going to request a printout from them on Monday. I'll e-mail it to you. Have a great weekend. Bye."

Monday, 0900 hours, Daily Briefing, The Pentagon Press Room, Washington, D.C.

"Good morning, Ladies and Gentlemen of the press. As you know from the wire reports over the weekend, our training force stationed at Camp Liberty, North of Rhamadi, Iraq came under mortar and light arms fire at approximately zero two thirty hours, local time. The defense perimeter was manned entirely by Iraqi Security Forces. The attackers were able to breech the Camp and attack outlying buildings and vehicles with grenades and explosives. ISF casualties are two killed, six wounded. NATO casualties are eight wounded. The wounded were medivaced to our air base in Landsduhl, Germany where all fourteen wounded are listed in guarded, but stable condition. That is all I have on this situation, right now. I'm sure there will be more details tomorrow. In Syria, an Air Force Predator drone fired Hellfire missiles at a known al-Shabbah meeting house. Local authorities have indicated that six suspected terrorists were killed in the explosion. Also, in you briefing packet is a follow up on our humanitarian efforts in Bangladesh. The *Bonhomme Richard,* a quick strike Helicopter Carrier, is sending its helicopters to the flood affected areas of the country and moving citizens to high ground. They are also providing medical help and dropping MRE's, as well as packaged drinking water. That is all I have as part of the formal briefing. Are there any questions?"

"Yes, Mitchell."

"Alex, Mitchell Andres, CNN News here. On Friday, you told us that you were going to follow up and get us some background on the missile lock-on by the *U S S Simpson* off Nassau. What do you have for us?"

"Yes, Mitchell, and I'm certain that Kelly Lockwood is interested in this, too --- the Defense Department has directed all inquiries regarding this situation to the National Security Director's Office in the White House. The operation in the Bahamas was handled by NSD and not the DOD. That is all I have for you."

"Alex, come on. Who is running our Navy ships? I thought it was the Secretary of Defense through the Joint Chiefs followed by the Office of Naval Operations --- now, all of a sudden, our fleet is being run by the NSD --- that just doesn't compute," retorts Kelly.

"I'm sorry Kelly --- and the rest of you. You'll have to take this matter up with NSD. The Department of Defense has no further comment on this operation."

"Hell, Alex, you know it will take a Freedom of Information Request to get anything from NSD --- and that can take months," responds Kelly.

"Sorry --- any other questions? Yes, Phil."

"First, did the ISF kill or capture any of the attackers? And, second, has anyone taken responsibility for the attack on Camp Liberty?"

"No, as of this moment, I have no information on killed or captured or any group from Iraq on taking responsibility --- perhaps by tomorrow's briefing. Any other questions? Okay, none --- see you tomorrow."

"Hey, Kelly," shouts Mitchell.

"Yea, Mitch --- what's up?"

"Follow with me to the corner where no one can eves drop. Now, copy this down --- its audio and video from YouTube. Play it. Don't tell anyone that I gave it to you. My handler at CNN has asked me to back off on this story. And --- it's really your story. I hope you get some traction on this --- I smell smoke and you know what that means."

"Thanks, Mitch. See you tomorrow."

Connie Newsom's Office, Fox News
Washington Bureau, Washington, D.C.

"Oh, hi Kelly --- thanks for the heads up phone call from the Pentagon briefing. I've got my computer up and ready to copy the YouTube address. Here's the feed ---." Connie enters the YouTube address into her computer and hits enter.

"Hello people back there in civilian land --- this is your cub reporter, Whirlybird, reporting to you from the U S S Simpleton --- oh, by the way, that's the name we enlisted ranks gave to our ship --- it's actually a guided missile frigate of a similar name --- I'm sure you can figure it out. Well, anyway since the Navy won't tell you, your erstwhile reporter will have to. We've been operating near Bahamian Territorial Waters --- yeah, the infamous Bermuda Triangle --- and we've been chasing some bad dudes. So, listen carefully and you'll hear what a real chase at one hundred-fifty knots sounds like. Cue the tape, Charlie boy."

The video is grainy and bumpy --- like it was shot with a cell phone. The audio is poor. There is lots of helicopter engine background noise.

"*Sea Fan --- Acrobat 12. Affirmative. Slowing this bird and maintaining angels three --- have acquired the target and are locked on. Awaiting your order and standing by.*"

"*Excuse me, Mr. Secretary. With all due respect, whiskey-tango-foxtrot is taking you guys so long --- another minute and all hell is going to break loose on New Providence Island --- the loss of life could be staggering.*"

"*Hey Sea Fan --- we share your pain. They're trying to connect to the VPOUS as the President's golf cart commo is down and he's a mile from the clubhouse.*"

"*Oh crap, what the heck is going to get these people off their asses and make a decision?*"

"*Sea Fan Base --- Acrobat 12 here. The target has turned away from the harbor entrance and is going directly South toward the opening into Paradise Beach. Advise status for firing one Penguin missile.*"

"*Justin --- tell him thanks for the update. Stand by one.*"

"*Acrobat 12 --- Sea Fan Base. Thanks for the update. Stand by one.*"

"*Acrobat 12 is standing by.*"

"*Sea Fan ---- we got ahold of VPOUS --- the Vice President --- permission granted. You are authorized to shoot. I say again --- okay to fire.*"

"*Roger that Sit Room. Sea Fan, out.*"

"*Justin --- tell the heli to shoot.*"

"*Acrobat 12 --- Sea Fan Base. Affirmative --- fire your missile. I say again --- launch your missile.*"

"*Sea Fan --- Acrobat 12 --- we're too late. The bad guys beached the boat at high speed and it blew up. All we can see are flames and heavy black smoke. The beach is in chaos --- bodies everywhere and people are running into the water to get away from the flames. We're staying upwind at angels five, as we have air traffic going into Nassau International. Over."*

"Roger, Acrobat 12, return to base."

"So my friends in Civilian Land --- sleep well tonight. The Navy is here doing its job. Now, as far as the Civilian Government is concerned --- our Commander in Chief is busy playing golf while his Islamic Extremists friends are effing the world. 'Remember the score --- bad guys, fifty --- good guys, one. Keep your Glocs locked and loaded. 'Til next time, this is your suffering servant and cub reporter, Whirlybird --- OUT!"

"Wow, Kelly --- there's the smoking gun --- if this video is real. Where did this come from?"

"Sorry Connie, can't divulge my source. Now, as they say, our job is to connect the dots. We've got Sabrina's call. We've got the loose tongued Navy helicopter mechanics at the bar --- and, now this."

"Fortunately, this YouTube site is fairly obscure --- but, it is in the public domain and anyone could turn this thing viral in a minute. I think we need to go to Richardson with this. I think we need to discuss how we get our story out --- perhaps, as early as tonight's Evening News.

"Speaking of Sabrina, did we ever get the phone printout from Chicago?"

"Let me check my e-mail. Oh, here it is --- WFLD. TV - CHICAGO. I'll print it out."

"My goodness, it's four pages --- single spaced. Looks like this will take some detective work to find Sabrina."

"Kelly, you've got more important things to do. I'll assign the research to one of the interns."

"Good idea, Connie. We'll talk later."

"Oh, Hi Kent. I don't think there's time for you to view the video. Here's the story in capsule form. Some bored enlisted men on the *Simpson* made a YouTube video. It runs about six minutes. The audio consists of messages going between code name 'Sea Fan' and 'Acrobat 12'. 'Sea Fan' seems to be running this operation --- CIA, NSA, White House ---who knows?. 'Acrobat 12' is obviously a Navy helicopter. The copter is following some bad guys --- al-Qaeda types in an outboard boat outside Nassau harbor. They've locked a missile on the bad guys, but since this is Bahamian Territorial Waters, the pilot is requesting permission to shoot from some higher up Civilian Authority. Smart guy, this pilot. CIA calls State ---Secretary of State Randall is walking up the boarding ramp to board Air Force Two, so she's out of touch. They try to reach the President, but the communications on his golf cart have gone down and he's on his Blackberry while heading back to the clubhouse. Finally after what seems like an eternity, State reaches the Vice President and he gives permission to shoot the missile --- only problem is, it's too late. The bad guys drive their boat onto Paradise Beach, explode it and let off a cloud of sarin gas --- you know the rest."

"This all sounds good --- let me recap. We've got the phone call to WFLD. I read your e-mail report on the info that Neil got at the bar in Florida Beach and now, we've got this audio/video from YouTube. I'm thinking we should lead with it on the Evening News. Do me a favor, forward the YouTube address to my computer --- and send a copy to Bentley in New York. Jot him a note and ask him to call me after he's seen it. I'm thinking we need to get this down to the art department, so they can edit it and see if they can clean up the audio a bit. Figure we need to delete the CIA names --- and, I think I'll give my old friend Ned Bates at the NSD's office a call to tell them what we're going with tonight. We'll have Alex Smith cut to Kelly here in the studio -- you'll give the background and play the video. Sound like a plan?"

"Yes, but what do you think the NSD is going to say, inquires Kelly.

"Here, I'll dial up Bates and see what he says -- heck it's on YouTube and it's not like they can erase it. I'll put him on speaker. Mr. Bates, please. This is Neil Richardson of Fox News."

"One moment, I'll ring Mr. Bates' office."

"Bates here, what can I do for you, Richardson?"

"Write this down --- it's a link to a YouTube video. It was recorded aboard the *U S S Simpson,* last week. We're going to run with this story tonight on the Evening News. We'll delete your agent's name and the Ambassador's name. Let me know if you have anything to add or delete."

"I've already seen it. There's nothing more I can add. It was just one of those situations --- you know, a SNAFU --- and, it is not the duty of the CIA, or any intelligence agency, to stand in front of the truth and protect the President. I say, let the chips fall where they may. Thanks for running this by me. Fox is the only news organization that would even think of doing this. Good luck with your story --- this should provide the Conservative talk show hosts with plenty of fodder for the next couple of weeks. I can see the cartoons already --- the President's golf cart racing down the fairway with sparks coming from his radio. Have a good evening. Bye."

"Well --- there you have it. There's no protecting the President from this. The White House will try to spin this, but the golf thing is going to be his undoing. While terrorists are blowing up Jewish-American Citizens, the President is putting out on number eight. Kelly, you get to your writing. Connie, send this YouTube thing to the artists and see if they can clean it up --- or perhaps we need to subtitle it, if the background noise is too much. Okay? Good work, ladies. See you later."

Fox News Channel, 7:00 P.M. Eastern Daylight Time, The Evening News with Alex Johnson

"Good evening. It's the top of the hour and time for the top of the news, fair and balanced, from Fox News. I'm Alex Johnson. We have breaking news and our lead story is a follow up to the terrorist sarin gas attack on Nassau. For this news, we go to our Pentagon Correspondent, Kelly Lockwood, in Washington. Kelly."

"Good evening, Alex. This is some really shocking news. Fox News has learned that the U. S. Navy was within seconds of destroying the al-Qaeda terrorist boat before they could inflict casualties at Paradise Beach, in the Bahamas. The order to fire a missile from a helicopter didn't come in time to save one hundred eight Jewish-Americans and hundreds of Bahamians from a horrible death. We have audio and video of the Navy operation. The video and audio are of poor quality. We have added sub-titles, so you can understand what the pilot of the helicopter is saying. To protect their identity, we have deleted the names of any intelligence agents and State Department employees. To help you follow the audio, 'Acrobat 12' is a SB-60 helicopter from the guided missile frigate, *U S S Simpson*. 'Sea Fan Base' is a U.S. Intelligence Agency that is running this operation. Here, have a listen to this tape ----. The YouTube video has been edited down from six minutes to four minutes.

"So Alex, as you heard, the audio indicates that the pilot of 'Acrobat 12', the helicopter, was waiting for permission to fire his missile in Bahamian airspace. The intelligence agency tried, but was unable to reach the Secretary of State and, the tape indicates that they tried to reach the President, but his communication on his golf cart, was down. Finally, the Intelligence folks got ahold of the Vice President and this was when the order was given --- an order that arrived too late for one hundred eight Jewish-Americans, as well as dozens of foreign tourists and hundreds of Bahamian Citizens, who also died. Back to you Alex."

"That's quite a bombshell, Kelly. How many minutes did the pilot wait for the order to shoot?"

"Assuming the audio was in real time, Alex, we timed it at two minutes and fifty-six seconds."

"Thank you Kelly. So, there you have it. Our civilian command structure was out of contact with the U.S. Navy for almost three minutes. One would think that there is going to be an inquiry into this. And, with the election only eighty-two days away, this could have an impact, on the final debate. We have calls in to the Senate Majority Leader, as well as the Senate Minority Leader and the Speaker of the House. We hope to bring their reaction to you, live, later in the program."

223

"Now, for more reaction we go to Matt Nemer on the South lawn of the White House. Matt."

"Good evening, Alex. There has been no official announcement from the White House, however, senior administration officials have told me privately that they are prepared for any Congressional inquiry into this event, and they emphasize that the President was never out of communication with the Intelligence Community, or the Joint Chiefs, at any time last week. Alex, that is all we have from the White House, until the daily briefing tomorrow morning. Back to you."

"Thank you Matt. Now we go to Heather Shanahan who is with the Minority Leader, Senator Jim Donnelly of Ohio. Heather."

"Thank you Alex. I'm here with Senator Donnelly, the Minority Leader. Senator, what do you think of this revelation?"

"Well first, Heather, I would again like to extend my sympathies to the families of the Americans --- as well as the other tourists and Bahamians that lost their life last week in the al-Qaeda gas attack. As you know, the Republican Party has been quite outspoken regarding this President's global travel and his seemingly excessive vacation time. Our enemies are awake twenty-four seven, just waiting for an opportunity to attack our country. It is inexcusable for our President to be out of contact with the civilian authorities ---er, someone who could have authorized a missile attack and, I'm certain there will be an investigation. Thank you, Fox News for bringing this matter to the attention of the American public and God Bless America."

"Thank you Senator Donnelly. Alex, I extended an invitation to both the Majority Leader and the Speaker of the House for an on air interview and they declined."

"Thank you, Heather. And now to the rest of the news............"

CIA Headquarters, The Conference Center, The "Friends of Freedom Banquet"

"Ladies and Gentlemen. Please rise for the singing of the Canadian National Anthem, 'O, Canada' and remain standing for the singing of the Star Spangled Banner."

The entire conference room rises to their feet and a huge American flag is unfurled behind the podium, side by side with the Canadian Maple Leaf.

"As your Director, it is with extreme pleasure and gratitude that I introduce to you a great friend of the Agency, Scott Lindsay and his lovely wife, Addie. Scott is a Canadian citizen who was born in Milwaukee --- and Addie, an American Citizen, was also born in Milwaukee. They come to us from their sailboat, *Caribe Dreamer*, that cruises the beautiful azure waters of the Bahama Islands. Please give them a warm, welcoming round of applause." As the applause dies down, the director continues. "Scott --- Addie, it is with great pleasure that I present you with these medals and plaques from the Central Intelligence Agency, as well as a personal letter from the President. And, lest I forget, in this envelope is a check in the amount of $10,000.00, as a reward for your help in the capture of a person of interest to the United States. In so many cases, 'Friends of Freedom' are often husband and wife teams. Many times the situations confronting them can cause tension and hardship in a relationship. Scott and Addie went through all of this turmoil and, as they told me, their marriage, today, is stronger, now, than ever. Scott, while you were born in Milwaukee, as a child your parents emmigrated to Canada. After graduation from college, you served your country, as a Canadian Army Forces Paratrooper. Many of the skills you learned in the military, as well as your hobby --- amateur, or Ham radio, as we refer to it in the U.S., helped the United States Government recover a valuable piece of military hardware and simultaneously shut down a group of terrorists who planned to attack the United States, from their secret base in the Bahamas. And, I am told, this is the second time you assisted the Agency. For these actions, we present you with your awards. Additionally, it is my understanding that you have received commendations from both the Government of Canada, as well as the Government of the Commonwealth of the Bahamas. Thank you, Scott and Addie Lindsay. Give them a round of applause. Would you like to say a few words?"

"Thank you, Director. First, I would like to thank my wife, Addie, for her support. There were some difficult times for our marriage, as this situation played out, but Addie gave me just enough rein to do the job --- thanks, hon. I also want to thank Albert Alton, my long time Bahamian friend for his assistance. As you know, all three of us make our living in the Bahama Islands. The islands are a piece of God's paradise and I encourage you to visit these beautiful islands soon, and see for yourself. As recent terrorist events have shown, even a paradise can become home to the bad guys. We must never let down our guard --- we must be ever vigilant and we --- that is, the freedom loving people of the world --- must develop the best intelligence apparatus on the planet and back it up with the best military on the planet. Thank you, the United States of America for showing the world that you will not shirk from your responsibility to root out the bad guys, wherever they may be. Again, thank you."

Scott and Addie are escorted by the Director, arm in arm to the edge of the stage to a standing ovation.

The Main Gate, China Lake Naval Weapons Laboratory, California

"Good morning, sir. May I see some identification? And, sir --- would you mind exiting your vehicle, so we may inspect it?"

"Certainly, sailor --- here's my Virginia Driver's License and my Navy Identification Card."

"Thank you, sir. Please step inside where it is cool," replies the Shore Patrol sailor.

"Sir, I see from your I.D. that you will be retiring from the Navy, next month. What business do you have on this base, sir?"

"I'm picking up my fiancé at the Everen Electric Contractors Building. I think she has informed you of my arrival."

"Oh, yes sir. We were expecting you. A Susan Jean Barton sent us an e-mail yesterday --- I have your authorization to visit her location, right here. You'll need a map and I'll highlight the route to Everen, sir. I'll need to fill out some paperwork and we'll have you quickly on your way. What did you do in this man's Navy, Commander Anderson?"

"Oh, I was the Executive Officer aboard the *U S S Topeka*, an attack submarine."

"I'll bet you saw some action --- chasing down those Russian Subs?"

"Unfortunately sailor, all that kind of stuff is still classified --- but there were some hairy times."

"Sir, just put this green card on the driver side of the dashboard --- facing outward. You can be on base for one and a half hours --- which will be until fourteen-fifteen hours. You need to report to the exit gate and return this card. Here's your map. Just outside the gate, is a four-way stop. Turn left --- that's Nimitz Avenue. Take Nimitz to the first stoplight. Turn right on Ditch Avenue. Drive four miles. You will see a group of beige Quonset huts on your right. There will be a SP on duty at the gate. Just show him the green card. He will pass you through the gate and you will see signs leading to visitor parking. Any questions, sir?"

"No questions. Thank you very much. You have been quite professional. I'll put in a good word for you with your Commander."

"Thank you sir, and have a great day."

"*Nimitz, Forestall, Spruance --- there must be a street named after them on every Navy Base in the world.*" thinks Kevin as he accelerates the Audi T-Type through the gate. "*Ditch Avenue --- now that's original. Ditch your multi-million dollar aircraft in the sea? Where did this name come from,*" questions Kevin, wondering aloud.

"*Ah --- beige Quonset huts on the right. That must be it. Stop at the gate and show the SP the green dash card,*" he reminds himself.

227

"Good afternoon sir," says the SP while reading the dash mounted card. "You may proceed. Just follow the signs to visitor parking. Thank you and have a safe day."

The Quonset huts were obviously leftovers from the nineteen forties. Almost every window had an air conditioner hanging from it. It is hot in China Lake, but desert cold at night.

"Okay, visitor parking right next to the visitor's entrance. How convenient. ---- Everen Electric above the door. This be the place," Kevin mumbles to the car's interior. Removing his hat, he enters the door.

"Good afternoon, ma'am Kevin Anderson to see Ms. Barton," says Kevin to the civilian female, occupying the reception desk.

"Have a seat, I'll see if Ms. Barton is available," she replies as she dials the phone.

"Ms. Barton --- a gentleman named Kevin Anderson is here to see you. Okay, I'll tell him. Bye."

"Ah, Mister Anderson --- Miss Barton will be right out. I'm Linda Higgins --- one of Jean's best friends here at China Lake. I'm thrilled to meet you. We've been on pins and needles all day --- waiting."

"Thank you, ma'am. It's very nice to meet you."

The office door creaks open and Jean runs across the reception area jumping into Kevin's arms, smothering him with a kisses.

"Wow, that's quite a reception, young lady. I've missed you, too. Say, I think you should know that my pass says I have to be back to the main gate in less than an hour. Show me your luggage and let's get out of here --- I've made reservations for us in Bakersfield--- in the Old Towne area. A La Quinta Inn with a fabulous view of downtown --- I stayed there last night."

"Kevin, that sounds great. Let me wheel my luggage up front. I'm certainly hoping we can get it all in the Audi."

"Yeah, me too --- I packed light and put most of my stuff in the boot. There's plenty of room in the back seat --- and, as long as we don't put the top down, we can use the trunk. You wheel, I'll pack the trunk --- okay?"

"Yes, and ---- I can't wait to talk --- there's so much to tell you."

The two small, red, wheeled carry-on bags fit perfectly in the trunk. The matching large suitcase barely makes it into the back seat. Two armloads of hanging clothes go on top of the suitcase, but there is still a view through the rear window. Jean comes out into the reception area, for the last time. She has a small package in her hand.

"Linda, thank you for everything you did to help me get moved out of this place. I couldn't have done it without you. Here's a token of my appreciation --- don't open it until I leave. We'll keep in touch --- I would so like you to be in our wedding."

The ladies hug and both wipe tears from their eyes.

"Bye, Linda --- I love you."

"Bye, Jean, I love you, too --- I'll email you and let you know when your separation is official."

Kevin holds the passenger door for Jean --- he notices her short skirt and beautiful legs. He walks around to the driver's seat and touches the ignition button. The Audi's engine roars and immediately the air conditioning and the radio come to life. Jean leans to her left and they kiss and touch --- just for a few seconds. They leave the contractor's area and head for the main gate --- returning their green dash card and finally connecting with U.S. Route 395 to Bakersfield. Jean sits in complete silence holding and stroking Kevin's right hand. Kevin breaks the ice.

"So, the future Mrs. Anderson --- you look beautiful. Your hair is a bit shorter --- I really like it."

"Oh, that sounds wonderful ---- Mrs. Susan Jean Anderson. And, Kevin ---- sorry about the silence, but I have so many thoughts going through my head --- you know Linda and all the Everen people who helped me with my garage sale and selling my car. And then, the inquiry --- all the stuff I told you about on the phone. It was awful --- and very stressful. I'm just glad it is over and I can crawl into your arms --- and have a good cry."

"We've got lots of time to talk. No pressure from me. And, you can have my right shoulder for a good cry --- there's a box of tissues in the glove compartment."

"Thanks, Kevin. All I need right now is the touch of your hand. Let me know if you need both hands on the wheel."

"Okay, babe. Temperature okay? Music okay?"

"Yes --- finally everything is okay."

"Mind if I talk some Navy shop," queries Kevin.

"No, the scenery out the window is ugly --- talk away."

"I've been thinking about our shrinking Navy and especially the sub force. Our older boats have only a few more years before they are too old, or too noisy. The SALT treaty is changing the look of the submarine force. We're no longer allowed to have all the 'boomers' we once had. I've got an idea --- what about converting them to conventional boats that fire Tomahawk's? They wouldn't count under SALT and would be stealthy enough to get close to the enemy's shore."

"Kevin, that's the germ of what could be a great idea. This is something that Bill Wilson at the Pentagon should hear about. We could simply cut a boat in half, remove the launch tubes and replace them with Tomahawks -- brilliant. I think General Dynamics, Electric Boat Division would be very interested in this."

9:15 P.M., The Barton Residence, on a quiet cul-de-sac in Petaluma, California

"Hi, Jean. Well, you guys finally made it --- safe and sound."

"Hi Mom. Hi Dad. This is Kevin."

"Hello, Tom and good evening, Diane. It is so nice to finally meet you. And, here --- we stopped long enough at a Cracker Barrel and got a couple of bottles of Rodney-Strong Chardonnay -- I understand that you and ---- ah, Diane like whites."

"Well, first off Kevin --- let's stop all this formal stuff and you call me Dad and call Diane, Mom --- Deal? And, thank you very much for the wine. Rodney-Strong is one of our favorite whites -- their winery is just East of us over the hill. Let's get these chilling. How about we move the party inside, so we can talk, Commander?"

"Dad, you chill the wine. Kevin and I need to get our luggage out of his car."

"Okay, Jeannie --- I'll do the wine, you young people do the heavy lifting --- Mom's got you two in the guest apartment."

"Thanks, Dad --- and by the way, Commander is still appropriate. I've got thirty days of leave before my resignation can take effect."

Kevin and Jean moved their luggage and hanging garments into the guest apartment.

"Wow, Jean --- this is some house your folks have. A guest apartment with a sitting room, kitchen, bedroom and a full bath -- nice digs."

"I'm thinking it would be best for you to keep your clothes in the sitting room --- at least until I sound out Mom on how she and Dad feel about you and I sleeping together --- and, you need not worry, there's no lock on the bedroom door."

"Darling, that's seems like a good plan. I don't want to get off on the wrong foot, as they say. I need to visit the bath and brush my teeth --- I can feel the fur on them."

"Good idea --- I'll follow you and be down to share a toast with you and my folks, in a few minutes. It won't be a long visit --- this is way past their bedtime."

Petaluma, California, The Barton's Living Room

"So, Son --- fill Diane and me in on the details of how you two met."

"Oh sure, my pleasure. I was the Executive Officer on the attack submarine, *USS Topeka*. Our boat -- ah, that's how we refer to a submarine in the Navy -- was sent to AUTEC. As you know, that's located on Andros Island in the Bahamas. Our mission was to test a new weapon --- and, I'm sorry, but the weapon is still classified Top Secret, so I can't say anything about it. Your daughter was Everen's contact with the Navy and I was assigned to coordinate our boat's testing with her. We met on a Friday afternoon and she dragged me to an island joint called Big Big's--- she showed me the sights of Andros Island and I took her sailing. In a nutshell, that's how we met."

"That's a wonderful story, Kevin. We know from talking and e-mailing Jean that there was some trouble with the test, but the important thing is that, despite the time apart, you have been able to continue your relationship. "Oh, hi Jean. Your father has been itching to have a toast with this lovely Chardonnay. Here's a glass for you and one for Kevin."

"Tom, would you do the honors and toast our daughter and about-to-be son-in-law?"

"Sure, honey. To Kevin and Jean, I wish you all the happiness in your life together. The same joyous love for the Lord, as He has so blessed our own marriage. May your life be exciting and fulfilling and, we would be proud to become --- someday, --- in due time, grandparents. Here, here," exclaimed Tom, as he raises his glass in a toast.

"Okay, Tom. Enough about having grandchildren. Let this young couple decide on that without pressure from us."

"Okay, Diane. Okay, I know."

"Jean, what do you two want to do about breakfast? Dad and I are up about eight o'clock to read the paper and watch the European stock market," announces Diane.

"Kevin will be up early --- probably six --- he's still operating on Navy time ---and he'll want to go for a jog. So, nine thirty, or so, for breakfast --- if that's okay with you and Dad?"

"That's perfect, darling --- I'll make my Southern French Toast --- plus some fried ham and, if Kevin's still hungry, we can always do eggs. After breakfast, Dad would like to take Kevin by the club, as it is his regular golf game. That way, you and I can talk about the wedding details. Kevin, it might get a little cool tonight so, I put an electric blanket on the bed. It has dual controls, if you're like my Tom, you can keep your side cooler if you prefer."

"Thank you, Mom --- I'm used to sleeping in a perfect seventy-two degree temperature. It will feel good to have a window to open --- there are none of those on a submarine! Good night, see you in the morning."

Kevin and Jean walked down the narrow hallway to the guest apartment.

"Well, that electric blanket comment certainly eliminated any discussion regarding where you are sleeping tonight"

"Yes, hon. Your Mom and Dad are pretty hip for a couple of Senior Citizens."

Monday, 10:00 A.M., Tom Barton's black, E-350 Mercedes Sedan en route to the Petaluma Country Club

"You know, Son --- Diane and I have only one worry. Both of you are unemployed and in this lousy economy, finding a job is going to be difficult."

"Well, Dad ---- the good news is that Jean and I work in a growth industry --- war. As the Russians, Chinese, North Koreans and Iranians continue to upgrade their military, we need to keep two steps ahead of the bad guys --- not to mention the trouble from al-Qaeda and ISIS. I have a degree from the Naval Academy in Nuclear Engineering. I'm a submariner --- an insider who has lots of knowledge that any number of contractors will be willing to pay for. Your daughter is somewhat in the same position. She's a techie. She has a Top Secret Cryptographic clearance --- and the best part is, she's a woman. So, I don't think we'll have any trouble finding jobs. Our biggest problem will be to decide where to land --- The East Coast, Florida or The West Coast? --- that will be the challenge."

"That certainly is reassuring. On another subject, Kevin, what's the feeling inside the Navy about President Collins?"

"I would say that out of ten enlisted men, two -- maybe three support his policies and would probably vote for him. Among the officers, it would be less than ten percent who would consider voting for Collins. As far as I'm concerned, the only good thing he has done is not to gut the military spending. --- although with our huge deficits, down the road, the defense budget will have to be reigned in."

"Glad to hear that, Kevin. I'm a fiscally conservative Republican and I think that you and I can have some great political discussions. You know, of course, that Jean is our only daughter. Her Mom and I have been waiting years, for the announcement of her engagement. I have been very fortunate in business --- and this country allowed me to make, and keep, some of my money. Diane has dreamed about Jean having a large country club wedding --- but, we don't want you and Jean to be forced into something that you don't want. So, we would like to make this offer --- a full fluff wedding at the club --- or a small ceremony and reception at our church, with a few close friends and a check, to the two of you, for forty thousand dollars. Think about it. Talk it over with Jean. I'm sure Diane is making the same offer to her right now."

"Dad, that is an extremely generous offer. I agree, we should talk it over ---- think it over. However, I'm pretty certain that Jean is leaning toward the full fluff, country club wedding."

"Okay, and speaking of the club --- we're here."

Your Wedding Planner a storefront in downtown Petaluma, California. Sandra Brown, owner.

"Now, Jean --- have you decided on a theme for your wedding --- you know like chocolate or Wine Country --- or black and white or something like that?"

"Actually, I am thinking of an old-fashioned theme --- like a throwback to the sixties or seventies where the groom doesn't see the bride, on her wedding day --- and they get married in a church by an ordained minister --- not some justice of the peace. You know, where the bride carries something old and something new --- and the guests throw rice, not bird seed. Is that something you can help me with, Sandra?"

"Well, of course. This certainly wouldn't be your typical California wedding, but I know that, with proper planning, we could bring it off and it will be lovely."

"So, Mom --- how does that sound to you?"

"Jean, it sounds wonderful and I'm certain Pastor George at First Methodist, would concur."

"Then, if this is all agreed on, we need to get started -- with a date. A date that your church is available for the ceremony."

"I've already checked with Pastor George and the church is available the first Saturday in October ah, October 4th," chimes in Diane.

"My goodness --- that's only two and a half months from now," blurts out Sandra. We will need to rush the dress and of course, the invitations --- this will be a very tight schedule --- especially the dresses. But, it certainly can be done. There may be some extra charges for UPS next day --- and the like. And, then there is the problem of the reception."

"Don't worry, Sandra. I have spoken to Charles, the manager at the club and he has assured me that he can accommodate us on the first Saturday in October. My husband and I only have one daughter and I don't think that any extra costs will be a problem. So, perhaps we can see some wedding dresses and then work toward the attendant's dresses?"

"Oh, certainly, Diane. I will have Danielle bring in some style books, while I get Jean's measurements."

4:30 P.M., The Barton Residence, Petaluma, California.

"Hi, Dad, Hi, Kevin --- so, how was your golf game, questions Jean, as she closes her bridal magazine and rises from the sofa to greet Kevin with a big hug and kiss.

"Go ahead, Dad --- tell them," adds Kevin

"Okay, I beat Kevin by one stroke when I chipped in on eighteen! I don't think I've chipped in during the last five years. Pure luck --- I do say."

"Your Dad played a hell of a game --- needless to say, I am a little rusty. But, most importantly we had a good time and I got a chance to see the club. It's a beautiful place and a perfect setting for our wedding. I met Charles and he penciled us in for October 4th. What did you ladies find out from the wedding planner?"

"She was very nice and accommodating. She freaked a bit when Mom told her our wedding date is October 4th. --- but, she got over it. She's loaded me up with lots of magazines and I'm supposed to get back to her with the wedding dress style, as well as the bridesmaids dresses --- all before noon, tomorrow. So, Kevin --- we need to talk."

"You two talk, while Dad and I change into some comfortable clothes. I'll make the cocktails and you can go to the sitting room and talk in private," states Diane.

"Mom, we're fine, right here. We don't need privacy --- is that okay with you, Kevin?"

"Right, hon. First question ...."

"Here's the checklist from Sandra. Mom and I split it up --- she's doing invitations, flowers and all the little details for the reception. I need to know from you about the best man, as well as, the groomsmen."

"This should be easy, since most of my good friends from the *Topeka* will be underwater somewhere in the Atlantic on October 4th, my father will be the best man and then, my roommate from Annapolis, who went Marine --- he's at the Pentagon --- Alex Goodyear. He will be a groomsman. Do I need more?"

"No, two is absolutely perfect. The wedding party will be small. My cousin, Kathy, will be Maid of Honor and Linda Higgins, from China Lake, will be an attendant."

"Question two. What about tuxedos --- or are you going to wear your uniform?"

"I'd prefer uniforms. October 4th --- I'll be assigned to a Reserve Unit, so I can still wear my dress whites. Alex will be in his Marine dress blues. What about your Dad?"

"I guess I didn't I tell you? --- Dad made it to Lieutenant Colonel in the Army. I need to check with him to see if he can rent a set of dress blues --- he's put on a few pounds since Vietnam."

"Okay, I'll check that off the list, but with a question mark about Dad wearing his uniform. Next questions in your column --- bachelor party."

"No wild, drunken brawl for me. I'd rather have a nice steak dinner, at the club, with some really good California wine and perhaps, an after dinner cigar. That would be perfect."

"Okay, so no to the stripper? --- I can check that off?"

"That's not really on the list, Jean?"

"No, Kevin --- just kidding. Next question --- just for you to think about. Groomsman gifts."

"Hmm --- I'll have to think about that a while. You know, I heard of a great gift --- a quarter ounce of gold. A paperweight --- with our names and the date inscribed on the back."

"Hmmm. Sounds expensive. Last question before cocktails. The honeymoon --- that's in your column, Hon. However, the more I think of it, this should be in the 'both' column."

"I agree. Dad took Mom to a Bahamian out-island. There was no electricity, no running water and only one restaurant --- and, Mom didn't know how to cook! Dad had to do all the meal planning and that's where Mom started learning how to cook."

"Come on --- no electricity, no running water. You have to be kidding?"

"No, Jean. I'm not kidding. This little cottage had a refrigerator that ran on propane. The lights also ran on propane and you pumped water by hand into a tank, which allowed you to have water pressure at the faucets and to flush the toilet."

"So, is this where you're taking me," questions Jean

"No, Hon. I wouldn't consider any kind of wilderness experience. But, I have been thinking about a luxury cruise on a charter sailboat. Last week, I picked up a copy of *Sail Magazine*. There's an article on cruising in the Abacos --- which is an island chain in the Northern Bahamas. I thought it would be a chance for us to get back to the Bahamas --- without the pressure of a secret Navy weapons program. There's a young couple that charters a fifty-two foot catamaran, out of Marsh Harbour in the Abacos. He captains, and she cooks. They've responded to my email. Looks interesting. The name of the boat is *Tres Amigos*. I'll fire up the computer and show you their website, later tonight."

"Hon, tell me how much bigger is fifty-two feet than the little craft we sailed out of Andros?"

"Oh, it's about twice as long and five times as wide."

"Oh, really --- it's five times as wide?"

"No, I'm not kidding --- catamarans have twin hulls, spread wide apart. Their beam, or width, is what makes them the perfect party platform --- lots of cabin space and deck space --- and plenty of privacy, since the sleeping quarters are in the separate hulls."

"Here, I'll bring up the web site and you can check the photos."

Sunday, June 13th, aboard a Gulfstream V approaching Marsh Harbour International Airport, Abaco Bahamas

"Scottie, hold my hand. I'm never really comfortable when we're making a landing"

"Addie, we couldn't be in better hands -- these pilots are top notch, they fly the Director and lots of CIA types, all over the world."

"Wow! Look at all that beautiful azure water --- the Cherry Blossoms in Washington were beautiful, but that Bahamas water looks fabulous. I sure missed it."

"Ah, MHH Unicom, this is Gulfstream nine-five golf. We're six miles Northwest of 'The Marls' at one-five hundred feet, inbound for runway nine -- squawking one, two, zero, zero."

"Gulfstream nine-five golf, Marsh Unicom --- da wind she be one-one two degrees, at nine knots, da barometer is three-zero, decimal seven-one. I got no other traffic to report. You be squawkin twelve hundreh. Clear ta land."

"Roger, Marsh Unicom, Gulfstream nine-five golf on left base to runway nine --- now passing through one thousand, cleared to land. Marsh --- ah, Gulfstream nine-five golf on short final to runway nine."

"Marsh Unicom, Gulfstream nine-five golf is on the ground and taxiing to Customs. Have a great day."

"Well, babe, --- look out the window. I'll be tarred and feathered --- there's Pinder, the old codger, right on time. And, there's his ugly VW bus --- as usual, he's parked in the Commissioners private parking space. Looks like we've got a ride to the ferry."

"I can't wait to get back to *Dreamer* and to curl up with you and Mittens."

"Me, too, babe --- let's get our bags and get through this chaos they call Customs. You go left --- I'll go right."

Monday, October 6th on board *Caribe Dreamer,* at anchor in the American Harbour at Frigate Cay

"Hey, Scott. We'd better get some fenders over the side. The ferry should be coming through the cut any minute. You know --- I'm really looking forward to cruising with some younger people."

"Me, too, Hon. Enough of these retirees with their 401k money -- I'm ready to party with that young couple from Chicago."

"Well, here's to your Chicago couple -- look at the *Davie* flying through the cut --- he's already making his right turn after passing the marker --- stand by, our guests are arriving," says Addie as the ferry captain skillfully pulls alongside *Dreamer.*

"Hi Will. Hi Amber--- welcome aboard *Caribe Dreamer.* I'm Scott and this is my wife Addie. Here, let us help you with your bags."

"Wow, Scott, just like the guide book says, this is a perfectly protected harbor," remarks Wil.

"Yep, sure is. The cut you came through was carved out by hand, more than one hundred fifty years ago. You'll find the Abaco natives to be hard workers. They've survived out here for over two hundred years. No job is beyond their abilities."

"Scott, once we're situated, Amber and I would really like a briefing on the origin of these settlements and this place you call the Abacos."

"Sure thing -- a history lesson is always included with your charter. Addie and I will help make you at home --- on our home. While Addie makes up some rum punch, I'll give you a tour. First, you'll need a lesson on using the marine water closet --- the toilet."

"Couldn't be too different from the toilet on my Pearson 35, Scott"

"Probably not, Kevin --- hey, good to know you're a sailor"

"Yeah. I was almost born --- actually I was probably conceived, on a sailboat."

"This small room is known as the 'head'. This is the water closet, as it is known on a ship. It is very similar to a toilet on your Pearson. Put nothing down it except waste and this special toilet paper. Do your business and then press the button. You should see a blue liquid cleaning the bowl. When you push the button, count to five --- that should be sufficient. You'll hear the vacuum system pump working --- that is the only noise this toilet makes. We hold the waste aboard, until we are out in the ocean. This system composts the waste before it is pumped overboard. Any questions?"

"Like you said, Scott -- just like an airplane," responds Wil.

"Let's move forward to your cabin. Note the location of the light switches --- they toggle two ways. One way you get bright, white light -- the other gives you red light, for night vision. The switch on the starboard

239

bulkhead turns on the floor lighting. It is on a rheostat, so you can adjust it to the brightness you desire. Above your bunk are twin reading lights. Don't worry yourself about using too much electricity. We have twin wind generators, as well as solar panels. And, if the wind and sun fail, there is always the generator. In the evening, we turn on the air conditioning. It is optional --- you may prefer the breeze coming down the hatch. Speaking of hatches --- notice the large hatch on the inboard, or left side of your bunk. This is the emergency escape hatch. All catamarans are required to have such a hatch, in every sleeping compartment--- just in case. Simply pull both handles down. The hatch is hinged and will fall outboard. Exit with your head and left shoulder and roll into the water. The good news is that we haven't used any of the emergency hatches --- ever! That's the end of the tour of the starboard hull. My suggestion is that you freshen up, hang your clothes in the lockers --- change into something tropical and meet up in the cockpit. Then, we can decide where we want to go, tomorrow. Okay?"

"Sounds like a plan, Scott. Both of us slept on the plane, so I don't think we'll need a nap. Besides, Frigate Cay is such a beautiful place, I'd like to sit in the cockpit and take in the sights until dark. We'll change and be up to join you in about fifteen minutes."

"Great, Amber --- Wil. See you topside in about fifteen minutes. I want to introduce you guys to our dog, Mittens"

Scott retreats back through the passageway and up the stairs to the salon where Addie is fixing snacks and drinks.

"So, what do you think of our guests," whispers Addie.

"They're going to be great. Wil's a sailor --- he owns a Pearson 35. You saw his sailing credentials. He's sailed Lightnings, Snipes, Lasers, R Boats, as well as, a Sabre 38. He's done the Bermuda Race and a number of Mackinac Races. You name it, he's sailed, crewed or raced it."

"Amber's a little quiet, but I figure a couple of your rum punches should loosen her up."

"Hey, mister. Give the lady a chance. She's only been married for a couple of days."

"Okay, Addie. I know --- Wil made the arrangements for the honeymoon and she's not sure how this is going to work out. We'll show them the best honeymoon --- ever!"

"Scottie, how about getting Mittens out of the head, so she can meet our guests."

"Hi, Amber. Hi, Wil. Pick a seat close to a table, so you have plenty of room for your drink and snacks," suggests Addie. Scott is bringing the dog to meet you. Please be truthful with us -- do you like dogs? Perhaps you hate dogs or are allergic to dogs? Don't worry, Mittens has a male dog friend on Frigate Cay and she'd probably prefer to spend some time on dry land."

"Oh, Addie --- Wil and I both grew up with dogs. I'm sure we'll get along with Mittens, responds Amber."

"We'll, I'll warn you --- she'll steal your heart. We've had a few charterers who wanted to take her home!"

"Scott -- do you have her?"

"Sure do --- I'm holding her tight, cause I know she'll go straight for Wil."

"Wil --- Amber, this is Mittens. She's a Soft-Coated Wheaten Terrier --- and, she doesn't bite, have fleas or shed."

"Oh, what an adorable dog, states Amber. I can see why people want to take her home."

"Yep, just like you said. She wants to curl up on my lap," adds Wil, as he pets Mittens behind her ears.

"Now that we have the Mittens intro finished, we need to find out what you prefer to drink. I'm the bartender and we have everything from a Doctor Pepper to a cocktail called 'Sex on the Beach'. Sometimes, after a day of flying to get here, our guests simply prefer bottled water. Addie has mixed up her Bahamas punch. And, right now, there's no rum in it, so you can have it virgin --- if you prefer."

"Okay, Scott, what's in a 'Sex on the Beach' cocktail --- or am I simply falling into some kind of a joke?

"No, Wil. This is for real --- especially in the Bahamas where 'it' happens quite often. Here are the ingredients: a couple of ounces of Vodka; an ounce of Peach Schnapps; a splash or two of Crème de Cassis; fill with three ounces of Orange Juice and three ounces of Cranberry Juice. Put it in a cocktail shaker with some ice and serve with a slice of orange and a maraschino cherry."

"Scott, I'll try the 'Sex on the Beach' --- but go easy on the Vodka. First, I'd like to start with a bottled water?"

"Oh, certainly, Amber. And for you Wil?"

"I'm a Scotch drinker. I can take it straight on the rocks, or with a little branch water --- or with club soda and a lemon twist, if you have one."

"Well, I'll be --- another Scotch drinker. I've got Chivas Regal, Ballentines, J & B, or Dewar's. And, I've got club soda or bottled branch. I think Addie picked this sour orange today. Tastes just like a lemon --- so I can give you a twist."

"Sounds good. Dewar's, club soda and a twist. Thanks, Scott."

"Okay, Mister Bartender --- are you finished? I want our guests to know what we have for snacks. We're going kind'a mild for this evening. With all the wedding pressures and the flying, we've found that our guests don't want a bunch of rich seafood like conch --- or lobster, the first day. So, I've put together a cheese and apple plate, as well as some avocado slices that have been drizzled with lime juice and some really delicious Brazilian grapes. You can put the cheese on these wonderful English crackers --- or, just smother the cracker with this tasty English orange marmalade, or raspberry jam."

"Will and Jean, you both said you wanted a history lesson about the Loyalists and the Abacos. Don't worry, if I get long winded, Addie will give me 'the look' --- and I'll stop."

"Here goes. In 1783, after the end of the Revolutionary War, the Colonists did some nasty things to the Loyalists who supported The King of England. We hung some of them, we took their land and livestock. Things were pretty bad for Loyalists, so many of them congregated in New York, which was held by the British until late in 1783. An influential Loyalist, who shared their same sorry lot, petitioned King George the Third for relief. So, reluctantly, the King sent some British Navy ships to New York harbor, to rescue the sorry bunch. The Loyalists were given the choice to go to Canada, Jamaica, Florida or the Bahama Islands. Advertisements ran in the New York newspapers telling of the wonderful land that awaited the Loyalists. The Bahamas were painted as being very fertile --- bring your livestock, your chickens, your slaves --- said the advertisements. So, hundreds of them did and they landed just to the North of what is now called Treasure Cay. They named their settlement Carleton, for Sir Guy Carleton, the British military commander in New York. As soon as they stepped off the beach, they sank into two feet of rotting pine needles --- there was little topsoil. There was no open land for cattle --- nothing but dense pine forests. There would be little farming until the land was cleared, so they had to abandon their slaves and their cattle. The Loyalists saw lots of schools of fish, through the clear water. Rather than starve, they quickly became fishermen."

"Okay, Mister History Buff, come up for air and let's see if our guests need a refill --- or perhaps have a question."

"Right, Babe. Amber needs a refill. Got that, Hon? And, both Wil and I have nothing but cubes in our glasses --- how about a second, Wil?"

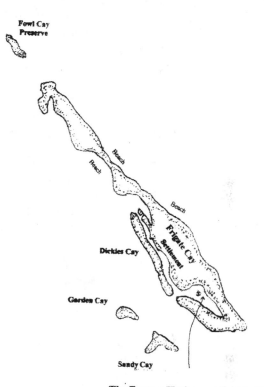

The Eastern Harbour at Frigate Cay

"Sure, Scott. Kind'a of interesting that our American History books never mentioned the Loyalists."

"Yea, makes you wonder what else they left out," says Wil.

"Scottie, time to get out the conch shell --- sunset is in two minutes."

"Okay, babe --- bring me the horn."

"Blowing the conch horn at sunset is a tradition in most yachting anchorages --- especially in the Eastern Harbour of Frigate Cay," reminds Scott.

"Okay, Hon -- give me the count down."

"You've got a minute and a half -- so pucker up."

"I'm already puckered, on just one Scotch."

"Okay, --- twenty seconds and counting."

Scott puts the conch shell up to his mouth and practices placing his lips on the small hole in the shell.

"Five, four, three, two, one --- do your thing, Scottie."

A moaning, screeching sound emits from the conch shell. More similar sounds come from other parts of the harbor accompanied by laughing and clapping and some boat horns honking.

"Now, attention guests. The blowing of the conch is NOT the signal to go to bed. It is the signal to start partying. Anybody ready to party?"

"Hey, babe --- ready to party," shouts Wil.

"Wil, who wouldn't want to party --- a beautiful anchorage, great music, food, drink --- lots of drink. --- lets party. How about we crank up the volume on the music and dance," shouts Amber.

"Okay, crew --- don't forget we've got to decide where we want to go tomorrow with this yacht," states Scott.

"Hell, we could just stay here and trade sea stories --- yah know --- yacht racing stuff versus cruising tales," says Wil.

"Hey, Addie --- click on the overhead light and let me lay out the charts."

"Okay crew, here's Frigate Cay --- we're here in the Eastern Harbour. How about we spend the morning here --- in the Settlement. You know, the ladies can go to The Studio Shop. Then, we can walk over the hill to the beach --- stop by the cemetery and the post office --- and the school. Then, we'll have lunch at Dock 'n Dine. Finally, we'll up anchor and head for Foul Cay for some snorkeling and beach combing. How's that sound?"

"Sounds like a plan --- I could go for some snorkeling and a little beach time," says Wil

"Me --- I'm along for the ride. Whatever the captain decides is okay with me --- hey, what about a little more volume on the music -- and, is there more of that Bahama punch," asks Amber.

"Okay, Amber, baby --- let's dance. You need to burn off some of your excess energy."

Tuesday morning at anchor in the American Harbour at Frigate Cay, aboard *Caribe Dreamer*

Scott sits alone in the cockpit with Mittens by his side and a cup of coffee in his hand. *Wow! These Chicagoans sure know how to party, thinks Scott while rubbing his hung over, aching head. This could be a really interesting cruise. So much for an early morning walk through the Settlement. And, where the heck is Addie? She was in the shower right after me. I thought she was going to make crepes for breakfast?*

"Morning, Wil. I see you found the coffee pot."

"Yea, good morning, captain. Are you and I the only people up?"

"Seems like it --- I thought my wife was right behind me. She is planning crepes for breakfast. Oh, speaking of my wife, here she is. Need a cup of coffee, Hon?

"I'm thinking more like a V- 8 or a virgin mary. What time did we get to bed --- does anyone know?"

"It definitely was late," remarks Scott. "How about helping me get the inflatable into the water, Wil?"

"Sure Scott. Just give me some orders."

2:30 P.M. Aboard *Caribe Dreamer* anchored in the American Harbour, Frigate Cay, Abaco, Bahamas

"Okay crew, enough goofing off. This is a cruising charter --- and, it's time to get cruising. Wil, you're in charge of the inflatable. Let her ride out about ten yards when we're under sail. When we prepare to anchor, bring her up tight to the transom, so we don't get the painter caught in the prop."

"Yes sir, captain," responds Wil.

"Amber, you sit right here in the cockpit and look pretty. Addie will be at the helm and I will take care of the anchor --- we'll get underway for Foul Cay."

"Yes sir." says Amber, mimicking her husband.

Addie starts both diesel engines and Scott makes his way to the forward trampoline to winch up the anchor. Soon, *Caribe Dreamer* is powering through the Frigate Cay cut and out into the Sea of Abaco. A turn to the North and they are on course for Foul Cays, a marine undersea park, where you cannot anchor --- all yachts must pick up mooring balls. The moorings protect the fragile coral reef from damage caused by anchoring.

Looking off to port, Addie says, "Hey, Scott. Looks like Bob Malone and the *Tres Amigos* have picked up a mooring. They must have a charter."

"Yeah, hon. You can't miss that wide beam on the Lagoon 52. Gosh, she's a monster. I doubt that he can only get through the Frigate cut at low tide."

"Think you're right about that --- and, we know how Bob and Mary love to party. Don't think we'll be getting to bed early tonight. I'll give him a call on the VHF and see what kind of party people he has aboard. That will determine if we pick up a mooring close to him, or anchor in the lee of the Cay."

"Good plan, Scott."

Scott picks up the microphone to the VHF radio and calls. "Ahoy, *Tres Amigos*. Hey, Captain Bob -- this is Captain Scott on *Caribe Dreamer* calling on Channel nine --- you copy?"

"Roger, Scottie --- let's go to Channel seven-three, over."

"*Caribe Dreamer* to channel seven-three."

"Hey, mister. How's your charter going?"

"Having a great time, Scott. I've got some California newlyweds aboard and I've been hung over for the last two nights --- these Californians can really handle their wine, over."

"We've got a newlywed couple from Chicago --- and my head still hurts from last night. How about I pick up the mooring ball to the East of you and we'll raft the boats together?"

"That sounds like a plan, Scottie. I'll put fenders out to port. Just throw me a line after you're secured to the mooring and our guests can simply walk between the boats. With all these bodies, we probably should party in my cockpit, tonight. Okay?"

"Sure thing. We're probably ten minutes to you. See you then. *Caribe Dreamer* clear with *Tres Amigos* on Channel seven-three and standing by on Channel zero nine."

"Okay, Amber --- time to put you to work. In the starboard seat locker are some inflatable fenders. We call them "Dollie Partons" --- and the reason will become obvious.

Party goers on Catamaran Sailboat

The charter crew of the Tres Amigos joins Caribe Dreamer at the Foul Cay Underwater Preserve.

They have pieces of rope attached to them. There's a knot in the end of the rope. Grab two of them and give one to Wil. Hold the rope in front of the knot --- don't let the knot pass through your hands or we'll be diving in to retrieve Dolly. I'll need you and Wil on the starboard rail up by the mast. Your only job will be to hold the fenders between our boat and *Tres Amigos*. Don't fend off with your arms or feet --- just use the fender. We don't want anyone getting hurt."

"I'm pretty sure I can do that --- captain Scott," says Amber with a salute.

Addie picks up the mooring ball with the boat hook and runs a length of five-eighths inch nylon line through the loop in the slimy, crustacean encrusted, mooring pennant. Scott is watching the process and, as soon as Addie stands up, he puts the wheel hard over to starboard and shifts into reverse. Slowly, *Caribe Dreamer* begins to move closer to *Tres Amigos,* whose crew is standing on her port deck --- holding the same Dollie Parton fenders that Amber has in her hands. Scott advances the throttle of the starboard engine for a few seconds and soon, only two feet separates the catamarans. As the boats settle together, it's time for introductions.

"Ahoy *Tres Amigos*, I'm Scott and up on the bow trampoline is my wife, Addie. Our charter guests are Amber and Wil from Chicago."

"Thanks, Scott. On board *Tres Amigos*, we have Jean and Kevin from Petaluma, California. I'm Captain Bob Malone and the pretty lady next to me is my wife, Mary. Wil, if you will toss me that spring line, we'll get these two ships lined up, so we can just walk through the gates from one boat to the other."

"Heads up, Captain Bob --- here comes the line."

"Hey, nice toss, Wil. Now, take up some of the slack until we touch the fenders. Yea, that's good. Cleat the line with a figure eight --- and, Scottie, you can shut down your engines."

"Roger that, Captain Bob. It's p-a-r-t-y time. Let the good times roll. Hey, Mary give us some volume on the stereo. --- and how about a snorkel before we have cocktails," inquires Scott.

"Good idea, Scottie, the tide is slack and the sun is still high enough for some good visibility. Maybe your guests would like to SCUBA--- or at least put on a mask and simply float over the coral head. Lots of fish life out here. Anyone game?"

"Jean and I are game," responds Kevin.

"I'm already in my suite, but I think I'll just float with one of the noodles," says Addie.

"Hey, Captain Scott, any chance we can catch some supper, asks Wil.

"Not here, Wil --- this is a Bahamas National Seashore Park and we can only look. The West boundary is just over there beyond that little coral spit. How about we lower the inflatable and go and get us some Yellowtail for supper, responds Scott.

"I'm just about ready --- all I need is my floppy hat and some SPF 30. Hey, gang --- it might be a good idea to lather up with sunscreen, before you get in the water. Red only looks good on a lobster in the pot, not on the crew," shouts Bob.

5:00 P.M., Cocktail hour aboard *Tres Amigos* on a mooring ball in the Foul Cay Preserve five miles North of Frigate Cay, *Carib Dreamer* is tied to the port side.

Scott and Addie have been in the galley for an hour fixing snacks and preparing their part of the dinner, while their cruise guests shower and nap before cocktails. Addie is marinating conch strips in lime and sour juice while Scott fills the cooler with ice and an assortment of beers, Kalik, Sands, Heineken and Red Stripe. The boat's generator is humming as the water maker is cycling and the ice machine is running full blast.

"Scott, you probably should knock on our guest's door and tell them fifteen minutes. Okay?"

"Yea, we don't want them to nap too long, or we'll be up till four A.M. tonight. Maybe their snorkel and the fishing trip took some of the fight out of them --- I can only hope." Scott flips the switch on his radio to 'intercom' and presses the talk button. "Now hear this, now here this. This is your captain speaking. Cocktails are served aboard *Tres Amigos* in fifteen minutes. I say again, cocktails and hors d' oeuvres are served in the cockpit in fifteen minutes."

Scott's announcement is met with the sound of hair dryers and running water, as the guests ready for cocktail hour. Scott and Addie begin the process of carrying the food across the deck to *Tres Amigo's* cockpit. Shortly, Wil appears dressed in starched, white Bermuda shorts and a Guy Harvey fishing shirt. He wears sailing sandals on his feet and gold chains hang around his neck.

"Good evening, captain and good evening Addie. Permission to come aboard, Captain Bob."

"Permission granted, Wil. Are you dining by yourself, tonight?"

"No, my lovely wife is getting more lovely, --- and mind you, that takes time --- right, Mary?"

"Yes, I remember those days -- hair, makeup. I finally had permanent makeup tattooed to my eyelids and this short haircut takes only minutes to fluff dry. But, I understand. You spend lots of time looking good for your wedding and you want to keep up the good looks into the honeymoon. Well, looks as if our guests are ready to party. Hi guys. Pick a comfortable place in the cockpit."

"Good evening, Bob --- Mary. Good evening, Wil. Good evening, Scott and Addie -- only one person is missing -- Amber."

"Oh, hi Amber. You look lovely," says Mary.

"Okay, since we're all assembled, let me run through the drink selection. First, the hard alcohols --- Canadian Whiskey, Kentucky Bourbon, ah, Jack

Daniels, as I recall. Three brands of Scotch, chilled vodka, gin, as well as vermouth for martini's, Roses Lime for gimlets and Grenadine for color. We have four rums, including coconut rum, as well as 200 proof rum. For mix, we have Schweppes soda water, and tonic. For soft drink mix, we have Canada Dry ginger ale, Seven Up, Coke, Diet Coke, Cherry Coke, Pepsi Zero, Sierra Mist --- and maybe a few others. And, of course we have reverse osmosis filtered branch water. In addition, we have red, as well as chilled white wines. I also have Kahlua, Peach Schnapps and Crème de Menthe, I'm pretty certain there's a half a dozen bottles of Domaine Chandon champagne in the fridge. And, to top our selection off, I've made a pitcher of Bahama Mama's, and I can make up a pitcher of frozen margaritas or daiquiri's in a few minutes. And, we also have local beer --- Sands and Kalik as well as American light beers. I've even brought in some "Old Style" for our Chicago guests. So ---- what will it be? Ladies?"

"Okay, Bob. Since were in the islands, I'll start it off with a Bahama Mama," says Amber.

"I'll try one of your frozen margaritas," chimes in Jean.

"Bob, I'm sticking with my tried and true Old Style beer -- no glass, right out of the can," responds Wil.

"Captain, I'm going to sip my favorite scotch, Dewar's -- on the rocks with a splash of branch water," says Scott.

"Okay, gang. I'll be right back with the drinks. Meanwhile, let's play the 'get acquainted' game. I'll start first. I was born and raised in Chicago and met Mary while playing 'beer baseball', during a layover in Saint Joe, Michigan, while racing my sailboat. Mary was the pitcher and every time you walked or got a hit, you had to go behind the mound, tap the keg and chug another beer. I can't remember if I was a great hitter or Mary was a lousy pitcher, but we both got really drunk and she ended up sleeping on my boat. We got reacquainted in Chicago at the Chicago Yacht Club and found we both loved sailing."

"So, let's start with Jean. What brought you and Kevin together?"

"Bob, you'll be sorry you asked --- it was a nuclear submarine."

"Come on, Jean --- you don't expect us to believe that. Is that true, Kevin?"

"Yes, sir. She's telling the truth. It was here in the Bahamas, that we met. My sub, the *USS Topeka*, was docked in Andros Island --- that's the big island just West and South of Nassau. Jean invited me to join her for dinner at a native joint on the North end of the island."

"Well, Kevin, that's a better story than Amber and me. We met in a famous Chicago bar, just off of Rush Street --- called Butch McGuire's. It was just before Christmas and Amber was helping to decorate the bar. They had this model train that went around the bar --- up by the ceiling --- and Amber, while attaching decorations, accidently knocked one of the cars off the track. I made a lucky stab for it as it fell and caught it a couple of inches above the floor. She was quite impressed. We discovered that we were both going to DePaul University at night --- working on our MBA's. Amber was a whiz in statistics and I did really well in calculus --- so we made quite the pair."

"How about you, two --- Scott and Addie," shouted Wil.

"Oh, we met the old fashioned way, we met on a blind date. One of my patients in the dental practice, where I was a hygienist, was the matchmaker. Scott was her boat captain and 'The Countess', as we called her, was determined to get Scott married off. I was the lucky person."

"Okay, gang. The best story, if we can believe it is from Jean and Kevin. We need some more details, 'caus no one here has ever heard of two people getting married because of a submarine. Who wants to tell us the naked truth --- Jean or Kevin?"

"I'll tell the story, volunteers Kevin. It's actually a pretty interesting story since our getting married had a lot to do with the Bahama Islands. I'll give you the short version. I was the Executive Officer on the *U S S Topeka*, which is a hunter-killer submarine. The boat was in dry dock for three months in Norfolk, where she was modified to carry the first, top secret weapon. *Topeka* was ordered to the Atlantic Undersea Testing Base, that is located on Andros Island --- to undergo sea trials and test the weapon. My commanding officer assigned me as the project officer and, just after we docked, I was sent to see a 'S. J. Barton' --- turned out to be Jean. Unfortunately for us, the test of this new weapon did not go well --- and the weapon disappeared, after hitting a reef, just South of here."

"Holy blank, Kevin! --- exclaims Scott. I was involved in the search for that 'vehicle' as they called it. I had the thing tied to the side of one of the Frigate Cay ferry boats --- heck, I've still got the lat and lon stored in my GPS."

"Scott, you've got to be bushing me. Both of our careers were ended because of that test failure. Jean and I were dragged before an Administrative Investigation Board. I lost the possibility of my own submarine command and left the Navy. Jean lost her job with Everen Electric. Why did those lying bastards on the board tell us that the vehicle had been destroyed by some Navy carrier jets --- to keep it from falling into the hands of a foreign power --- and now, sitting in *Tres Amigos* cockpit, Scott tells me that he has the GPS position of the wreck! This is more than a little freaky."

"Sorry Kevin, I didn't know that this little piece of information would hit you so hard."

"It's not a problem, Scott. I've got mixed emotions about this discovery. I'm going to have to sip on my Scotch for a little while --- and sort this out. This is like a nightmare --- it's unbelievable. The evidence to clear our names and get to the truth may be stored in Scott's GPS."

"Scottie, darling. Hold me tight --- this revelation is really tearing me up. The Navy lied to us --- thank God we had the faith to move on with our new careers. I hope our new friends understand that we spent countless hours reassuring each other that our relationship had nothing to do with the failure of that test."

"So, Scott, what is the chance of going to the site and see if the vehicle is still there. If it is, we need to let the Navy know so they can retrieve it --- and keep the electronics from falling into the hands of our enemies," asks Kevin.

"Well, I'm game to go South --- that's the opposite direction I had planned, but it's doable. We can head down to Lynyard Cay. This Cay has some of the most beautiful beaches in the Bahamas. Lynyard will put us close to the location where we dumped the vehicle."

"So, come on --- let's party. Tomorrow, we sail early, out in the ocean, to Lynyard Cay."

"How's everyone's drink ---?"

9:00 A. M., *Caribe Dreamer and Tres Amigos* are anchored on the West side of Lynyard Cay just South of the North Bar Channel Passage.

"Okay, ladies and gentlemen. This is the day Jean and Kevin have been waiting for. We're going to all suit up and get our SCUBA gear or, for those that prefer, just mask, snorkel and fins. Ready ----," asks Scott.

"We'll put the SCUBA divers in the inflatable and we'll tow a couple of lines so the snorkelers can join in the fun. Our objective is to try to move enough sand to find a piece of the vehicle. Once we've done that, we'll call in the *Argonaut* which is a treasure vessel that uses Marsh Harbour as its home port. They can put their prop wash into a particular area and move feet of sand in the matter of minutes," states Addie.

"Remember, the vehicle is painted with orange day-glo stripes. If you see anything orange or made of metal, it doesn't belong on the bottom of the ocean -- it may be our vehicle. Signal me, or Addie and we'll check it out for you. Keep in mind, this test vehicle is packed with explosives, in case it went missing or sank, so safety is of primary importance. Scott, anything to add?"

"No, Addie, I think you covered it. Let's get loaded, or into the water. For our snorkelers, if you get tired or have some problem with your gear, just raise your hand and we'll stop and help you. If you think we're towing you too fast, give us the thumbs down signal. Okay? Let's go!"

Bob and Mary and the snorkelers follow Scott and Addie in the inflatable, as they make their way to the deep North Bar Channel Passage and out into the ocean. Scott has his GPS set to the coordinates he loaded just five months ago. Memories of that day and the action aboard 'Davie Seven' flash through his mind as he powers, ever so slowly toward the intersection of the latitude and longitude of the last known position of 'the vehicle' Scott circles with his hand as he throttles back and puts his engine in neutral. The roll of the ocean is gentle and the late morning sun is shining brightly --- perfect weather to see something on the sandy bottom.

"All my SCUBA divers, have your diving buddy check your equipment. Check your regulators and descend to the bottom. The tide should be flowing in from the Northeast, so stay with me. We'll dive Northwest of the plotted location and this will prevent us from kicking up the bottom and the water will remain clear in front of us. Let's roll over the side and meet at the bottom."

Three divers join Scott on the bottom and he motions them to spread out in a North to South direction. Scott begins fanning the sand and his fellow divers join in. Small pin fish and fry appear above the sand, feeding on the plankton stirred up by their gloved hands. Seconds turn into minutes and after twenty-five minutes of stirring up the bottom, Scott signals to the frustrated divers to surface. The divers remove their equipment and hand it up to Addie in the inflatable. An aluminum step helps the divers get aboard the slippery sides of the dinghy. Wil starts the conversation.

"There's at least two feet of sand where I am digging. I think Kevin and Jean should decide if we are going to bring in the big equipment -- you know the *Argonaut* --- the ship with the big props to wash away the sand. And, if you don't mind me saying this --- I would think the U.S. Navy would do the work for free --- except, as we all know, it's our tax money," says Wil.

"Wil, I'm in agreement --- with one big caveat, I'm not certain that the Navy wants to find this thing. The transcripts of the investigative proceeding are probably buried in a file box, in some dusty warehouse in Norfolk," says Kevin.

"Okay, since this is a vacation for most of us, I would propose that we stop at the sand bar at Pelican Cay for lunch and a great warm water swim. The guests that want to snorkel or SCUBA at the Sandy Cay undersea park can go in *Tres Amigos* inflatable. I'll go with Kevin and anyone else who wants to join us and try another area East of where we were digging today."

"Scott, Addie and I have decided that our predicament seems to be overshadowing our honeymoons. This is supposed to be fun and laughs and time to see the beautiful Bahamas. We'd like to call the whole thing off and get to sailing, cruising, cocktails, beaches and sunsets. After lunch, I propose that we go back to *Dreamer* and get out the charts and plan our next port of call."

"Well said, Kevin. I think you're right. We're in this way over our heads. I'll copy down the lat and lon and you and Jean can decide if you want to let the Navy in on our secret. Addie has planned a great lunch. I'll go back to the boat and get the charts. We're only a few miles away from Little Harbour. This is a 'must see' port of call on a cruise in the Abacos. The Johnstons came here in the 1950's and opened their foundry, where the senior Johnston cast large bronze statues using the lost wax method. The foundry and 'Pete's Pub' are interesting attractions of the Abacos. I'll be back in twenty minutes with the charts --- Addie, save me some lunch."

Epilogue

Mr. Daniel F. Justice, Secretary of the Navy

The Pentagon,

Washington, DC 20112

Dear Secretary Justice,

Please be advised that equipment belonging to the U.S. Navy can be found at the following location in the Bahama Islands: 26 degrees, 26 minutes, 8 seconds North; 76 degrees 52 minutes, 35 seconds West. Copy of nautical chart is attached.

Sincerely,

A Former Commissioned Naval Officer

About the Author

Long before provisioned, luxury charter boats existed, the author's parents sailed extensively throughout the Caribbean and Central America.

The author spent much of his youth and adulthood aboard numerous types of sailboats, racing, crewing and also, cruising aboard his own vessel.

The family's love for the Bahamas influenced the purchase of property and construction of an out-island cottage in the Abacos. The cottage became the "go-to" destination for the author during high school, college and subsequent vacations.

After graduating from Miami University, Oxford, Ohio with post-graduate studies at De Paul University, Chicago, the author enlisted in the Illinois Army National Guard where he became a communication specialist. He saw active duty with the 33rd Infantry Brigade Combat Team.

These experiences, as well as his life-long fascination with naval warfare history, led to the writing of this fictional story of terrorism, intrigue and passion.

A native of Chicago and a "dreamer" himself, the author currently resides in Southwest Florida with his wife, daughter and their 31' Bristol sloop.

Printed in the United States
By Bookmasters